You Might As Well Die

**Center Point
Large Print**

Also by J. J. Murphy and available from
Center Point Large Print:

Murder Your Darlings

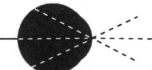

**This Large Print Book carries the
Seal of Approval of N.A.V.H.**

You Might As Well Die

An Algonquin Round Table Mystery

J. J. Murphy

CENTER POINT LARGE PRINT
THORNDIKE, MAINE

This Center Point Large Print edition
is published in the year 2012 by arrangement with
NAL Signet, a member of Penguin Group (USA) Inc.

The text of this Large Print edition is unabridged.
In other aspects, this book may vary
from the original edition.
Printed in the United States of America
on permanent paper.
Set in 16-point Times New Roman type.

ISBN: 978-1-61173-432-4

Library of Congress Cataloging-in-Publication Data

Murphy, J. J. (John Joseph)
You might as well die : an Algonquin round table mystery / J.J. Murphy.
— Large print ed.
p. cm. — (An Algonquin round table mystery) (Center Point large print edition)
ISBN 978-1-61173-432-4 (library binding : alk. paper)
1. Large type books. I. Title.
PS3613.U735Y68 2012
813'.6—dc23

2012008670

To Bill Murphy and Stephen Murphy

Résumé

Razors pain you;
Rivers are damp;
Acids stain you;
And drugs cause cramp.
Guns aren't lawful;
Nooses give;
Gas smells awful;
You might as well live.

—Dorothy Parker

Author's Note

Dorothy Parker reportedly said, "I don't care what is written about me so long as it isn't true." Following her advice, this book is almost entirely a work of fiction, even though it is populated with many real people. The members of the Algonquin Round Table never seemed to let the truth get in the way of telling a good story—and I hope you won't let it get in the way of enjoying this one.

PREFACE

In the 1920s, there was no Internet, no wireless phones, no satellite TV—no TV at all. Even radio wasn't commonplace until the later twenties. Instead of text messages and e-mail, people sent telegrams or employed messenger boys. For music at home, they listened to a Victrola or sang around a piano.

For entertainment, New Yorkers had dozens of theaters in which to see plays and a number of movie palaces where they could see silent films. ("Talkies" didn't arrive until the later twenties, too.)

For information, New Yorkers lacked twenty-four-hour cable news networks. But they did have a dozen daily newspapers to choose from. Presses ran day and night, printing morning editions, afternoon editions and special editions *("Extra! Extra! Read all about it!")*.

At this time, the people who wrote the news also became the news. A new class of writers, editors and critics emerged. A loose-knit group of ten—and their assorted friends—gathered around a large table for lunch at the Algonquin Hotel. They went to the Algonquin because it welcomed artists and writers—and because it was convenient and inexpensive. Their daily lunch gatherings were known more for wisecracks and witticisms than for the food they ate. But they buoyed one another with merriment and camaraderie. They thought the fun would never end.

Chapter 1

H ave you ever wanted to kill yourself?"

Dorothy Parker looked up to see the eager face of Ernie MacGuffin hovering just inches away. MacGuffin was a third-rate illustrator and a first-rate nuisance.

"Mrs. Parker," he whispered again, only more urgently. "Have you ever wanted to kill yourself?"

"Matter of fact," she sighed, "I'm thinking about it right now."

It was just after lunchtime at the Algonquin Hotel. Dorothy sat at the Round Table in the hotel's dining room. She had been searching in her purse for a cigarette when MacGuffin suddenly appeared. Her usual lunch companions, sometimes called the Vicious Circle, had gotten up from the table. They were saying their see-you-laters and heading back to work for the afternoon. Helplessly, she watched them go.

"Seriously," MacGuffin said, hurriedly taking the seat next to hers. "I want to know."

She looked at him. He was a skinny scarecrow. Messy, nut-brown hair. Cheap necktie. Paint-stained fingers. Dirty fingernails. A small smear of egg salad at the corner of his mouth. She felt both pity and disgust for him.

"Suicide?" She lit her cigarette. "Sure, I've

tried it. Who hasn't these days? It's like the Charleston—everyone's doing it."

"I knew it!" He leaned closer. "What happened?"

"What happened?" Her cigarette almost fell from her mouth. "Can't you guess? It didn't stick."

He nodded as if he was about to suggest how she could get it right next time.

"What's this all about?" she asked.

MacGuffin inhaled deeply. He was clearly debating whether he could trust her with something.

MacGuffin was a poor man's Norman Rockwell. He aspired to paint covers for *Collier's*, *Vanity Fair* and *The Saturday Evening Post*, but most of his works were for pulp magazines like *True Crime* or *Old West*. He was not an invited member of the Round Table. Instead, he rode on the coattails of Neysa McMein, a first-rate illustrator and one of the few women besides Dorothy who were welcome at the Round Table.

Unlike Dorothy, Ernie MacGuffin took this conversation very seriously. "Your suicide—were you afraid?"

"I was afraid I would wake up." She brushed aside the brunette bangs that shadowed her pretty face. "Again, what's this all about?"

He seemed to come to a decision. "I knew you knew all about it. Now I know I can trust you. Here." He handed her an envelope. "Don't open it until midnight. Promise me."

No one took Ernie seriously. Not his friends, not the art world, not the public. She looked at the plain white envelope and handed it back.

"Nothing doing," she said. "If you mean to commit suicide, don't get me involved. If you go toes up, I don't want that on my head."

He looked disappointed and confused.

She softened. "Don't kill yourself, Ernie. Take it from me. Attempting suicide after lunchtime will simply ruin your whole day."

Ten minutes before midnight, Dorothy and Robert Benchley, her closest friend, were at Tony Soma's, their favorite speakeasy.

Earlier in the evening, Tony had been waltzing around the loud and lively crowd, chatting with all the customers, singing opera and pouring drinks. Now he approached Dorothy and Benchley. His smile had disappeared.

"Mrs. Parker. Mr. Benchley," Tony said sternly. "There's a little matter I'd like to discuss. It's about the bill."

"Ah, yes." Benchley rocked back on his heels, nearly spilling the drink in his coffee mug. "Our cups and our tab runneth over."

"Tony, you know we're good for it," Dorothy said, gently swatting him on the arm. "We'll pay in full next time."

Tony's deep-set eyes turned darker. "That's what you said last time. It's been weeks since you paid."

He slid his hand inside his vest pocket. Dorothy, less than five feet tall, instinctively edged behind Benchley.

Tony pulled out an envelope. "Your bill."

Benchley glanced at Dorothy. He reluctantly took the envelope and gingerly pried it open.

This prompted Dorothy to remember Mac-Guffin's envelope. She hadn't given him a single thought since lunchtime. She didn't care much for Ernie, but she hoped he had gotten over whatever itch had been bothering him.

Benchley gasped when he read the bill. Dorothy grabbed her purse and quickly pulled out her horn-rimmed glasses. She scanned down the long column of numbers to the total. . . .

Four hundred and eighty-five dollars! Her big, dark brown eyes grew wide. That was well more than she earned in a month.

"Have we really drunk all this?" Benchley asked her.

She silently returned his glance. Of course they had. The bill was only a column of prices. It didn't list the many different types of drinks. But she could imagine—double scotches, whiskey sours, gin martinis, gin rickeys, gin and tonics, sidecars, orange blossoms, Tom Collinses, Rob Roys, old-fashioneds . . . and more Manhattans than they could remember.

Dorothy felt unsteady. She needed a cigarette—and another drink. She reached into her purse for her pack of Chesterfields, but her hand touched paper. She pulled an envelope from her purse—MacGuffin's envelope.

"What's that, Mrs. Parker?" Benchley asked, his thin mustache twitching. "Another bill?"

"You pay mine first," Tony said, folding his arms over his barrel chest.

"Might be nothing," Dorothy said, holding it in her quivering hand. "Might be something."

MacGuffin must have slipped it into her purse after lunch. He had told her not to open it until midnight. She grabbed Benchley's arm and looked at his wristwatch. Just a few minutes until midnight. Something told her to open it right now.

She ripped it open, unfolded the plain white paper and skimmed through the handwritten note.

To whom it may concern. At midnight tonight . . . will meet my fate in the waters beneath the Brooklyn Bridge . . . My last will and testament . . . Once I am dead and gone in this life . . . A new and better life awaits me. Good-bye, cruel world.

"Oh crap!" She clutched Benchley's arm. "It *is* a suicide note. That Ernie! Come on, we have to go."

She stepped forward, but Tony blocked her way. "Sorry. I cannot let you leave until you pay."

"Tony, what is this?" she said. "A friend of ours—well, a man we know—is about to kill himself. We have to stop him. We have to leave now."

Tony shook his head. "Nobody leaves until the bill is paid up."

Benchley was puzzled. "We don't carry that kind of money around with us. How can we get you any money if you won't let us leave?"

Tony merely kept his arms folded and jutted out his round chin.

"Please, Tony," Dorothy said. "A man might be dying. Right at this moment."

He shrugged, indifferent.

"Oh, Tony, old pal—" Benchley began kindly; his eyes were merry and twinkling.

Dorothy interrupted. She had had enough. "Don't make me make a scene," she said quietly, but Tony heard every word. "Really, is that what you want? A short, hysterical woman shrieking in your speakeasy?"

Underneath it all, she knew Tony was a softie. His tough facade cracked. His eyes changed from unforgiving to apologetic.

"My friends, I'm so sorry," he sighed, his hands cradling his sagging cheeks. "It's the wife, Mrs. Soma. She's on my back day and night. No more freeloading, she says."

"Freeloading?" Dorothy gasped. "Well, I never." She eyed Mrs. Soma across the room. Mrs. Soma returned Dorothy's glance with an icy glare.

"Look around," Tony said, exasperated but with a touch of pride. "We've paid for a lot of improvements. If we get raided, we put in trapdoors behind the bar where the bottles can drop out of sight."

Benchley nodded approvingly.

Tony continued. "See all these new potted plants with the big ferns? If the cops bang on the door, you dump your drink in there, and we fill up your cup with tea or coffee. And don't forget all the palms that need to be greased—the patrol cops, the lookouts, the city officials. I can't run the place on goodwill!"

"Of course," Benchley said. He held out a few bills. "Take this for now. We'll pay you the rest as soon as we can."

Tony took it and stepped aside. "Go on. Go help your friend. But please bring in the money soon, okay?"

"Sure," Benchley said, patting him on the shoulder. Dorothy kissed him on the cheek.

They hurried outside and down the steps of the brownstone. They looked in vain for a taxi. The darkened street of town houses was quiet as usual.

"Stop right there!" Mrs. Soma shouted from the doorway. "You pay your tab or you'll never drink in this club again!"

Tony grabbed her arm to drag her back inside. She shook him off easily and pushed him away.

Dorothy and Benchley paused only a moment. Then they turned and ran.

Mrs. Soma yanked off her apron and threw it back inside. "Tony Jr.! Get your backside out here and catch these scroungers! Now!"

Chapter 2

Tony Jr.!" Mrs. Soma yelled again.

Dorothy looked over her shoulder. She expected to see a dark, strapping, muscle-bound young man appear in the doorway of the speakeasy. Instead, she saw a boy only about twelve years old.

Tony Jr. spotted them. Even from such a distance in the dark, Dorothy could see him smile like a wolf on the hunt. The boy's dark eyes sparkled. His huge grin was full of big white teeth. Suddenly, he tore down the steps, his jacket flying, his mother hurrying down the steps after him.

"Wait for me, you little rat!" she called.

Tony Jr. bounded across the sidewalk in one long leap, then flung open the door of a parked Studebaker. He jumped into the driver's seat. He could hardly see over the steering wheel. Mrs. Soma hurried into the backseat as the boy started the engine roaring.

Benchley and Dorothy reached the street corner but stared back in amazement at the scene in front of Tony's speakeasy.

Tony Jr. yanked the wheel and gunned the engine, and the car shot forward.

Benchley turned to Dorothy. "I think we need a taxi."

"I think we need a flying chariot," she said. "But a taxi will do."

They turned toward the busy traffic of Sixth Avenue, their arms flailing to hail a cab—any cab. In the street behind them, they could hear the car with Tony Jr. and Mrs. Soma speeding closer.

A cab slowly pulled in front of them and came to a leisurely, agonizing stop. Frantically, they jumped in.

The man behind the wheel was old, fat and gray. "Where to?"

"Brooklyn Bridge, and step on it," Benchley said.

"What's the big hurry? You going to turn into a pumpkin at midnight?"

"If only," Benchley said. "We have a blood-thirsty adolescent and his wicked, speakeasy-running mother after us."

Dorothy said, "And we have to stop a mediocre illustrator from drowning his sorrows in the river. Please hurry."

The cabbie turned to face them, annoyed and sarcastic. "Are you a couple of nuts, or have you had too much to drink?"

"A little of both," Dorothy said. "Please hurry."

At that moment, the Somas' Studebaker turned onto Sixth and came parallel with the cab. Tony Jr. stuck out his tongue at them.

"Jeez, what is this?" the old cabbie yelled.

Then the boy turned away, reaching for something.

"My word," Benchley said. "You don't suppose he's got a gun?"

"A gun?" the cabbie cried. His anger had given way to fear.

Suddenly, something splattered on the passenger window. The cabbie visibly jumped in his seat. "Holy—!"

"Just a tomato," Dorothy said.

They looked at the pulpy red burst. As it slid away, it revealed the grinning, fanged face of little Tony Jr.

The cabbie, breathing heavy now, threw the taxi in gear, stepped hard on the gas and pulled away fast into the swiftly moving traffic. Dorothy and Benchley turned to see the Somas' car quickly follow them.

Dorothy looked down to see the suicide note still clutched in her hand. Ernie MacGuffin's sprawling, loopy penmanship was more like that of a teenage girl than an artist.

"May I see that?" Benchley said. She handed it to him.

She had only skimmed it before. He read the whole thing aloud by the light of the quickly passing streetlamps.

" 'To whom it may concern,' " he began. " 'At midnight tonight, October twentieth, I will meet my fate in the waters beneath the Brooklyn Bridge. I hereby make my last will and testament. To my wife, I bequeath all my paintings, including those well-known to the public as well as the vast majority of finer ones the public has rarely seen. Once I am dead and gone in this life, perhaps these superior yet unknown works will speak for me in the afterlife. Then the world will know I'm not a hack. A new and better life awaits me. Good-bye, cruel world.' "

"Hello, cruel afterlife," Dorothy said.

Benchley shook his head. "Why would a guy like Ernie try to kill himself?"

"Why would anyone? Sometimes life is just too much."

Benchley, who was almost always cheerful, didn't seem to comprehend this answer. Dorothy tried a different one. "Clearly, he thinks no one takes him seriously as an artist."

"But suicide?" Benchley said. "Not Ernie. I've rarely met a more eager beaver."

"That's true. Ernie's about as melancholy as a newly adopted puppy. He certainly didn't have the blues this afternoon."

Something thumped loudly. The taxi lurched forward.

"Jeez," the cabbie cried. He was almost in tears. "That damned kid rammed into us!"

Dorothy and Benchley peered out the rear window at the vicious face of Tony Jr. dangerously close behind them.

Turning around, Benchley handed the note back to Dorothy.

"I don't know what Ernie hopes to achieve," Benchley continued. "He thinks no one takes him seriously now? Just wait until he kills himself. Certainly no one will take him seriously then."

"I don't know about that," Dorothy said. "Nothing's more serious than suicide."

Bang! The taxi lurched again as Tony Jr. rammed the Studebaker into it.

The cabbie wailed, "Stop it, you dirty little monster!"

"Give him a break," Dorothy said primly. "He's only a child."

Benchley, who had two boys of his own, shook his head. "Why is that child up this late on a school night? Some parents have no control of their children."

From behind them, they could hear the shrill voice of Mrs. Soma. "Stop playing games, Tony Jr., and run them off the road!"

On a street corner ahead, the cab's headlights illuminated a policeman on a motorcycle.

"Oh, thank the Lord!" the cabbie sobbed. He drove right for the cop and brought the taxi to a lurching halt inches from the motorcycle. The cop peered in the window.

"Help, Officer!" the cabbie pleaded breathlessly, his words tumbling out almost too fast to make sense. "There's a damned boy monster. And his mother. Trying to kill us!"

The policeman put his gloved hands on his leather-belted hips. "You drunk, buddy?"

"Officer Compson, is that you?" Dorothy called from the backseat. "It *is* you! Don't you recognize me? From the printing plant?"

The young officer rolled his eyes. "Oh yeah, I remember you."

"Officer," Dorothy said, all business now. "There is a colleague of ours who is about to throw himself off the Brooklyn Bridge at this very moment. Please call in a squadron of squad cars and an army of ambulances."

Mrs. Soma and Tony Jr. had pulled their car alongside. "You won't need an ambulance once we get ahold of you," she spat. "You'll need a hearse."

"Arrest them!" the cabbie babbled. "They're a menace!"

Officer Compson ignored this. He replied to Dorothy. "The Brooklyn Bridge? Is that where you're headed in such an awful hurry? And what's that kid doing driving that Studebaker?"

"Never mind them," she said. "A man's life is at stake."

"All right," Compson said. "Let me call it in. Then I'll lead you to the bridge."

His motorcycle was parked next to a police call box. In less than a second, Compson dismounted the cycle, popped open the small door of the call box, and grabbed the telephone receiver in his

26

hand. He talked quickly, closed it up again, and jumped back on his motorcycle.

Siren on, lights flashing, Compson kick-started the cycle and took off, waving the taxi to follow.

The fat old cabbie sat stupefied. "Isn't he going to arrest them?"

"Follow him!" Dorothy said.

The cabbie jumped again in his seat, threw the cab in gear and hurried to catch up to the motor-cycle cop.

"See?" Tony Jr. jeered as he drove alongside. "Even the cops won't help you. Give it up now and call it quits!"

The cabbie ducked his head down and gunned the taxi's engine.

About twenty blocks farther, with Officer Compson parting traffic before them, they reached the approach to the Brooklyn Bridge. The bridge was brightly lit—like a stage, Dorothy thought. And MacGuffin was making his final bow. If he hadn't made it already.

Compson slowed his motorcycle and took out a flashlight, which he shined toward the railing of the bridge. He crept along the length of the bridge, the taxi following. At the midpoint of the bridge, Compson halted.

The taxi driver was visibly shaking. He stopped the cab. He turned to face Dorothy and Benchley. His skin was pale, sweating.

"Okay, you nuts, we're here. Brooklyn Bridge. Now get the hell out of my cab."

They got out. The cabbie reached back and pulled the door closed.

"Wait," Benchley said, reaching for his wallet. "Your fare."

"Forget it," the man said. "Just never get in my cab again."

The cab sped off, tires squealing.

"Huh." Benchley shrugged. "Who says New York cabdrivers are rude?"

"Look out!" Dorothy shouted.

The Somas' car came hurtling toward them. Dorothy and Benchley ran around behind Officer Compson's motorcycle for protection. Tony Jr. hit the brakes. The car screeched to a halt just inches from the motorcycle.

Next came an ambulance and six squad cars, lights flaring and sirens wailing.

Dorothy turned to Officer Compson. "Did you find something?"

He nodded and pointed the beam of his flashlight toward the railing. An unframed painting leaned against it. Compson lowered the flashlight beam and illuminated a beat-up pair of brown wingtip shoes. The shoes were positioned neatly side by side.

Dorothy sighed. "We're too late. He's gone."

A booming voice called from behind them. "Well, look who it is."

Dorothy and Benchley turned to see a plain-clothes police detective. The big man wore a light brown suit and a brown derby hat; both were a size too small.

"O'Rannigan," Dorothy said.

"Got a report of a suicide," the detective said. "Too bad it wasn't either one of you. So what do you think you're doing here?"

"Don't look at us," Benchley said. "We're as innocent as two little white lambs."

Mrs. Soma yelled from the window of her car. "Innocent, my eye! You pay your liquor tab, you lousy freeloaders. Or else!"

"Or else you're a rotten egg!" Tony Jr. cackled, and flung something white.

The rotten egg—they could smell it instantly—missed Dorothy but splattered O'Rannigan's tight trench coat.

"The yolk's on you," Benchley said meekly to the detective.

"And I guess I have egg on my face," Dorothy said, wiping away a few flecks from her cheek.

O'Rannigan looked like a volcano about to erupt. He moved toward the Somas' car, but Tony Jr. quickly stepped on the gas and the car sped away in a small cloud of exhaust. O'Rannigan signaled to one of the squad cars, which zoomed after it.

"Now," the detective said, turning back toward them and addressing Officer Compson, "what do we have here?"

Dorothy glanced over the handrail at the inky rippling water of the East River more than a hundred feet below. Then she looked across to the buildings that lined the Brooklyn side of the river. They were lit as if in miniature, like an elaborate toy train setup in a darkened room. She saw a factory with an illuminated clock, which read ten minutes after midnight.

"Well?" O'Rannigan barked.

"Forget it," Dorothy said. "It's water under the bridge."

Chapter 3

At lunchtime the next day, Dorothy absent-mindedly dunked a popover in her coffee. She and Benchley were gathered with the other members of the Round Table in the dining room of the Algonquin Hotel.

Dorothy dropped the popover back on her plate. She didn't feel like eating.

She was depressed, more so than usual. She was depressed about not being able to return to her favorite speakeasy for the foreseeable future. She was depressed that she didn't even earn enough money to pay her bar bill. But mostly, she was depressed about Ernie, that she hadn't been able to do anything to help him.

Alexander Woollcott—the imperious, over-weight *New York Times* drama critic and occasional mother hen of the Vicious Circle—eyed her narrowly through his spectacles. "Dottie, if you're going to be a bump on a log, then go back out to the forest. Don't dishearten our *déjeuner*."

Dorothy ignored him. She was mulling over Benchley's question from the night before. "Why *would* a guy like MacGuffin take his own life? I don't understand it."

George Kaufman, a successful Broadway playwright and perpetual worrywart, said, "Who knows why anybody does anything? You can never know what's inside someone's head."

"MacGuffin?" Woollcott sneered. "If he ever had a thought in his head, it would have died of loneliness."

"Aleck, what would we do without you?" Dorothy sighed. "How I'd love to find out."

Robert Sherwood turned to her. "Mrs. Parker, forgive me for saying so, but I'd think if *anybody* would understand why MacGuffin would take his own life, it would be you."

Benchley shifted uncomfortably in his chair.

"Yes, Dottie," Woollcott said, "you attempted to cross the river Styx with an overdose of sleeping pills. So surely you understand what would compel the erstwhile MacGuffin to such an extreme."

"Oh, I understand suicide, all right," Dorothy said. "Just not Ernie MacGuffin's suicide." Then she turned to Neysa McMein, who sat next to Kaufman. "Neysa, you knew MacGuffin the best of any of us. He orbited around you like the moon. Did he ever talk about suicide?"

Neysa shook her head. "I'm as surprised as anyone. Frankly, I would have said Ernie was too shallow to commit suicide. He was self-absorbed and self-pitying, certainly. But self-loathing? Not a bit."

Dorothy leaned back in her chair. "Suicide is not done only by the Vincent van Goghs of the world—the geniuses, radicals or deep thinkers who carry sorrow around like a heavy suitcase. It's also done by regular people who just can't stand to get out of bed one more day and face the ugly world."

There was a moment of uncomfortable silence. No one looked at Dorothy. Benchley, who hated to discuss such topics (especially in reference to Dorothy, his closest friend), ostentatiously clapped his pipe in his palm and got up to go outside for a smoke. Dorothy felt like a fool.

Then Neysa considerately picked up the conversation where Dorothy had left off. "Ernie wasn't a deep thinker, that's true. But afraid to wake up and greet the world? I think not. You all know what he was like. He was full of energy. Always bugging anyone who could help him for a leg up. Always had another idea he was working on."

"Maybe this was simply his last idea," Kaufman said morosely.

Dorothy shook her head. "No. Neysa hit the nail on the head. MacGuffin wasn't a misunderstood genius, nor was he a dope at the end of his rope. When he last talked to me, he seemed—I don't know—*excited* by the idea."

"Could it be," Sherwood asked, "that he was so fixated on the idea of fame and notoriety that he killed himself to achieve it?"

"I don't think so," Neysa said. "Success seemed

like the thing he wanted most in this life, not in the next. What good is success if you're not alive to enjoy it?"

"Exactly," Dorothy said.

"Pshaw!" Woollcott fluttered his hands. "A fool like MacGuffin? Suicide is the ultimate selfish act, and MacGuffin was a self-absorbed nincompoop. It doesn't surprise me in the least that he would take the coward's way out. It makes perfect sense to me."

"I don't know," Dorothy said. "It takes more than a coward to jump off the Brooklyn Bridge."

Franklin Pierce Adams, the elder statesman of the group, spoke contemplatively from behind his cigar. "Can you please read his note again?"

Dorothy simply handed it to Adams, and he read it aloud. "'Then the world will know I'm not a hack. A new and better life awaits me. Good-bye, cruel world,'" Adams finished.

Woollcott wiped jelly from his mouth and sneered, "He writes like a melodramatic teenage girl."

"Takes one to know one," Dorothy said.

Woollcott frowned. "Highly amusing. You should submit that riposte to a suitably intellectual journal, such as *Boys' Life*. That aside, all that young fellow MacGuffin needed was a healthy outlet for his energy, such as a dose of vigorous exercise. Would have perked him right up."

Everyone looked skeptically at Woollcott, who

was notoriously—almost proudly—as fat and round as an overfed baby.

"And what would you know about exercise?" Dorothy asked. She was still annoyed by his comment that *suicide is the ultimate selfish act.*

"I know everything about exercise. I'm madly taken with it." Woollcott beamed through another mouthful of jelly tart. "I'm disappointed that no one here has noticed the phenomenal changes in my physique, all thanks to healthy exercise. My spirits are soaring. My skin is pink and glowing. My weight is down. My appetite is up."

"Haven't noticed any change in your healthy appetite," Dorothy said. "And none of those other changes you mentioned either."

"Aleck," Sherwood jeered. "The only exercise you get is exercising your right to free speech."

Adams asked, "What sort of healthy exercise are you talking about? Skewering playwrights? Elbowing out old ladies at Macy's?"

Woollcott laid his hands on the table and pronounced, "Croquet."

They all laughed.

"Croquet is not exercise," Adams declared. "It's puttering in the yard wearing a bad sweater."

"Croquet is just an excuse to wander around the lawn drinking gin and lemonade," said Marc Connelly, who was Kaufman's writing partner.

"Croquet requires all the physical exertion of a game of checkers," Dorothy said.

Woollcott sneered, "Not the way we play."

"*We?* We who?" Adams said.

"Harpo Marx and I."

Again they all laughed.

"You can't play croquet with Harpo," Dorothy said. "That's not a game. It's a circus."

Harold Ross, another member of the Round Table, came rushing into the dining room, followed by Benchley.

"Big news, everyone," Ross exclaimed. "Raoul Fleischmann had a great second quarter in the baking business. So he's finally going through with the loan. My magazine for New Yorkers is officially in business. Now, who wants to write an article for the inaugural issue?"

They had been enjoying heckling Woollcott and now extended their scorn to Harold Ross.

"Ross," Adams said, "you've been talking about launching that magazine for years. Do you really think we believe you'll get it off the ground now?"

Ross was born out West and still retained some of the earnest sincerity of a country boy. "Why, sure! Now, come on, who wants to contribute to the first issue and make history?"

"Forget it," Dorothy said. "Even if you do launch it, that magazine is going to sink faster than the *Titanic*."

Ross looked over the group seated around the table and eventually turned to the good-natured Benchley.

"Benchley, you can do it. You can write something light and funny and urbane."

"Such as?" Benchley said.

Dorothy spoke. "Give it a rest, Ross. We're busy with something just a bit more serious right now."

Ross said, "More serious than a dream that I've been trying to make real for years?"

"Yes, believe it or not, more serious than that," she said. "We were wondering why a chipper fellow such as Ernie MacGuffin would suddenly throw himself off a bridge."

Ross' bright expression darkened. He rubbed his big chin, thinking. "Yeah, I heard about that. MacGuffin is the talk of the town." Then Ross snapped his fingers. "That's it, Benchley! Write a story about why MacGuffin committed suicide."

"That's what you mean by light and funny and urbane?" Benchley said drily. "I'd hate to see what your more serious articles will cover."

Ross was unperturbed. "That's just what such a story needs. Your light touch. Not irreverent, just witty. Respectful yet affable."

"Aff yourself, Ross," Dorothy said. "It's a macabre idea."

"No, it isn't!" he insisted. "You just said you were asking yourselves why a guy like MacGuffin would throw himself off a bridge. Everyone in town is wondering the same thing. Now here's your chance to find out. You and Benchley can write it together."

Dorothy and Benchley looked at each other.

She said, "I couldn't possibly write such a thing."

"Five hundred bucks says you can," Ross said.

That caught their attention. Everyone at the table sat up.

Ross didn't stop there. "Come on, Benchley. You can do it. And, Dottie, if you don't want to write it, you can help him out with interviewing MacGuffin's friends and next of kin. Then the two of you split the fee however you want."

Dorothy and Benchley looked at each other again. They were thinking the same thing. Five hundred would pay off their liquor bill at Tony Soma's, with money to spare.

"Come on," Ross implored. "This story needs you. And you need this story."

"Oh, do it," Adams cried, "if only to shut Ross up."

"Fine," Benchley said. "I'll do it."

"Great," Ross said. "I need it in a week."

A week? Dorothy thought. Benchley looked equally doubtful.

Woollcott said, "Well, you have your first story, Ross. But do you even have a name for this new magazine of yours?"

Ross nodded. "*New York Life.*"

"Sounds like an insurance company," Kaufman said. "Do you have any other ideas?"

"*The Metropolitan?*"

"Another insurance company," Connelly said. "Anything else?"

Ross ran a hand through his thick hair, which stood on his head like an upturned bristle brush. "*Our Town.*"

Woollcott snorted. "Sounds like a Rotary Club newsletter. Come, come, Ross. You can do better than that."

Ross folded his arms over his chest. "You're all so damn smart. You tell me what to call it."

John Peter Toohey, a Broadway press agent and an occasional member of the group, spoke up. "Your magazine is for New Yorkers, by New Yorkers, and about New Yorkers. Why not call it *The New Yorker*?"

They all turned to look at Ross, who exhaled in frustration. "That's the dumbest thing I ever heard."

Chapter 4

Together Dorothy and Benchley left the Algonquin, silently and slowly strolling along Forty-fourth Street toward the Condé Nast building, which housed the offices of *Vanity Fair*.

Dorothy inhaled the last of her cigarette and dropped it into a street sweeper's ash can. "Making money from MacGuffin's suicide in order to pay our tab at Tony's . . ." She sighed, exhaling the smoke. "That doesn't seem right."

"Don't feel bad just yet," Benchley said brightly, puffing on his pipe. "We haven't made a red cent. We still need to write the darned article, and soon."

"There's the rub," she said. "How do we begin? Who do we interview?"

They looked at each other. Neither one had a good answer.

A brown sedan pulled to the curb. They recognized it as Detective O'Rannigan's car because the detective opened the door and got out. "Just the folks I was looking for."

Dorothy frowned. "You managed to track us down in front of the Algonquin after our well-known and usual lunchtime? Incredible police work, Detective."

"Funny business is over." He rounded the front

of the car and stood in their way. "I want to talk to you about Ernest MacGuffin, the painter."

Benchley looked around uncomfortably. "Shall we take this inside? Not quite civil to discuss suicide on the sidewalk."

They went back inside the Algonquin and found a small table in a dark corner of the hotel's luxurious lobby. Dorothy dropped into one of the plush lounge chairs. "MacGuffin's dead. What's so urgent?"

O'Rannigan tilted his small derby back on his balding head. "Explain to me why he gave you his suicide note."

"I was wondering the same thing myself," Dorothy said.

"I should have collected it from you last night." O'Rannigan held out a large hand, palm up. "Give it over. It's police evidence."

Dorothy grabbed her purse and held it tight. "Like hell it is. MacGuffin gave it to me. Go get your own suicide note."

O'Rannigan snapped his fingers and held out his palm again. Dorothy grudgingly dug the note out of her purse and slapped it in O'Rannigan's hand. He unfolded it, glanced it over and folded it up again. "Now talk. Why did MacGuffin give this to you?"

"We'll talk if you will," Dorothy said.

"What's that supposed to mean?"

"Quid pro quo," she said. "We tell you what

41

we know, and you tell us what you know."

O'Rannigan leaned back in his chair, arms folded. "You don't make deals with the New York City Police Department."

Dorothy clucked her tongue. "What are you afraid of? Or maybe you just don't know anything."

"I ain't afraid. But you're right—I don't know anything. I mean, I can't tell you anything. Now you talk."

So Dorothy talked. She told him simply that Ernie MacGuffin gave her the suicide note because he knew that she had once tried to commit suicide.

"Oh—yeah?" O'Rannigan seemed unsure whether to make fun of her or feel sorry for her.

"Yeah," she answered, not wanting either reaction from him. "And that's all I can tell you. Now your turn. You talk."

"There ain't much I can say. What do you want to know?"

Dorothy leaned forward. "His body? Did you find it?"

"Nah, not yet," O'Rannigan said. "We had a couple boats out this morning looking for it. No luck so far. But don't worry. He'll turn up eventually. They almost always do."

"Almost?"

"Well, the East River flows out to the bay and then directly to the Atlantic Ocean. I can't guarantee that the body didn't catch a current and is halfway to Spain by now. But probably not."

"Probably not?" Dorothy asked. "Probably what, then?"

"Probably the body will rise to the surface in a few days, bloated and blue, maybe with a few bites out of it, and wash ashore somewhere."

Bloated and blue, maybe with a few bites out of it? The thought made Dorothy sick. She choked the thought down.

But something—just a little something—had been bothering her since last night: MacGuffin's shoes. They were placed so neatly, side by side, at the rail of the Brooklyn Bridge. In appearance, MacGuffin had always been unkempt. Messy hair, paint-stained hands, rumpled jacket. It was odd that he placed his shoes so neatly—

"Mrs. Parker," Benchley said softly, "is anything the matter?"

"I'm not sure." She turned to the detective. "You don't think MacGuffin may have been the victim of foul play?"

"Foul play?" O'Rannigan laughed. "Didn't he stuff this suicide note in your purse? Exactly what kind of foul play would make a man willfully write a suicide note and then jump off a bridge?"

"You're the detective," Dorothy said. "You tell us."

"No kind of foul play, that's what," he

43

answered. "We get dozens of dumbasses jumping off bridges every year. This MacGuffin is just another name to add to that list." He stood up to leave and held up MacGuffin's note. "Thanks for the evidence."

Dorothy pondered a moment. "Evidence of what, Detective?"

But O'Rannigan was already out the door.

Moments later, Dorothy and Benchley were back on the sidewalk. The early-autumn afternoon was bright and sunny as they strolled along. The warm sunshine came at an angle, lighting the busy street with a golden glow. The air, which usually smelled of car exhaust and horse droppings, was now fragranced with a whiff of chimney smoke. A spinning cluster of dried leaves, animated by a cool breeze, danced across their path. Dorothy parted the dust devil of brown leaves with her little scuffed shoe.

She didn't feel like going back to work on such a glorious afternoon, especially after their disheartening chat with O'Rannigan.

"You know," Benchley said suddenly, as though reading her mind, "I don't feel like going back to the office. Let's go have a drink."

She looked up at him, at his funny bow tie, his kind smile, his twinkling eyes. She glanced at his soft, gentle hands and slid her arm through his as they walked together.

"Have a drink? Where? Not Tony's, certainly."

"Somewhere outdoors," he said with a sigh. "It's so enjoyable to have a drink in the autumn sunshine."

"That's all well and good. But, again, where? Should we get a bottle of bootleg hooch from a drugstore and plop down on the grass in Central Park like a couple of vagrants? The vagrants wouldn't stand for it."

They mulled this over as they strolled to a stop in front of a combination betting parlor and ticket shop. The window was covered with advertisements, placards and posters for different events—horse races, boxing matches, tennis matches, football games—all with large, screaming headlines.

"Look at this," Dorothy said. "The first-ever professional football match in New York is being held today. 'The National Football League presents the New York Football Giants versus the Frankford Yellow Jackets.'"

"*Professional* football?" Benchley scoffed. "Who wants to watch a bunch of washed-up players fumble around and lose a game when we can go see my alma mater's team fumble around and lose a game?"

"I do, if it means a drink," she said. "Didn't Sherwood say that's why Heywood Broun couldn't make it for lunch today? Broun is reporting in the press box for this game."

"The press box? Those boys can drink." Benchley inspected the poster. "New York Polo Grounds—there *is* no finer place to drink in the autumn sunshine than at a sporting event. On we go!"

Chapter 5

They arrived at the enormous and crowded stadium just as the first half of the game ended. They pressed through the crowd, climbed three flights of concrete stairs, and shuffled down a dim side corridor until they finally entered through a battered door to the shabby press box.

The box was about twelve feet wide and three rows deep. Several sports reporters—jackets off, sleeves rolled up, hats tilted back, cigarettes hanging from their mouths—clacked the keys of portable typewriters or scribbled in notepads. Heywood Broun turned and, seeing Dorothy and Benchley, greeted them with a cheer. As usual, the big, burly sports writer looked disheveled, like an unmade bed.

"Mrs. Parker! Mr. Benchley! What a grand surprise." Broun beamed. "Sit right down. You're just in time for the halftime show. Houdini's here. He's going to make something disappear."

They sat down and Dorothy asked Broun if he had anything to drink.

"I had a bottle here a moment ago. We were handing it around." He stood up and addressed the other reporters. "Hey, boys, who's got the bottle?"

A bottle of rum was passed hand to hand back to Broun. He held it up. It was empty.

"No surprise, I guess," Dorothy said down-heartedly. "Sunny afternoon in a reporter's box. You boys work up a thirst watching the pigskin fly."

"Don't fret," Broun said, dropping the empty bottle into a dustbin. "Liquor bottles are like subway trains around here. Miss one and another will show up in a few minutes. So, what brings you to the Polo Grounds?"

It seemed preposterous to explain that they had traveled a hundred blocks for a nonexistent drink.

"It's a nice day, so we gave ourselves the afternoon off," Dorothy said.

"You just missed Edna Ferber," Broun said, referring to the bestselling novelist and infrequent attendee at the Algonquin Round Table. "She went down to talk to—"

A voice burst over the loudspeaker. *"La-dieees aaa-nnd gen-tle-mennnnnn . . ."*

They looked down at the center of the football field. On a hastily erected stage, a dark-haired man in a tuxedo stood beside an enormous wooden box. "You know me as Houdini the escape artist, who has baffled millions around the world. I have escaped from all types of handcuffs, manacles, ropes, straitjackets, cages, jails—and even coffins. Although imprisoned and hand-cuffed, I am no criminal. But as every criminal knows, there is no escape from"—he paused dramatically as a policeman on horseback climbed

48

the short flight of steps up to the stage—"the law."

The crowd laughed and jeered at the policeman. The horse, a Clydesdale, stretched its neck and whinnied.

"Even I can't outrun the law," Houdini continued good-humoredly. "Or can I . . . ?"

The crowd, clearly on the side of lawlessness, cheered again.

Houdini swept across the stage to the horse and policeman. "Officer," he said, "would you kindly dismount this majestic creature?"

The policeman hesitated. The crowd jeered. The policeman slowly, resentfully climbed down from the horse.

Houdini took the horse's reins. "La-dieees and gen-tle-men, what you are about to see is merely a sampling of my phenomenal, phantasmagorical presentation at the Hippodrome, opening next week. Buy your tickets now because, I guarantee you this, they will not last long. This will be the most sensational exhibition ever presented at the Hippodrome, or anywhere else in the world!"

Dorothy turned to Benchley. "He's got a knack for quiet understatement, don't you think?"

"Watch closely," Houdini continued. "To outrun the law, one must take away his means of swift transport."

The policeman started forward, but Houdini held out his hand and the policeman stopped. Houdini walked the Clydesdale into the open end of the enormous wooden box, which was big enough for only the horse. Houdini stepped back, patted the horse on the rump, closed the door and threw the sliding lock, bolting the box shut.

Houdini again addressed the audience. "Your patience, please, as I make this policeman's beautiful steed disappear!"

On the sidelines, the New York Giants' marching band struck up a rousing rendition of Sousa's "Stars and Stripes Forever." On the small stage, the policeman made several attempts to reach the big wooden box. Houdini blocked him and held him back each time.

Heywood Broun shook his head. "We live in an age of mania. Everywhere you turn, there's someone doing a lamebrained stunt or lunatic spectacle or frenzied endurance contest. Last month, a man sat for days on the top of a flagpole. Today, a bunch of college boys are seeing how many of them can stuff themselves into a Model T. Tomorrow, party boys and flappers are dancing themselves to death in a twenty-four-hour Charleston contest."

As he spoke, Edna Ferber appeared, sat down beside Broun and picked up the conversation as though she had never left.

"And don't forget hypnotic trances, mystical séances and the all-night Ouija board readings," Edna said. "Thank goodness these absurd, manic pursuits haven't infected our little group."

Dorothy looked down to the football field. "Perhaps you spoke too soon."

The crowd erupted in a roar. On the stage, Houdini and the policeman had frozen as they watched two figures carrying croquet mallets zigzagging across the field. Dorothy recognized them instantly as Alexander Woollcott and Harpo Marx. As they ran, Woollcott and Harpo knocked croquet balls every which way. A group of stadium officials appeared on the field and chased after them.

Edna, abruptly turning away from the spectacle on the field, addressed Dorothy and Benchley. "So, what brings you two here?"

"I already asked them," Broun said. "Some nonsense about enjoying a sunny afternoon."

Edna nodded thoughtfully. "So what *really* brings you here?"

"Other than playing hooky?" Dorothy asked. Then she explained about Ernie MacGuffin, the subsequent article assignment from Harold Ross and his fledgling magazine, and their puzzlement about how to proceed.

"Everyone's talking about MacGuffin," Broun said. "I wish Ross was paying *me* five hundred dollars for an article. I'd spend it on one of MacGuffin's paintings. The investment could be worth double in no time."

"We're not so much interested in the paintings as in the man," Dorothy said. "Anyway, the five hundred is earmarked for our tab at Tony Soma's, not some crummy painting of cowboys and Indians."

"They say MacGuffin had a storehouse of real art—not just lurid illustrations for magazines," Edna said.

"You're no football fan," Dorothy said. "What brings *you* here?"

Edna pointed to the man on the stage. "Him."

"Houdini?" Benchley said. "You're a Houdini fan?"

"Believe it or not, we're from the same hometown—Appleton, Wisconsin," Edna said. "I interviewed him twenty years ago, one of my first assignments as a cub reporter. I went backstage just now to say hello. Would you believe he remembered me? He said he even saved the clipping of my article in his scrapbook."

She blushed.

Dorothy glanced at Benchley. They were both guilty of thinking the same thing. Edna Ferber was wildly successful as a popular novelist, but she was not a great beauty. If Houdini did indeed remember her, it was despite her looks, not because of them. (Edna had once appeared in a tailored suit at the Round Table. "You look almost like a man," said Woollcott. Edna quickly replied, "So do you.")

On the field, the marching band ended their tune with a wave of Houdini's arms. Woollcott and

Harpo were nowhere to be seen—presumably they had been chased off the field. Houdini addressed the impatient crowd of nearly thirty thousand people.

"Ladies and gentlemen, thank you for your patience. Please direct your attention to the massive container behind me. Inside, the horse has disappeared. Evaporated. Vanished!"

The policeman stood to the side with his arms folded, in scorning disbelief.

"You don't believe me, Officer?" Houdini said. He ran to the big box, tugging on some hidden bolts or fixtures. "See for yourself!"

Houdini stepped away as the sides of the box fell outward, landing on the stage with a loud clatter. The policeman jumped backward, almost tumbling off the stage.

The horse was gone.

The crowd exploded into thunderous cheering and applause. The noise was so loud that Dorothy had to cover her ears.

The policeman ran to the floor of the wooden box as though a trace of the horse might still be there. Then he jumped off the waist-high stage and looked under the bunting that covered its side. Apparently seeing nothing, he threw the bunting down in disgust, hoisted himself back up and stalked threateningly toward Houdini. The magician didn't move an inch. He merely smiled.

All this time, the crowd continued to roar and applaud. Houdini raised his hands and gestured for quiet.

"If you thought that was stupendous, come see my exhibition at the Hippodrome next week!" As Houdini spoke, he began to lift the sides of the enormous wooden box, aided by the policeman. Together they reassembled it—all the while, Houdini kept up his patter about the wonders to be seen in his stage show.

Then, seemingly as an afterthought, Houdini opened up the front of the box, reached in—and led out the horse by its reins! The crowd made a collective gasp, and then again burst into thunderous applause, even louder than before. The stunned policeman took the reins and then hugged the horse around the neck. The crowd cheered even more wildly.

After many bows and waves, Houdini finally left the stage, followed by the policeman on his horse. The crowd didn't quiet down until the magician had disappeared through one of the tunnels under the bleachers.

Dorothy leaned back in her seat and lit a cigarette. "Maybe we should recruit Houdini to make our problem disappear."

"Problem?" Broun said. "What problem?"

Benchley spoke. "We don't know exactly what to do. We don't know who to talk to. Besides Neysa McMein, we can't think of anyone who befriended MacGuffin. Even she didn't like him much."

"He must have had an agent or something to sell his artwork. Neysa could find out," Broun said. "And of course he had that tall, beautiful, vapid wife."

"MacGuffin had a beautiful wife?" Dorothy said. "Never seen her."

"Not beautiful like a showgirl," Edna said. "Beautiful like a statue."

"Well, when you put it that way," Dorothy said, "now she sounds really approachable."

Dorothy glanced at Benchley, who raised his eyebrows. The idea of interrogating a grieving widow—a beautiful statuesque widow—for a puff piece in Ross' little hobby of a magazine seemed almost unconscionable.

But of course, they knew that was where they had to start.

"Heywood," Dorothy said, "when does that next bottle of rum get here?"

Chapter 6

The following morning, Dorothy and Benchley planned to meet bright and early across the street from Ernie MacGuffin's house. Dorothy and Benchley knew each other too well to actually show up bright and early. It was ten o'clock before Dorothy arrived, just moments after Benchley had.

MacGuffin lived on East Fifth Street, a quiet tree-lined street near Greenwich Village, the artists' district in lower Manhattan.

"That's the address," Benchley said, gazing across the street at the narrow, three-story town house. "Which apartment is it?"

"Neysa said bottom floor," Dorothy replied. "Street level."

But they stood a moment longer. They were in no hurry to chat with MacGuffin's widow. Benchley puffed on his pipe, and Dorothy smoked a cigarette.

"What should we say, exactly?" Benchley asked thoughtfully. " 'Good morning, we're here to ask you why your dead husband committed suicide'?"

"Perhaps a bit more subtlety is in order. Let's just tell her who we are and see where it goes. Ready?"

They strolled across the empty, sun-dappled street.

"You'd think an artist would need more light," Dorothy said as they advanced toward the building's stoop. "I wonder why MacGuffin took a shady apartment on street level."

"Maybe he had a fear of heights."

Dorothy thought of the long distance between the highest span of the Brooklyn Bridge and the dark water below. "I think he got over it."

They stood side by side on the top step as Benchley knocked on the door.

A very tall, elegant woman answered. She had luminous pale skin and long, straight, jet-black hair. The woman's expectant, breathless smile changed to an expression of dismay. "Oh. Hello."

Clearly, she was expecting someone else, Dorothy thought.

Dorothy and Benchley introduced themselves. Midge MacGuffin shook hands politely, delicately. She wore a silk sapphire blue dress, which seemed cheerfully out of place on an ordinary Wednesday morning in late October.

"Sorry to show up unannounced," Dorothy said, feeling outclassed in her old maroon jersey jumper. "Were you expecting someone?"

"No, no one special," Midge said, though she glanced up and down the street. "What can I do for you?"

"We'd like to talk to you about your husband," Benchley said.

"And offer our condolences," Dorothy added.

"We work for *Vanity Fair* magazine. We've been assigned to write an article about Ernie."

Dorothy sensed Benchley look at her in surprise. True, they worked for *Vanity Fair*. And, true, they were assigned to write this article—but by Harold Ross, not the editors of *Vanity Fair*. But Midge MacGuffin didn't have to know that.

"We didn't know him very well," Benchley continued. "But we knew him well enough to write such an article with care and affection."

While Benchley spoke, Midge busied herself with inserting a pair of pearl earrings.

"Oh," she said, indifferent. Then she looked imploringly at Benchley. "Can I trouble you to help me with my necklace?"

She handed Benchley a short string of pearls and turned around. Benchley, after the briefest of quizzical pauses, draped the string of pearls around her neck and clasped it easily. Dorothy was mildly surprised. Benchley was usually all thumbs with such things.

Midge faced them again, smiling, evidently pleased that her outfit was now complete. "Thank you."

"May we come in?" Dorothy said.

A shadow of concern darkened the woman's porcelain complexion. "Actually, now's not a good time. Perhaps you could come back later?"

She backed away, grasping the doorknob to close the door.

"Sure," Dorothy said. "When?"

"Whenever you please. Phone me later. I'll be happy to set up an appointment with you."

As the woman retreated through the door, Dorothy stepped forward. Dorothy knew the woman was bluffing them. "So we can telephone you later this afternoon, then?"

"Yes, that's fine. Good-bye," Midge said, closing the door, clearly anxious to end this conversation.

Dorothy grabbed the edge of the door. "Just a moment."

"Yes?" Midge almost let her impatience show.

"May we have your telephone number?"

"Of course. It's Klondike-5-6789." She rattled the numbers off quickly, and then closed the door on them.

They stood there a moment, staring at the closed door.

"How much do you want to bet she made up that phone number?" Dorothy asked.

"I'll bet five, six, seven, eight, nine bucks," Benchley replied.

They turned and strolled away.

Dorothy said, "Did you get the feeling she had something else on her mind?"

"Some*one* else, you mean?" he asked. "Not her recently departed husband, that's for sure. Our endeavor to write an article about her husband didn't seem to disrupt the grieving widow one tiny bit."

"Grieving? She wasn't wearing a scrap of black. Unless you count lacy black undergarments."

A wide-shouldered man carrying a big bouquet of white roses marched in their direction. He didn't waste a glance on them. He eyed the house numbers—and nearly bumped into Dorothy.

With little more than a grunt of apology, the large man hurried by them, continuing to look up at the buildings. They caught the scent of roses and dime-store cologne as he brushed by.

Dorothy and Benchley stopped in their tracks. Without a word to each other, they turned and followed the man at a distance.

Dorothy sized him up. The man wore a fitted gray plaid suit that emphasized, rather than hid, his large, muscular frame. His thick neck was as large as his head, which was topped by thinning, grizzled, dark blond hair under a gray hat. Dorothy hypothesized that he was a man who had spent the early part of his career in hard physical labor but had since worked his way up to some level of authority and prosperity.

As they expected, the man strode up to Midge MacGuffin's door. He straightened his hat and the knot of his necktie, squared his wide shoulders and knocked loudly and confidently.

Midge, now fully primped and ready, threw open the door. Again she was breathless with expectation. But this time, her expectations were correct.

Dorothy and Benchley withdrew into the shelter of the closest doorway, out of Midge's line of vision.

"Mr. Clay! So good to see you after all these years!"

"And it warms my heart to see you," the man gushed. His voice was husky, choked with emotion. "But 'Mr. Clay'? You knew me too well once to use surnames now, dear Harriet."

Dorothy and Benchley silently mouthed the name to each other: *Harriet?*

"Very well, Bertram." Her chuckle was as gentle and melodious as a wind chime. "Please do come in."

He stepped forward, holding out the bouquet of flowers. "Here, my dear Harriet—these are for you."

"Oh, Bertie, my favorites. You remembered! How thoughtful of you."

She closed the door. Dorothy and Benchley could hear only the fading sound of her lilting laugh.

Dorothy looked up at Benchley's raised eyebrows.

"Did you notice those flowers?" she said. "White roses, not white lilies."

"Maybe the grieving widow has an allergy to lilies?"

"Or maybe she's not doing a lot of grieving."

Chapter 7

That afternoon, in the quiet office of *Vanity Fair*, Dorothy stared at a blank page in her typewriter. For the tenth time, she gazed at the glossy black-and-white photos on her wooden desk. The photos showed a brand new briefcase.

She hated writing photo captions. Nothing came to mind. In frustration, she punched the typewriter keys to see what her brain would spit out.

Important date? Carry an extra pair of briefs in this handsome, genuine cowhide, leather-stitched Luxembourg briefcase.

That would not do. Clearly, the rendezvous between Midge MacGuffin and Big Shoulders Bertram was still on her mind.

She yanked out the sheet of paper, inserted a new one and typed again.

Important date in court? Carry your legal briefs in this handsome, genuine cowhide, leather-stitched Luxembourg briefcase.

Not great, but it would suffice for now. She crumpled up the first attempt and tossed it at Benchley, who was leaning back in his chair, mouth agape, snoozing at his desk. The paper ball bounced off his forehead.

"Fred, wake up."

He rubbed his eyes and stretched. "Whatever for?"

"We need to figure out what's going on with Midge MacGuffin and Bertie the Mystery Man."

"Oh, that. Wake me when you find out." He lowered his head to his chest and closed his drooping eyes.

Dorothy was about to toss another paper ball at Benchley when the door flew open and their friend and fellow editor Robert Sherwood entered.

"Good afternoon, boys and girls," Sherwood said as he took off his overcoat and his straw boater and hung them on the coat stand.

He hesitated before he sat down, sensing he had interrupted something between Dorothy and Benchley. "What's with you two?"

Dorothy explained their all-too-brief meeting with Midge MacGuffin that morning and their puzzlement about the appearance of Bertie. "We're supposed to find out what kind of man MacGuffin was. But now it seems like we have to find out first what kind of woman she is."

"Did you call her this afternoon as she told you to do?" Sherwood asked.

Dorothy shook her head. "She gave us a phony number."

"Look her up in the city directory," Sherwood said.

Dorothy had already considered that. "What good would it do? She'll give us the brush-off on the phone even easier than she did on her doorstep. No, we need to think of something else."

They were silent for a long moment, thinking. Then their editor's office door opened, and a stately gray-haired gentleman appeared. Frank Crowninshield, born of high society and educated with high standards, was a perfect match for the fashionable, erudite style of the magazine he edited.

Crowninshield stared at the three editors stretched out in front of him. Dorothy slouched in her chair, staring sullenly at nothing. Benchley had his feet up on his desk, his hands laced together behind his head, his eyes closed. Sherwood sat with his long legs angled from his chair; his chin rested on his hands, which were folded on his desk.

"I was alarmed by the uproarious silence," Crowninshield said in his honeyed, cultivated voice. "What are you young whelps up to out here? Very little, I see."

They didn't answer. They barely moved.

"Dillydallying again? I've just about had enough." Crowninshield sighed, more disgusted than angry. "You treat this office as your backyard tree house—you come and go as you please.

You're gone for hours at lunch. When you do deign to come in, you lollygag and let your deadlines fly by like swallows heading south for winter—"

Sherwood stood up. He held out a thin envelope.

"What's this?" Crowninshield said, alarmed.

Sherwood spoke for the three of them. "It's two tickets to Houdini at the Hippodrome."

Crowninshield gently accepted the envelope. "Houdini?"

"That's right," Benchley said quickly. "We know he's your favorite. This is his final tour before he retires. They're for next Thursday's show, which is Halloween night. Should be fantastic."

Crowninshield blushed. "You really got these for me?" He looked at the tickets and made an attempt to recover his composure. "You're not giving me these just to embarrass me into silence? To curry favor?"

"Certainly not," Dorothy said. "They're a gift, freely given. No strings attached. No favor curried. No chicken curried either."

Crowninshield's eyes began to well with tears.

Benchley said, "We sent Sherwood out into deepest midtown just to acquire those for you. We know how you like a magical spectacular."

Crowninshield's fingers trembled as he held the tickets. His voice was choked. "You damned young whelps. I thank you and I would love to go.

But unfortunately I cannot make it next Thursday night. I have a social event to attend." He handed the tickets to Benchley. "Here, you go. Take Mrs. Parker. Review it for the magazine. Put the cost on your expense report."

Crowninshield removed an immaculate handkerchief from his breast pocket and dabbed at his damp eyes. With a sob and a sneeze, he withdrew into his office and closed the door.

Sherwood broke into a grin. He stood and bowed.

Dorothy muttered, "That was quick thinking, you giant son of a bitch."

Benchley was not as pleased. "If he had kept my tickets, I would have taken it out of your paycheck."

"And now you can expense them, thanks to me," Sherwood said.

"And now I have to write yet another review, thanks to you," Benchley said.

"Oh, you would have been assigned it anyhow," Sherwood said with a wave of dismissal. "You may return the favor at your leisure." He glanced at the clock on the wall—nearly four o'clock. "Now, let's celebrate, shall we?"

"Where?" Dorothy asked.

Sherwood stood, retrieving his hat and coat from the stand. "Tony Soma's, of course."

"We can't," she said sourly. "We're *personae non gratae*."

Benchley said, "That's pig Latin for *et-gay ost-lay*."

"You don't say." Sherwood dropped into his chair, disappointed. "Then where?"

Chapter 8

Dorothy and Benchley spent nearly a week fruitlessly trying to get in touch with Midge MacGuffin and trying to find someplace to get a drink.

Why is it, Dorothy thought, *that when you're denied something, you only want it more?*

"This is New York during Prohibition," she cried. "There's practically a speakeasy on every corner. Why is this so difficult?"

Benchley shushed her. This was not the place to make such exclamations. They stood in a long line at the pharmacist's counter at the rear of an enormous drugstore off Times Square. They had heard that this druggist made and sold hooch over the counter for ten bucks a pint. Not cheap, but cheaper—for now—than paying off their bill to Tony and Mrs. Soma. Fortunately, they hadn't run into Mrs. Soma and Tony Jr. since that night on the Brooklyn Bridge.

"Mrs. Parker, Mr. Benchley," a woman's voice said. "What are you doing here?"

They turned to see Neysa McMein followed by Franklin Pierce Adams, enshrouded in a cloud of cigar smoke.

"Just buying a pint of 'medicine,'" Dorothy said. "What are you doing here at seven o'clock on a Monday night?"

Neysa nodded toward Adams. "Just dropping by to pick up some cheap cigars for the star columnist of the *New York World*. What's that phrase? 'What this country needs is a good five-cent cigar'? Well, he just bought a bundle of them."

Adams frowned. "There are plenty of good five-cent cigars in this country. The trouble is, they each cost a quarter."

Dorothy waved away the pungent smoke. "No, the trouble is, they smell like hell."

"Anyway, I'm so glad we bumped into you," Neysa said. "I asked everyone in the art scene and it took me forever, but I finally found out the name of Ernie MacGuffin's agent."

"Swell. What's his name?"

"Abraham Snath. He's a lawyer, an artists' agent, an art dealer, you name it. Not a very sweet fellow, I'm told."

"Are any of them?" Dorothy asked.

"His office is near the old armory, off Lexington," Neysa said. "But there's something else."

"Next!" the pharmacist said gruffly.

Benchley apprehensively approached the high counter and mumbled something unintelligible.

"What? Speak up!" the irritable pharmacist barked.

Benchley flinched.

"Cripes!" Dorothy said to Benchley. "He's not a Supreme Court judge." She turned to the impatient pharmacist, who exuded authority with his high-collared white smock and his high perch behind the counter. She spoke sweetly. "A pint of your finest medicine, if you please, sir."

The pharmacist scowled. "Got a prescription?"

"A *prescription?*" She blinked. "Is that honestly necessary?"

"This is a licensed pharmacy, you ditzy lady. No prescription, no medicine," the pharmacist said with finality.

Benchley slammed his hand hard on the counter. He spoke so loudly that everyone in the store could hear. "Don't you dare talk to her like that!"

The store went quiet. Everyone's eyes were on them. The pharmacist froze.

"You need a prescription?" Benchley again slammed his hand down on the counter, leaving a five-dollar bill on top of Dorothy's ten-dollar bill. "There's your prescription. Good enough? Now, give the lady what she asked for."

Without a word, the pharmacist disappeared among the shelves behind him and quickly reappeared with a large brown glass bottle with no label. "I'm fresh out of the usual. This is all I have," he said humbly. "It's, uh, 'cough medicine.'"

As the pharmacist spoke, he put the bottle in a white paper bag, folded down the top of the bag neatly and placed it on the counter in front of Dorothy.

Benchley, Neysa and Adams turned to leave. Dorothy picked up the bag. She spoke as sweetly as before. "I suppose we each got a taste of our own medicine." She turned on her heel and followed her friends.

They strolled to the marble-topped soda counter at the front of the store. Dorothy caught up to Benchley and squeezed his arm. She whispered, "Thank you for standing up for me to that thug of a druggist."

"I'm now both anti-thug and anti-druggist. I'm anti-thuggist."

"Gesundheit."

Neysa took a seat at the soda fountain. Adams, still in a cloud of cigar smoke, sat down next to her. Benchley and Dorothy joined them.

"You were telling us about MacGuffin's agent," Dorothy said to Neysa. "And you were about to say something else before we were so rudely interrupted."

"Why, yes." Neysa's beautiful half-lidded eyes widened. "Guess where we're off to. You'll never guess."

"No, I certainly won't," Dorothy said impatiently. "Just tell."

"A séance. Can you believe it?"

Dorothy and Benchley looked back and forth between Neysa, whom they knew as a savvy, worldly-wise woman, and Adams, a hard-nosed veteran newspaperman.

"No," Dorothy said, stupefied. "I can't believe it. A *séance?*"

"Not just any séance," Adams said, puffing cigar smoke. "A séance of Ernie MacGuffin. Some sorceress or voodoo priestess claims to be conjuring up MacGuffin's disembodied voice."

"Come along with us," Neysa said, playfully. "It'll be a lark."

"A lark?" Dorothy said. "Sounds like a crock."

"Of course it's a crock," Adams said, smiling. "But it's good material for my column."

Dorothy shook her head. "I need a drink if I'm going to hear any more of this." She motioned for the young, pimply-faced soda jerk. "Soda water, please."

"Same for me," said Benchley.

Neysa asked for a root beer float. Adams ordered an orange phosphate.

After the soda jerk delivered the drinks, Dorothy reached for the white paper bag with the brown glass bottle. She pulled out the stopper and sniffed. It even smelled like medicine.

"Maybe you *should* come with us to the séance," Adams said. "Might be something there you could use in your article for Ross."

"Ugh, that article for Ross," Dorothy groaned, and poured some of the druggist's hooch into her soda water. "We don't even want to think about it."

"Not going well?" Adams asked.

"Our only contact so far has been Midge MacGuffin, but we can never pin her down. She's likely been busy with Bertram the Mystery Man all week."

"Well, now you know the name of Ernie's agent," Neysa said. "That should get the ball rolling."

"Thanks to you," Dorothy said, raising her glass. "Let's make a toast to that numbskull himself. To Ernie MacGuffin. May his death have been easier for him than it's been for us."

They raised their glasses and clinked them together. "To Ernie MacGuffin."

They all drank deeply. Suddenly Benchley gagged. Dorothy coughed violently.

"Mrs. Parker, Mr. Benchley, are you all right?" Adams asked. "Something wrong with the 'cough medicine'?"

"Damn right, there is," Dorothy choked, slamming her glass to the counter. "It really *is* cough medicine. That lousy pharmacist actually put medicine in my medicine bottle."

Chapter 9

The next morning, Dorothy and Benchley skipped work. They wondered how the séance had been the night before. But they would ask Neysa and Adams about it another time.

Today, they were off to see Harold Ross to ask for an advance. Ross had offered to pay them five hundred for the article. So, why not collect it now rather than later? Once they paid off Tony Soma, then they could focus on writing the article—and know they would have an oasis to go back to after writing it.

Dorothy and Benchley found their way to Ross' new office in the Fleischmann Building on West Forty-fourth.

As they rode up in the elevator, she thought again about how Benchley had defended her in the drugstore. It wasn't his gallantry that impressed her—she was a thoroughly modern woman and could speak for herself. She didn't need a man to do that.

What impressed her—what warmed her heart—was that she knew Benchley usually avoided such confrontations. He hated "scenes." And yet, he spoke up for her, without even a moment's hesitation. She wanted to grab his hand and squeeze it tight. Damn it, she wanted to kiss him! But Benchley was a married man. And even if he wasn't, there was an elevator operator standing right there in front of them.

Before she could give it another thought, the doors opened. The operator said, "Twelfth floor," and they stepped into a wide, well-lit hallway.

A few paces away, a workman in stained painter's overalls was busy lettering the new magazine's name on the door's opaque glass window.

"*The New Yorker*?" Dorothy read aloud. "A rather generic name."

The painter turned on her and spoke with a hard Brooklyn sneer. "What should it be called? *The Pittsburgher*?"

The painter yanked open the door. They went in, and he slammed the door behind them.

Dorothy had pictured a posh, bright office with many sharp, young editors hard at work. Instead, they were in a tiny, dingy, windowless office with three old desks. Only one of the desks held a typewriter. On a second desk stood an old telephone. At the third desk was a young woman with a smart, boyish haircut and a tired expression.

Dorothy and Benchley recognized her as Jane Grant, a journalist for the *New York Times* and also Ross' wife. She was the only person in the room and was busy erasing numbers from a large ledger book. She paused a moment to blow away the erasures. She appeared frazzled as she looked up and noticed them. "Mrs. Parker. Mr. Benchley. Whatever are you doing here?"

They said their hellos and asked to see Ross.

"He's not in," she sighed, exasperated. "He's down in the dumps."

"Poor old Ross," Benchley said sympathetically. "The magazine is having problems so soon?"

"Yes, we are, as a matter of fact," she said, throwing down her pencil. "We've had no electricity until yesterday. We have no office supplies. We have no staff. And every time I talk on the phone to a vendor or supplier—or just anyone who knocks on that door—I have to explain what *The New Yorker* is."

"Very sorry to hear that," Dorothy said. "I guess that's why Ross is down in the dumps."

Jane shrugged. "I guess so."

"In any case," Dorothy continued, "we'd like to speak to him. Can you tell us where we can find him?"

She looked at Dorothy incredulously and spoke impatiently. "Didn't you hear me? I just told you. He's down in the dumps."

Dorothy and Benchley stepped off a hired boat onto a long wooden pier at Rikers Island. To either side of the pier, weather-beaten garbage scows unloaded steam shovels full of rancid trash, which had been shipped up the East River from Manhattan and the other boroughs.

Dorothy and Benchley looked around. Mountains of garbage filled the landscape. Trash covered nearly every inch of ground. Above them, squadrons of seagulls rose and then dived like warplanes in a dogfight. Somewhere on this ever-expanding hundred-acre island wasteland was a small prison farm, but it was nowhere in sight. Nor was Harold Ross.

The putrid stench of decomposing garbage, combined with the sulfurous odor of the river, was overpowering and nauseating. Benchley handed Dorothy a clean handkerchief, which she thankfully used to cover her nose and mouth.

"How will we ever find him?" she wondered aloud, her voice muffled. "And what is he even doing out here?"

In the distance, a flock of seagulls suddenly rose en masse, as though startled by something.

"Let's check over there," Benchley said.

They cautiously followed a rough dirt path that had been forged by bulldozers. Dorothy's little blue pumps were not made for walking on the bumpy, muddy terrain. At one point, her shoe got stuck in the muck. She stood on one leg, holding her bare foot aloft, while Benchley reached to retrieve the shoe. It made a sucking sound as he freed it from the gluey mud.

They followed the winding path as it twisted between the mountains of garbage. They eventually found themselves in a ravine, with high slopes of trash on either side that blocked out the sunlight.

In the narrow ribbon of smoky blue sky overhead, a red object soared in a gentle arc through the air. They couldn't see where it landed. Above the sound of the seagulls and steam shovels, they seemed to hear voices. Familiar voices.

They emerged from the ravine and saw that the path in front of them rose uphill. They climbed the short ascent and saw a figure at the top of a hill.

The man had his back to them, but they recognized his hunched shoulders, his spiky straw-colored hair, his hands jammed sullenly in his pockets. He stood at the edge of an overlook. Dorothy and Benchley approached him silently.

Harold Ross didn't move. His mournful eyes looked down at the clearing below. The clearing was a wide area of bare ground studded here and there with monolithic objects of junk—a claw-foot bathtub, a rusty spring mattress, the carcass of a Model T, and many others.

On opposite ends of the field, two figures in white athletic sweaters and pants ran around helter-skelter. Dorothy identified them right away—Alexander Woollcott and Harpo Marx, playing their crazy game of croquet.

"Hello, Ross," Dorothy said casually.

Ross barely turned to glance their way. He didn't seem at all surprised to see them.

"Hi, Dottie. Benchley." His voice was melancholy. His gaze returned to the game. "What brings you here?"

We could ask you the same thing, Dorothy thought. Instead, she took a deep breath, which she quickly regretted, and spoke up. "We came to ask for an advance on the fee for the article."

Ross didn't look at her. "An advance?"

She thought he was asking for an explanation. "There have been certain expenses—" she began.

"Expenses?"

"Yes, expenses. You know, related to research. Telegrams. Telephone calls. Research fees. And the like."

"Sorry," he sighed, his shoulders drooping further. "Can't help you out. Fleischmann is tightening the terms of the loan."

"Ah," Benchley said. "That's not good news."

Ross shook his head. He spoke as though talking to himself. "Starting up a magazine is damned expensive! I never realized the amount of the investment involved. The money is just running through my fingers. You need money for putting down deposits for paper at the printer. For creating promotional mailers to send to advertisers. For purchasing a mailing list to find initial subscribers, and then for printing up a notice to send to them, plus the postage on top of that. Then there are the day-to-day expenses. Leasing the office. Buying desks and typewriters and office supplies. Installing telephone service—"

"Again, sorry to hear that," Dorothy said. She did feel bad for him. But she also didn't want to make this lousy trip out to Rikers Island for nothing. "We understand you're stretched. But could you at least help us out a little?"

Ross shook his head again. Then he looked at them directly for the first time. "Matter of fact, I'm glad that you're here. I wanted to talk to you. I have to reduce the fee for the article. Instead of five hundred, I can only offer you four hundred." He turned back to watch the game. "You can shorten the article accordingly. It's not like we need a helluva lot of editorial pages to balance out the few ad pages. This goddamn magazine—" He cursed loudly. "Damn! It went right down the toilet."

"What?" Dorothy and Benchley said together.

"Harpo's croquet ball." Ross pointed toward the field. "Just went down an old toilet."

"Oh, right," she muttered softly. "I know exactly how it feels."

Chapter 10

That afternoon, Dorothy waited on East Twenty-fifth Street with her dog, Woodrow Wilson, a bat-eared, bug-eyed Boston terrier. They loitered in front of an ancient limestone office building—a narrow, grim, dark and dreary old mausoleum of a place. *Like something out of a Dickens novel,* Dorothy thought. She looked up at it. On the grimy, sooty windows of the third floor was painted in peeling gold-leaf letters: ABRAHAM SNATH, ESQ.: ATTORNEY/ARTIST'S AGENT/ART DEALER/NOTARY PUBLIC.

"And pants pressed while you wait," Dorothy said aloud. The dog looked up at her quizzically.

That morning, as she and Benchley had left the city dump of Rikers Island and took the hired boat back to Manhattan, they realized they had only one option left—they'd better get their article written and done with before Ross cut the fee any further.

They also realized they stank like sweaty fishmongers. So Dorothy went back to her apartment at the Algonquin, and Benchley took the train back to his home in the suburbs, to clean up and change clothes.

She was frustrated. She felt thwarted by the situation with the article. With Harold Ross. With Tony Soma—and his wife and son. With Ernie

MacGuffin. With the whole damn lot of them!

But right now, she was annoyed at Benchley the most. He had to take the train all the way back to Scarsdale. For what? To get a bath and put on a new suit? Couldn't he do that in the city?

She had to admit to herself (and not for the first time) that she didn't like having to share him.

Why is it, Dorothy thought yet again, *that when you're denied something, you only want it more?*

But how absurd! She knew she was being unreasonable. *Share him?* Benchley was a faithfully married man. She was a single woman. He simply wasn't hers to share. The pleasure of his company was all she could ask for. And frankly, that was all she needed.

Woodrow Wilson tugged on his leash. A slim young woman with a peroxide blond permanent wave and a short, tight blue skirt approached Dorothy and the dog. Woody wagged his little tail; his wide-set eyes bulged even more and his bat-like ears perked up.

You horny little pervert, Dorothy thought, looking at the dog. *Just like a man.*

"Cute pooch," the woman said as she handed Dorothy a flyer and kept walking. Dorothy didn't look at the leaflet; she turned and watched the woman saunter away. Dorothy had an instant, and admittedly unfounded, dislike for the voluptuous blonde. Every man who walked by the woman gave her a good look up and down. She handed a flyer to each of them. Dorothy saw Benchley coming. He tipped his hat at the woman but didn't ogle her. He hardly gave her a second glance. Instead, he looked at the paper she handed him.

Damn that Benchley. Just when she was getting good and ready to be angry at him, he had to act like a gentleman.

Now Woody wagged his tail as Benchley approached. Benchley scratched him behind the ears. "And how is President Wilson today?"

"He refuses to take a leak," Dorothy said. "I don't know how he can hold it so long."

"Well, some tasks simply cannot be rushed." Then he spoke excitedly, holding up the flyer. "Did you see this?"

"No. What is it?"

"Look at it. It's a leaflet for that séance—the one for Ernie MacGuffin."

Dorothy looked at the cheaply printed handout. It pictured a crude line drawing of the platinum blonde herself seated at a small table in a darkened room. Her eyes were closed in rapture, her arms extended upward. A spectral face, shadowed in smoke, floated in the air above her.

Dorothy read aloud: " 'Mistress Viola Sweet— Spiritualist, Mentalist, Clairvoyant, Interlocutor of Paranormal Manifestation—conjures the voice from beyond the grave: famed artiste and victim of suicide, Ernest MacGuffin. October 31, Halloween night, eight o'clock and again at twelve midnight. Arrive early—only a few true believers will be permitted inside. Donations gladly accepted.'"

"That was her!" Benchley said. "Mistress Viola."

"More like Lady Godiva," Dorothy muttered. "She looks like a showgirl, not a spiritualist."

Benchley checked his watch. "Well, we can discuss it later. We're late for our meeting with this lawyer fellow."

Dorothy and Benchley, with Woodrow Wilson in the lead, ducked inside the old limestone building, then up two flights of once-grand but now well-worn stairs, and found the lawyer's office. No one sat behind the secretary's desk in the musty, poorly lit waiting room.

Heavy double doors led to the lawyer's office. One was partially opened. Inside, they could see a large figure moving about.

"Yes?" the man called. His voice was deep, resonant—and impatient. "Are you here from the secretarial agency? You're late."

Benchley pushed open the creaky door and stepped aside for Dorothy to enter. She paused at the doorway and looked around the large, high-ceilinged office. Woody cowered at her feet. Unframed paintings were everywhere. Some two dozen canvases of different sizes were stacked against the tall bookcases lining the walls. Another dozen stood on the floor leaning against the lawyer's massive, old-fashioned mahogany desk. More canvases filled the old crimson velvet chairs, and even more were piled on a wide wooden table beneath the large soot-stained windows.

"I said, you're late," the man snapped.

For the moment, she ignored him and continued to look around at the paintings. Some pictured scenes fit for pulp magazines—cowboys, gangsters, women in danger. But others were simpler, more artistic, more conceptual—like the one Ernie MacGuffin left on the Brooklyn Bridge.

Did MacGuffin leave all these paintings behind? she wondered. Surely, they couldn't *all* be his?

The lawyer suddenly stalked toward her and towered over her. He was tall and imposing and wore an expensive, well-cut black suit over his large frame. His salt-and-pepper hair was slicked back above menacing black eyebrows. His long, thin nose tapered down toward a chin so narrow and pointed, you could use it to chip ice, Dorothy thought. And from his demeanor, maybe that was exactly what he did, she thought.

The man inhaled deeply through large nostrils, panting like a bull in a bullring. "You expect to work for me, yet you show no respect for punctuality? You bring a mangy mongrel with you into a professional office? And you call yourself a secretary?"

"No," Dorothy said quietly. "I don't."

"You *what?*" The lawyer's face screwed up in indignation. "The impertinence—!"

"I'm not from a secretarial agency," she said calmly. "We're journalists. From *Vanity Fair*. We called earlier and made an appointment?"

His demeanor changed immediately. His vicious stare softened. His scowl transformed to a wide, solicitous grin.

"My humblest apologies." His deep voice was now a purr instead of a growl. "I beg your pardon. Yet another secretary quit, at the busiest of times. What gets into these infernal young women?" He swooped away behind his desk, amazingly light and agile for so large a man. "Abraham Snath, Esquire, at your service," he said with a nod and a dramatic sweep of his hand.

Dorothy and Benchley introduced themselves.

Snath said eagerly, "Journalists, you say? Well, well, I gather you want to know about the auction, then?"

"Auction?" Dorothy said.

"Of Mr. MacGuffin's works. A very prestigious affair, I assure you. Exactly the kind of event the readers of—*Vanity Fair*, was it? Exactly the kind of event your affluent and discriminating readers will want to attend."

"Actually," Benchley said, "that's not why we're here—"

Snath bristled. "It's not?"

His moods change faster than a traffic light,

Dorothy thought. She spoke quickly. "What Mr. Benchley means is that we're here to ask you about Ernie MacGuffin—for a story *to accompany* a notice about your auction."

Snath nodded, flashing his smile again. "Very well. Please forgive the disastrous appearance of my humble chambers." He glided quickly toward the chairs facing his desk, deftly lifted the piles of canvases from them, and gently stood them against the others on the floor. He gestured for them to sit down. "What is it you would like to know?"

"The obvious," Dorothy said, taking a seat. "Why did MacGuffin commit suicide?"

Snath descended into his chair and spoke gravely. "To improve his sales, of course."

Dorothy glanced at Benchley. Was this some sort of joke?

Snath maintained a somber expression, then finally cracked a smile. "Pardon the gallows humor. I'm speaking in jest, of course."

"Oh, sure." Benchley chuckled nervously. He didn't sound at all sure.

"Despite the sudden interest in Mr. MacGuffin's works, I cannot fathom why he did what he did, God have mercy on his eternal soul," Snath said gravely. "Frankly, my association with Mr. MacGuffin was a business relationship rather than what you might call a personal one."

"You didn't get along?" Dorothy asked.

"Oh yes, certainly we did. Very cordial, I assure you. But we only discussed matters of business, and even then we only met in person on occasion. You see, most of my business is easily conducted through letters and correspondence, perhaps a telephone call now and then." Snath leaned forward. His hospitality showed signs of strain. "What kind of background story are you writing exactly?"

Dorothy and Benchley glanced at each other again. Why did they never get their story straight ahead of time? Dorothy wondered.

She recovered quickly. "We're writing the story everyone wants to read. That is, what kind of man *was* Ernie MacGuffin? A lot of people seemed to know him—and yet, no one seemed to know him, if you know what I mean."

"Indeed I do. Please continue."

"In life, Ernie was . . . Well, let's face it—he was dull as a rock. And a bit of a nuisance," she said. "Hell, he was a pain in the ass. But in death—in death he's become a man of mystery."

Snath arched his black eyebrows. "I like that—a man of mystery. That's very compelling. Be sure to include that in your article when you write about the auction. What else can I tell you about him?"

"Tell us about his career before he died."

"A very workmanlike painter, and I mean that as a compliment. A very pragmatic man, especially for an artist. These temperamental artists so rarely appreciate the financial side of the art business. But not Mr. MacGuffin. He understood that the art business is, well, a business, after all."

"How sensible of him," Dorothy said dryly.

"Just look at that cover illustration of the two gunslingers there." Snath pointed. "He did that in less than two days. *Old West Magazine* had hired another illustrator—some hack who didn't deliver on deadline. I telegrammed Ernie—Mr. MacGuffin—on a Friday afternoon. On Monday morning, he delivered this. We demanded the magazine double the fee, of course, because it was a rush job."

"How much was the fee for that one," Dorothy asked, "just out of curiosity?"

"Oh, a hundred dollars, I believe. But don't quote me on that. His typical fee for such an illustration was fifty."

A measly fifty, Dorothy thought. She knew Neysa McMein got hundreds for her illustrations for the covers of more prestigious magazines. "And how much will it be auctioned for?"

Snath grinned. "How much? The sky's the limit. The *minimum* bid for that one is eight hundred. But that's a MacGuffin classic. I expect it will eventually fetch at least fifteen hundred. Maybe two thousand."

That made Dorothy indignant. Now that MacGuffin was dead, who would get the money for his work? Not the artist himself; that was for sure.

Snath continued. "But these—these genre works were MacGuffin's bread and butter. No, his much more valuable works are these over here. See these?"

The lawyer went to the paintings resting by the tall bookcases. He flipped through them, holding up one after another. Most of them were predominantly cobalt blue with a swirling effect—as though MacGuffin had adopted the look of Van Gogh's *Starry Night* and gotten far too carried away with it, Dorothy thought. Many were figures. Several were nudes. A few of them looked like Midge MacGuffin, Dorothy thought. Benchley looked at her knowingly—he was thinking the same thing.

Snath briefly held up one nude—an image of a slender woman with a platinum blond permanent wave. But the face was indistinct—like the others, this painting was impressionist in style. Before Dorothy could get a better look, Snath had put it down and held up a different one, a cubist-style abstract of what might be the Brooklyn Bridge.

"Aren't they wonderful?" Snath said effusively. "During Ernie's lifetime, I never could get a gallery to show them. But his death—pardon my candor—changed everything. Thursday night's auction will be to a standing-room-only house. Some of these more serious works could fetch upward of three thousand. Maybe five. Maybe even more." Snath was almost bubbling with excitement.

Inwardly, Dorothy was furious. She mentally willed Woody to pee all over the paintings. But Woody just lay quietly at her feet. That dog never came through when you needed him to. Just like a man.

"Again, don't quote me on those figures. They're merely estimates," Snath said, sitting down and leaning back contemplatively in his leather chair, looking heavenward. "Ah, Mr. MacGuffin would be proud if he could only see what his career had become. Such joy." He awoke from his reverie and leaned forward again. "So, this article will appear in the next issue of *Vanity Fair*? And when will that be available? Probably not tomorrow, I gather. Thursday, then, the day of the auction? That's quite soon, isn't it?"

Dorothy and Benchley realized their mistake. To come out in print, *Vanity Fair* took three weeks from when they sent the issue to the printer to when it hit the newsstands.

This realization began to dawn on Snath as well. He rose from his chair and moved quickly toward the door, blocking their exit. The warmth disappeared from his voice. "How is it possible to print a magazine in so short a time?"

At the ominous tone in Snath's voice, Woody huddled nervously against Dorothy's ankles.

"Actually," she said with a confidence she did not feel, "this article will appear in a brand-new magazine, *The New Yorker*. The first issue will come out very soon."

"This is *not* for *Vanity Fair*? And this won't be printed in time for the auction on Thursday?" Snath growled, his fists clenching. "You have the arrogance to come in here and waste my valuable time?"

Benchley mumbled, "We may be wasting your time, but we're certainly not being arrogant about it."

Snath had quickly become enraged. "You vermin! You cretins! You scum! Who put you up to this?"

He began ranting about a rival auctioneer or rival art dealer. Dorothy couldn't tell—she could barely follow what he said. She glanced at Benchley, who seemed to be amused rather than intimidated.

"I'll crush you!" Snath ranted. "God help me, I'll crush you into the ground. You vile—"

There was a knock on the door. Snath spun around. "Not now!"

The door opened anyway. A dapper young British man entered. He wore a finely tailored Savile Row suit, an Eton striped repp tie, and expensive black leather brogues.

He looked so slick, he nearly glistened, Dorothy thought. She knew the man on sight: Jasper Welsh. He was an editor for Waterloo Books, a disreputable publisher of tawdry dime novels and dubious get-rich-quick guides.

Snath calmed himself instantly. He smoothed his hair and tugged at his shirt cuffs. "Ah, yes, Welsh," he purred. "Do come in."

"Am I interruptin'?" Welsh said. "Well, who do we 'ave 'ere? 'Allo, Mrs. Parker. Mr. Benchley."

For all his phony upper-crust affectation, Dorothy thought, he couldn't quite lose his coarse East End of London accent.

Before she could respond, Snath turned on him viciously. "You're acquainted with these infidels? These charlatans?"

"Indeed I am," Welsh said brightly. "Are you ready to make a book deal, Mrs. Parker? My offer still stands. Beggars can't be choosers, you know."

Several months ago, Jasper Welsh had asked her to put her poems together for a book, for which he offered her a paltry hundred dollars plus ten cents for each book sold. She'd be rich—in about a thousand years of steady sales.

"Forget it, Jasper. I'm destined to remain a beggar," she said. "Speaking of beggars, what are you doing here?"

"Mr. Snath and myself 'ave a major business deal we're workin' on," he said smugly. "Somethin' very big in the publishin' world. A masterstroke, if I say so myself. Mind you—Oh my God!"

God? Well, maybe He answers our prayers after all, Dorothy thought as she looked down and saw her dog peeing on the man's fancy leather shoes.

While Snath and Welsh stood stunned, Dorothy quickly pulled Woody and Benchley away. They hurried out of the office without another word.

Chapter 11

Once outside of Snath's dilapidated office building, Dorothy stopped on the busy sidewalk and searched in her purse for a treat for Woodrow Wilson.

"Good boy," she said as the dog snatched a piece of dry kibble from her hand.

With relief, Benchley looked up at the grimy windows of the lawyer's office. "Mr. Snath, Esquire, had very little to tell us about Ernest MacGuffin, painter. Now what do we do?"

"Do you still have that leaflet?" Dorothy asked.

Benchley pulled the flyer from his pocket and read it aloud. "'Mistress Viola Swect— Spiritualist, Mentalist, Clairvoyant, Interlocutor of Paranormal Manifestation—'"

"And pants pressed while you wait."

"She's near Washington Square, in Greenwich Village."

"Then let's see how much she knows about our pragmatic and workmanlike pal Ernie. Come on, Woody."

"I remember you." The platinum blonde chuckled as she opened the door and patted the dog lightly on the head.

Woody's stubby tail wagged so vigorously that his little behind moved back and forth. Again

Dorothy silently cursed the little dog for its lasciviousness.

Viola no longer wore the tight blue skirt. Now she had only a pink satin robe wrapped tightly around her shapely body. Her sultry eyes showed that she remembered Dorothy and Benchley, too. "You're here to ask about the séance?"

"Boy, you really can read minds, can't you?" Dorothy said.

"You have my flyer in your hand," Viola said wryly, glancing at the leaflet. "Can I have your names for the list?"

"The list?" Dorothy said.

"The list of participants. The séance is for participants only. No gawkers. There's a five-dollar deposit. You can pay the balance of the donation when you arrive."

"The balance?"

"Twenty dollars. So twenty-five altogether."

"Mesmerism, clairvoyance and arithmetic, too. You're quite a talent." Dorothy looked over the storefront. The large sign read HUDSON RIVER SCHOOL OF ART. "What is it you do here? Are you an artist?"

"I'm an artist's model."

"A clairvoyant, a math whiz *and* an artist's model? You're quite a Renaissance woman."

"Being a medium is new for me, just since Mr. MacGuffin's spirit began speaking to me."

"Speaking to you?" Benchley asked.

"Well, speaking *through* me. It's his voice. I'm just a mouthpiece."

That's not the only kind of piece you are, sweetie, Dorothy thought. But she said, "So, you knew Mr. MacGuffin?"

"Oh no. We never met."

Dorothy remembered one of the paintings in Snath's office—the one of the platinum blonde. Surely it couldn't be a coincidence?

"There's a big auction of Ernie MacGuffin's paintings on Thursday night—Halloween night, the same night as your séance," Dorothy said. "We just had the opportunity to look over the paintings. I could swear that you were pictured in one, and dressed quite informally, I might add."

"*Quite* informally," Benchley said merrily.

Dorothy asked, "How could he have painted a picture of you if you didn't know him?"

"I told you I'm an artist's model. I pose nude." Viola didn't sound defensive, but her voice took on an edge. "Maybe he was in a class or an artist's group and I was the model. In any case, I never met him personally."

"But his voice speaks through you now?" Dorothy asked.

"Yes. When summoned."

"And why does he speak through *you,* if you never knew him?"

She smiled, as though back in familiar territory. "A number of people have asked me that. All I can say is that I'm the conduit, the channel through which he chose to convey his message."

"And what is his message?" Dorothy asked. "What does he say when he speaks through you?"

"I don't know exactly." Viola's smoky eyes took on a faraway look. "I go into a trance when it happens. People who have come to the séance tell me afterward that Mr. MacGuffin's spirit says things—details—only he would know. They walk away convinced that it's his true spirit."

"Yes, I'm sure you show them a lot of spirit," Dorothy said. "What kind of details?"

"All kinds," Viola said, smiling again, confident in what she was saying. "He talks about his most well-known paintings. What kinds of brushes he used to paint them. When he painted them. Which models he used to get the exact effect. I learned that he once used Popsicle sticks to prop up a dead cat as a model for a painting of an attacking mountain lion. This was for the cover of *The Outdoorsman* magazine."

Dorothy sensed Benchley's posture stiffen. That story about the cat was a telling detail. They'd heard MacGuffin tell Neysa that exact same tidbit before.

Dorothy took a different tack. "And has he said why he took his own life?"

"Not that I know of. But you can ask him yourself."

"Right now?"

"No." The woman chuckled good-naturedly. "Halloween night. Just a five-dollar deposit each."

Benchley took out his nearly empty wallet and handed her two fives.

Viola produced a clipboard. "Your names?"

"Mrs. Becky Sharp," Dorothy said.

Viola scribbled it down, then turned to Benchley.

"Fred"—Benchley gazed around for inspiration, his eyes settling on Woody—"Wilson. Fred Wilson."

Viola wrote down the names. "We'll see you at midnight on Thursday."

"One last thing," Dorothy asked. "What does this *donation* go toward?"

The woman spoke with sincerity. "To further the search for a better connection to the spirit world."

To further the search for a better peroxide dye job, Dorothy thought. Instead, she said, "Can you tell us anything else about what MacGuffin says?"

"You'll have to come see for yourself. Bye." She began to close the door.

Dorothy spoke impatiently, desperately. "I think you know more about Ernie MacGuffin than you're telling us."

Viola paused. Her smoky eyes now glittered with resentment.

Dorothy continued. "I think you knew him. I think you knew him quite well."

For the first time, Viola didn't speak so sweetly.

"Mr. MacGuffin was a married man, *Mrs.* Sharp."
Her eyes darted accusingly between Dorothy and
Benchley. "If you want to know more about him,
go ask his wife."

She slammed the door.

Chapter 12

"Harold Ross is going to have to reimburse us in shoe leather," Dorothy said to Benchley. Woodrow Wilson had tired, so Dorothy now carried the dog in her arms. They trudged across busy Fourth Avenue on their way to pay Midge MacGuffin another visit. They walked in shadow. Overhead, the elevated train rumbled by.

She and Benchley hadn't spoken about what Viola had said to them—that taunt about Ernie being a married man, implying by association that Dorothy and Benchley themselves were involved in an illicit affair. As they walked together in silence, Dorothy wondered if she should say something about it to Benchley to clear the air. Perhaps she should make some joke about it in an effort to deflate it—to nullify it.

She glanced up at Benchley. He smiled back and took Woody out of her arms. "Let me help. The poor creature must be getting heavy for you."

The moment was gone. Benchley had cleared the air on his own, although the question remained unresolved.

"Thank you," Dorothy sighed. "So, do you believe Ernie's spirit can speak through Mistress Viola?"

"Not a ghost of a chance. Not even the ghost of Ernie."

"What makes you so sure?"

"Oh, come on, now." Benchley smiled warmly, his merry eyes creasing. "She's a nude model and self-proclaimed paranormal clairvoyant. Her head is clearly full of stuffing. I'm surprised she can even speak for herself, much less MacGuffin."

Dorothy shook her head. "I disagree. She had a good head on her shoulders—to match the rest of that body of hers. But I wonder, is she sharp because she has the clarity of a true believer? Or because she's a conniving opportunist?"

Benchley's face clouded. "She did say that Ernie's spirit spoke about that dead cat posed as a mountain lion. We know that's for real. Ernie mentioned it several times. How could Viola know about it? To be honest, it spooked me a little."

Dorothy wouldn't believe it. "Ernie told that tidbit to anyone who'd listen. Viola could have picked it up anywhere, especially through artistic circles. Hell, Neysa and Frank Adams went there for the séance the other night. Neysa could have let that information slip, and now Mistress Viola is using it in her act."

"Maybe. But if Viola does have a connection to the spirit world—"

"Which she doesn't," Dorothy said emphatically.

"But supposing she does, why would Ernie's spirit choose her?"

"Why not her? She's gorgeous. Any man would

like to be inside her. Even a dead one. It's the only way MacGuffin ever could." Dorothy stopped. They were within sight of Midge MacGuffin's house. Two people stood by the doorway. "Look, there's Clay. He's leaving."

Bert Clay was on the stoop, a childlike grin on the bulky man's face. Dorothy couldn't hear what Clay was saying, but he was apparently taking his sweet time saying good-bye. Midge, standing at the door, looked equally reluctant to see him go.

"Here, give me Woodrow Wilson," Dorothy said, grabbing the dog from Benchley. "You follow Clay and talk to him. I'll question Midge."

Benchley looked doubtful. "Won't he be suspicious?"

"You'll figure something out. Now, go."

He shrugged, smiling. "Go I shall."

As Clay finally walked away from the house, Benchley nonchalantly followed several paces behind him.

Dorothy, carrying the dog in her arms, strolled to the bottom steps of Midge's house. The tall woman lingered in the doorway, her eyes fixed on the retreating figure of Bert Clay.

Dorothy recalled something unusual that Clay had said the last time she had seen him on Midge's doorstep. "Hello there, Harriet—oh, I'm sorry," Dorothy said. "I mean, hello there, *Midge*."

The woman froze. Her expression was guarded,

though her face showed neither surprise nor alarm. "Hello? Yes?"

"It's Mrs. Parker." Dorothy ascended the stone steps. "Do you remember me? I stopped by a few days ago? Last Wednesday, to be exact. I've also called you on the telephone several times. And I sent you two letters and a telegram."

Midge now looked a little nervous. She took a half step backward.

Why should she be nervous? Dorothy thought, looking up at the tall woman, who towered over her like a marble statue. *She's a titan compared to me.*

"Oh yes," Midge said warily. "Of course."

Dorothy moved closer. "Would you have time to talk now?"

Midge backed away. "Actually, now is not a good time—"

Dorothy smiled knowingly. "I understand, Harriet." Her hand flew to her lips. "Sorry. I mean *Midge,* of course. Perhaps tomorrow—"

Midge's wary expression became one of puzzlement. "How did you know my name is—was Harriet?"

Dorothy moved back down the steps. "Oh, silly old me. Don't let me bother you one bit. If you don't have time to talk now—"

Midge reconsidered, glancing up the street. Clay was long gone. She held the door open. "Actually, now's as good a time as any. Won't you come in?"

Benchley couldn't lose sight of such a large, broad-shouldered, athletic man as Bert Clay. On the busy sidewalk, Clay stuck out like a big brown bull amid a herd of docile dairy cows.

But Clay walked fast. Benchley realized Clay was outpacing him. Eventually, Benchley would lose Clay in the crowd.

Benchley looked down at his shoes, willing them to move faster. His shoes were still caked with dark mud from the morning's trek through the garbage dump on Rikers Island. He hadn't yet had a chance to get them cleaned up.

Suddenly, he had an idea. He stopped a moment to think as he watched Clay move farther away.

Yes, it could work, if only—

He was shocked out of his reverie by a messenger boy on a bicycle who nearly knocked him down. *That's what I get for standing on a crowded sidewalk staring at my shoes,* Benchley thought. He watched the messenger boy hop off the bike, lean it against a lamppost and then disappear inside a candy shop. Ignoring his conscience, Benchley grabbed the bike, got on, turned it around and raced down the busy sidewalk in the direction that Bert Clay was headed.

Dorothy Parker followed Midge MacGuffin into her small sitting room. Dorothy was surprised—

this wasn't at all the type of fleabag apartment typically kept by a third-rate artist such as Ernie. The room was decorated with sleek, new, expensive-looking art deco furniture—all curves and angles and zigzag designs.

"Please sit down," Midge said.

Dorothy sat in a plush, angular armchair and found that it was surprisingly comfortable. Woodrow Wilson plopped down on the thick rug by her feet and fell asleep immediately. It was a good thing the dog had relieved himself earlier at Snath's office, Dorothy thought, because she didn't want him peeing here.

Because Midge was home on a Tuesday afternoon, Dorothy figured that she did not hold a job. Without an income and without Ernie to provide for her, how would Midge continue to live this kind of lifestyle? In a strange way, Dorothy felt sorry for her.

To add to the lavishness, the room smelled and looked as wonderful as a florist's shop—every flat surface held bouquets and vases of brilliant flowers. Many of these were roses, in every tint and variety.

"Wonderful flowers," Dorothy said with sincerity.

"Oh yes." Midge smiled, though it seemed as if she had forgotten about them or taken them for granted. "Thank you."

Roses, Dorothy thought. Clearly they weren't

funeral flowers given in memory of Ernie. Could they all be from Clay?

Midge stared directly at Dorothy, though her expression was blank. If she was suspicious or angry, she didn't show it.

"So how did you know my name was Harriet?" she asked. "Have we met?"

"No," Dorothy said weakly. "I suppose you just look like a Harriet."

"Really? I do?" She turned and looked into a gilt-framed mirror.

"I confess you don't." Dorothy took a stab in the dark. "Perhaps Ernie had said it once—by accident."

"That wouldn't be like him. He preferred to call me Midge."

"Midge. Now, that's a cute nickname. Is it short for Harriet?"

"No."

"Margaret? Is that your middle name?"

"Oh no. It's short for *midget*. In our hometown, where Ernie and I are from, I was teased all the time for my height. So they called me midget. I suppose they were trying to be funny. But I didn't think it was funny. But still, I prefer Midge to Harriet."

"Young people can be so cruel," Dorothy clucked. "So you and Ernie came here together from the same town?"

"Yes."

"What town?"

"Elmira. Upstate."

Dorothy pictured a provincial, working-class town. Not a great place for a beautiful but tall woman. Or, for that matter, a budding artist whose ambition exceeded his talent.

"I suppose you and Ernie were high school sweethearts?"

Midge's expression, which had been as blank as the face of a statue, now clouded over. She turned and gazed at the flowers and was quiet for a long moment.

Benchley pedaled quickly, urging the bicycle as fast as he could make it go. He weaved his way dangerously through the pedestrians on the crowded sidewalk, leaving their shouts and curses in his wake. He pressed on and rounded the next corner. He was circling the block, racing to get ahead of Bert Clay.

Benchley's favorite shoe-shine stand was dead ahead. He glanced over his shoulder and spotted Clay coming toward him. When Benchley reached the shoe-shine stand, he braked hard and hopped off the bike, leaned it against a fire hydrant and jumped up into one of the stand's two empty seats.

"Hi, Rudy," Benchley panted, out of breath. "Can I ask a favor?"

Rudy, a middle-aged black man in a tweed cap, looked up from the sports page of the afternoon newspaper. He scrunched up his weathered face. "Do I know you?"

"Rudy, you remember me," Benchley gasped. "I stop by every week."

"I don't look at faces. I look at shoes," Rudy said, carefully folding up his newspaper and evaluating Benchley's oxfords. "Oh, I know these shoes. Man almighty, what have you done to them?" Rudy scowled as though Benchley had kicked his kitten.

"No time for that now," Benchley leaned down and whispered quickly. "Look behind you. No, don't look. Do you see that big man in the light brown suit? I said don't look! I need you to stop him. Give him a free shoe shine."

"Are you out of your mind? I don't give out free shoe shines."

"Don't worry; I'll pay. But you stop him. Get him up here. Give him a shine. Say it's for free. Then I'll pay you later."

"Doesn't sound right." He frowned, still eyeing Benchley's muddy shoes. "Is this some kind of con job?"

"Rudy, it's me. It's sweet old Benchley."

"I said I don't know you. I only know your shoes. And I don't like the way you've been treating them."

"Please, I'm begging you. Here he comes," Benchley begged. "Please, if not for me, do it for my shoes. They need your help."

This seemed to make sense to Rudy. "All right," he agreed. "For your shoes."

Rudy turned and stepped right in front of Bert Clay, whose eyes narrowed.

"Excuse me, sir," Rudy said with a winning smile, a master salesman now. "You look like you need a shoe shine."

"Can't you see I'm in a hurry?" Clay growled, trying to sidestep. "I don't have time for a shine."

"Always time for a quick shine," Rudy said, not letting the big man pass. "Come on. It's on the house."

Clay paused. "On the house?"

"Sure. If you like it, you come back. If you don't like it, what have you lost?"

Clay looked down at his shoes. "All right." He climbed up and plopped down into the other chair. He didn't even glance at Benchley.

Rudy handed Clay the sports page; then he grabbed his brush and a can of Shinola and went to work on the man's big shoes.

Benchley sized up Clay. The man was a few inches taller and was built much larger—probably a good forty or fifty pounds heavier. Benchley, who was just under six foot and built rather slender, couldn't help but feel intimidated by the larger man.

Now Clay was looking back at him out of the corner of his eye. "What are you looking at?" he snarled.

Benchley didn't know what to say. He stammered, "Bert Clay, right?"

"Yeah. Who wants to know?"

"We met at the—the Elks Lodge fund-raiser?" Benchley heard himself say.

"Elks Lodge? I'm not an Elk."

"Oh no?" Benchley asked, eyeing him up and down. "You certainly look like one."

"Not a chance in hell! I'm a Freemason. Dyed in the wool."

"Oh yes, of course. That's how I know you. I should have recognized a fellow Mason."

He offered Clay his hand, which Clay grasped with his much larger one. Benchley guessed at a secret Masonic handshake—attempting an elaborate mancuver of rotating his thumb around Clay's thumb, his pinkie inside Clay's palm, and pumping his hand up, then up higher, and then down with a wrist-wrenching drop.

Clay yanked his hand away from Benchley. "What kind of dimwit, knuckleheaded lodge are you from?"

Midge continued to stare at the glorious array of flowers.

Dorothy wasn't sure if Midge had even heard her, so she repeated the question. "You and Ernie were high school sweethearts?"

"No, *we* weren't."

"So how did you meet Ernie?"

111

"Oh, I had a silly idea I wanted to go to college."

"That's not a silly idea. I wish I'd gone to college," Dorothy said sharply. It was one of her biggest regrets, but she didn't have the money. And it wasn't easy for a girl to attend college, especially during the years of the Great War.

"You know how it is when you're eighteen," Midge sighed, taking no notice of Dorothy's sharp reply. "You put on a dress and you think you're a woman. You put on a tennis skirt and you think you're a tennis pro. I put on a plaid wool skirt and I thought I should go to college."

"You wanted to leave the small town and live life in the big city."

"Exactly. But we've been here five years, and I haven't been much of a student. I've taken a few classes, but I'm a long way from graduating. Perhaps I never will. Did you come from a provincial little town, too?"

"I certainly did, if you consider the Upper West Side a provincial little town, which I do."

Midge smiled politely, but she didn't get the joke or didn't think it was funny. "So you're a native New Yorker?"

Dorothy nodded. Actually, she was born while her family was on a seaside vacation in New Jersey. But this wasn't the time to split hairs. She wanted to keep the focus on Midge—and Ernie. "So Ernie was your ticket to New York?"

"Yes. I felt I stood out in Elmira. I'm five foot

eleven, so I thought I would blend in among the skyscrapers. Ernie said we could get married and go right away to New York. Of course, there were other boys back in Elmira."

"Of course," Dorothy said. *Such as Bertram Clay, perhaps?*

Midge clasped her hands in her lap. "But Ernie was a talented artist, with a lot of big ideas. I could see he was really going somewhere. He offered to take me with him. He offered me a new last name. He offered a chance for me to change. So I took it."

"And you regret it?"

Midge looked away. "Now I do."

"I think I understand. I once married a man named Parker, a nice clean last name. Only good thing he ever gave me."

"It didn't work out?"

How could she explain that Eddie Parker had gone off to war just days after they were married, and then came home a couple of years later a changed man? And while he was off becoming shell-shocked, Dorothy had changed also. She was building a name for herself using his clean last name. When Eddie Parker finally did come home, he was a broken man. And Dorothy was a woman he didn't recognize and, truthfully, no longer much cared for. His addiction to morphine didn't help. Things went downhill from there.

But Dorothy couldn't explain all this to Midge. She merely nodded. "No, it didn't work out."

"I'm sorry."

"But look at us now!" Dorothy smiled and gently slapped Midge's knee. "We're both women who reinvented ourselves. Put on a new dress and you feel like a new woman. Put on a new name and you are one."

Midge smiled wistfully. "My name was Klausner. Harriet Klausner."

Dorothy kept her smile plastered on her lips. *Harriet Klausner?* Not a fitting name for such an elegant woman. "Well, now you're Midge MacGuffin." Dorothy looked around the nicely furnished room. How would Midge keep herself in such style without a job and without a husband? Dorothy foresaw her returning to Elmira. "You've made quite a transformation."

Midge sat up straight. "But I haven't! I had a new name, but I found out I was still the same old me. In Elmira I had felt outlandish, and I thought I had outlandish ideas. But it turned out I had nothing of the kind. I had no ideas in my head whatsoever. New York didn't change me at all."

"If that's true, you're the first person in New York history to be unchanged by it," Dorothy said cynically. "So then what happened between you and Ernie?"

"Nothing."

"Nothing?"

"Everything was fine. I loved him, in my own way. And he seemed happy with me, though he was very focused on his career. As time passed, I started to feel adrift. But we never once had a harsh word. Even until the end."

"When he killed himself?" Dorothy spoke gently. "I guess that took you quite by surprise?"

Midge looked away, like a child caught doing something wrong. Was she thinking of the obvious affair with Bert Clay so soon after Ernie's death?

Or, Dorothy began to wonder, was there something else?

Chapter 13

Rudy was polishing up Bert Clay's second shoe, and soon Clay would get up and leave. Clay was studiously ignoring Benchley.

Despite the cool October breeze, Benchley began to sweat. He racked his brain for engaging conversation. What do Masons talk about? Secret rituals? Initiations? Robes and rings with special symbols?

Then Benchley noticed Clay squinting up at a skyscraper under construction, a latticework of girders and beams.

Masons talk about buildings, of course!

Benchley cleared his throat. "Great new sky-scraper, isn't it?"

"You like it?" Clay smiled, full of pride. "It's mine."

"Yours?"

"You got it. I'm the chief engineer on the project. Been working on it for three years."

Benchley gazed up at the building with new interest. "Ah, yes, of course. Great girder work. Delightful I beams."

"You think so?"

"I do indeed. I beam at your I beams."

Clay guffawed as though he never heard anything so funny. "You're all right, fella."

He slapped Benchley on the back with such

force that Benchley thought he dislodged several vertebrae.

Dorothy spoke with gentle care. "So you were as surprised as we were that Ernie committed suicide?"

Midge replied with equal caution, picking her words hesitantly. "Well, yes and no."

Dorothy was sympathetic. "I know this is difficult to talk about. . . ."

Again Midge displayed that guilty look. "It certainly is."

"Did Ernie give you any clue about what he was planning to do?"

"As a matter of fact, he did."

"What did he say?"

Midge stared off into the middle distance. Again she picked her words carefully and deliberately. "He said that everyone would be so surprised when they heard that he'd jumped off the Brooklyn Bridge. Everyone would think completely differently about him." Midge turned to Dorothy. "I guess since you've come here to ask about him, to write an article about him, then it proves that he was right, doesn't it? People are interested in him now."

All of a sudden, Dorothy felt manipulated. Had MacGuffin orchestrated this whole thing? Had he given her the suicide note knowing full well she'd be the one sitting in his art deco armchair a few days later talking to his wife in order to write a feature magazine story about him?

Goddamn MacGuffin. Had that second-rate twerp really been so calculating?

Benchley realized he had opened Pandora's box. Once Bert Clay started talking, he would not shut up.

"So they delivered ten barrels of three-inch rivets instead of five-inch rivets," Clay blathered. "Of course, they wouldn't take them back. And waiting would put us two weeks behind schedule. So I said, you deliver those five-inch rivets to the work site tomorrow or I'm going to shove every last one of these three-inch rivets right up your you-know-what."

Benchley forced a chuckle. "You said that, did you?"

"Damn right, I did. And you know what?"

"No, what?" But Benchley knew exactly what.

"At sunup the next day, here comes the truck with ten barrels of five-inch rivets." Clay took out a handkerchief and blew his nose loudly. "Now, it turned out that on the work order, I had specified three-inch rivets after all. But *they're* the ones in the rivet business. No matter what we specified, they should have known we needed five-inchers, not three-inchers. How could they think we would build a seventy-story skyscraper with three-inch rivets? Ridiculous!"

Benchley shook his head sympathetically. "It certainly is. Well, you had the last word with them, didn't you? Speaking of the last word—" He rose to leave.

"Hold on." Clay grabbed Benchley's arm, pulling him back into his seat. "I didn't tell you the best part."

"The best part? I hope you saved the best for last," Benchley said truthfully. "Really I do."

Dorothy was dumbfounded. "So Ernie told you beforehand he was going to commit suicide? Did you try to talk him out of it?"

"No," Midge said simply.

"No?"

"Well, I would have. . . ." Midge's words tapered off.

"Yes?"

"It's rather complicated."

"You mean you didn't believe Ernie would go through with it?"

"No, I believed him. He was dead set on it."

"He was? So then you felt you couldn't talk him out of it?"

"That's right. His mind was made up."

Dorothy was stunned. Who in his right mind could be so certain about suicide? She pictured MacGuffin whistling a merry tune as he strode purposefully to the Brooklyn Bridge, to his doom.

But, at the same time, this information gave

Dorothy a bit of relief. She hadn't quite realized until this moment how guilty she had felt about MacGuffin's death. He had handed her his suicide note. He had picked *her* specifically. Until now, Dorothy had been thinking that if she had been more suspicious—if she had found and opened the letter earlier, despite Ernie's directions not to do so—she would have been able to intervene, maybe even stop him.

But Midge's account contradicted this. If his wife couldn't talk him out of suicide, how could she?

Dorothy said, "He gave me his suicide note."

"Yes, I know. Ernie told me you and he had a connection because you had once tried suicide."

Dorothy couldn't believe this woman. She spoke so bluntly, as though talking about the weather, not death. Was she still in shock? Dorothy decided to speak as straightforwardly as Midge.

"I must admit," Dorothy said, "suicide did Ernie a hell of a lot more good than my attempt did for me."

"What do you mean?" Midge asked, with a blank, curious look.

Dorothy explained about the auction, about how Ernie's paintings could sell for a hundredfold of what Ernie was originally paid for them. "Ernie's more successful now than he ever was," she concluded.

"Oh yes," Midge said, finally showing some enthusiasm. She was clearly gratified. "I've heard from Mr. Snath on several occasions. I'll receive quite a pretty penny if the paintings sell as well as Mr. Snath expects."

Of course, Dorothy thought. Midge would be Ernie's primary beneficiary. So Midge—and Snath, through his hefty commissions—would be rolling in dough. Meanwhile, Ernie would get his long-awaited recognition. And even Mistress Viola, charging twenty-five dollars a head, was getting a piece of the action.

Dorothy spoke ruefully. "Ernie's death seems to have worked out pretty well for nearly everyone."

Midge smiled. "Yes, I suppose in a strange way it has, hasn't it?"

Everyone except me and Benchley, Dorothy thought, feeling the article deadline looming heavily over her head.

Benchley chuckled weakly. "And that's the best part, is it?"

Bert Clay smiled smugly. "The icing on the cake is that we stuck it to those Polack bastards. They have a stranglehold on the rivet business."

Benchley winced. He hated slurs. Time to wrap things up. "Well," he said diplomatically, "you certainly seem to be a man of strong passions."

"Hell yes. A man has to be passionate about life,

doesn't he? You have to love what you do. Otherwise, what's the point? Why even bother to get up in the morning?"

"I asked myself that very question today," Benchley sighed.

Clay looked up dreamily at the skyscraper. "A building is a work of art, you see. People just don't understand that. Look at me. I call myself an engineer. But really I'm an artist."

"I can see that. You certainly have the temperament."

"Only my art is steel and concrete, not paint and paper," Clay spat.

Benchley had had enough of Bert Clay. But unfortunately, he sensed that Clay had more to say about this subject, which could indeed be related to Ernie MacGuffin. So reluctantly, he goaded Clay on. "How right you are. Give me reinforced concrete any day. You can have your van Goghs and Gaugins. I'll take granite and glass."

"Now you're talking," Clay said, slapping Benchley jovially but roughly on the back.

"That makes two of us," Benchley winced.

Midge sat with a dreamy smile, her head either completely empty or else filled with thoughts that her comfortable lifestyle not only would continue uninterrupted, but would significantly improve.

Dorothy couldn't help but want to burst her

bubble. "So, why would your husband want to kill himself?"

Midge turned white. "You know why. You read the note."

"So you read it, too?"

"Of course. I helped him write it."

"You *helped him* write his own suicide note?" Dorothy nearly shouted.

Midge cringed. "Well, yes."

Dorothy softened. She needed answers, and yelling was no way to get them. "Exactly how did you help him write it?"

"Being a painter, he was never very good with words. He held the pen, of course, but I helped him compose his thoughts and put them on paper."

"You ghostwrote his suicide note?"

"No." Midge was dismayed, in over her head. "I just helped him articulate what he was thinking."

Dorothy felt outraged. "And what the hell was he thinking?"

Midge closed her eyes and put her hands to her forehead. "I'm feeling flushed all of a sudden. Will you excuse me? I think I had better go lie down. I don't feel well at all."

"You and me both. I'm sick to my stomach," Dorothy said, and she meant it. She scooped up Woody and made her way to the door. "Hope we both feel better soon."

• • •

"A skyscraper is a fine thing. A fine American thing," Clay declared. "Some people say they're an eyesore. They blot out the sky and make the streets shadowy."

"Nonsense," Benchley answered.

"Nonsense is right. A skyscraper is a monument to the forward movement of modern civilization. Onward and upward, thrusting up to the sky. Skyscrapers are nothing less than the embodiment of men's dreams. We literally reach for the stars when we build a skyscraper."

Benchley decided to hit closer to home. "You talk like a man in love."

"Is it that obvious?" Clay blushed, which Benchley found nauseating.

"It's not just a love of skyscrapers, is it?" Benchley asked. "You have a sweetheart."

"You got me dead to rights, mister—what did you say your name was?"

"I didn't," Benchley said briskly. "Tell me, who's the lucky girl?"

Clay gazed up at the sky again. "Ah, she's an angel. I've had my eye on her for years, waiting for another chance with her. She's well worth the wait. More beautiful now than when we met as kids."

"As kids? Have you known her that long?"

"As teenagers, I mean. You know how teenagers fall in love? They fall completely. Heart, mind, body and soul. But as you get older, they say you lose that passion, right? Like, those kinds of feelings get watered down?"

"'Youth is hot and bold. Age is weak and cold,'" Benchley said, quoting Shakespeare.

Rudy the shoe-shine man gave Benchley a peeved look. Rudy had finished their shoe shines some time ago, yet Clay made no move to leave.

"Not for me, buddy. I'm still hot and bold," Clay said. "I fell for her and I fell hard, and I've never gotten over her. I still feel like I did when I was young, and I always will. I built a skyscraper in my heart, and she lives in it."

Benchley coughed to stifle a groan. Yes, that was quite enough of Bert Clay. He stood up and said by way of conclusion, "You're not just an artist. You're a poet. It was my pleasure to meet you."

"Aw, enough about me," Clay said with a wave of his hand. "I'm boring you, I can see that. Don't go just yet. Tell me about yourself."

"I'm a messenger boy. Come to think of it, I'd better get back to work. Reams of telegrams to deliver." He hurriedly shook Clay's hand, stepped down from the shoe-shine stand and slipped Rudy two bucks, which was more than enough to cover the cost. "Wonderful speaking to you, Mr. Clay. Let's do it again."

"Sure. When?"

"I'll send you a telegram," Benchley said with a wave. Then he hopped on the bike and sped away, disappearing into the busy stream of people on the crowded sidewalk.

Chapter 14

Dorothy Parker had been at the office of *Vanity Fair* for just a few minutes before Benchley arrived—sweaty, rumpled and tired. She had been filling in Mr. Sherwood about their day's many events: their morning at the garbage dump on Rikers Island, their harrowing visit with the lawyer Snath, their strange conversation with the nude model and spiritual medium Viola, and Dorothy's unsettling chat with Midge MacGuffin.

She wondered aloud, "Why would Midge be so indifferent to her husband's death?"

"Perhaps because she's got another poker in the fire?" Benchley said, wiping his forehead with a handkerchief.

"What's that supposed to mean?" Sherwood asked.

Benchley explained about his conversation at the shoe-shine stand with Bert Clay.

"Clay has a skyscraper-sized infatuation for Midge," Benchley concluded. "If you have an hour or two—or seven—he'll be happy to tell you all about it."

Dorothy frowned. "I don't doubt there is some kind of hanky-panky going on between those two. But as for Midge herself, I think she's got some bats in the belfry."

"How so?" Benchley said, and drank deeply from a glass of water.

"She ghostwrote Ernie's suicide note, for Pete's sake. She's got a screw loose somewhere."

"I never thought so," Sherwood said, lighting a cigarette and leaning back in his wooden chair. "As a matter of fact, I don't think there's much hardware up in her attic to come loose." He tapped his temple.

"That's what Mr. Benchley said about Viola." Dorothy looked from Sherwood to Benchley. "What is it with you boys? Do you think a pretty face automatically means there's no brain behind it?"

"You're the exception that proves the rule, Mrs. Parker," Benchley said gallantly. She smothered a smile.

Sherwood raised an eyebrow. "In regard to Midge, do you disagree?"

"I guess not," she sighed, remembering the woman's vacant stare. "You're right. Midge did strike me as something of a simpleton."

Benchley asked, "What did she say about Clay?"

"Nothing, really. I left before I could ask her." Dorothy explained how she got fed up with Midge's implacability. "Mr. Sherwood, I can understand how you said she looks as beautiful as a statue. She's made of stone, too."

"What do you mean?" Sherwood asked.

"She looks at the world like a statue would,

watching it all pass by without it affecting her in the least," Dorothy said, in a world-weary mood. "Rains may come and winds may blow, but unless the weather affects her personally, she doesn't seem to care a whit. She seemed to care very little about Ernie, at any rate."

"Well, speaking of caring a whit, who would care to wet their whit-stle?" Sherwood asked. He stood up, took his suit jacket off the back of his chair and slid it on. "This has been a long day for you two. I think we could all use a good stiff drink. How about we improve this discussion by continuing it at Tony's?"

Dorothy groaned. She reminded Sherwood of their debt to Tony Soma.

"All right," Sherwood said, undaunted. "This is Manhattan during Prohibition. There's a speakeasy on every corner. How about Jack and Charlie's? Or Club Durant? Or even the Roxy Grill?"

"I suppose so," Dorothy said without enthusiasm. "Certainly, you're right. But it's not just the drink. Tony's is our regular place."

Benchley sighed. "That's true."

"Then what?" Sherwood asked.

Dorothy brightened. "Allow me to be optimistic—"

"That's unlike you," Benchley said with a gentle twinkle in his eye.

She cast him a superior look and continued.

"Allow me to be optimistic and suggest we give Tony's another try. Perhaps Mrs. Soma and that little devil Tony Jr. are away at their Tuesday afternoon coven, and Tony will take pity on us for just one drink."

Benchley shrugged. "It's worth a go."

But Mrs. Soma herself met them at the door of the speakeasy. She clucked her tongue. "Well, look who it is! Do you have our money?"

Dorothy hesitated. "Actually—"

Mrs. Soma screamed over her shoulder. "Tony Jr.!"

Benchley chuckled. "No need to summon the little dickens. What we were about to say—"

Dorothy interrupted. "What we were about to say is that we have your money."

"We do?" Benchley said.

"You do?" Sherwood asked.

Mrs. Soma folded her arms across her chest. "What is this? Do you have it or don't you?"

"We do," Dorothy said confidently. "I mean, we don't actually have it on us. Would you like to meet us at the bank around the corner and we'll withdraw it for you?"

Tony Jr. came running, grinning his wolfish smile. Mrs. Soma wrapped a thick arm around the boy's narrow shoulders. "Meet you at the bank?" she asked. "Why didn't you withdraw it before you came here?"

Dorothy leaned in and spoke low. "It's quite a sum, and we're not comfortable carrying such an amount of cash. You, on the other hand, have nothing to fear with your own little personal bodyguard." They both looked down at Tony Jr. "What's more, you have your car to bring the money home. You're not obliged to go on foot, as we are."

"It's a trick, Ma!" the boy blurted out. "Don't fall for it."

"Shut up, you." She cuffed him on the head. "Do you run this business?"

"But, Ma—!"

"No back talk. Get out and start the car." She pushed him along.

The boy skipped down the steps, casting a malicious glance up at Dorothy, Benchley and Sherwood.

Now Mrs. Soma leaned in close, holding a stubby finger up to Dorothy's face. "It's one thing to try to pull a trick on me, but if you make me look like a fool in front of my little Tony Jr.'s eyes, God help you."

"God help me?" Dorothy said philosophically. "He already did once today. I don't want to press my luck."

Mrs. Soma ignored this. She was already at the bottom of the steps, about to get into her car. "I'll see you at the bank."

Benchley rubbed his chin as the car pulled away.

"I'm about to have a twinge of remorse. Should we go through with this?"

"Certainly. I'm about to have a twinge and tonic," Dorothy said. "Come on. Let's go in."

But at that moment, the bootlegger Mickey Finn and his moll, Lucy Goosey, the former striptease dancer, emerged through the door of the speak-easy.

"Mrs. Parker! Mr. Benchley! Fancy meeting you here." Finn smiled, and his teeth were just as yellow and rotten as when Dorothy and Benchley had last encountered the gangster.

"Not fancy at all," Dorothy said sourly. "Lousy meeting you here, actually. What brings you out of your hideout?"

Finn cackled. He was a redheaded devil—devilishly handsome and devilishly dangerous, Dorothy thought.

"Not a social visit. Purely business," he said in his faint Irish brogue. "I'm sure you recall very well that I supply Mr. Soma with his finest liquor, smuggled down from Canada. I have to constantly check on my interests, don't you know."

"I don't know and I don't care," Dorothy said, turning to go inside. "My only interest in your interests is in imbibing them."

Finn smiled as he stepped aside to let her in. "A word of warning, Mrs. Parker. You won't want to quench your thirst here very long. My darling Lucy spotted Izzy and Moe leaving as we entered."

132

"Izzy and Moe?" Dorothy asked. The names sounded familiar. Had she read about them in the newspaper? Were they gangsters—or worse, Prohibition agents?

Mickey Finn confirmed her suspicions. "Aye, they're government agents who enforce the Volstead Act. They always come in disguise. Today they were dressed as a priest and a rabbi. How do you like that? A priest and a rabbi walk into a bar—"

"A priest and rabbi walk into a bar," Dorothy said. "And ten minutes later, it turns into a raid."

Benchley asked Lucy, "How can you be sure it was Izzy and Moe?"

"Cop shoes," Lucy said. "Even a penniless priest wouldn't wear those cheap black shoes that cops always wear."

Mickey Finn cackled again, patting Lucy on the behind. "She's a smart lass, ain't she? Well, enjoy your relaxing little drink. Just make sure it's little."

Finn turned and guided Lucy down the steps.

"Wait," Dorothy said. "Did you warn Tony?"

"I daresay I didn't." Finn paused at the bottom of the steps. "When there's a raid, the owner dumps all the liquor. Then, of course, he has to buy more. Why would I pick my own pocket? See you around." He steered Lucy toward his waiting white limousine, parked across the street.

Benchley turned to Dorothy and Sherwood. "I

guess that's that. We don't want to be here if the place is about to be raided. The party's over before it even got started."

"No, that's just it," Dorothy said. "This is our ticket. Come on."

Chapter 15

Inside the dark speakeasy, they spotted Tony at the bar. He saw them, too.

"No, no, no!" Tony hurried toward them, wagging a long piano player's finger. "If my wife sees you here, we all catch hell."

Dorothy held up a hand. "You'll thank us when you hear what we have to tell you. You're about to be raided. Mickey's girl saw them here a few minutes ago."

Tony frowned. "You're certain?"

"If Mickey Finn wouldn't know, who would?" she asked. "Did you have a rabbi and a priest in here a short while ago? They were Prohibition agents."

Tony's face darkened; then he swung into action. "Carlos, get rid of that liquor!" he yelled to the man behind the narrow bar. "Put on the coffee and tea. But first, give these three each a drink on the house. Make it quick."

Carlos nodded, moving quickly and without question.

Tony turned and addressed the room. The speakeasy wasn't as crowded as it would be on a Saturday night, but there were enough people to make the place seem lively.

"Ladies and gentlemen, please drink up," Tony said, his arms raised in either supplication or surrender. "We have it on good authority we're about to be raided."

Several people groaned, fatigued by this nuisance. Only a few bothered to get up and leave.

"There's no cause for alarm," Tony continued in his most reassuring voice. "Carlos will be around with tea and coffee. So please drink up quickly or dump your drinks into the potted ferns. That's what they're there for."

"I guess that's how they came to be potted," Benchley said.

Tony hurried back to Dorothy, Benchley and Sherwood. "Now I got to go get the lockbox. Those damn cops will want a handout." Then he looked at them hopefully. "Unless you have the money?"

Dorothy and Benchley shook their heads, and Tony hustled into the back room.

They moved to the bar. Carlos already had a teacup for each of them. He deftly poured a measure of top-shelf Scotch into each one. He put the bottle back on the shelf and then pulled a hidden lever. The shelf of bottles descended through a trapdoor, as though on a dumbwaiter. Once the bottles were out of sight, the trapdoor closed and Carlos covered the shelf with a cloth; on top of the cloth he placed a large, ornate, silver coffeemaker. Then he grabbed a silver carafe and moved quickly around the room, filling up patrons' cups with hot, freshly brewed coffee.

Amused by the hubbub all around them, Dorothy, Benchley and Sherwood cheerfully raised their cups and clinked them together in a silent toast.

Just then, the door burst open. Government agents in long trench coats swarmed in.

To Dorothy's surprise, Carlos had reappeared behind the bar. He grabbed their teacups of Scotch and dropped them into the sink behind the bar. He quickly filled up new cups with steaming hot tea.

Tony now stood at the door. The agents swarmed past him. "Gentlemen, what's the meaning of this?"

A humorless man—the senior agent—stepped forward. "This is a raid. We know you're violating the Volstead Act."

"Hogwash!" Tony said, removing the cashbox from underneath his arm. "This is nothing but a quiet coffeehouse. Can't we discuss this?" Tony ushered the senior agent into the back room.

Two homely, stocky men—one wearing a priest's frock and one in a rabbi's hat and ringlets—sidled alongside Dorothy. She glanced at their cheap black shoes. Damn it, but Lucy Goosey was right.

"Are you enjoying a nice cup of tea?" said the one dressed as a rabbi in a friendly tone.

She looked into the steaming, dark liquid in her cup. "Yes, it *is* a nice hot cup of tea, as a matter of fact. It's *only* tea, thanks to you. So take your cheap shoes and go for a walk."

Dorothy, Benchley and Sherwood left the speakeasy before Mrs. Soma and Tony Jr. could return and make things worse.

Once they were back on the sidewalk, the long white limousine pulled up alongside them. Mickey Finn's face leered out the window. "How was your relaxing little drink?"

"It didn't suit me to a tea," Dorothy said.

"Ah, better luck next time," Finn said, and cackled a mischievous laugh.

Inside the car, Lucy whispered something to Finn.

Dorothy followed Lucy's line of sight to Benchley. Dorothy was dumbstruck. The last time they had encountered Finn and Lucy, Benchley couldn't stop ogling her. Now it seemed the tables had turned. What fresh hell was this?

"Well, why not?" Finn said to Lucy; then he spoke to Dorothy. "Would you three care to come back to my little sanctum sanctorum for a wee drink?" He opened the limousine door.

Benchley said, "I wouldn't mind a wee drink or two."

"Or thwee," Sherwood said. "And I've heard a lot about this hideout of yours, Mr. Finn, but I've never seen it."

Sherwood formally introduced himself to Finn.

They shook hands as he and Benchley stepped inside the limousine.

Benchley sat down next to Lucy. She moved close to him, not taking her eyes off him. Benchley didn't even seem to notice.

What's going on here? Dorothy wondered. She stood resolutely on the sidewalk.

"Come on, lass," Finn said. "We'll let bygones be bygones."

Just then, Mrs. Soma and Tony Jr.'s Studebaker came racing around the far corner. Dorothy thought she could hear the woman screaming even from this distance.

"What madness is that?" Finn said.

"A very mad Mrs. Soma."

"Aye, poor Tony," Finn said. "That woman would drive a sober man to drink."

Dorothy hopped inside the car, squeezing herself in between Benchley and Lucy. "Drive this sober woman to drink, instead."

The limo cruised through a forlorn and dilapidated section of the Bowery. An alley cat, curled up in one of the potholes of the empty street, looked up peevishly and sped out of the way of the oncoming limousine. Dorothy saw it turn and make an angry hiss as they drove by. They cruised alongside a shuttered brewery building, then turned a corner to another desolate street of boarded-up and dilapidated storefronts. The limo stopped beside the one shop that still appeared to be in business: Prof. Oddball's Magic & Novelty Emporium.

Dorothy gazed up at the sign. "Emporium? Not exactly truth in advertising."

"How do you mean?" Finn said, holding a hand out to Lucy. But as Lucy emerged from the car, she still had eyes only for Benchley.

"How can you call it an emporium when you never get a customer?"

Finn approached the shop and opened the door. "That's where you're wrong. The advantage to this place is that it *never* gets a—"

Finn stopped in his tracks. Inside the shop, a well-dressed man stood near the front counter, perusing the shelves.

"A customer?" Dorothy said.

Finn angrily pounded his silver-tipped shillelagh on the tiled marble floor to attract the man's attention. "Who the devil might you be?"

Sherwood knew the man immediately. "Jesus Christ!" he cried, before the man could answer.

"No, but I thank you for the compliment," the man said. "I also perform miracles; however, mine are merely illusion."

Though she had seen him only from afar, Dorothy recognized him, too. It was none other than Harry Houdini.

Chapter 16

Mickey Finn growled, "Mister, if you don't want to find yourself locked in a box at the bottom of the river, you'll explain your presence here."

Houdini was less than six feet tall. His expensive, well-fitted suit enhanced his powerfully built physique. He had a wide, friendly smile that was perpendicular to his angular features. Despite his youthful physicality and energy, he had crow's-feet at the corners of his eyes and gray hair at his temples, which indicated what Dorothy already knew—that the man was in his fifties.

Houdini smiled genially, completely unafraid of Finn. "I've found myself locked in innumerable boxes and tossed in many a river. As evidenced by my presence here, I've escaped every one."

Finn advanced threateningly. "Enough games, man. Explain yourself."

Lucy Goosey spoke up. "It's Harry Houdini, you jackass."

Lucy—and only Lucy—could speak to Finn this way. Thus he ignored the insult.

"Mr. Houdini!" Finn was flabbergasted. His ruddy face reddened further, but he recovered quickly. "You grace us with your presence in my humble shop."

"Humble indeed," Houdini said with an amused

smile, looking around. "These tricks went out of fashion decades ago, although anyone could tell as much by the thick coating of dust on—well, everything."

Like many powerful men, Finn groveled before those even richer and more powerful than himself. "You hardly need to visit a magic shop, Mr. Houdini," he said with a bow. "Is there something you're needing, then? I have many resources."

Houdini returned the bow. "I make it my business to know every magician and every magic shop in the city, if not the world. But I've had a house in New York for twenty-odd years, and I've never visited this particular shop. It has managed to evade my notice. I now see why. And, my curiosity satisfied, I need never visit it again. Thank you."

Houdini put on his top hat (Dorothy wondered if it had any rabbits inside) and moved toward the door, intent to leave.

"Ah, just a moment, there, Mr. Houdini." Finn wouldn't let such an influential man leave without trying to impress him. "I myself have a few tricks up my sleeve, and I wager you haven't seen everything this shop has to offer."

Houdini turned, and Dorothy detected a hint of condescension in his warm smile. "I've walked every aisle of your shop—without the oversight or assistance of any shopkeeper or salesperson, I might add—and found nothing to pique my curiosity." He was goading Finn. "What more could you possibly offer that would be of interest?"

Finn answered confidently, "Follow me."

Finn seemed to have forgotten all about Dorothy and everyone else except Houdini. He led the magician through one of the dim, musty aisles toward the back of the store, which was even darker. They followed Finn and Houdini and found them standing before a fun-house mirror.

"Go ahead," Finn said. "Give her a shove."

Houdini gently pressed the mirror with both hands. It silently slid backward, revealing a dark passageway.

Finn led the way. Houdini stood aside to let the ladies enter, and then he, Benchley and Sherwood followed.

They entered an enormous, brightly lit room as big as a banquet hall. It had been the cafeteria and employee bar of the shuttered brewery. Now it was Finn's lair, where a party was almost always in swing. On seeing Finn enter, a small band of musicians in the corner jumped to their feet and struck up a merry Irish tune. A silver-haired, steely-eyed bartender stood behind a long and beautifully polished bar. An assemblage of gangsters, henchmen and scantily clad beauties mingled about the room.

"Well," Houdini said to Finn, suitably im-pressed, "this is indeed quite a wondrous place. I literally take my hat off to you, sir." And he did.

Finn, his yellowed teeth grinning widely from his little triumph, now turned to his other guests. "Allow me to make formal introductions, Mr. Houdini. This is my girl, Lucy." She made a sort of bow. "And some fellow visitors today from the literary world, Mr. Benchley, Mr. Sherwood and Mrs. Parker."

"I've read your amusing articles," Houdini said to Benchley and Sherwood, shaking their hands. "And, Mrs. Parker, you are also making your name as a woman of letters."

"Afraid so," she said. "And those letters are IOU."

Finn clapped his hands together. "Now, how about that wee drink?"

"Now you're playing my tune," Dorothy said. "I'll have a Rob Roy."

"And you, sir?" Finn said to Sherwood. "A tall drink of water for a tall drink of water?"

Sherwood said gratefully, "A martini would be grand."

Lucy Goosey stood at Benchley's side. "Can I wet your whistle?"

Dorothy moved closer, waiting for a chance to get between them. She wouldn't let Lucy *touch* his whistle.

Benchley said, "How about that delightful beer I had once before?"

Lucy smiled. "Coming right up."

Finn tossed his hat, his jacket and his shillelagh to one of his helpers, then turned to Houdini. "And you, sir? Name your pleasure."

Houdini answered graciously. "The pleasure of your mysterious company, sir, is all I desire. I'll be satiated if you tell me more of your secrets."

Finn reddened, his emotions turning on a dime. "My secrets?" he snarled. "Come, come. Is that how you answer my hospitality? You drink or you get out!"

"I meant no offense, sir, I assure you." Houdini showed no fear. He answered Finn as if talking to an ill-tempered teenager. "But I have to keep my senses as sharp as a knife. Thus I rarely drink. A sarsaparilla or a lemonade would be perfectly suitable—or simply soda water if you have neither of those."

Finn's face flushed again, this time in embarrassment. But instead of lashing out at Houdini, he channeled it into despotic authority over the others in the room. "The great Harry Houdini has spoken! In deference to our exalted guest, we'll all have soft drinks."

A low-browed man with hairy knuckles had just handed Dorothy a cocktail glass. It was half-full of a deep amber fluid with a delightful smoky smell.

"Take those drinks away," Finn commanded. "Sarsaparillas all around."

For the second time that day, the drink was

yanked from her fingertips. In no time, someone else handed her a tall, cold glass of bubbly, foul-smelling *root beer.*

Not quite defeated, she sneaked over to the bar and winked at the bartender, an old man with silver hair and bushy black eyebrows.

She whispered, "Could you sneak a few drops of rum into mine?"

"Not on your life," he answered. "Because that would be the end of it."

Chapter 17

A beer-stained, green velvet love seat and several matching armchairs formed a circle in the center of the hall. Mickey Finn sat down in the nicest of the armchairs and the rest of the group followed. Benchley sat down at one end of the love seat. Before Dorothy could take the other seat, Lucy quickly slid in next to him.

Dorothy looked at Finn—Lucy typically sat on the arm of his chair, like a house cat. But Finn either didn't notice or didn't care about the change in seating arrangements, and Dorothy— feeling glum—slumped into the only armchair left, between the love seat and Finn.

Benchley, oblivious to Lucy's presence next to him, spoke to Houdini. "Mrs. Parker and I saw you at the halftime show at the pro football game last week. That was quite a disappearing trick with the police horse. We can't wait to see your performance on Thursday night."

"The Halloween show!" Houdini smiled tauntingly. "Yes, you'll be very entertained."

Finn said, "Can you show us a trick—or is it only for the paying customers?"

Dorothy felt insulted on Houdini's behalf. She muttered to Finn, "Don't make him sing for his supper—or even for this stale sarsaparilla."

"No trouble at all, Mrs. Parker." Houdini stood

up. "I'm happy to oblige. As a matter of fact, I'd be insulted if our host *didn't* request a trick. Here's a little one I always carry with me."

He took something from his pocket and opened his hand in front of Finn. Dorothy saw it clearly. Houdini held a handful of sewing needles, perhaps two dozen.

"Examine them, please," Houdini said confidently. "You'll see that they're completely normal sewing needles, easily obtained in any five-and-dime."

Finn did so, picking up several needles and holding them up to the light.

Houdini showed them to each person in the circle. Standing in front of Finn again, the magician said, "Are you satisfied they're genuine, and quite ordinary?"

Finn grunted in agreement.

"Please return them to my hand," Houdini said.

Finn did as he was told.

Then Houdini surprised them all. He clapped his hand to his mouth and began to chew. Lucy gasped. They could hear the clink and clatter of the needles as he gnashed them with his teeth. Dorothy thought she even glimpsed a glint of shiny metal as Houdini chewed, his smile wide and self-assured.

"How do they taste?" Dorothy asked.

"A little sharp," Houdini responded with a smile.

Then Houdini closed his eyes and gulped, swallowing hard. He opened his eyes and let out a deep sigh, as though he had eaten the best meal he'd ever tasted.

"That's quite a trick." Finn laughed. "But I think that's all it was. Just a trick."

"You haven't seen the best part," Houdini said cheerfully. "But first, would you care to examine my mouth for any needles I may have missed?"

Before Finn could agree or disagree, Houdini opened his mouth wide and stood directly before Finn. The bootlegger didn't hesitate. He gazed deeply into Houdini's mouth, looking in every corner.

"Clean as a whistle," Finn said.

"Then let's proceed." Houdini now withdrew a long strand of white thread from his pocket and handed it to Finn. "Would you please examine this thread? Would you agree it is ordinary white thread, easily purchased in the notions department in any home goods store?"

Finn nodded, fingering the thread. Houdini then showed it to the others.

"The needles were tasty," Houdini said, "but I always need a little something to chase them down." Then he put the end of the thread in his mouth and began chewing it up. They watched as the strand grew shorter and shorter. Eventually, only a tiny bit was left, which he slurped up like a piece of spaghetti.

"Swallowing a handful of needles was something," Finn said. "But anyone could eat up a line of thread, if he wanted to."

Houdini listened patiently and nodded, as though conceding defeat. "I suppose you're right, Mr. Finn," he sighed. "My little display has failed to entertain you. Permit me a moment to retrieve my materials and return them to my pocket."

Houdini reached his thumb and forefinger into his mouth and pulled out the end of the string. Finn jumped to his feet at what he saw next. Tied to the thread was a needle. Houdini pulled out two more inches of thread, and another needle appeared. Houdini tugged again and there was another needle—and another and another, all tied to the thread. Each needle was tied about two inches from the next. Houdini pulled the thread out faster, the needles tinkling against his front teeth. Dorothy counted the needles—twenty-five of them—as the last of the string emerged from the magician's mouth.

Houdini handed the string of needles to Finn, who dropped it like it was a snake. Dorothy could see that the string was wet from Houdini's mouth. The magician picked it up and held it out, stretched between both hands, for the others to examine. Then he returned it to his pocket.

"Astounding!" Sherwood said, clapping.

"Encore! Encore!" Benchley cheered.

Dorothy saw Lucy lean against Benchley.

"That's nothing," the former stripper whispered in Benchley's ear, but loud enough for Dorothy to hear. "I know a swallowing trick that'll really knock your socks off."

Stunned, Dorothy dropped her glass. It hit the wooden floor and shattered. Shards of glass, chunks of ice and sticky soda exploded around her feet.

Everyone looked at her quizzically—everyone except Lucy, who looked like the cat who swallowed the canary.

Dorothy stared back at them blankly. Had she been the only one who heard Lucy's remark? Apparently she was. Even Benchley appeared oblivious.

"Whoops," Dorothy said, after a long, quiet moment.

Immediately, the bartender appeared with a bar rag and a dustpan and cleaned it all up.

Ignoring the disruption, Sherwood resumed the conversation with Houdini. "I'm glad to see you're still up to your old tricks."

"Some old tricks," Houdini acknowledged, sitting down, clearly pleased with himself. "But also many new ones. I'm constantly trying to improve my act. So I'm always trying new things."

Finn growled at Sherwood, "Who the hell are you to accuse this world-famous magician of doing old tricks? Ignore this ignoramus, Mr. Houdini. You do all the old tricks you want."

"No, it's quite all right," Houdini said, smiling generously at Sherwood.

He hands out smiles like the Easter Bunny hands out eggs, Dorothy thought.

"But speaking of new tricks," Houdini continued, excited, "there's a truly amazing trick you'll see if you attend one of my sold-out shows at the Hippodrome this week. Are you ready for this? I make an elephant disappear. I'm the only magician to have ever accomplished it. And believe me, plenty of my imitators have tried and failed."

"Forgive me," Sherwood said, "but is that so new? You made a horse disappear last week in front of thirty thousand people. Is that so different from an elephant?"

Finn growled again, baring his yellow teeth. "You watch your mouth—"

"No, no, Mr. Finn," Houdini said soothingly, holding up a hand. "If one has never seen the Vanishing Elephant, one would be inclined to believe it's merely a variation on that old standby, the Lady in the Cabinet trick. But I assure you, Mr. Sherwood, if you see it, you will be astounded. It's a feat like no other, I guarantee you."

"I didn't mean to offend," Sherwood said. "I only meant that I'm pleased to see that you're still doing magic tricks at all. I've read so much about how busy you've been debunking the spiritu-alists, challenging mediums and exposing all that mystical mumbo jumbo."

"That's quite true," Houdini said gravely. His benevolent smile disappeared. "Revealing fraudulent spiritualists has become quite a passion of mine. I gather you've read about the five-thousand-dollar challenge in *Scientific American*?"

Both Sherwood and Benchley nodded.

"Five thousand dollars?" Finn sputtered. "I must have missed that particular issue of that illustrious journal. Can you enlighten me please, Mr. Houdini?"

"Most certainly I can, Mr. Finn," Houdini said solemnly. "I am a member of a research committee intent on studying psychic and spiritual phenomena. Last year, the committee published a challenge in *Scientific American* magazine. If any spiritualist, medium, clairvoyant or what have you can demonstrate objective evidence of a psychic manifestation under rigid test conditions, then the committee will award that person five thousand dollars."

"I'd speak to ghosts for five thousand dollars," Dorothy said. "I'd talk their damned ears off."

Houdini cracked a smile. "It's a very rigorous examination, believe me, Mrs. Parker. And at every one of my performances, I repeat the challenge. Despite this determined pursuit, I've found no credible evidence of the spirit world so far."

"That's a dangerous game you're playing, Mr. Houdini," Finn said.

"What game is that?" Houdini asked.

"Taunting spirits. That's asking for trouble, that is."

"I've had no complaints so far." Houdini smiled, not offended. "Except from phony flimflammers and fake fakirs."

Finn leaned forward. "You mean to say you don't believe in the spirits? You don't believe in heaven and hell?"

"And you do?" Dorothy said.

"Certainly I believe in heaven and hell!" Finn snapped at her.

Dorothy shrugged. "I'm surprised that someone so in danger of eternal damnation would be so determined to believe in it."

Finn's face grew red. He was about to rake her over the coals, but Houdini intervened.

"I believe in the afterlife, Mr. Finn," Houdini said sadly. "More than anyone I believe in the afterlife."

Hearing this, Finn cooled down. "You do?"

Houdini nodded. "A few years ago, I lost my dear sainted mother. How I miss her! I look forward to the day when we shall be reunited in paradise," he sighed. "Meanwhile, I've been earnestly searching for a way to communicate with her through the veil of death. The spiritualists promise that hope. But I'm afraid I have never yet seen any demonstration that the afterlife makes its presence known in *this* life. To my view, they are indeed separate worlds. The only crossing over is the final one."

Dorothy wondered how she might be able to convince Houdini to accompany her to Viola's séance for Ernie MacGuffin. "Well, aren't you the afterlife of the party?"

Finn narrowed his ice blue eyes at her. "Another county heard from," he sneered. "Surely you don't believe in spirits, you damned dirty heathen?"

"Surely I do, you damned dirty bootlegger," she said. "But the spirits I believe in are the ones behind your bar." She stared miserably at the liquor bottles. "And like heaven itself, they seem eternally out of reach."

Chapter 18

At lunchtime the next day, Neysa McMein spoke excitedly to the others gathered at the Algonquin Round Table.

"It was *his* voice. *Ernie's* voice," she said. "There was no mistaking it. It gave me chills."

Frank Adams nodded sagely. "Neysa's right. If I hadn't heard it for myself, I wouldn't have believed it. I don't know how that beguiling platinum blond witch did it, but it was Ernie speaking through her pretty little lips." He shoved the wet end of his smoldering cigar in his mouth, as if this concluded the matter.

Dorothy looked around at the faces of the others at the Round Table—Heywood Broun, Marc Connelly, George Kaufman and even Sherwood and Benchley. Neysa and Frank Adams had them almost completely bamboozled.

"Where's Alexander Woollcott when you need him?" she asked to no one in particular. "He wouldn't let this nonsense go unanswered."

Kaufman said, "Aleck and Harpo are out wandering the city again, playing their oddball game of croquet."

Benchley was insulted. "Mrs. Parker, you don't believe we're swallowing this whole, do you?"

"That means you're swallowing it a little bit," she said.

Frank Adams sat bolt upright. He yanked the cigar from his mouth. "Mrs. Parker, are you calling me a liar, or are you calling me a sucker? I don't care for either accusation."

"I'm saying you can't expect us to believe this woman talks to ghosts," Dorothy said. "That's poppycock."

Adams spoke through clenched teeth. "I never said she talks to ghosts. I only said she talks just like MacGuffin. I don't know how she does it, but she does it."

Dorothy folded her arms.

Neysa said, "Dottie, you really have to see it for yourself. It was spooky. I asked her questions only Ernie could answer. And she answered them. In his voice. You should have gone with us."

"We should have," Benchley answered. "But Mrs. Parker and I are going to go tomorrow night, after the Houdini show. I know you're convinced, Neysa, but it still sounds fishy to me."

"That's not the only thing that's fishy," Dorothy said. She explained about the incredible number of paintings in Snath's office. "I can't believe Ernie painted so many. Some of them, if not all of them, must be fakes."

Neysa shrugged. "Ernie always had an angle. He was always trying to sell a new painting. Always trying to get a new client."

Adams said with a smirk, "Ask him yourself tomorrow night."

"Very funny," Dorothy said. Then she thought better of it. She spoke thoughtfully, "But maybe you're on to something."

"What do you mean?" Heywood Broun said.

"I can think of one way Ernie can speak from beyond the grave. But we need one of his paintings."

"One of his paintings?" Neysa said.

"Perhaps steal one from Snath's office," Sherwood said playfully.

Dorothy shook her head. "No, thanks. He probably has snarling, ravenous guard dogs roaming the place at night. But maybe we can buy a painting at the auction?"

"Buy one?" Neysa said.

"Dottie," Benchley said, exasperated, "what the devil are you getting at?"

"We buy one of the paintings at the auction and have it authenticated. That shady solicitor Snath is pulling a fast one, I'm sure of it. If the painting's not a forgery, I'll eat my hat."

Frank Adams was skeptical. "So, let's say you have it authenticated—or inauthenticated, as you believe. Now you have a worthless painting on your hands. What good does that do you?"

"I'd return it first, then report Snath to the police."

Kaufman spoke sharply, "Buy a thousand-dollar painting and then just return it? It's not a dress off the rack from Gimbels."

"Besides," Benchley said, "where would you get the money?"

Marc Connelly grinned. "Maybe Harold Ross can loan it to you. If Raoul Fleischmann lent Ross enough dough to launch his loony magazine, maybe Ross would finance your idea."

Dorothy chuckled. "Ross is in such bad straits with his magazine, he couldn't lend me a pencil. Still, it's worth a try."

Sherwood raised an eyebrow. "Maybe that bootlegger could loan you the money?"

Harold Ross arrived at the table and sat down in his usual chair. "What bootlegger?" he said.

"Never mind that," Dorothy said. "You're just in time. Could Fleischmann loan us the money to buy one of Ernie MacGuffin's paintings?"

Ross frowned. Clearly, this was a sore subject. He didn't answer her question directly. "Speaking of money, I need to talk to you and Benchley about the article—"

Dorothy sighed. "You're not cutting the fee again, are you?"

Ross cleared his throat. "Well, how about this? What if you also write a book review, and I won't lower the fee?"

"A story about MacGuffin and a now a book review—all for four hundred?" Dorothy said.

"You got it," Ross nodded, taking this as her acceptance of his offer. "But you'll love this book. It's a memoir. Guess who just wrote it?"

"If you say Ernie MacGuffin, I'll rip your nose off," she said.

"Close, but no cigar. It's by Midge MacGuffin. The book comes out on Friday."

Dorothy's eyes went wide. "What? I just had a visit with her yesterday, and she didn't mention any memoir! Matter of fact, I had to drag her story out of her. And now she wrote a book?"

"Well, yes," Ross stammered.

She railed on. "And it's coming out on Friday? For Pete's sake, Ernie killed himself hardly a week ago. How did she find the time to write it—*and* get a publisher?"

"Shucks," Ross said. "I thought you'd be happy for her. You know, a fellow female writer."

"Happy for her? She's no writer. She—" Dorothy stopped. Midge *did* ghostwrite Ernie's suicide note.

"What is it?" Benchley asked.

Dorothy also remembered that there was some other subject that Midge didn't want to talk about. It must have been about her memoir, of course.

"Mrs. Parker, what is it?" Benchley asked again.

"Of all the crummy things," Dorothy muttered and slumped in her chair. She had been pecking away on her typewriter for years now, and what did she have to show for it? The only one who had shown any interest in publishing her work was that British bastard Jasper Welsh, who offered only pennies—

Dorothy sat up. "Fred, what did Welsh say? He had something big?"

"Don't call me Fred," Benchley said. "But, yes, Welsh said he and Snath had a big deal coming up."

"Damn!" Dorothy pounded her tiny fist on the table. "Midge is publishing with that Cockney snake in the grass."

"That's right," Ross said. "Her book is coming from Waterloo Press. Welsh probably did make the deal."

"How did Midge MacGuffin get mixed up with that slimy limey Welsh?" Benchley asked.

"Through Snath," Dorothy said. "He's Ernie's agent. Maybe Welsh pitched it to Snath, and Snath talked Midge into it. I can't imagine she'd come up with the idea herself. She's no operator. She's as green and as dense as an emerald."

Ross was unfazed. "So, will you review it?"

"This whole thing stinks," she said, ignoring him. "Maybe I will go ask Ernie all about it at the séance. What do I have to lose?"

"What time is the séance?" Sherwood asked.

"Midnight," she said.

"Midnight on Halloween night?" Kaufman cried. "Have you lost your marbles?"

"It's trick-or-treat," she said. "We'll find out how Viola does her trick, and revealing it will be a treat."

Sherwood ran a finger around the rim of his

coffee cup. "I thought you two were going to Houdini's show tomorrow night."

Dorothy said, "Houdini's show will be over before the séance begins. Maybe we could even convince Houdini to join us for one of his famous debunkings."

"Good idea," Benchley said. "Houdini *is* the famous debunk king."

Adams waved his cigar, creating a plume of smoke. "What about Snath's big auction of MacGuffin's works? You said you wanted to buy a painting at the auction and have it authenticated. Isn't that tomorrow night as well?"

Dorothy frowned. Adams was right. She couldn't be in two places at once. She'd have to forgo the auction and put aside the thought of exposing those paintings as forgeries. At least for now.

Sherwood shrugged. "I'd offer to go to the auction in your stead. But there's a big Halloween party at Texas Guinan's. And—"

"And what?" she demanded.

"And—well, you don't have the money to buy a painting."

Benchley turned to Dorothy. "Maybe we *could* borrow the money from Mickey Finn. It wouldn't hurt to ask."

"Yeah, sure," she said. "That violent, volatile gangster wouldn't hurt a soul. What's the worst that could happen?"

Chapter 19

Mickey Finn laughed, "Not in a million years."

Dorothy Parker and Robert Benchley sat together in the love seat in the middle of Finn's hideout. Outside, through the smoked-glass windows, a late October twilight descended. Inside, Dorothy was pleased that Lucy Goosey had reclaimed her usual house-cat seat on the wide arm of Finn's armchair.

"We're not asking for much," Dorothy said, trying to sound convincing. She wasn't sure how firmly she wanted to make her case. She wouldn't beg Finn for the money. She certainly wouldn't stick her neck out if he insisted on being a gangster about it. "Just enough to buy one painting. A few hundred dollars, at most."

"Listen," Finn said, wiping tears of laughter from his eyes. "I like you brainy birds. I don't have many society types come in here. And certainly not magazine writers—except a few nosybodies looking to sell a juicy story about me. But they get tossed out on their ear because I don't want *any* stories written about me. I just want to be left alone to enjoy myself and take care of my business enterprises. I think you understand that."

"No one has to know you lent us any money," Dorothy said.

"I said, I like you," Finn repeated, more sternly. "We're old friends, right? As a rule, I don't lend money to friends. It's bad for business and bad for friendship. Bad things tend to happen to the people I lend money to. I don't want anything bad to happen to my friends."

Benchley took a different approach. "Don't think of it as a loan. Think of it as an investment."

Finn's laugh was as sharp as a boxer's jab. "I've heard that one before. They say, 'Buy into this racehorse, Mr. Finn. He's a guaranteed money-maker. He can't lose.' They tell me, 'It's not a loan, Mr. Finn. A stake in this nightclub is a sure thing.'" Finn laughed. "Let me tell you, no business is a sure thing. There are no guarantees, other than the ones you ensure by force. And I don't want to have to get into the kneecap-busting business with you. What kind of investment is that?"

Dorothy was almost insulted. Even a gangster didn't want to get into business with her? "I've been told my kneecaps are just divine, thank you very much."

Finn leaned forward. "Then let's keep them that way and drop this whole thing."

He leaned back in his chair and sucked on a large cigar, blowing smoke up at the ceiling.

Meanwhile, Dorothy saw Lucy look meaning-fully at Benchley. What was that all about?

"You know, Mick," Lucy whispered in his ear,

"that crazy son of a bitch's paintings are expected to sell for ten times their original asking price. Investors are going to make out like bandits."

Dorothy knew Lucy was the only person Finn ever listened to.

"Ten times?" Finn stood up, moved slowly to the bar, grabbed a shot glass and a bottle of Irish whiskey, poured himself a neat snort and tossed it back. Lost in thought, he didn't offer them a drink. "You know what tonight is?"

"Wednesday?" Benchley said.

He shook his head.

"Pinochle night?" Dorothy said.

"Wash night?" Benchley suggested.

"Sir Gawain and the Green Knight?" Dorothy asked.

"No, no, and not even close." Finn chuckled throatily. "It's October thirtieth, Mischief Night."

They waited silently for him to elaborate.

"When I was a lad in Belfast," he continued, "we used to get up to all kinds of shenanigans on Mischief Night."

"Do tell," Dorothy said, sensing he had something rich to share.

"I remember one Mischief Night very clearly." Finn sat down, a storyteller's twinkle in his ice blue eyes. "I was nine. Me and some of the other lads went to an old graveyard to carry on and scare ourselves silly. I said, let's dig up some old bones. Well, this notion frightened the bejesus out

165

of the other boys. But I was full of hell. I didn't care. Me and another lad, Tommy Connor, dug 'em up anyways. So we took these old bones, buried probably two hundred years, and we carried them to the house of Mrs. Parsons. Now, her husband, Mr. Parsons, was a tough, angry bastard, or so we thought at the time. If I were to meet him today, I suppose he might seem a decent and upright—if rather angry—sort of man. But there's no chance I would meet him today, because at that time he had recently died. Mrs. Parsons had just buried the bastard the week before."

What does this have to do with the price of MacGuffin's paintings? Dorothy wondered. But she kept her thoughts to herself.

Finn continued. "Anyhow, it was the kind of October night that ghost stories are made of. Fog. Drizzling rain. Wind howling like a banshee. The other boys had run on home. So now it was just me and Tommy Connor. We carried with us the bones of one arm and the skull. We peeked into the Widow Parsons' sitting room window. She sat in a rocking chair, cuddling a crying baby. Now, Tommy Connor, he had a heart as hard and black as coal. He took true joy in the misery of others. Back then, I didn't know any better, and he and I were thick as thieves. He wanted to scare Mrs. Parsons right then—and maybe we'd get to see one of her teats as she fed the baby. I said no, let's wait for her to put the baby in the cradle."

"How considerate of you," Dorothy said dryly.

"I thought so at the time." Finn shrugged. "Finally, the baby is done crying and feeding. Mrs. Parsons lays the baby in the cradle. That's when we take the skull, see, and we take what's left of the bones of the one arm, and we start tapping—gentle, oh so gentle—on the window, with the finger bones. Tommy is holding up the skull in front of the window, so when she opens the curtain—*Aaaah!*—there's a skull staring at her with its black, dead eyes. Its hand is scraping at the window to get inside. That's our plan, anyhow. So we hear her shuffle toward the window; then she draws back the curtain—and then—"

"Then what?" Dorothy said.

"Then nothing," Finn said. "No scream of terror. No sound at all."

"Could she even see the skull in the dark?" she asked.

"She saw it, all right."

"How do you know?"

"Because," Finn continued, "the next sound we hear is a terrific explosion. And the window blasts to pieces and the skull is suddenly gone. And gone, too, is Tommy's hand, which had been holding it up."

"His hand?" Dorothy asked.

"Shot clean off. With a shotgun. Almost point-blank range, from right inside the window. Mrs. Parsons must have taken it off the mantel and fired it the moment she saw that skull."

"What did you do?" Benchley asked.

"Nothing at first. I'm staring at the stump at the end of Tommy's arm. And I see him screaming, but no noise comes out of his mouth. I realize my ears are ringing—I was stone deaf from the shotgun blast. Then all of a sudden Mrs. Parsons is standing above us, lowering the barrels of the shotgun at us. Next thing I knew, I'm tearing hell down the lane. I left Tommy behind and I didn't give a tin shit if he lived or died. I just wanted to save my own precious little arse."

Finn took a long drag on his cigar.

"And then what?" Dorothy asked.

"Then nothing. The next morning, my uncle was leaving on the steamer for New York. I begged and pleaded that he take me with him. Been here ever since."

"And your friend?" Benchley asked gingerly. "What happened to him?"

"He survived, I heard. But he wasn't the same. Even more belligerent than before. Got himself into any fight that came his way. When there was no fight, he would start one. In another year or so, he got kicked in the head by a horse and died."

Again Dorothy wondered what this had to do with an investment in a painting. "So?"

"So when I was a boy, I thought grumpy Mr.

Parsons was an old man. But I'm about the same age as he was when he died. Funny how your point of view changes. One thing didn't change. On that long, filthy voyage to America, I had a lot of time to think. I swore to myself that I'd never knowingly trick anyone ever again." He held his arms wide, to encompass not only the clandestine brewery but also his citywide bootlegging empire. "And that's been the secret of my success. I'm an honest man working hard in an honest business."

"That was a tremendous story," Dorothy said. "But you do realize you're a ruthless gangster running an illegal racket."

Finn shook his head. "It's the law that's wrong, not the business. Not me. I'm not like those undercover Prohibition agents. I don't trick or swindle. I set reasonable market prices and I deliver quality products when I say I will. Play fair with me and I'll play fair with you—that's my slogan. You call it Mischief Night, but now it's just another night for me."

Dorothy sighed. "So I guess that's a really, really, really long-winded Irish way of telling us no."

"No," said Finn. "It's a really long-winded Irish way of telling you yes."

"Yes?" Dorothy and Benchley said in unison.

"Aye, yes," Finn said. "I don't like the notion of this slick lawyer fellow swindling fools with a dead man's reputation. You catch him in the lie.

You write a big magazine article on it. You expose him as a fraud." He held up a hand. "But first, you sell off the painting and you give me my tenfold profit. Does that sound like a fair deal?"

Dorothy considered this, though she wished she had a drink to think it through. "Buy a painting at auction? Show that it's a fake? Sell it to some rich sucker at a big profit? And expose Snath in print? That's our deal?"

Finn nodded seriously. "That's our deal."

Benchley was ready. "So, can you give us cash?"

Again Finn barked in laughter. "Ha, you think I keep my money here in a coffee can under the floorboards, like some petty criminal or little old lady?"

"If I had any money," Dorothy said, "that would do for me."

"I keep it safe in the bank, like any good businessman," Finn said firmly. He spoke directly to Benchley. "So I'll give you my bank credit number. That should satisfy any transaction."

Benchley was puzzled. "I-I'm not handling any such transaction."

Dorothy spoke up. "You can give the account number to me. I'll do the bidding at the auction."

"You?" Finn laughed derisively. "A woman? Not on your life. Who would believe a woman would buy a fine painting?"

"I know a couple women who *paint* fine paintings."

"It won't work." Finn wiped a tear of laughter from his eye. "They'd laugh when you go to pay and you have to give the name Michael Finnegan. No, Mr. Benchley will take care of it, won't you?"

Benchley tugged at his bow tie. "I'm not so certain—"

"Certainly you're certain!" Finn leaned his fists on his knees. Lucy Goosey took out her compact and powdered her nose.

Benchley cleared his throat. "What if Miss Goosey accompanies me?"

Lucy turned and raised one eyebrow.

Dorothy gasped, "Nothing doing, Fred!"

Finn ignored Dorothy. "Good idea, Mr. Benchley." He chuckled and then winked at Lucy. "Lucy goes with you—to ensure my investment is safe. She'll make sure you don't spend my money at the nearest speakeasy, and make sure no unfortunate occurrence may befall you."

No unfortunate occurrence befall Benchley? What could that mean? Dorothy didn't like the sound of this. She felt that disaster was looming. She also felt a sharp pang of envy. She didn't like that self-satisfied look in Lucy Goosey's sultry eyes.

"Miss Goosey accompany Mr. Benchley?" Dorothy stammered. "But everyone knows she's your—your companion! People will talk."

Lucy cast a dark glance at Dorothy. "I can dress up as fancy as you please. I can look like the wife of any Park Avenue millionaire—don't you worry. I'll dress the part and do up my hair. No one will recognize me in a million years."

Finn gently patted Lucy's leg. "In that case, cut back on the makeup, doll."

Lucy folded her arms grumpily. Dorothy was pleased to see her at least a little upset. Still, she had to talk them out of this.

"Mr. Benchley *can't* go to the art auction," she said. Her voice sounded weak even to her own ears. "We have tickets to see Houdini at the Hippodrome tomorrow night. Mr. Benchley is assigned to review the performance for *Vanity Fair*."

Finn looked angry again. "You came to me. Now you don't want my money? You think you can waste my time like this?"

Lucy patted his arm to calm him down. "So Mr. Benchley and I go to the auction, and Mrs. Parker goes to see Houdini. She can write the review." Lucy looked down at Dorothy. "You are a writer, aren't you?"

Dorothy couldn't bring herself to answer to this former stripper–turned–gangster's concubine. It took her a moment to respond. "Well, I'm as good a writer as you were a stripper. Does that answer your question?"

Lucy glared at her.

"That answers the question for me." Finn smiled. He pointed his cigar at Lucy and

Benchley. "You two go to the art auction and multiply my investment." He aimed the cigar at Dorothy. "And you go see Houdini and write your little magazine article. Now, all of you get the hell out. I have work to do."

"Of course you do," Dorothy said, standing up. "Those kneecaps won't break themselves."

Chapter 20

The next night, Halloween night, Houdini stood onstage, waved his hands, and opened the giant box. The crowd gasped. The five-ton elephant was gone.

Dorothy sat in the third row of the massive Hippodrome auditorium. She could feel the air being sucked past her as the five thousand people in the audience simultaneously drew in their breath.

Then, like the rest of the crowd, Dorothy applauded and cheered. The sound was thunderous. She automatically looked to her right, as she usually did when attending shows, to smile in mutual approval at the merry face of Benchley.

But Benchley wasn't there, of course. The seat was empty.

Benchley stood waiting at the curb in front of Pennsylvania Station. At home, he had dressed in his tux and tails, bid his family good-bye, and boarded the evening train. Now here he stood on the noisy, bustling sidewalk, with people rushing by behind him, traffic jostling along Seventh Avenue in front of him, and the exhaust from buses and cars blowing on him, waiting for Lucy Goosey to arrive in Mickey Finn's white limousine to pick him up.

How do I get myself into these messes? he wondered. Why couldn't he have simply had a relaxing, enjoyable evening with Mrs. Parker, sitting together watching Houdini's magical spectacle? *Oh well,* he contented himself, *at least* she *must be enjoying herself.*

Soon, the long white limo cruised up to the curb like a yacht docking in a boat slip. Benchley opened the door and found only Lucy Goosey inside. "Permission to come aboard?"

She waved him in. He sat down and closed the door, and the car eased back into traffic.

Lucy Goosey had been right about her ability to look like a millionaire's wife. Benchley had always admired her. But here she looked absolutely stunning. Too bad Mrs. Parker wasn't here, he thought. Mrs. Parker would have a quip about Lucy going from harlot to starlet, or something like that. He smiled at the thought of it.

Lucy asked, "Do you know anything about art auctions?"

He shook his head. He now eyed the limo's little bar, stocked with top-shelf liquor. But she didn't invite him to have a drink.

"Don't be fooled," she said. "Art is a business. Just as cutthroat as any other." She told him she had learned everything there was to know about art auctions.

"So, then," he asked politely, "you're not that fond of art?"

"You think just because I was a striptease artist that I can't appreciate the finer arts?"

"Please forgive me, Miss Goosey. I didn't think any such thing." However, he admitted to himself, that had been almost exactly what he had thought. He asked, "So you're an art lover, are you?"

She frowned at this term but nodded. "And you?" she said doubtfully. "Do you appreciate art?"

"Most assuredly," he said, stealing another glance at the minibar. "I like them all—Monet, Manet, Tanqueray."

"Oh dear. Not Monet. I hate the Impressionists. So simplistic."

He chuckled, trying to keep the mood light. "Well, you know what they say. Monet isn't everything."

"You can keep your Impressionists. I prefer the Baroque artists."

"Every artist I ever met was br-oke."

She frowned again. "Not broke. *Baroque*."

"Again, you know what they say. If it ain't Baroque, don't—"

"Don't say it," she said, dismissing his jest. "I particularly like Rubens. Do you like Rubens?"

"No, thanks. I like the corned beef but can't stand the Russian dressing."

She was smiling now. "Rubens is not known for his dressing. He's known for his *un*dressing. His nudes."

"Nudes?" Benchley was now on shaky ground. He didn't like where this was going.

"Yes, nudes. Do you like nudes?" She leaned toward him. Her intoxicating perfume enveloped him. She wore an elegant dress, but it was decidedly low cut at her—her—her bustline. He forced himself to look her in the eye.

"I asked you," she said, "do you like nudes?"

"Well, no," he said nervously. "No nudes is good nudes."

He glanced out the window at the busy sidewalk, wishing to be back out there. Just how *did* he get himself into these messes?

After Houdini's show was over, Dorothy elbowed her way through the crowd toward the backstage area of the Hippodrome, intending to find his dressing room. The Hippodrome Theater, located directly across the street from the Algonquin, was the most massive auditorium in New York—it took up nearly half a city block. The stage itself was double the size of a baseball diamond, big enough to fit an entire circus. Below the stage, Dorothy knew, was a glass-walled water tank the size of a swimming pool, which could be raised onstage and then lowered as needed. As a teenager, Dorothy had seen performances of horses diving into that tank. The Hippodrome had been in its glory back then.

As she made her way backstage, she could

see how the theater was now showing its age. The well-worn plank floors were dusty and dilapidated. The ropes and cables for raising and lowering the scenery looked thinned and frayed. Stagehands and crew members pushed past her. They had an air of weary indifference about them, as if they weren't a part of the theater's storied past or had no sense of pride in working under its roof. No one questioned her. No one asked why she was backstage. This indifferent attitude discouraged her from asking directions, so it took her some time to navigate her way.

As she went along, she considered what she would say to the magician. Houdini had closed the third act of his show with the vanishing elephant trick. But he had spent most of the second act lecturing about spiritualism (denouncing it, really) and demonstrating the tricks that bogus spiritualists and mediums used. Then he restated his challenge, with the five-thousand-dollar prize, for any medium to show him scientific proof of spiritual manifestation.

For Dorothy, this challenge confirmed that Houdini simply *had* to accompany her that night to Mistress Viola's séance. Besides, it was Halloween and, superstitions or not, she did not want to go alone.

A burly stagehand suddenly blocked her way.

"Just where do you think you're going, lady?"

"I need to see Mr. Houdini."

"Yeah, you and a thousand other adoring female fans." The man brushed sawdust off his brawny forearms. "You want to reach him, send him a postcard. No visitors backstage."

She ignored him with a wave and attempted to brush past him. But the man grabbed her arm with a meaty hand. She was about to launch a sharp insult but realized this would do little to disarm him. Then a thought occurred to her.

"Don't touch me," she gasped in her most dramatic voice—which was not very dramatic at all. Kind of austere and raspy, as a matter of fact. "I commune with the dead."

The man dropped his hand. "W-what'd you say?"

"I am a spirit guide," she said, doing her best to create a mysterious look in her eyes. "I traverse the stygian boundary to bring back the messages of those who have gone before us to the—the land of the spirits."

The man's initial surprise was wearing off. "Oh, yeah, sure, lady. Whatever you say."

She cranked it up a notch. "I am here to accept the challenge of Herr Houdini. I will show him his proof that the ghost world does indeed exist within this material world."

"Oh, will you, Frau Parker?" said a voice behind her.

Dorothy turned around to see Harry Houdini standing in the doorway of the makeup room, wiping the greasepaint off his face with a cotton cloth.

Houdini stepped forward, hand extended. "Good to see you again, Mrs. Parker."

"Ah, I didn't see you there, Mr. Houdini. Did you hear . . . all of that?"

"I certainly did," Houdini said with a grin. "An atrocious performance. But you pulled it off with panache. Good for you. Great showmanship is more than half the battle of winning over your audience. And you had big Danvers here fooled." He patted the burly stagehand on the back.

Big Danvers gave Dorothy a surly look and walked away.

Dorothy smiled at Houdini in return. "You'll have to forgive me, Mr. Houdini—"

"Just Houdini. Not *Mr.* Houdini. Not Harry. Everyone, even my wife, calls me Houdini. Now, what can I do for you?"

She batted her big, brown, soulful eyes. "Well, Houdini, I wondered what you're doing after the show."

Now it was Houdini's turn to be flustered. "Well, now, Mrs. Parker, I'm a happily married man."

"Fine with me. Your wife can come along. Come one, come all."

"Mrs. Parker!" Houdini was insulted. "Exactly what sort of proposition are you making?"

"No, no, it's nothing like that." She smiled,

letting him off the hook. She enjoyed getting his goat. "Who do you think I am? Some floozy who would try to get you alone and get my hands on your—your magic wand?"

He realized she was teasing him. "I had no such illusions, at least not illusions of the extramarital sort, I assure you."

"Well, good. Now that we've settled that, enough playing games. Time to get down to business. You want proof of the afterlife? Let's go."

"Go? And where might we be going?"

"To meet a friend." She grabbed his arm and tried to pull him along. But even though he was twice her age, he was still as strong as a rhino. He could not be moved.

"And who might this friend be?"

She dropped his arm. "Just a friend—who's a ghost."

Chapter 21

Arm in arm, Benchley escorted Lucy Goosey through the stately entrance of Piddle Brothers, the famous auction house off Fifth Avenue. It was not truly a "house"—it was built more like a ballroom or ornate auditorium—but it had the luxurious furnishings of a mansion, with high-domed ceilings, crystal chandeliers, long white columns, gold-brocaded drapes and plush crimson carpets.

"Over there." Lucy discreetly pointed one of her white-gloved hands. She steered Benchley toward a long, wide table marked REGISTRATION.

"Is that where we get our table-tennis paddle?" he asked. Lucy ignored this.

Not a very lively companion, he thought. Mrs. Parker would have had the courtesy to roll her eyes at least, or respond with a typical, "That's enough, Fred."

As they made their way to the registration desk, Benchley took in the crowd. Everyone was dressed to the nines. Mostly stiff old rich gents and their powdered matronly wives, noses in the air. Well-to-do names from the Social Register. But there was some "new money," too. Benchley spotted at least a couple of famous athletes, a number of gadfly actors and actresses he knew and more than a few high-level gangsters and bootleggers, deliberately ignoring one another. None of them seemed to recognize Lucy, or at least they pretended they didn't know her. Buzzing around the hall, in and out of the mostly formal old crowd, were a few packs of rich young lads in their baggy tuxedos, arm in arm with their flapper girlfriends in their swishing beaded dresses, laughing loudly and carrying on.

Benchley wondered if this was what Ernie MacGuffin had really wanted. Certainly, MacGuffin had desired popularity and admiration. But from *these* people? Benchley shrugged his shoulders, unable to make sense of it.

The man behind the registration desk asked, "Your name, sir?"

"Robert—"

Lucy elbowed him in the ribs, and Benchley remembered.

"Did I say Robert? How silly of me. That was my mother's name. The name is Michael Finnegan," he said, with an attempt at an Irish lilt.

Lucy gave him a warning look. But the man behind the desk nodded deferentially. "Here you are, sir."

The man handed Benchley a small card with the letter *N* on it.

"What's this?" Benchley asked. "Where's the paddle?"

"No paddles, sir. We've modernized."

183

"I'd say you've miniaturized." He held up the card. "I gather I'm supposed to bid with this?"

"No, sir." The man looked deferential again. "It's a totally modern bidding system. All state-of-the-art electronic devices now. You simply push a button."

Benchley inspected the card carefully for a button. He saw nothing but the letter *N*, printed in black ink.

"I beg your pardon, sir." The man behind the desk spoke helpfully, pointing in the direction over Benchley's shoulder. "Behind you, you'll see a number of bidding devices within the gallery. Yours is marked with the letter *N*. It's over there—near the back, on the right side. Once the auction begins, you simply push the green button on the device to bid on an item you desire. The auctioneer will acknowledge you by your letter. Discreet, yet much more effective than the antiquated paddle method."

"How so?"

The man smiled. "Now there's no question whether a bidder is making a bid—or swatting a fly. That was sometimes a problem with the former paddle system." The man waited expectantly for a laugh. Benchley didn't. The man nodded, the smile gone. "Good luck, Mr. Finnegan. And happy bidding."

"Likewise," Benchley said, letting Lucy drag him away.

Benchley stopped short. Making a beeline toward them was a handsome, self-assured, middle-aged man with a jaw like the prow of a ship. *Oh dear,* thought Benchley.

"Here comes Horace Liveright," he whispered to Lucy. "He's a big-shot publisher in the book world. But *don't* mention his kidney infection."

Lucy frowned and muttered, "Why in the world would I mention—"

"Bob!" Liveright smiled and extended a manly hand to Benchley. "How's things, old boy?"

Benchley decided to copy the man's collegial gregariousness. "Oh, Horace, old bean. How are you, old kid. Old kidney bean."

Liveright looked puzzled. Perhaps even perturbed. "Just fine, Bob. How are you? How's *Vanity Fair*?"

"Not blad," Benchley said merrily, still shaking Liveright's hand. "I mean, not bladder. I mean, you know how things go from bad to bladder—I mean, from bladder to worse."

"Sure." Liveright detached his hand from Benchley's, nodded at Lucy and strode away, shaking his head.

"That went just swell," Lucy said.

"At least you didn't mention his kidney infection," Benchley said, mopping his perspiring brow with his handkerchief. "Well-done."

"Don't look now," Lucy muttered. "It's the heat."

Benchley lowered his handkerchief to see Captain Church of the New York Police Department hobbling by. Church had a wooden peg leg below his right knee. He had his pants leg cuffed as if to display it.

Benchley stiffened at the sight of him, which caught the police captain's attention.

Church turned toward him. "Mr. Benchley, is that you?"

"Ha, you've got me pegged." Benchley cut his laugh short and quickly added, "What brings you here, Captain? A police investigation?"

Captain Church ignored this. He scrutinized Lucy. "Miss Goosey?"

"No, no, no," Benchley interjected, and tried to stand between the policeman and the former stripper. "This is a foreign lady. A duchess, in fact. Duchess County."

"Duchess *County?*" Church asked. "The same as Dutchess County, the municipality along the Hudson River?"

"Ha!" Benchley had his handkerchief in hand again, patting his profusely sweating brow. "Did I say Duchess County? Silly me. I meant, this is Countess Dutchie. From the Netherlands."

But Benchley knew this wouldn't wash. Church folded his arms, looking skeptical and insulted. Benchley couldn't stand up to cross-examination. He silently hoped for a flood or an earthquake or some other natural disaster to suddenly occur and get him out of this sticky situation. But Church merely took out a notepad and pencil from his inside jacket pocket. He turned and walked away, carefully jotting down something as he glanced over his shoulder at Benchley and Lucy.

"He's not an art lover," Benchley said. "He must be here for a reason."

Lucy sighed. "Let's find our seats."

Making their way through the swelling crowd, Benchley halted once more. "Not another one!"

"Now who?" Lucy said.

"See that dapper, silver-haired gent over there? That's my boss, Frank Crowninshield. He knows I'm not supposed to be here. The lovable old dear assigned me to go to see Houdini tonight."

"He's not looking this way," Lucy said. "He hasn't seen us yet. Come on."

She grabbed Benchley's hand and they hustled through the well-to-do attendees, moving toward the back of the auditorium. They found the bidding device marked *N* and sat in the chairs placed before it. Benchley picked up his auction catalog and held it up directly in front of his face, trying to hide behind it.

He found himself staring at a startlingly lifelike painting of a young nude woman. A platinum blond young nude woman, to be exact. It was Mistress Viola.

"Oh dear, oh dear, oh dear." Benchley quickly turned the page.

Houdini balled his hands into fists and planted them on his hips. "I'm not going anywhere until you tell me what all this is about. Now, come sit down and explain yourself."

He turned and strode into the makeup room, pointing Dorothy toward one of the makeup chairs. He looked about and spotted a champagne bottle chilling in a silver bucket filled with ice. He grabbed it and deftly popped the cork. It bounced off the vanity mirror, cracking the glass.

"Here." He held out a glass. "Have a drink."

She stared at the shattered mirror. "That just earned you seven years' bad luck."

"I don't believe in such superstitious curses."

She took the glass he offered and drank a big gulp.

"Curses!" she cried. "What is this?"

"Sparkling white grape juice." He sipped from a glass. "Not alcoholic. What do you think?"

"What do I think?" She set the glass down on the crowded makeup counter. "You don't need to be a mind reader to guess what I think."

"Sorry." He found a metal pitcher and poured her a glass of cold water. "Now, curses aside, what is all this about?"

She explained about Ernie MacGuffin and how he had committed suicide. She explained about Ernie's lawyer, Snath, who was at that very moment selling a pile of what might be forged paintings—so many paintings that MacGuffin couldn't possibly have painted them all himself. She explained how Mistress Viola, who claimed she never knew Ernie, held séances at which she very convincingly spoke with Ernie's voice and answered questions only he could answer.

"So you debunk these things," she said. "How would you like to debunk this one?"

The excited gleam of a hunter came into Houdini's keen eyes. "Off the top of my head, I can think of three ways this Mistress Viola is performing this trick. I wonder which one it is— or if she's come up with a new one altogether."

"So you think she's a fraud?"

"I prefer to see her with my own eyes. But from what you've told me, I suspect she is."

"Oh, you'll get an eyeful." Dorothy was relieved. "So you'll go to the séance with me?"

Houdini rubbed his hands together. "I will indeed. Let's get dressed."

"Get dressed?"

Houdini checked his pocket watch. "It's nearly eleven thirty. You say the séance starts at midnight? We don't have much time to prepare."

"Prepare? Prepare for what?" She hopped out of the makeup chair. "Let's just go."

"But we need disguises." He pulled on a heavy old coat and looked at himself standing stoop shouldered before the mirror. Satisfied, he reached into a box and found a small iron gray wig. He wrestled it onto his wide head, smoothed it down and instantly looked twenty years older. He picked up a makeup pencil and expertly exaggerated the lines at the sides of his eyes and mouth, giving his hard, marble-like features the sagging and imperfect appearance of old age. Then he donned thick spectacles with heavy black frames. In a few moments, he had transformed himself from a stocky, virile man to a slouching, doddering, elderly geezer.

He turned to her excitedly. "Now you."

"Nothing doing." She backed away. "Why in heaven's name do we need disguises? She's already seen what I look like."

Houdini frowned. "And you gave her your real name?"

"Well, no." Dorothy had given Viola the name Becky Sharp, the female protagonist of the book *Vanity Fair* by William Makepeace Thackeray.

Houdini smiled. "So you instinctively gave her a false name? You did not want to taint your reputation as a journalist by associating your real name with such a dubious enterprise as a séance. Isn't that right?"

Well, that was partly right. She liked this Houdini guy. He appeared to be earnest and cheerful, but he was really just as cynical and suspicious as she was. She shrugged. "All right. What's my disguise?"

He turned and she followed him out of the makeup room, down a hallway and into an enormous costume room, which was stocked with racks and racks of dazzling clothes, costumes and circus outfits. He moved along the racks and pulled out a pair of baggy knickerbocker shorts, a dingy argyle sweater, a rough canvas jacket and a floppy, tweed newsboy's cap.

"You want me to be a golf caddy?"

He handed her the clothes. She took them but didn't put them on.

"Well," he said impatiently. "Get dressed."

She looked apprehensively at the boy's clothes, then looked around the large room.

"Go on," Houdini insisted, standing before her.

She looked askance at him. "Don't you think it's time we talk about the elephant in the room?"

"What do you mean?"

"That elephant! Right there," she said, pointing to Jenny, the five-ton elephant slouched in the corner.

"Never mind her," Houdini said. "She's as tame as a house cat. She has the run of the place."

"Still," Dorothy said, "it's awkward to take my clothes off in front of another girl if we haven't been properly introduced."

Houdini directed Dorothy to a small changing room and waited outside. He continued talking as she put the clothes on.

"What distinguishes a magician from a

medium?" he asked. He didn't wait for her to make a smart-aleck answer. "A magician is but an actor playing the part of a magician. A fraudulent medium is the same. The only difference is that people expect to be tricked by a magician."

"Sure," she said. "The fun is in wondering how it was done."

"Exactly! There really is no magic in our magic. It's purely art and entertainment. The only magic, should you want to call it that, comes from the art of the presenter. But phony mediums dress themselves in religious robes, pretending that their tricks are real. So, unlike the magician, their trickery is deceitful and reprehensible."

She stepped out of the changing room and looked at herself in a floor-to-ceiling mirror. She was no longer a petite young woman. She looked like an adolescent boy—any one of the city's countless newspaper boys or errand runners.

Houdini appeared behind her, speaking in a mumbling old man's voice. "You're now my assistant, my footman, my manservant."

"I've been a man's servant before, but never like this." She spoke to his reflection in the mirror. "Don't you find it odd that we're being deceptive to reveal another's deception? Is the irony lost on you?"

"Not at all," he said, resuming his usual voice. "I know all about deception. But, unlike these phony mediums, we're not out to steal another man's money. Just the opposite." He leaned over her shoulder, as if whispering a secret in her ear. "It takes a flimflammer to catch a flimflammer."

Chapter 22

Benchley slouched in his seat, peeking over the auction catalog. He switched between looking out for Crowninshield and suspiciously eyeing the bidding device—a polished wooden and brass box on an iron pedestal. Seated next to him, Lucy scanned the legal mumbo jumbo in the back pages of the catalog.

"Look at this." She pointed to the dense page of fine print. "It's a disclaimer of authenticity."

"A what?" Benchley was barely paying attention.

"They don't guarantee that what they sell is authentic. That means they won't even stand by their own goods. A pawnshop in Harlem is more trustworthy than this fancy Fifth Avenue auction house."

Benchley was simply relieved she was no longer discussing nudes. Anything was better than that.

A smooth voice came over the loudspeaker. "Ladies and gentlemen, your attention, please. We will now begin the evening with an explanation of the newly installed, and very modern, bidding device in front of you."

Benchley looked at the device warily.

The voice continued. "The old-fashioned bidding paddles have been replaced with this state-of-the-art push-button system. Be aware that very few disputes have ever occurred in our sixty-year history here at Piddle Brothers Auctioneers. To prevent disputes in the future, the decision was made to modernize to this novel electronic system, which eliminates the possibility of human error entirely."

Benchley looked it over. The wooden box itself was a cube, about half the size of a shoe box. On the top face of the box, like two brightly colored candies, were a green button and a red button. There was also a large, flat, brass letter *N*. That was all.

"When you wish to bid on an item," the smooth voice continued, "simply depress the green button. Your bid will be automatically and electronically registered here, at this control panel."

Benchley shifted his focus to the stage, on which stood a long-faced gentleman—the smooth-voiced man. The auctioneer. The man stood behind a wide wooden tabletop, the surface of which was covered with metal buttons and gizmos, like a horizontal telephone switch-board.

Benchley sank even farther down in his seat. Among his weaknesses, he always had trouble with mechanical things. They were somehow out to get him, he had decided after many bad experiences. Even the simplest of devices—a footlocker, an egg timer, a revolving door—gave him fits on a daily basis. But more complicated mechanical contraptions—a typewriter, a radio, an elevator, the crank starter of an automobile— were positively seeking his destruction.

And he did not like the look of this newfangled bidding instrument. Not at all.

The auctioneer smoothly continued. "When the bidding price of the auction item is raised, you may depress the green button again to raise your bid. It's that simple. Shall we begin with the first lot?"

It was not that simple. Someone down in the front of the audience raised a hand and posed the same question that Benchley wanted to ask: What was the red button for?

"Ah," the auctioneer replied with some hesitation, his smoothness momentarily disturbed. "The red button is not yet functional. That feature will be implemented at a date very soon."

What feature? he wondered. The red button would likely be used to cancel a bid. Of course, *that feature*—the one he would most likely need—was not yet functional.

For distraction, he turned to Lucy Goosey, who still scrutinized the catalog's fine print and disclaimers.

"So," he said, "about those nudes . . ."

The charcoal gray Rolls-Royce—Houdini's private car—rolled along Wooster Street in Greenwich

Village. "Stop here," Houdini commanded his chauffeur.

Houdini turned to Dorothy. "We'll walk the last two blocks. We don't want to call any extra attention to ourselves. And this car is rather noticeable."

"Yeah? I hadn't noticed," she said dryly as she got out of the car, looking at the large silver *HH* embossed on the side of the Rolls.

Houdini jumped out and walked in the direction of Viola's residence. He was entirely convincing as an elderly gentleman, yet he still moved fast. She could barely keep up with him.

"What's the big hurry?" she asked. "If Mistress Viola really speaks for the dead, then there's no need to rush. It's not like the ghost of Ernie MacGuffin is going anywhere."

"I want a good seat in the circle, preferably right next to Mistress Viola, so I can hold hands with her."

"Hold hands with her? That's what all the boys say."

"No, that's how I can best catch her in her act."

"Her act? So you don't believe in any of this voodoo bullshit, huh?"

He spoke sternly. "I never said that. I'm not a foe of spiritualism, only of fraudulent mediums."

"But at Mickey Finn's hideout, you said—"

He stopped and turned to her sharply. "I said, I have yet to see any convincing evidence that people in our world can communicate with those in the spirit world."

Dorothy was confused. In her mind, there were usually two types of people: cynics and suckers. "So you do believe?"

She couldn't see his face in the dark, but his shoulders sagged lower. He spoke softly. "To be quite honest, I want to believe. I'd give away my entire fortune to have one word from my dear sainted mother."

"One word? She says 'Hello.' That's one word. Now, pay up."

Houdini chuckled. "Mama never spoke English. Only German." He started walking again, but not as quickly as before. "Do you know of Arthur Conan Doyle?"

"Of course. He wrote the Sherlock Holmes books. What about him?"

"He and I used to be friends."

"You *used to be* friends?" *Boy,* Dorothy wondered, *who and what else did this man have up his sleeve?* "What happened?"

"We had a falling-out. You see, Doyle is an avid and totally committed supporter of spiritualism."

"You're telling me that the man who wrote about Sherlock Holmes—a detective who relies on deductive reasoning—believes in spooks and séances?"

"He does indeed," Houdini said. "Two years ago, he brought his family on a tour of America, and they had a summer holiday in Atlantic City. My wife and I had the occasion to visit him and his family."

"Sounds pleasant enough."

"It was, until Lady Doyle sat me down and told me she could perform a spirit-writing séance. She was not being duplicitous. Lady Doyle knew of my love for my dear departed mother, you see. And she thought she was doing me a favor. Like her husband, Lady Doyle is a true believer. For my part, I attempted, in the spirit of friendship and in a hope against hope, to participate fully in the endeavor to contact the spirit of my mother."

The spirit of his mother? Dorothy's mother had died when she was only five. But Dorothy wouldn't ever consider trying to reach her in the great beyond. *Rich people like Houdini,* she thought, *are no different from the rest of us. They want what they can't have.*

"So what happened?" she asked.

"We sat in a darkened room. Lady Doyle sat across the table from me. Her husband stood behind her for support. After several supplications to the spirit world, Lady Doyle started writing on a notepad, telling me it was the words of my mother. And she read them to me. There was never a more ghastly display. The words she spoke were in English."

"You just said your mother spoke only German."

"Exactly. And later I told them as much." His soft voice now took a venomous tone. "But, oh, they were so convinced, those Doyles. Sir Arthur gave me some patter about how the spirit speaks through the ether, without the filter of an earthly language. The spirit's meaning comes through no matter which language you speak."

"But you didn't buy it?"

"Not in the least. As a matter of fact, that was just about the turning point for me. I still want to believe, but now I'll accept only absolute proof."

"You were close to your mother?"

Houdini looked up at the few visible night stars. "Every day was Mother's Day for me. It still is."

Dorothy nodded, wondering what the recent practice of psychoanalysis would make of this guy. Dr. Freud would have had a field day.

"All the same," she said, "I'm pleased that you're willing to challenge Mistress Viola."

"I suppose that she performs her act in the dark?"

"That seems like her line of work, yes."

Houdini smiled. "I gather that she's an attractive woman?"

Dorothy explained that, by day, Viola was a nude model. "Then again, if I had a body like Viola's, I'd take my clothes off as often as possible, too."

"But as a medium," he asked, "she holds séances in the dark?"

Dorothy thought a moment. "I don't know. My friends didn't mention that."

"That's usually how they work. In the dark, they can hide their tricks. Not at all like a magician. A magician, such as myself, is proud to do his amazing feats before the bright lights of the stage and in front of an audience of thousands."

Dorothy found his self-admiration to be both a little endearing and increasingly irksome.

Houdini continued. "In a typical séance, everyone sits in a small circle and holds hands, and then the lights are extinguished. Holding hands is supposed to create the spirit circle, they say. But it's also supposed to assure you that the medium isn't up to any chicanery."

"So if both of Mistress Viola's hands are held, she can't perpetrate any tricks?"

"That's what you're naturally *supposed* to assume. But phony mediums always use some device, or they employ an assistant—or even use their feet—to ring a bell, lift up the table, knock on the floor. They'll try any trick to simulate a spiritual manifestation. And the closer we sit to her, the better we shall uncover her duplicity." Houdini paused in front of Viola's house. "Is this the place?"

Dorothy pulled the flyer from her pocket and glanced at the address printed on it. "This is it."

She reached for the door, but Houdini stopped her. He turned to her and laid his big hand on her shoulder. Even in the dimness, his piercing eyes stared intently into hers. "Now, let me warn you. Despite all I've said about trickery, everything changes once we get into that room. When the lights go out and we sit there in utter darkness and unnatural silence, it's very easy to succumb to a very real, primordial fear. I myself have felt the creeping hand of terror crawl up my back on more than one of these occasions."

"I've felt that creeping hand in a darkened theater. It was usually some man I was with."

"This is not a joke."

"Not to worry. I don't scare so easily. Don't think I'm a pushover just because I'm a woman."

Houdini held up his hand. "Woman, man, young, old—none of that matters when you are in the dark and you're told that the dead are silently standing there beside you. And then—then you hear a tortured voice from beyond the grave—"

"And the voice says, 'What the hell are all these people doing in my living room?'"

Houdini smiled wryly. He opened the door. "Come on. It's time we met your dead friend."

Chapter 23

On the stage of the auction house, the first item came up for bid. It was a medium-sized painting of an American soldier in green fatigues rushing forward, with the glinting steel of his rifle's bayonet pointing toward the drooling, open maw of an attacking Russian bear. Benchley glanced at the catalog. This was one of Ernie MacGuffin's first professional paintings, perhaps the first he ever sold. It had been the cover of an old issue of *Boys' Adventure* magazine. The description in the catalog said that MacGuffin had sold it for twenty-five dollars. The starting bid was listed as five hundred.

"Never bid on the first one," Lucy said. "That's for amateurs."

"Is it, now?" Benchley's eyes were fixed on the glamorous female assistants who stood on either side of the painting. He heard the auctioneer's voice.

"This exciting piece," the auctioneer said, "has increased in value more than twentyfold since its creation. Some have described the subject matter as overly dramatic or even juvenile, but please do not be fooled. Experts have commented that this painting exhibits a deceptively complicated, dynamic composition, with a bold choice of colors and masterful brushwork. Its value will surely continue to quickly multiply."

Lucy clucked her tongue. "Listen to that carnival barker's patter. Look at those busty assistants. This whole thing's a racket. They know how to get you all worked up so you lose your sense of proportion. They want you to get caught up in the excitement of it. Then you're not thinking with your head, you're thinking with your—*Benchley!*"

He had pushed the green button. He simply couldn't help himself. He didn't want to let this painting get away.

"Our first bidder!" the auctioneer announced. "Thank you, N. The bidding stands at five hundred dollars for bidder N. Do I have six hundred?"

A blond battleship of a woman—about Houdini's age, Dorothy estimated, but nearly twice his weight—met them at the door when they entered, clipboard in hand. Dorothy guessed she was Viola's mother. Viola was built, Dorothy thought, but her mother was built like a brick wall. She had no neck. Her chin disappeared in the solid mass of flesh above her thick chest.

"Your name?" the woman said in a rough voice.

Dorothy, dressed as an errand boy, couldn't state her name as Becky Sharp—the name she had given to Viola the day before. But Houdini solved the problem. He simply asked, in a quavering elderly voice, "How much?"

"Fifty," the woman grunted.

Dorothy wanted to mention that she and Benchley had already paid a deposit of ten, so they owed only forty, an amount that was still outrageous. But Houdini, acting as the stoop-shouldered elderly gentleman, produced a money purse with palsied fingers and offered the woman the full amount. She snatched the bills and, without another glance at them, pointed toward a small, cozy parlor.

The little room was dimly lit and furnished in an old-fashioned style, with dark, spindly furniture and thin, worn carpets. In the middle of the room was an oblong table, adorned with a crimson tablecloth and a single candle in a tall brass stand.

Mistress Viola sat at the head of the table. Dorothy had somehow expected Viola to again be wearing that revealing satin bathrobe and maybe a bejeweled swami's turban on her platinum blond head. Dorothy was surprised to see that the young woman was conservatively—even plainly—dressed in a shapeless brown frock. Her white-blond hair appeared newly shellacked.

Viola reached out a hand as they entered. "Welcome," she said soothingly. "Please sit."

To Viola's right sat a sullen, thin-faced man. A woman with an equally narrow, sallow face—Dorothy took her to be the man's wife—sat at

Viola's left. In either seat next to this pair sat another couple, a slick-haired young man with a sharklike smile and, across the table from him, his very young, doe-eyed girlfriend—Dorothy saw that her hand had no ring. At the end of the table, the last two chairs sat empty. Viola gestured toward them.

"Please sit," she said again.

Houdini coughed and stammered, playing the role of the elderly gentleman. He leaned heavily on his cane and spoke in a wheezy croak, addressing the narrow-faced couple. "My hearing isn't what it used to be, I'm afraid. Could I impose on you to give up your seat to an old man, so that I may better attend to Lady Viola?"

"It's *mistress,*" Viola said, "not *lady.*"

She's no lady, that's for sure, Dorothy thought.

" 'Mattress'?" Houdini asked crankily.

"Not *mattress,*" Viola enunciated carefully, still in her calm voice. *"Mistress."*

" 'Mischief'? No, no. Mischief Night was last night, was it not? Tonight is Halloween night." He turned to Dorothy. "Isn't that right, Master Timothy?"

"Right you are, sir. It's Halloween night," Dorothy said in her best imitation of an adolescent boy's voice. She didn't care whether she was convincing or not. What the hell? This was starting to be kind of fun.

The narrow-faced man got tired of all this

206

fluster. He stood up and waved his wife to stand. "The spirits won't speak with so much distraction," he said peevishly. "Here, old man, take my seat." He and his wife moved down to the end of the table and grumpily sat down in the last empty chairs.

"Much obliged, my good fellow," Houdini wheezed. He hobbled around the table and lowered himself carefully into the seat next to Viola. Dorothy plunked down in the seat on Viola's other side.

Clever, Dorothy thought, admiring Houdini's ploy. Now they were each positioned to hold one of Viola's hands. The woman could pull no wool over Houdini's eyes now.

"Quiet, please. Let's begin," Viola said in that gentle tone. Dorothy wondered if Viola's lullaby voice and the dimness of the room might put her to sleep.

But Houdini made her immediately dismiss such a thought. He didn't quiet down at all. In fact, he spoke up, introducing himself to the others as Henry Hossenfuss and Dorothy as his faithful valet, Timothy. Dorothy nodded but said nothing. The fish-faced husband was annoyed by the delay and grudgingly admitted to being Mr. Tibbet and wife. They were true believers, Dorothy surmised. They probably went to séances with the frequency that other middle-aged married couples went to the movies.

The slick young man and his even younger girlfriend introduced themselves as Sylvester and Cissy. Dorothy figured they were there for a lark, some not-so-cheap thrills. Sylvester's idea, for sure, Dorothy thought. He probably brought her to this event just to put a scare into her, show her that he was unafraid, console her afterward and, likely as not, take advantage of her while she was at a weak moment. That creeping hand again.

"Now let us begin," Viola said, still with that calm voice. *Where did she pick up this Gypsy act?* Dorothy wondered. From the mother, perhaps.

Viola nodded to the old blond battleship, who now stood at the parlor door. The woman switched off the single overhead bulb, which left only the flickering glow of the candle on the table. Then the lady left, closing the door behind her.

Even in the dimness, Dorothy could tell Houdini was somewhat surprised by the candlelight. Fraudulent mediums used the cover of total darkness to hide their tricks, he had said. *Well,* Houdini's expression seemed to say to her, *now we'll see what she's up to.*

Viola intoned, "We create a circle of spiritual energy by holding hands. Please, hold each other's hands."

Dorothy had a moment of panic when Viola's other hand reached for hers. Dorothy had the soft, thin hands of an indolent, adult female writer, not the grubby, rough hands of a hardworking young errand boy. However, Viola encircled Dorothy's hand in hers and didn't seem to notice.

But on the other hand—literally—Sylvester gave Dorothy a curious look. He knew a girl's hand when he held one, Dorothy figured.

Viola closed her eyes and spoke up toward the ceiling. She was going into her trance. "We now call upon the departed spirit of Ernest MacGuffin."

They waited a long, silent moment in the gloom. But there was no response.

"Ernest MacGuffin," Viola spoke, "when you flung your body into the river, you committed your soul to an immortal no-man's-land, trapped between this life and the next. Visit us now. Unburden your suffering among willing listeners. Enlighten us with your visions of the great beyond."

Dorothy looked at the candlelit faces around the table. Mr. and Mrs. Tibbet both had their eyes shut tight, as though anticipating some glorious rapture, or some hideous terror, or both. Next to Dorothy, Sylvester had his leering eyes locked on Cissy. The young girl had the half-wondrous, half-anxious look of someone riding up that first incline of a roller coaster.

Next to Cissy, Houdini appeared to be on the verge of falling asleep. Dorothy wondered if he actually might.

"Ernest MacGuffin," Viola said softly again. "We call upon you with sincerity and faith and hope. Visit us now. Show us a sign."

Then—Dorothy almost couldn't believe her eyes—the candle sputtered. Not merely a flicker—the flame almost snuffed itself out.

Dorothy glanced at Viola to see if she had surreptitiously blown on the flame. But Viola's expression was as shocked as every other face at the table.

Dorothy started to feel uneasy. She didn't believe in ghosts. But something here was not right. Not right at all. There was something amoral, even wicked, about this whole business. This was no fun, after all.

Not for the first time, Dorothy felt guilty and despicable. MacGuffin had put his suicide note in her purse, and she had been unable to save him. Now here she was, participating in this séance tomfoolery. She felt as though she had been caught doing cartwheels over Ernie's grave.

"Ernest MacGuffin." Viola's voice was nearly a whispering moan. "Speak to us." Then her body seemed to stiffen.

"Speak to us," Mr. Tibbet pleaded, rocking slightly back and forth, his eyes shut tight.

Dorothy felt sick to her stomach. She just wanted to get up and leave.

Then a voice—Ernie's voice!—filled the room. "I'm here."

Dorothy went cold. Her first thought was to get up and run. But she was frozen in her chair.

Her next thought was, *Where the hell is Benchley when I really need him?*

Chapter 24

Lucy Goosey watched Benchley vigilantly. But Benchley sat motionless. He was afraid she would break his arm if he even so much as raised his hand to scratch his nose.

"Bidder N has the first bid at five hundred," the auctioneer said in his smooth, articulate voice. "Do I hear six hundred?"

At the edge of the auctioneer's platform, Benchley spotted MacGuffin's agent and lawyer, Abraham Snath, who stood poised like a smiling fox at the door of a chicken coop.

A small light flashed on the control panel in front of the auctioneer. "Six hundred for a new bidder, Bidder D. Thank you, Bidder D. Do I have seven hundred?"

Benchley followed the auctioneer's glance into the audience. Was that his boss, Crowninshield, down there? Benchley could see only the back of the bidder's head. But the man turned to make a comment to someone sitting next to him. Yes, it was Crownie! The lovable old dear had saved Benchley by outbidding him. And he didn't even know he'd done it.

The bidding continued, back and forth between Crowninshield and some other bidder. Eventually, Crowninshield won the auction to the tune of eighteen hundred dollars. Benchley wondered what Crowninshield would even do with such a painting. His wife wouldn't let him hang the garish thing in their living room. Perhaps Crownie would put it up in the office. Benchley and Dorothy could throw darts at it. Benchley smiled. Yes, that would be fun.

A waiter came by with a silver tray filled with champagne glasses. Benchley nodded his thanks to the waiter and reached for a glass.

Lucy grasped his wrist with a silk-gloved hand. "We got out of that one. But don't make a screwball bid like that again."

Benchley's smile withered. He glanced at the waiter, who tried to appear as though he hadn't seen or heard Lucy.

"The wife," Benchley muttered to him. "She holds the purse strings even tighter than she holds my wrist."

Lucy released her grip. Benchley picked up two champagne glasses and smiled appreciatively to the waiter, who nodded and moved away. He handed one glass to Lucy.

"A toast," he said. "May the road rise up to meet you and the wind be always up your skirt." He clinked his glass with hers.

They were momentarily distracted as the next painting came up for bid. It was one of Mac-Guffin's abstract works. The starting bid was one thousand dollars.

"I don't know much about fine art, but I know it

when I see it," Benchley said. "And I'm not seeing it."

He took a gulp and winced.

"It's not that bad," Lucy said, studying the painting.

"Yes, it is!" Benchley sputtered, holding up his glass. "It's cream soda! What a dirty trick."

Lucy sniffed her glass, shrugged and set it down. "This ain't a back-alley speakeasy. It's a hoity-toity Fifth Avenue auction house. Serving champagne is against the law."

"Then let's leave this hoity-toity auction house and find a back-alley speakeasy."

She folded her arms and stared straight ahead. Benchley didn't exactly know how to respond to this, or whether he should respond at all. Dorothy Parker never gave him the silent treatment. This was no fun without her. He would much rather go to a back-alley speakeasy, with or without Lucy.

But then again, Mrs. Parker needed him to get one of these paintings. And he usually did just about anything to please Mrs. Parker.

He turned his attention to the bidding on the abstract painting. The bidding price was rising quickly. It was thirteen hundred, then fourteen hundred, then fifteen hundred. Maybe he had misjudged this painting, he thought. Maybe it was worth something after all. These other bidders certainly seemed to think so. And they ought to know because they must have done this before.

They must know how much such a thing could be worth—

"Sixteen hundred for Bidder N," the auctioneer said in their direction. "Thank you, Bidder N. Do I have seventeen hundred?"

Benchley found himself with his finger on the green button. Without looking, he felt Lucy clutch at his shoulder. Her breath in his ear was hot.

"What the hell are you doing?" she hissed. "You're using Mickey Finn's money! Do you know what will happen to you if you squander Mickey's money? Do you know what will happen to *me* if I let you squander—"

"Seventeen hundred for Bidder B," the auctioneer said. "Do I have eighteen hundred? Thank you, Bidder K. Eighteen hundred."

She exhaled in relief. "We have to find something to cover that button so you can't bid willy-nilly. Then I want you to sit on your hands."

Benchley nodded. He gulped his cream soda. Then he turned the glass upside down and set it over the green button, like a little dripping dome.

After a moment, Lucy spoke softly. "Listen, you have to use your head, or you'll lose your head. Mickey will see to that."

Benchley appreciated that she was speaking more reasonably. "I just can't help myself. They're going like hotcakes and I don't want to miss out. Mrs. Parker would be so disappointed if I came back empty-handed."

"They want you to feel that pressure. That's how they jack up the bids." Lucy looked up at the chandelier, as though taking the whole place in. "See, an auction house has the deck stacked against you. They have all the key information. They know the original price of the painting. They know the current estimate of the painting's value. And of course they have their reserve price—"

"Reserve price?"

"The reserve price is their minimum asking price, but they keep it secret. If no one bids as high as the reserve price, they won't sell it."

"That's fair enough."

"No, sir, it's not, because they don't tell you what the reserve price is. The auctioneer won't say, 'Sorry; we haven't reached our reserve price, so we're taking this painting off the stage.' Instead, the auctioneer acts like somebody made a bid in order to make other bidders interested."

Benchley turned to her in disbelief. "They wouldn't do that. That's dishonest."

"Yeah, it *is* dishonest. Unfortunately, it's all perfectly legal. Every auction house does it, big and small."

"How do you know all this?

Lucy hesitated. "I also once dated a wealthy art collector, right before I was with Mickey."

"Oh, is the man here?" Benchley looked around the enormous room.

"Who?"

"The wealthy art collector. Wouldn't he be at a function such as this?"

"Not a chance."

"Why not?"

"He's dead."

"Oh," Benchley said. "I'm very sorry to hear that. Was it sudden?"

"It sure was," Lucy said with a wry grimace. "I suddenly met Mickey, and then the wealthy art collector suddenly met the sidewalk, starting from his penthouse window."

Benchley gulped. "A very quick breakup."

Dorothy stared at Mistress Viola. The woman's eyes had rolled back—only the whites were showing. Her lips trembled as the hollow sound of MacGuffin's voice again filled the room.

"This is Ernie MacGuffin speaking through the mouth of this—this beautiful young woman. Hear me, and heed my warnings."

Sylvester's hand was clammy. Dorothy looked at him. His face had turned pasty white. His shark's smile was long gone. He stared at his girlfriend for reassurance. Cissy, on the other hand, looked like a kid at a birthday party, happily expectant to see what surprise would happen next.

Next to Cissy, Mr. Tibbet's whole body quaked with excitement, a kind of religious fervor. "Spirit of MacGuffin, what do you see in the ethereal void?"

Viola's lips moved as MacGuffin's voice said, "The ether—the etherea—uh . . . What did you say?"

"The Great Beyond, spirit," Tibbet nearly yelled. "Tell us what you see. Tell us where you are."

"I am floating up on the clouds." Viola's mouth moved only slightly, not always in sync with Ernie's voice.

Did the words come from Viola's mouth—or elsewhere? The Great Beyond? In the dim, flickering candlelight, Dorothy couldn't be sure.

"Bright light is all around me," Ernie's voice said. "Golden harps play all day long."

As Ernie's voice was heard, Houdini watched the enraptured Viola. Then he bent and peeked under the table. He straightened up. He didn't seem to find what he was looking for.

"Why her, Mr. MacGuffin?" Houdini wheezed. "Why do you speak through *this* woman?"

"Hossenfuss, please!" Tibbet hissed. "Respect the solemnity of the spirit circle." Then he called out, "Spirit, do not depart because of the disrespectful observers here. Pay them no heed. Rather, give us your wisdom."

"My wisdom, yes, of course," the voice said. "Allow me to share my—my wisdom."

Dorothy's fear had quickly faded away. It had been replaced by indignation and downright spite. Real or unreal—alive, dead or undead—she was going to give MacGuffin a piece of her mind.

"Your *wisdom?*" she blurted. "You had none when you were alive, Ernie. How the hell did you get so wise in the afterlife? Did St. Peter pass you a crib sheet as you went through the pearly gates?"

"Shut your trap, boy," Tibbet snapped. "Or I'll shut it for you."

Viola's eyes peeked at Dorothy a moment, then quickly rolled back again as Ernie's voice answered. "Who is that? I know that voice."

"You bet your disembodied ass you know me," Dorothy said. "You gave me your suicide note—don't you remember?"

Dorothy watched Houdini's eyes roam around the room. *What was Houdini looking for?*

"Ohhhh," Ernie's voice said.

"I've been carrying that damned thing around like a deadweight since you jumped off the Brooklyn Bridge. Who the hell do you think you are to dump that kind of responsibility on me?"

"Dottie? Is that you?"

"Damn right it's me. Who do you think it is? Or were you handing out suicide notes like valentines, and now you don't remember who you gave them to?"

Tibbet stood up. His narrow face looked enraged. "Be quiet, kid! You're annoying the spirit."

Ernie's voice said, "Well, I—I thought if anyone would understand, you would."

"Understand?" Dorothy said. "I told you to forget it, don't you remember? Don't kill yourself, I said. And now look where it got you. You're playing parlor tricks for twenty-five bucks a head. Is that any way to spend eternity?"

Tibbet rounded the table. "Boy, I said that's enough!"

Dorothy ignored him. "Ernie, you turned this blond nudie model into your own personal public address system from heaven—or wherever the hell you are. Is this what you were expecting from the afterlife? Some life, Ernie. What the hell was your hurry?"

Viola's eyes rolled down, from white to their usual blue, and stared angrily at Dorothy.

Ernie spoke, but Viola's lips didn't move. "Now, hold on just a gosh-darn minute, Dorothy!"

"Dorothy?" Tibbet grabbed her shoulder.

"Dorothy?" Viola said in her own voice, and not the soothing one.

"Dorothy!" Houdini yelled. "Get up. Now!"

Dorothy and Houdini jumped to their feet.

"I am Houdini!" he yelled, pointing at Viola. "And you are a fraud!"

He yanked the tablecloth. The single candlestick went flying. The flame went out. The room plunged into absolute darkness. Both Mrs. Tibbet and Sylvester screamed. Cissy laughed.

Then all hell broke loose.

Chapter 25

The auctioneer raised his hammer. "Going once . . . Going twice . . ."

The eighteenth painting, out of a collection of twenty-five, was on the block. Benchley's fingers reached for the glass, tipped it up, felt for the button.

"Don't you dare." Lucy grabbed his hand and jammed it between her knees. "That'll hold you."

"No more bids?" the auctioneer said. He banged the hammer lightly, just one knock. "Sold to Bidder G for twenty-seven hundred dollars."

Now that the painting was sold, Benchley tried to free his hand from between Lucy's legs, but she was too strong. He felt as though he had his hand trapped in a silky vise.

"It's wet," she said. "And sticky."

"Excuse me?"

She was fumbling with the champagne glass on top of the bidding mechanism. "It's all wet and sticky. There must have been some sugary soda left in your glass. I hope it didn't leak down into the—the thingamajig."

Benchley thought of the wealthy art collector who had a final run-in with a sidewalk. What would Mickey Finn do if he found out Benchley's hand was jammed in between Lucy's lovely legs?

"You can let me go now." He tried to free his hand again. "I get the point."

"Not just yet." She smiled devilishly. "I've got you just where I want you."

I'm caught, he thought, *between the devil and her petite, cute knees.*

In the chaos and blackness, Houdini yelled, "Dorothy, follow me. Quick!"

Follow him? She couldn't even see him. Wisely, she had remembered to stow her cigarettes and a box of matches in the pocket of her boy's britches. She dug out the box and lit a match.

She nearly jumped. Tibbet was standing right over her. Almost on top of her. He grabbed for her. Dorothy dodged away, cupping the lit match in her hand.

Houdini stood at the doorway, holding a wire in his fingers.

"Look there," he yelled to Dorothy and pointed at the table. "It's a built-in radio speaker."

Dorothy glanced at the bare wooden table. In the center was a large hole, as wide as a plate. Set inside the hole was some kind of loudspeaker.

Ernie's voice emanated from the speaker. "Dorothy? Viola, darling, are you all right? What's going on in there?"

Dorothy's gaze traced a wire that went from the speaker beneath the table, along one of the table legs, and into a hole in the carpet. The wire ran under the carpet to the opposite side of the room. At the edge of the carpet stood Houdini, tugging the wire in one hand and flinging open the door with the other.

"Come on. Our spirit is somewhere at the end of this wire!" Houdini disappeared into the dark hallway.

Dorothy sprang forward to follow him, but something held her back. Viola had grabbed onto Dorothy's short jacket, digging her nails into the leather.

"You ruined my séance. You can't go anywhere."

"You bewitched my dog," Dorothy said. "You can go to hell."

Dorothy flung the match at Viola's platinum blond hair. Dorothy had intended only to make her flinch so Viola would let her go. But with so much shellac, pomade or whatever was in the fake medium's hairdo, it caught fire. The room lit up like daylight. Viola screamed so loud, Dorothy's ears hurt.

Again Dorothy leaped to follow Houdini, but now Tibbet clutched her by the arm. He brought his fish face close to hers.

"Infidel! You've trespassed on our sacred ceremony."

"Let me go," Dorothy said, trying to wriggle free. "Let me go, you mesmerized moron."

Viola continued to shriek, the blue and white flames dancing above her head like a halo, burning the chemical fumes more than her actual hair.

From the corner of Dorothy's vision, she saw someone enter the room, sweep up the tablecloth from the floor and quickly wrap it around Viola's head. The blazing fire went out, and the room fell into inky blackness again.

Dorothy then heard someone else stumble into the room. She recognized the clomp of Houdini's heavy, old man's shoes.

"You charlatan," Houdini yelled. "Come back here. You can't escape the World's Foremost Escapist so easily!"

Cripes, Dorothy thought, *even at the direst moments, he's busy promoting himself.* Again she tried to free herself from Tibbet's grasp. "Houdini, get over here. I'm in the clutches of a zealot."

Dorothy heard Houdini's walking stick knock against the edge of the table and whoosh through the air. It thudded against something. A man cursed in pain. But it wasn't Tibbet.

Stumbling footsteps thumped toward the far door and disappeared. Another door creaked opened and the room's bright overhead light flicked on. After the darkness, the brilliant light hurt Dorothy's eyes. She blinked and saw the blond battleship filling up the nearest doorway.

The lady bellowed, "My darling, your beautiful wig!"

Dorothy turned to look. Viola's charred blond

hair lay in a clump on the floor. Viola stood before it; her frizzy dark hair was matted down against her skull. Now Dorothy understood why Viola had chosen the platinum blond look.

In the surprise of the moment, Dorothy again tried to pull away from the tight grip of Tibbet's pincerlike fingers.

He snarled, "No, you don't. You sinned against heaven and you sinned against this poor woman. You're not leaving until your sins have been purged."

"*All* my sins?" Dorothy asked. "Honey, we don't have that kind of time. And this 'poor woman' wasn't sinned against—merely singed. And only her wig, at that. Now, let me go!"

But Tibbet didn't let go. He raised his other hand to strike her.

Houdini moved far faster than Tibbet. With the walking stick in his right hand, Houdini struck Tibbet's fist with a hard crack, as though swatting a fly out of the air. With his left hand curled into a wide fist, Houdini landed a precise hard jab to Tibbet's nose. It sounded like a twig breaking. Blood gushed and Tibbet yowled in pain as he clumsily covered his shattered nose.

Dorothy had never seen anything like it. Now, *that* was some trick.

"Come on," Houdini yelled to Dorothy, rushing again toward the far door. "The charlatan went this way."

Dorothy darted after him but was immediately stopped by Viola's big blond mother. The woman blocked her way, staring furiously down at Dorothy. Imitating Houdini, Dorothy shot a sharp jab at the large woman's large nose, but the lady brushed Dorothy's slender arm aside.

Then, with thick, flabby forearms, Viola's mother reached forward to grab Dorothy. But Dorothy dodged backward and realized she still held the box of matches. She quickly lit one and held it threateningly forward. The woman screeched and covered her big blond hairdo with her chubby bearlike hands.

Dorothy dodged around the big woman and hurried through the doorway after Houdini, tossing the dying match harmlessly to the carpet.

The hallway was dim and empty. Houdini was already way ahead of her. Dorothy spotted the loudspeaker wire snaking along the hardwood floor. She followed the wire to an adjacent room. No one was in the room. It contained only an old desk. On the desk was a big, shiny microphone mounted on a short tabletop stand. The microphone was plugged into a kind of black box, with dials and switches on the front and vacuum tubes on top—a radio mechanism or public address set.

Back out in the hallway, a door slammed. She heard Houdini's voice growl, "You coward!"

She raced back into the hallway and followed

the sound. She came into a tight, messy little kitchen. Houdini was hunched near the back door. He held what appeared to be lock-picking tools in his hands. He deftly manipulated the tools in the keyhole.

"The villain," Houdini said over his shoulder to Dorothy. "He locked the door from the outside. It's of little concern, however. I'll have this lock picked faster than a jackrabbit's sneeze."

Dorothy watched in wonder as he worked. *His fingers move as fast as Irving Berlin's on the piano,* she thought. "How did you know about the wire under the table? You spotted it in the dark?"

He glanced at her with a proud smile. "I felt it with my toes."

"Your toes?"

"I slipped off my shoes and felt around. I've trained my toes to be as nimble as fingers. I can tie or untie any knot with my toes."

She continued to watch, impatient now, as he worked on picking the lock. "Maybe you should use your toes to unlock that door."

He made a perfunctory laugh and kept fiddling at the keyhole.

"Let me give it a try," she said.

Before he could respond, Dorothy picked up his walking stick from the floor. She swung it. Houdini dodged aside, eyes wide. The end of the walking stick shattered the door's porthole-sized window. She carefully reached through the jagged

227

opening. The remaining blades of glass scratched lines on the sleeve of her leather jacket. She twisted the outside knob and the door opened.

"Well-done," Houdini said, amused and impressed.

"I'm just following your lead," she said. "So lead."

Houdini pulled open the door and they found themselves in a narrow, dimly lit alley. It was littered with trash, debris and dark puddles of muck. Footprints were just barely visible after the first puddle, and they raced forward.

Houdini, despite his age and cumbersome costume, was clearly as fit as an Olympic athlete. He shot down the alleyway like a greyhound. Dorothy, in spite of her youth, was hobbled by her heavy shoes and slowed by several years of smoking, drinking and physical inactivity. Houdini turned left down one side alley and then right down another.

He was soon well ahead of Dorothy. Within just a few dozen yards, he had rapidly outdistanced her. She feared she might lose sight of him. Lost and alone in the dark, narrow labyrinth of alleyways was not where she wanted to be after midnight on Halloween. She pushed herself to keep running. *Curse that MacGuffin! This was all his doing.*

Then she realized something. In her tirade at MacGuffin during the séance, she hadn't even asked him if the paintings at Snath's office—the same paintings at that evening's auction—were authentic.

Oh, the hell with it, she thought, quickly losing steam. She began to slow down.

From somewhere far ahead of her, Houdini egged her on. "Quick, Mrs. Parker. This way!"

She forced herself to keep going. The alleyway twisted and turned. Houdini was well ahead of her now. So when she lost sight of him, she followed his wet footprints. She dodged around battered trash cans and stacks of wooden fruit crates. She ran through discarded newspapers and over broken bottles. At some points she raced through pitch blackness and didn't know what she was running or stumbling through.

She suddenly found herself in a very small, filthy courtyard, dimly lit by the pale light from a high, narrow window.

Dorothy stopped. She needed to catch her breath. She leaned against the nearest damp brick wall. The hell with Houdini and the con artist they were chasing. She'd catch up to Houdini later. Or not. It didn't seem to matter.

She hadn't yet caught her breath, but she got out her pack of Chesterfields and the box of matches. She popped a cigarette in her mouth and slid open the matchbox.

The box was empty. She cursed silently and flung the box to the dirty pavement.

Then she heard a noise.

What fresh hell is this? She stood up straight and tried to quiet her breathing. She was about to call out Houdini's name, but she knew it wasn't Houdini. It was someone deliberately trying to move silently. She squinted into the darkness surrounding her.

Something moved. A shadow was creeping down the alley, moving in her direction. Several shadows. Coming closer.

She stepped back. There was nowhere to go. She was too exhausted to turn and run back.

The shadows neared the tiny courtyard. There were a half dozen of them. A gang. Angry faces. Aggressive stances. Looking for a fight. Tough young hoodlums. *Very* young hoodlums.

Dorothy recognized one, the one in front, who appeared to be their leader. His wolflike grin shined through the darkness.

Tony Soma Jr.

What were the chances of running into him?

Tony Jr. smiled. "We've been looking for you."

Looking for her? *Evidently, the chances were pretty good.*

Chapter 26

Tony Jr. took a step closer. "We came across an old man running like a bat out of hell. He said he'd give us each two bits if we could find you and bring you to him."

Dorothy did her best to sound like a rough young kid, too. "All right. So take me to him."

"Not until we find out exactly what you're worth."

"What I'm worth?"

"You must be worth a pretty penny if he'd pay us each two bits to find you."

The rotten little gangster, she thought. A shakedown in a side alley. What a night.

The gang of adolescent boys spread out, surrounding her, blocking any exit if she tried to make a run for it. Not that she could have—she was too winded.

She tried a bit of reverse psychology. She had read about it in a magazine article. "He'll pay you *more* than two bits if you play your cards right. The man is worth millions." She tried to speak casually. "But, fine with me if you don't want to take me to the old jerk. I was trying to get away from him anyhow."

Tony Jr. spoke in exaggerated baby talk. *" 'I was twying to get 'way fwom him any-ow.' "* Then he spat, "What's the matter with your voice? You some kind of queer?"

Dorothy looked at him squarely. Was that all? He wanted to trade insults? This, she could handle. She could speak insults in a variety of languages and dialects, including twelve-year-old pissant.

"Yeah, I'm queer, all right," she said, her voice as tough as she could muster, the cigarette dangling dangerously from the corner of her lip. "Bring your pretty mouth over here and I'll let you kiss my knuckles, the hard way."

Some of the other boys tittered.

She continued. "Say, anyone got a match for my cigarette? Wait a minute. I've got a match—his face and my ass." She pointed at Tony Jr. "Yeah, that's a perfect match."

The other boys laughed openly now. This level of humor, Dorothy thought, was right up their alley, so to speak.

Tony Jr. looked at his pals like traitors. "Pipe down, you mooks!" And they did. He turned back to Dorothy. "That old guy told us to bring you to him. He didn't say we had to bring you in one piece." He stepped forward, raising his fists.

Was he really about to punch her? She had belittled countless Broadway big shots and Manhattan matrons, any of whom would have gladly slugged her if given the chance. And here she was, about to get decked by a twelve-year-old boy who didn't even know she was a grown woman.

What if she took off her cap and unveiled herself? *You wouldn't hit a girl, would you?* But that might not be such a great idea. First, Tony Jr. would recognize her and perhaps drag her back to his ruthless mother. Second, there was no guarantee that they *wouldn't* hit a girl. Or maybe worse.

Tony Jr. advanced toward her, hunching forward to strike a blow.

Well, the hell with it. If he was going to punch her lights out, she'd at least make it worthwhile. "Your mother's an ugly, vicious warthog," she said. "And she buys her clothes off the rack—at Woolworth's!"

This last insult stopped Tony Jr. cold. He was more perplexed than offended. He slightly lowered his fists.

"How did you know that?" he asked, dismayed.

Dorothy had an idea. "I'm psychic."

"A sidekick?" asked a pimply-faced boy. Dorothy recognized him. He was the son of Carlos, the bartender at Tony Soma's speakeasy.

"A *psychic*," Dorothy repeated. "I can read minds. And tell the future."

Tony Jr. raised his fists again. "Every mook here knows your future. In one minute, you'll be eating pavement."

"Your father wouldn't let you talk like that, Tony boy," Dorothy said. "He'd smack your backside with his belt—and sing opera while doing it."

Tony Jr. went pale. "O-opera?"

"*Don Giovanni*," Dorothy said, naming Tony Sr.'s favorite. "And he'd use his best belt—the crocodile one with the gold buckle." This indeed was Tony's best belt. Benchley had given it to him late one night in lieu of payment.

Tony Jr. backed away, his eyes wide.

Dorothy next looked at the pimply-faced boy, Carlos' son. "Have you stopped wetting the bed yet, Charlie?"

The boy screamed. As a group, they turned and ran.

Dorothy watched them go. They moved fast, shoving one another forward, as frightened boys do. She knew they were her only way to find her way back to Houdini—if they indeed went back the way they came.

With a sigh of resignation, she threw down her unlit cigarette and hurried after them.

"Mr. Benchley," Crowninshield gasped, "what in heaven's name are you doing here?"

Benchley turned to see the waspish, mustached face of his boss, Frank Crowninshield, looking down at him. Then Benchley looked down at his hand stuck between Lucy's legs. He wondered to himself, *What in heaven's name* am *I doing here?*

"You are supposed to be at the Hippodrome seeing Houdini's show," Crowninshield fumed. "You are supposed to write a review of it for

234

Vanity Fair. You are not supposed to be here, with your hands tucked in that woman's—that woman's—"

"Cookie jar," Benchley stammered. "I mean, I guess you caught me with my hand in it. The cookie jar, that is."

Benchley couldn't help but notice the large painting that Crowninshield was holding. It was MacGuffin's depiction of the mountain lion—the one he had used the dead cat to create. Benchley cringed just looking at it.

"Please explain yourself, Robert," Crowninshield said. His face was red.

Benchley looked from Crowninshield's reddening patrician face, to the dead cat/mountain lion painting, to the sticky wet bidding mechanism covered with an upside-down champagne glass, to his hands stuck between Lucy's legs. He gave up.

"I simply can't explain myself, Crownie, old dear." Benchley sighed. "I don't even know where to begin."

Crowninshield was furious. His carefully trimmed mustache twitched with vexation. "Then I shall see you first thing tomorrow morning. In my office!" He walked away, shaking his head, his newly purchased mountain lion painting clamped under his arm.

"I thought I was in trouble before," Benchley said, again looking down at his hand clamped in between Lucy's legs. "Now I'm really in trouble."

"Trouble? You can say that again." The sense of alarm in her voice made Benchley look up.

"What do you mean?"

"We just made a bid for a thousand bucks."

Benchley glanced at the bidding box. The overturned glass hadn't moved. It still covered the green button. But on the stage, the auctioneer nodded approvingly in their direction, having just accepted a bid.

"Bidder N bids one thousand. Thank you, Bidder N. Do I have eleven hundred? Eleven hundred?"

Lucy said, "Our bidding box is making bids, but no one's pressing the button."

Nothing could surprise Benchley now. "Tonight *is* Halloween. Perhaps the darned thing's haunted."

"Boys, stop!" Houdini yelled from somewhere far ahead. *"Wait, come back here! Where is my lackey?"*

But the boys' footsteps did not stop. Dorothy followed the sound straight to Houdini. The magician stood alongside a stone wall, watching them run away. His back was to her as she panted slowly toward him.

"Your lackey," she gasped, out of breath. "Present and accounted for."

Houdini turned. He spoke impatiently. "So, there you are, Mrs. Parker. I've been patiently awaiting you for quite some time. The impostor went through here." He pointed to a low door in the middle of the stone wall. "I was nigh ready to sally forth all on my own."

"Glad you waited," she said. "It would be silly to sally on your own. What would people say?"

He grasped the doorknob. "Then shall we?"

She nodded. "Surely."

He threw open the door. It was a brightly lit, cluttered cellar room. No one appeared to be inside. They stepped in.

Houdini immediately began poking behind objects as Dorothy stood and looked around. The room smelled of paint, turpentine and—flowers? In the center of the room was an easel with a half-finished painting on it. Something in the style of van Gogh, Dorothy thought. More finished and half-finished canvases were stacked upright against the wall. Shelves were filled with small cans and tubes of paint, brushes, jars of mineral spirits and resin varnish. Despite the room's disarray, several objects—such as the paint-brushes—were lined up neatly side by side. They reminded her of MacGuffin's shoes on the Brooklyn Bridge, Dorothy thought.

Houdini stood with an ear against a tall cabinet, listening.

"Dorothy," he hissed and handed her his stout cane. "Prepare to pummel whomever I pull out of here."

She took the cane and nodded but prepared to do no such thing. She knew exactly who was in there.

Houdini counted silently on his fingers: *One . . . two . . . three!*

He yanked open the door, reached his big hand inside and pulled out a tall, gangly man, dressed all in black, like a thief.

"Here is our impostor!" Houdini shouted in triumph, holding the man by the neck.

"He's no impostor," Dorothy said. "That's Ernie MacGuffin."

Chapter 27

Do I have eleven hundred for this haunting abstract of the Brooklyn Bridge? Eleven hundred?" The auctioneer looked in their direction. "Bidder N, you just bid one thousand. You don't need to raise the bid to eleven hundred."

The auctioneer looked away from Benchley and Lucy and stared pointedly toward the center of the audience. "A new bidder—Bidder Q bids eleven hundred. Thank you, Bidder Q. Do I have twelve hundred? Thank you, Bidder N, twelve hundred."

Lucy hissed at Benchley, "*We* didn't bid twelve hundred. This lousy machine did. The button must be stuck."

"Must be the sticky cream soda," Benchley said, removing the glass. He smacked the side of the bidding box.

"Do I have thirteen hundred? Thank you, Bidder Q. That's thirteen hundred. Do I have fourteen hundred? Fourteen hundred for Bidder N. Thank you, Bidder N."

Lucy's expression turned from dismay to seething anger. "Did you see that? He's taking bids from the chandelier."

"Taking bids from the chandelier?" Benchley looked up. "Well, I hope the chandelier wants it more than we do. And good luck to it."

Lucy grabbed his arm. "No, no. That's what it's called when the auctioneer takes phantom bids."

"Phantom bids? Well, as I said, it is Halloween."

"I mean he's making it up. We're bidding against no one but the auction house. Who would want to be Bidder Q, anyway?"

"Oh, right." He thumped the bidding mechanism again.

"Thank you, Bidder Q. Bidder Q bids fifteen hundred. Do I have sixteen hundred?"

"Do something!" Lucy said. "Get his attention. Tell them it's malfunctioning."

Benchley waved his hand at the auctioneer. The auctioneer acknowledged him. "No need to raise your arm, Bidder N. Use your bidding box, please. Ah, I see that you have. Thank you. Bidder N bids sixteen hundred. Do I have seventeen hundred?"

Benchley dropped his arm. "Well, that didn't work." He looked down at the stage. He recognized the painting. It was the one that MacGuffin had left against the railing that night on the bridge.

"I wonder," Benchley mused, "what would Mrs. Parker do if she found herself in this sticky situation?"

"Forget what Mrs. Parker would do!" Lucy said. "Think about what Mickey Finn will do. He'll kill us both."

"Perish the thought, my dear," Benchley said, with a wave of his hand. "He wouldn't harm a hair on your head."

"He'll kill you, though."

"Oh, certainly." Benchley nodded. "That goes without saying."

The auctioneer continued. "Eighteen hundred for Bidder N. Do I have nineteen hundred?"

"Ernie MacGuffin?" Houdini said. "The painter? The suicide?"

"The one and the same," Dorothy said.

"Go ahead, Dottie," MacGuffin said miserably, his Adam's apple rising and falling. "Say something nasty. Let me have it."

She strolled slowly up to MacGuffin, cranked back her arm and, with all her strength, punched him right in the eye.

"Ow!" MacGuffin shouted. "That's not what I meant."

"You rat bastard," Dorothy said calmly. "That's for giving me that stupid suicide note and making me feel like hell for the past week."

"Jeez, first this guy clubs me with his cane. Now you sock me in the eye." He rubbed his eye. "How long have you known?"

"Since about two seconds after your voice came out of that phony medium's mouth," she said. "I should have suspected it long before. But I never thought you had it in you to pull such a stunt.

Didn't it occur to you that suicide is very serious?"

MacGuffin looked dumbfounded. She could guess his thoughts. *Dorothy Parker, of all people, says suicide is too serious to joke about?* Even she had joked with him about it.

Houdini was shorter than MacGuffin, but he shook the painter by the collar like a puppet. "You rapscallion. You knave. You milksop."

The skin around Ernie's eye was swelling and turning from red to purple. She had really popped him one. She felt strangely gratified—and ashamed. So what if he deserved it? Punching MacGuffin was beneath her. It was like kicking a scrawny alley cat.

"That's enough," she told Houdini, who stopped shaking MacGuffin but didn't let him go. "Would you care to explain yourself?"

MacGuffin nodded. "But first can I ask for your help?"

"My help? After what you've pulled?" Dorothy looked to Houdini. "Shake him some more. Shake some sense into him."

Houdini shook him vigorously.

"Thank you, Bidder Q. That's twenty-nine hundred. Do I have three thousand dollars?"

The audience grew quiet and tense with anticipation. This was the highest bid yet.

Benchley banged his hand on the bidding box

one more time, more out of desperation than anger.

"Three thousand for Bidder N!" the auctioneer said. "Thank you, Bidder N."

The auctioneer continued. "I shall now increase the bidding by increments of five hundred dollars. Do I have three thousand five hundred? Thirty-five hundred dollars for this exquisite, abstract rendition of the Brooklyn Bridge? The last sight that Ernest MacGuffin saw before his tragic death. Thirty-five hundred?" The auctioneer looked to the center of the audience but at no one specifically. "Thank you, Bidder Q. Thirty-five hundred dollars for Bidder Q. Do I have four thousand dollars?"

Lucy angrily shook the bidding box, which caused people nearby to raise their eyebrows and look askance at her. Benchley had given up. He leaned back lazily in his chair with his hands behind his head.

"Bidder N for four thousand dollars," the auctioneer said, looking in their direction. "Thank you, Bidder N. Do I have forty-five hundred?"

Lucy let go of the bidding box. She rammed her elbow into Benchley's ribs, which doubled him over. "Do something, damn it!"

Bent over, Benchley noticed a thick black wire coming from the bottom of the bidding box. The wire ran along the floor, where it met with other wires from other bidding boxes. Together, the wires ran under the seats and presumably toward the central switchboard on the stage.

"Bidder Q for forty-five hundred dollars. Thank you, Q. Do I have five thousand dollars? Five thousand? Allow me to inform you that this one-of-a-kind, never-before-seen painting was found at the scene of the artist's suicide. So it commemorates both the life and the death of Ernest MacGuffin, now recognized as one of our modern-day masters."

Benchley inspected the wire. It was coated in cloth and as thick around as a pencil. Did he have the strength to yank it out completely?

"Thank you, Bidder N. That's five thousand dollars for Bidder N. Do I have five thousand five hundred?

Lucy hissed, "Do something. Hurry!"

Benchley pulled the wire out of the box. It was as easy as pulling a blade of grass from the ground.

"No?" the auctioneer said. "Fifty-five hundred? Final call for five thousand five hundred dollars. Going once. Going twice . . ."

Benchley folded his arms and looked up at the chandelier: *Oh, now you're quiet.*

The auctioneer banged his gavel. "Sold to Bidder N for five thousand dollars! That's Bidder N."

"That's the bitter end, all right," Benchley muttered to Lucy.

"Mickey's going to have your head on a plate," she said.

"For five thousand?" Benchley asked. "He'll have my head, my feet, and everything in between."

Then Benchley spied Snath in the shadows, down at the edge of the stage. The lawyer was looking heavenward, nearly floating with joy, an impossibly wide grin on his narrow face.

Chapter 28

S-stop, p-please," MacGuffin said through clenched teeth, as Houdini continued to shake him like a rag doll.

"Okay, let's hear him out," Dorothy said.

Houdini stopped shaking him. MacGuffin eyed him carefully, then hesitantly began to speak. "I'm sorry I tricked you, Dottie."

"You didn't trick only me. You tricked the whole town. People would kill you for this—if you hadn't already committed suicide."

MacGuffin looked sorrowful.

"And that séance business," Dorothy said. "What would make you do such a shameful thing?"

"It was her—Viola's idea, not mine."

There was something about the way he said her name.

"She's your girlfriend," Dorothy said. "Mistress Viola is not just *a* mistress, she's *your* mistress. And she put you up to this hoax, didn't she?"

MacGuffin nodded. "I didn't want to do it. But I agreed in return for a piece of the money. And the notoriety. It was fun. At first." He smiled a moment. But his smile faded at their hard stares.

"Then why did you give your suicide note to *me?*" Dorothy asked. "Why not give it to her?"

"To Viola? She's an artist's model. It wouldn't look decent."

"And letting her use you as a ghost to make a quick buck is decent?"

MacGuffin shrugged.

Dorothy asked, "Then why not give the note to your wife? She helped you write the damned thing—"

Then Dorothy figured it out and understood why the room had the scent of flowers. The sitting room upstairs, where Dorothy had sat last week with Midge, was full of them. "We're in the basement of your house, aren't we? So your wife is in on it. That's why she showed no guilt when I asked her about helping you with your suicide note. She knew full well you weren't dead."

MacGuffin nodded. Then the words poured out of him. "Dottie, please. You have to help me. I'm in a tight spot. I'm at the end of my rope."

"Which is it? You're in a tight spot, or you're at the end of your rope?"

"It's both. I've dug myself in deep, and now I can't get out."

"Put yourself out on a limb, and you'll also be fresh out of metaphors. Now explain yourself. Why did you fake your suicide?"

"It was a career move, pure and simple."

"Faking suicide is neither pure nor simple," she said tartly.

"So I've learned. But all the same, that's why I

did it. To make myself famous. To raise the price of my work."

"I've heard of career suicide, but suicide to improve your career?"

"It's not career suicide. It's career success." MacGuffin brightened with the thought of it. "The moment everyone thought I jumped off that bridge, my work was suddenly in demand, even more than I had hoped. Overnight, I went from middling success to celebrity sensation."

She thought of the auction and the prices that Snath would be asking. "So this was all just for fame and fortune?"

"Exactly. And it worked—only too well."

"Too well?" she asked. "What's that supposed to mean?"

He saddened again. "Look at me. I'm at the top of my career, the talk of the town, with a high-priced auction going on at Piddle Brothers. But I'm hiding out in back rooms and basements. To make it work, no one can know I'm alive. Then again, if I can't enjoy the reward for my labor, it was all for nothing. The money and the accolades are pouring in, and I can't enjoy a bit of it."

"Slow down," Dorothy said. "Start over."

But MacGuffin didn't start over. He babbled on. "It's my agent and lawyer, Snath. He and my wife, and even Viola, they all have me over a barrel."

"You mean they're all in on it?"

"Not together, but individually, yeah."

"They all know you're still alive?"

"Yeah."

"And whose idea was it to fake your death? Yours, or one of theirs?"

"Well, mine, I guess."

"You guess? You don't know?"

"I was on the phone with Snath one day. He had gotten me a job to paint some cowboy cover or something. But it was a rush job, and the fee—well, the fee was hardly enough to cover the costs of paint and canvas, much less my time. So I said, if he kept me at this pace, he was going to kill me. And, for a laugh, I said if I died in the middle of painting this job, then it might really be worth something, if only for the sheer novelty of it."

"And that joke gave you the idea?"

"Sort of," MacGuffin said with a shrug. "Snath called me back a few days later. He said he was researching what I said, and generally a painter's worth increases immediately after he dies. The more successful the painter in life, the bigger the boost after death. I laughed and said, 'So I'd be worth more dead than alive?' And he agreed. And that's how it all began."

"So what's the problem? You're on easy street now. And if you're dead, I guess it's all tax free," she said sourly. "Enjoy it to your shriveled, atrophied heart's content."

"That's the problem. I can't enjoy it," Mac-Guffin moaned. "Snath hasn't yet given me a dime. He has me working like a dog, churning out painting after painting, which he's selling at auction. But I haven't seen a red cent."

Dorothy thought about Benchley at the auction at that very moment. And Lucy Goosey probably cuddled up next to him. Dorothy also angrily remembered Midge's recent book deal, which Snath had undoubtedly brokered.

Irritably, she said, "And what about your wife? Is she conspiring with Snath?"

MacGuffin shrugged. "Sort of. Midge helped me with the suicide note, but that's as involved as she wanted to be, she said. I promised her a piece of every painting sold after I, you know, died. And she agreed to that. But she said she didn't want to have to lie to anyone. So she wants me to stay away."

Dorothy thought of big, thick-necked Bert Clay and wondered if Midge had another reason for wanting Ernie to stay away. "So where are you staying?

"At Viola's house. I use the alleys to go back and forth, so no one will see me."

"And you're still using this studio to paint all your posthumous paintings? Here, in your very own house, with Midge upstairs?"

Ernie automatically lowered his voice. "I come and go by the cellar door there. I keep quiet and do my work and don't go upstairs. Midge simply pretends I'm not here."

"And that arrangement works for you all?" Houdini asked.

MacGuffin looked at him sorrowfully. "No, that's just it. It works for all of *them,* but it's killing me." He turned to Dorothy. "Please, you've got to help me, Dottie."

"Oh no." She held up a hand. "The last time you asked me that, you stuffed something that turned out to be 'police evidence' into my purse, and I got assigned to write a posthumous magazine tribute about you—and you're not even dead. You're more trouble than you're worth, Ernie. And right now, I just want to pretend you're dead, too." She turned to go.

"Dottie, please!"

She looked over her shoulder. "Don't worry. I won't tell anyone your secret —yet."

Houdini loosened his grip. MacGuffin pulled free and ran in front of her. He stood before the door, blocking the exit. "Please, Dottie, you have to help me out of this mess. Please! I don't have anyone else to turn to. Help a fellow out."

"You made your bed, you lie in it. You're pretty good at the lying part." She tried to shove him out of the way, but she couldn't move him.

She stepped back. "Okay, then, I'll go upstairs and out through the front door. I'll give Midge your regards on my way out." She turned toward the basement stairs.

"No, no, don't do that," Ernie said quickly,

251

moving away from the door. Dorothy turned around and grabbed the doorknob.

"Just one more thing," Ernie said, clearly trying to stall her. He touched the eye that Dorothy had punched. It was dark purple now, and Dorothy couldn't help but feel just a little sorry for him.

"What is it?" She took a cigarette out of her pocket.

"Can I—can I ask you just one question?"

She shrugged, grabbed a box of matches from the worktable and lit her cigarette.

"Can you tell me why," he asked slowly, "you're dressed like a newsboy?"

She almost kicked him in the shin. Instead, she yanked open the door and stomped out into the night, followed by Houdini, who slammed the door behind them.

"And good riddance," Houdini said, as they stepped into the darkened alleyway.

"You got that right," Dorothy said, exhaling smoke.

But she already felt lousy again—as she had before, on the night when she believed that Ernie had killed himself, and she hadn't been able to help him.

Chapter 29

It was very late when Dorothy and Houdini arrived at the Algonquin Hotel. On the street, they had passed several revelers and merrymakers in Halloween costumes—yet Dorothy still felt conspicuous and uncomfortable in her errand boy's outfit.

When they entered the hotel's lobby, they found Benchley slumped in a club chair, smoking his pipe. A tall, flat rectangle, wrapped in brown paper, leaned against the side of his chair. Dorothy was fully prepared to let him have it for going out with Lucy Goosey—even though she knew Mickey Finn had ordered Benchley to go. But here he was, sitting alone, staring gloomily ahead. Not at all his usual cheery self.

She tried to act nonchalant. "Oh, Fred, there you are. We drove by Tony Soma's, but you weren't outside as we agreed, so I knew I'd find you here."

Staring ahead, Benchley just nodded.

"Fred, are you all right?" she asked.

Benchley looked up slowly. "Hello, Mrs. Parker, Mr. Houdini. Did you have a wonderful Halloween evening?"

"Oh, very spirited. And your evening?" She bit her tongue to keep from asking about Lucy Goosey.

"A real dandy," he said morosely.

"I see you bought a painting."

That brought him to life a little bit. "Not just any painting. *The* painting." He explained it was the one that MacGuffin had left on the Brooklyn Bridge on the night of his suicide.

Dorothy dropped into one of the chairs. "Well, I hope you didn't pay too much, because we don't need it now."

Benchley's eyes went wide. "Don't *need* it?"

"Ernie MacGuffin is alive. His suicide was a fake. There's no need to have that painting authenticated. I can guarantee that it's genuine."

Benchley stared straight ahead. "Oh. Well."

She didn't like the looks of this. Benchley was never at a loss for a joke, no matter how bleak things seemed.

" 'Oh. Well.' Is that all you have to say? Nothing to add?"

Benchley shook his head. "I could add that I now owe a ruthless gangster five thousand dollars for a painting we don't need. I could also add that Crowninshield is going to fire me first thing tomorrow because I was not at Houdini's show as I was supposed to be, but instead had my hands between Lucy Goosey's legs—"

"Wait." She felt a wave of panic. "What do you mean, you had your hands between Lucy Goosey's legs?"

But Benchley continued. "I could also add that I

raised the suspicions of Police Captain Church. And I insulted Horace Liveright's liver. Or his kidneys. Or his bladder or giblets or something."

She gently laid a hand on his knee. "Go back. Tell me what happened at the auction."

So Benchley told her.

"Oh," she said when he was finished. "Well."

"You can say that again."

Houdini smiled optimistically and waved one of his large hands, as though brushing aside these problems like gnats. "Don't be so down in the mouth. You have the power of the press on your side, do you not? Bring this scoundrel's shenanigans to light. Expose the fraud. Then we'll see if his paintings still fetch five thousand dollars at auction." He leaned back in his chair. "Mark my words, they won't fetch five cents. There's your revenge. If you don't expose him, I gladly will."

"No, no, no!" Benchley sat up. "We can't tell anyone. Nobody, you understand? It's just like you said—if anyone finds out that Ernie's alive, the value of his paintings will plummet."

"Good," Dorothy said. "Serves him right."

"No, no, no! Not while I have this thing on my hands." Benchley pointed to the painting. "My name is already mud as soon as Mickey Finn finds out I cost him five grand for this painting. But if Ernie is exposed, and this painting loses even a nickel in value, my name won't be mud. It'll be on a tombstone."

Now she understood Benchley's dreadful mood. She turned to Houdini. "Mr. Benchley is right. We can't tell anyone."

"Tell anyone what?" said a strident, nasal voice. It was Alexander Woollcott, with Harpo Marx in tow.

Dorothy thought quickly. "We can't tell anyone about the croquet tournament. Happening at this moment on the sheep meadow in Central Park. But if you go right now, don't say you heard it from us."

Woollcott was wearing a big bumblebee costume. "I certainly shan't, because I'm not going."

She raised an eyebrow. "Oh, is croquet no longer the bee's knees?"

"It's still the bee's knees. It's the cat's pajamas even." He pointed to Harpo, who was dressed in a cat costume. "But Harpo and myself have taken the evening off our game of croquet to enjoy the frivolity of All Hallow's Eve." Woollcott looked Dorothy up and down. "Speaking of which, did you steal the clothes off the back of your latest romantic conquest for your costume?"

"Oh, queen bee, where is thy sting?" she asked. "Is that the best you can do, Aleck?"

Woollcott ignored her, looking instead at Houdini. "And who is this spindly old gent you've dragged out of his convalescent home?"

"This is Harry," Dorothy said.

Houdini jumped up and bowed deeply. "I

256

certainly recognize you, Mr. Woollcott. A pleasure."

"For you," Woollcott sneered, not recognizing the famous magician.

Harpo, in his cat costume, was struck dumb. He and his zany brothers were still a fairly recent success on Broadway, so the recognition of Harry Houdini, one of the greats of show business, standing right before him reduced the professional prankster to silence.

"What's the matter with you?" Woollcott said sharply to Harpo.

"Perhaps he's got his own tongue," Benchley said.

A few minutes later, they had adjourned to Dorothy's suite on the second floor of the Algonquin. Woollcott—still in his outrageous bee outfit—hadn't relented. He hated to be left out, to have secrets withheld from him.

"I've got a real me in my bonnet, Dottie. Tell me what you don't want to tell anyone. And, Benchley, open that parcel."

"No," Benchley said and pointed to Harpo, still standing mute in his cat costume. "I won't let one of him out of the bag."

"Never," Houdini said. "Never reveal your secrets. I never do."

"Don't listen to this old fool," Woollcott said haughtily. "Tell me, Dottie. Tell me. Tell me!"

It was late, and Dorothy knew her strength of will was weak. Also, she herself was rarely one to keep a secret. "Oh, why the hell not? Just please, Aleck, don't let this out."

"Yes, Aleck," Benchley said. "It's not a stretch to say my life is on the line."

"On my honor, I shall tell no one, especially if it means Robert's dear life!" Woollcott spoke with exaggerated drama, but Dorothy sensed he understood the seriousness of the situation. They then looked at Harpo, who mimed turning a key on his lips and throwing it away.

So Dorothy told them how Ernie MacGuffin had faked his death and was still churning out paintings for money. ("That cad!" Woollcott cried.) Benchley unwrapped the parcel and explained how he had gone to the auction, intending to acquire a painting so they could have it authenticated. But he had wound up with the most expensive painting of the lot.

"So you see," Dorothy said, "because the value of the paintings depend on Ernie's suicide, if anyone finds out he's still alive, the price of the paintings will plummet."

"And so will I," Benchley said, "out of a skyscraper window, if Mickey Finn loses his investment."

"Never fear!" Woollcott said, standing up, the fake antennae on his head bobbing up and down. "Not only is your secret safe with me, but I can

258

help you increase the worth of that despicable waste of canvas and pigment." He pointed to MacGuffin's abstract of the Brooklyn Bridge.

Dorothy regretted, as she thought she might, letting Woollcott in on the secret. But she was tired and just plain worn-out. "No, Aleck, don't trouble yourself."

"No trouble at all, my dear Dottie. You know I have perhaps the most-read column in all the newspapers of New York."

Benchley leaned toward her. "Emphasis on the *perhaps,*" he whispered. It made her feel better that Benchley was making jokes, or at least insults, again.

"I heard that, Robert," Woollcott said, examining the painting. "Nevertheless, I will save your hide from Finn the bootlegger by extolling, in my column, the beauty and modernism of this dreck, which will undoubtedly increase its value further. Then, after a suitable period of time, you can sell it at an increase in profit. You can thank me by naming your next child after me, Robert."

"Bumblebee Benchley?" Benchley asked.

"Aleck, please, don't get muddled into this," Dorothy said.

Woollcott held up a hand. "It's no trouble in the least, and it won't even interfere with our croquet game. Consider it done. Now, what do you plan to do?"

Dorothy considered this a moment. "I'd like to pay another visit to Midge MacGuffin, first thing in the morning. She knew all along that Ernie was alive, yet she allowed me to believe he was dead. Ernie may well have been painting in the basement as Midge and I were talking. I think she has some explaining to do."

As angry as Dorothy was about Midge's dishonesty, she was just as annoyed that Midge could have secured a deal to get a book published so quickly. Dorothy wanted to grill her about that, too. "Fred, will you join me?"

Benchley checked his wristwatch. "First thing tomorrow?"

"Yes."

"I'm supposed to meet with Crowninshield first thing tomorrow. I think he's going to fire me. So, considering that, yes, I will most certainly join you, Mrs. Parker."

Houdini chuckled to himself. "You people meet together for lunch. You gather together at night. You write articles about each other. And you skip work together. How do you ever get any real work done?"

Woollcott narrowed his eyes at Houdini. "I don't know who you think you are, but would you please just disappear?"

Houdini smiled and nodded. "As you wish." He turned to Dorothy. "Thank you for the interesting evening, Mrs. Parker. I'll see you again soon." He moved toward the closet, opened the door, stepped inside, and closed the door behind him.

"Ha," Woollcott laughed. "You'll see him again sooner than he thinks. The old coot doesn't know the difference between the closet and the hallway. Where did you find that rube, Dottie?"

"I found him backstage at the Hippodrome," Dorothy said, moving toward the closet. "He had just performed for an audience of five thousand."

She opened the door to the tiny closet. Houdini was gone.

Woollcott looked puzzled.

Harpo finally broke his silence. " 'I don't know who you think you are'?" he said in a perfect imitation of Woollcott.

"What do you mean?" Woollcott said, confused.

Harpo said, "That 'rube' was Harry Houdini, you idiot!"

Chapter 30

The next morning, by the ninth toll of the bell from St. Patrick's Old Cathedral several blocks away, Dorothy stood across the street from the MacGuffins' house in Greenwich Village.

Benchley soon arrived. "Look at you," he said. "You're rarely so bright eyed and bushy tailed in the morning. Usually you're bushy eyed and bright tailed."

Dorothy thought about how she hadn't had a drink in days. "It's not my fault. Sobriety is to blame."

"Perhaps sobriety agrees with you," he said as they strolled across the street toward the house.

"Unfortunately, I disagree with it," she said.

Sobriety had its place—Dorothy didn't disagree with that. For instance, she didn't like to drink when she had real work to do. But to go for days and days without any drink was simply no fun at all.

Then again, she had to admit that she did feel upbeat today. She figured her mood was also lifted by the prospect of spending the whole day with good old Benchley.

She banged on Midge's door.

Seconds passed. Dorothy and Benchley glanced at each other. After half a minute, Dorothy banged on the door again. They heard shuffling, scuffling, a moment's pause; then the door swung open. Midge MacGuffin stood there, blank faced and regal, like a tall, raven-haired angel in luxurious satin pajamas the color of expensive pearls. But as poised as Midge seemed, Dorothy noticed that her breathing was slightly quickened, as though she had to take care of something hastily before answering the door.

"Good morning, Midge," Dorothy said. "May we come in?"

"Actually—"

"Wonderful," Dorothy said, moving forward. Midge was forced to step backward into her front hall, but she kept the door open, one hand on the knob, signifying she wasn't willing to give them much of her time.

"What— " Midge began.

"Is there something you'd like to tell us?" Dorothy said politely but with gritted teeth.

"Tell you?"

Dorothy tried again. "Is there something else you think you should share with us, given that we're writing a glowing article memorializing your late husband?" She emphasized the word *late* but didn't bother to elaborate that they hadn't yet written a word of this article.

Midge's face was as blank as a plaster statue. "Something else to share? No, I don't think so—"

Dorothy smiled, looking up at the elegant woman. "I do believe we're short—"

"Short?" Midge said.

"Short on a few facts," Dorothy continued, still smiling. "One very pertinent fact, in particular."

"Yes," Benchley agreed. "One particular pertinent fact."

"What fact is that?"

Dorothy narrowed her eyes but continued with a smile on her face. *Would Midge* really *be so obstinate about this?* She tried a different approach. "The suicide note, the one you wrote for Ernie. It was a catalog of lies."

"Lies?" Midge said, a hand on her chest. "That's not true. Ernie meant every word we wrote."

"Every word about him being misunderstood, perhaps," Dorothy said. "But the part about him killing himself—that's a whole different story."

Midge's pale face finally registered at least some sense of alarm. "What exactly do you mean?"

"You know perfectly well what I mean," Dorothy said. "You lied. Ernie had no intention of killing himself. The whole thing was a fake. And you knew all about it when we talked last week. But you didn't say a thing. Your husband, Ernie, is alive."

Midge covered her mouth with her hand, trying hard to keep her composure and hide her alarm.

"Huh?" said a deep voice behind them.

Dorothy jumped at the voice. She and Benchley spun around in surprise.

Bert Clay, unshaven and in a tight white undershirt and baby blue boxer shorts, leaned halfway out of the hallway closet. He looked at Benchley in surprise. "Hey, you're that friendly telegram messenger. What are you doing here?"

Before Benchley could answer, Clay's expression turned menacing. He realized that Benchley was no friendly telegram messenger. Clay stepped out of the closet, all six foot two, 250 pounds of him.

"What are we doing here?" Benchley said, chuckling, backing away. "Why, we were just leaving. So nice to see you again."

He tipped his hat to Clay and Midge. Then he grabbed Dorothy's hand. They turned quickly, trotted down the steps and hurried away down the street.

Chapter 31

The next morning—Saturday morning—Dorothy and Benchley were at their desks in the editorial office at *Vanity Fair*. They had agreed to meet Robert Sherwood there. The three of them were the only ones in the place—except for Crowninshield, who was in his office, evidently doing actual work. Rain drummed on the windows. They were leaning back, sipping hot black coffee and talking—for the dozenth time—about all that had transpired at the séance and at the auction house on Halloween night, and what had happened the previous morning with Midge MacGuffin.

"I didn't even ask her about her rotten book," Dorothy said. "How the hell did she get a book deal so fast, and get it printed even faster?"

As if to answer that question, Harold Ross came in the door. "So here you are!" He had a book in his hand. "How's that story going on Ernie MacGuffin?"

"It was looking dead in the water for a while," Dorothy said. "But we were just talking about how it's come to life recently." She pointed at the book. "What's that you have there?"

"Glad you asked," Ross said, handing it to her. "It's Midge MacGuffin's memoir. Came out yesterday. How soon can you review it?"

Dorothy looked at the slim volume, glancing at the title, reading it aloud. "*Silence Speaks Volumes*. That doesn't quite apply to the author, does it?"

Ross shrugged. "The bookstores have ordered scads of them. They're expecting it to sell like hotcakes. There's talk that it will make it onto tomorrow's bestseller list in the *New York Times*."

Dorothy groaned hearing this. For the umpteenth time, she thought about how she had to struggle for weeks to write just one short poem, and here came blank-faced, empty-headed Midge MacGuffin about to break into the bestseller list with her slapdash memoir. Dorothy was reluctant, but also painfully curious, to look inside to see what dreck Midge must have written.

She opened the book. But the pages were blank.

"Ross, you dope," she said. "You picked up a misprint. Didn't you even look inside?"

She held up the book for all of them to see and flipped through its blank pages.

"That isn't a misprint, damn it," Ross growled, lighting a cigarette. "That's the idea."

"What's the idea?" Dorothy wasn't sure she wanted to hear the answer.

"You don't read it," Ross said. "You look at it and you think things. Get it?"

Dorothy, Benchley and Sherwood looked at one another. They didn't get it.

Ross reached out and took the book from

Dorothy. He licked his forefinger and turned to one of the first pages. He read aloud. " '*Silence Speaks Volumes*, by Midge MacGuffin.' " He turned to the next page and read in his gruff voice: " 'The pages of this book are as empty as my heart. I look at an empty page as though looking on an empty canvas, and wonder about the story that now won't be told or the picture that won't be painted. At other times, I recall the happy visions and dreams of yesteryear. I invite you to do the same, dear reader. Imagine what you long for. Think of thoughts of the future, and memories of the past, and envision your own story.' "

Dorothy jumped up and grabbed the book from Ross.

"That's it?" She flipped through the blank white pages in disbelief. "One screwy paragraph and then a hundred empty pages? That's her book?"

Ross nodded. "That's her book. That's how she got it printed so fast."

"And you mean to tell me it's going to be a bestseller?"

"Yup, it's all the rage," he said. "Folks are in love with the idea. It's a book that doesn't tell you what to think. It's for people who want to do the thinking themselves."

"It's for people who don't do *any* thinking themselves!" She dropped back into her chair. "Only an idiot would buy this book."

Ross was unconvinced. "Yet a whole lot of

people will, and I'm sure they'll get a lot out of it."

"Get a lot out if it? There's nothing in it!"

Ross exhaled smoke. "So, how soon can you review it?"

"Review it?" Dorothy almost screamed. "How am I supposed to review a blank book?"

"You'll think of something clever, Dottie," Ross said reassuringly. "That's what you always do."

"This will be the first-ever book review that's longer than the book!" she said.

Editor in Chief Frank Crowninshield opened his office door and leaned out his old head. "Mrs. Parker, what's all that ruckus?" Then he spotted Ross. "Harold Ross, you've got some nerve coming in here. Are you trying to poach my editors again for your little *New Yorkers* magazine?"

Ross stood straighter. "It's *The New Yorker*, Frank. And I'm not poaching anyone."

Still leaning back in his chair, Benchley said, "He's not poaching me, but he's got me scrambled."

Dorothy was simmering, looking at Midge's book in her hands. "He's got me fried."

"Glad you didn't say 'over easy,'" Benchley said to her.

Crowninshield gave Harold Ross his most severe patrician glare. "Ross, please remove yourself from these premises at once."

Ross glanced at the book in Dorothy's hand and exchanged looks with her. "Okeydoke. I was just removing myself anyhow."

Benchley sprang into action, jumping toward Ross. "Attaboy, on with your hat. There you are. Now go. Go on—you heard what the boss said." He nearly shoved Ross out the door and closed it quickly.

Crowninshield looked at Benchley approvingly and seemed to recall something from deep in his memory. "Benchley, didn't we have an appointment first thing yesterday? Where were you?"

"I was working hard on that Houdini review, you lovable old goat." Benchley smiled.

"But I saw you at the art auction," Crowninshield said slowly, his silver mustache twitching. "You didn't even attend the Houdini show the other night."

"I'd never let a little thing like absence stop me from writing a review."

"Or abstinence, for that matter," Dorothy said, thinking of Benchley's hands between Lucy's legs. She would certainly have to ask him more about that.

Crowninshield closed his eyes, shook his head with a sigh and retreated back into his office, shutting his door.

"I guess I'm not fired," Benchley said, smiling, once again leaning back in his chair. "Thanks to Ross, I got a reprieve."

Dorothy dropped the book on her desk. "And thanks to Ross, I gotta review."

The phone rang. Dorothy picked it up.

"Hello, my lass," Mickey Finn's voice said on the other end of the line. His voice was smooth, low and somehow extremely menacing. "Is your dear friend Robert Benchley there? I need to see you both. Right now."

Dorothy was about to make an excuse when Finn added, "Be on the sidewalk in five minutes. And bring the painting. I want to be there when you have it authenticated."

Finn hung up and Dorothy stared at the receiver. Then she looked at Benchley. "Your reprieve is over. Mickey Finn wants to have a little art-to-art talk."

Chapter 32

Dorothy spent the next few minutes frantically trying to reach Neysa McMein to ask her for the name of an art expert. "One who'll say the painting is worth a mint," Dorothy told Neysa on the phone.

Neysa gave her a name, and Dorothy scribbled it down. Then she told Sherwood to call the police if she and Benchley didn't come back by lunchtime. She was only half joking.

The next minute, she and Benchley stood on the West Forty-fourth Street sidewalk in front of the Condé Nast Building, waiting for Mickey Finn as though waiting to take the short walk to the electric chair.

So it was almost a nice diversion to see Mrs. Soma and Tony Jr. stroll down the sidewalk.

"You!" Mrs. Soma's tired eyes narrowed when she spotted them. She pointed a stubby finger at Dorothy. "You are a devil woman, Mrs. Parker!"

"Funny," Dorothy said. "That's what Mr. Parker used to say."

"You told me you'd meet us at the bank to pay off your debt. But you never showed up," Mrs. Soma seethed. "You tricked us. You lied!"

"Hmm," Benchley said. Dorothy turned and saw he had a very self-satisfied look on his face.

"What was that noise?" she asked.

"I just realized something quite ironic."

"And what is that?"

He tipped back his hat and chuckled. "Don't you see? You tricked Mrs. Soma, and then this morning you were so angry at Midge MacGuffin for tricking and lying to you. See? It's funny. And ironic, don't you think?"

Mrs. Soma snapped, "I don't think it's funny."

"Nor is it ironic, Mr. Benchley," Dorothy said airily. "Irony is when you buy stock in a company that makes pianos, and then a piano falls out of a window and crushes you to death—which is what I'm wishing for right now."

Mickey Finn's long white limousine cruised to a stop in front of them. The smoked-glass window rolled down.

"Get in," Mickey said.

Dorothy turned back to Mrs. Soma. "Our chariot awaits."

"You—!" Mrs. Soma sputtered.

Dorothy held up a hand. "We will get you the money—one of these days. There's no need to upset yourself."

Mrs. Soma ignored this. "I told every speakeasy owner in this town to keep you out. You're blackballed—do you hear me? I don't even care if you're friends with our liquor supplier." She jabbed her finger at Mickey Finn this time. "You're still blackballed in this town."

"Go home to your husband," Mickey Finn said to Mrs. Soma.

Dorothy looked at Tony Jr. "And you, stay out of those back alleys at night. You never know who you'll run into." She winked.

Tony Jr.'s eyes went wide and his jaw dropped as he figured out what she was saying.

Dorothy and Benchley climbed into the limousine. Dorothy watched Mrs. Soma swing her fist at Tony Jr. and yell, "What is she talking about? What are you doing in back alleys at night? Answer your mother!"

Tony Jr. covered his head with his arms in self-defense. Dorothy couldn't hear his response—if indeed he answered his mother at all.

The limo pulled away into traffic. In the backseat, Dorothy and Benchley turned to Mickey Finn. His ginger red hair seemed redder than usual. His ruddy face seemed redder, too. But his ice blue eyes were as cool as ever. Even cooler, perhaps.

"You two are getting in trouble all over town, aren't you?" he said with a grimace that showed his yellow teeth.

"It's nothing but child's play," Dorothy said. "We'll sort it out. Don't worry about it."

"Oh, I'm not worried," he said with a laugh, but his face wasn't smiling. "Not worried at all. I always get a return on my investments." He nodded to the flat, brown-wrapped parcel leaning against Benchley's knees. "Is that the painting?"

"Yes—" Benchley began. He unwrapped it and showed it to Finn.

"This is the painting you paid five thousand bucks for?"

"Y—" Benchley began again.

"Five thousand when you only asked me for, and I quote, *a few hundred?*"

"Y-yes."

"And how much do you owe Tony Soma?"

Benchley mumbled something.

Finn leaned forward. "Speak up, my lad. I didn't hear what you said."

"A few hundred," Dorothy said, repeating Benchley's mumbled words.

Finn leaned back in his seat and nodded. "Aye, you told *me* you only needed a few hundred and my investment would increase tenfold."

Dorothy frowned. They hadn't said that. Lucy was the one who said it.

Finn continued. "As I may have mentioned, I didn't get much formal education, so I never learned my multiplication tables very well. Tell me, what's ten times five thousand?"

Benchley gulped. "Fifty thousand."

Finn's blue eyes went wide in mock surprise. "Fifty thousand! Now, that's quite a payoff, ain't it? That'll be a tidy profit when we sell it—*if* we sell it." Finn's mouth was tight. His hands gripped the silver-tipped shillelagh lying across his knees.

Neither Dorothy nor Benchley answered. They knew Finn didn't really want a response.

Finn's seething anger finally boiled over. His face turned bright red and the veins in his neck went taut. He leaned forward and yelled, "Do you really think anyone will pay *fifty thousand goddamn dollars* for that *goddamn awful painting?*"

Dorothy's throat was tight. She gulped but didn't answer.

Finn leaned back in his seat, his anger at a low boil again. His voice was calm now. "Well, I guess we'll just have to find out. So, where is this art appraiser? And how good is he?"

Dorothy couldn't decide if she was more unsettled by the furious and raging Mickey Finn—or the calculating and even-tempered one.

Chapter 33

V ery well, let's take a look," said Hubert Cathcart, the art appraiser.

He laid the wrapped painting on an enormous worktable—more than twice the size of Dorothy's office desk—which took up most of the floor space in the back of the store.

Other than a soft clucking from deep in Cathcart's throat, it was surprisingly, unnervingly quiet in here, Dorothy thought. She could turn around in her chair and glance out to the plate-glass window at the front of the store and see the clogged sidewalk and the traffic on Fifth Avenue. But she couldn't hear any of it. This place— Cathcart's Fine Art, the sign had read—was somehow insulated against the sounds of the street.

Benchley, Dorothy and Mickey Finn sat next to one another in a short line of hard metal folding chairs that faced the big worktable. Finn was next to Dorothy. He sat up as straight as a flagpole, gently and methodically tapping the end of his walking stick on the floor. The sound reminded Dorothy of a dripping faucet, and she realized she could stand it no longer.

She stood up on the pretext of watching Cathcart unwrap the brown paper from the painting.

Hubert Cathcart looked like some kind of gaunt

flightless bird—an emu or an ostrich—that had spent its entire life in a small cage indoors, Dorothy thought. He was long, bony and stoop shouldered. He was young—possibly not much older than Benchley—but he wore his rimless, round bifocals on the end of his long, narrow nose like an elderly librarian. His skin was waxy and pale. He wore an expensive, slender blue suit— probably from a nearby men's clothier on Fifth Avenue—yet he barely filled it out.

Cathcart continued the occasional soft clucking sounds as he carefully peeled away the brown paper and examined the painting.

"Well?" Finn's voice was sharp.

Cathcart didn't respond—didn't even seem to hear him.

Finn stood up next to Dorothy. "Come on, man. Speak. Is it genuine?"

Cathcart didn't even look at Finn. "Sit, please," he said, his voice as soft as a whisper. "This takes time."

Finn considered this, and then agreed wholeheartedly. "Aye, indeed. Take your time. Take all the time you need. Do your best." He sat down again, leaned back in his chair and took a cigar out of his suit jacket pocket. He flicked a match on his thumbnail, and it flowered into flame.

Cathcart spun around. "Put that out!" he hissed. "There's no smoking in here."

The unlit cigar hung in Finn's open mouth. No one spoke to him that way!

But Cathcart had already turned back to MacGuffin's painting, as if the matter had been settled and even forgotten.

Finn didn't respond. He silently shook the flame out of the match and then placed the cigar back in his jacket.

Cathcart continued to make the soft clucking sounds as he examined the painting. He reached for a large magnifying glass that was attached to a pivoting, adjustable stand. He positioned the glass over the painting and stared through it.

The telephone rang. Dorothy scanned the art-covered walls and tabletops. She couldn't see the telephone anywhere. It rang a second time. Cathcart either didn't hear it or didn't care.

"Are you going to answer that?" Dorothy asked.

Cathcart shook his head, not looking at her. "Would you mind, please?"

He wanted *her* to answer it? Well, it would give her something to do. She skirted around the worktable and paused as the phone rang again. A glass-topped sales counter divided the store between the art showroom in front and the work area in back. The ringing seemed to come from there. She found the phone under the counter and picked it up.

"Hello. Cathcart Fine Fart," she said. Cathcart

didn't look up. "I mean, Cathcart Fine *Art*. May I help you?"

"Mrs. Parker? Is that you?" said a familiar voice.

"Mr. Sherwood? Why are you calling?"

"Why are you answering?" She was about to make some joke when Sherwood continued. "Never mind that. I have terrible news."

Oh cripes, Dorothy thought. *What now?*

She instinctively turned away from the men at the back of the store and spoke quietly into the phone. "Go ahead. Let me have it."

"It's Ernie MacGuffin," Sherwood said. "He's dead."

Dorothy was momentarily puzzled. Sherwood knew that Ernie's suicide was a fake. . . .

Then a chill ran through her.

"You mean," she whispered, "he's not just dead, but . . . *dead? Really* dead?"

"Yes," Sherwood said. "Really dead. His body was found this morning. The news just came over the wire."

"Are they sure it's him?"

"There were no details," Sherwood said. "Just that his body was found lying in the gutter on Water Street this morning. That's all."

Dorothy bit her lip. She looked over her shoulder at Finn, Cathcart and Benchley. Finn was staring directly at her. She turned away again.

Sherwood's voice continued. "As soon as I saw the news, I found Cathcart's number on your desk

280

and called right away. I'm glad you were the one who picked up the phone."

"I'm not," she said, covering the mouthpiece with her hand. "This is terrible. I can't believe it's true."

"If it is true, does it really make any difference?" Sherwood said. "After all, only you and a few others knew that Ernie was alive. The only difference is that his body hadn't been found before. But now it has."

"Before, he had jumped off the Brooklyn Bridge," she said. "Now his body is found in the street two weeks later. That's more than a little odd, don't you think?"

"More than a little, yes."

She didn't yet know what this might mean. She didn't quite believe it, yet she feared it might be true. When she'd seen Ernie the night before, he'd sounded so desperate. She remembered how he had begged for her help. If she had agreed to help him, would he be dead now—if he truly was dead?

She pushed the thought aside. She'd figure it out later. She thanked Sherwood and hung up. She crept back to her seat, trying to be unobtrusive.

But Finn's eyes were on her. "Who was that on the phone?"

"Wrong number," she said. "Some guy looking for a woman named Betty."

"Then why were you on for so long?"

281

"I wanted to know what's so great about Betty."

Then Cathcart straightened up, about to pronounce a verdict. Finn, Dorothy and Benchley looked at him expectantly.

"It's genuine," Cathcart said to them. "Although it's not his usual style, this is without a doubt an authentic MacGuffin."

Finn appeared momentarily satisfied. Dorothy felt a little relieved at least, even though she already knew that it was genuine.

"So how much is it worth?" Finn asked.

But before Cathcart could respond, the front door opened and an elegant older woman in a mink stole and a wide-brimmed hat came in. She swooped toward Cathcart, ignoring everyone else. She spoke through her nose, which was long and high in the air.

"Hubert dear, did you hear? It's the latest—the absolute *latest*. I just heard it on the radio. The body of Ernest MacGuffin has finally been found. Can you believe it? And found on the street, not in the river. Isn't that beyond the pale—the absolute *pale?*"

Cathcart swiveled his birdlike body from the painting on his worktable to the aristocratic woman and back again, and back yet again. He couldn't seem to reconcile this news to the painting in front of him.

"Yes," Finn said gravely, his eyes on Dorothy. "That is absolutely beyond the pale."

● ● ●

A moment later, Finn was on his feet, towering over the art expert and the fancy lady, demanding answers.

The lady spoke in a superior tone. "I don't know who you think you are, sir—"

Dorothy interrupted. "On the contrary, ma'am. Mr. Finn knows exactly who he thinks he is."

The woman silently mouthed, *Finn?* Her powdered face went even whiter.

Mickey Finn repeated, "Where was he found? *How* was he found?"

The lady took a half step backward. "The announcer didn't say *how* MacGuffin was found. Just that he was dead—absolutely *dead*."

Finn spun around to Dorothy. "You told me he jumped off the Brooklyn Bridge."

Dorothy didn't know what was going on, but she wouldn't let Finn talk to her like that— gangster or not. "I was there on the bridge. He left behind his shoes, a suicide note, and that very painting." She pointed to it on the worktable.

Finn turned back to Cathcart. "You were about to tell us how much it's worth, before this—this woman came in." Finn eyed the fancy lady. "So tell. How much?"

Cathcart gulped. There was no way he would tell Finn not to light a cigarette now. He'd probably happily strike the match for him.

"H-how much?" Cathcart repeated. "That—that depends."

"*Depends?*" Finn barked, folding his arms. "Tell us, what does it depend on?"

"Well." Cathcart blinked. "A moment ago, I would have quoted you one figure. But now—" He glanced at the fancy lady, clearly thinking of the news she'd just told. "Now that's changed."

"Changed *how?*" Finn said. "I want a number. A dollar figure!"

Dorothy slid her hand into Benchley's. Maybe they could sneak out while Finn focused his attention on Cathcart and his gossipy lady friend. She pulled Benchley toward the door.

"Just where the hell do you think you're going?" Finn yelled behind them.

Dorothy and Benchley turned. She told Finn exactly where she thought she was going. "To the police."

"The *police?*"

"Yes, the police," she said. "We have to find out what happened to MacGuffin. Captain Church will surely tell us."

"In good time," Finn growled. "For now, sit your backsides down! My investment comes first."

Dorothy didn't sit down. But she didn't move any closer to the door either. Benchley simply held her hand, ready to follow her either way.

The phone rang. Cathcart didn't reach for it. He looked to Finn as if for permission.

"Go ahead," Finn snapped. "Answer it."

Cathcart picked it up, his voice subdued. "Cathcart Fine Art. Hubert Cathcart speaking." He glanced at Finn. "Yes, I just heard. . . . Why yes, as a matter of fact I have one on my desk at this very moment." He turned to MacGuffin's painting, his voice gaining strength again as he focused on his work and not on Finn. "Yes, the one of the Brooklyn Bridge."

He paused for a moment, listening. Then he glanced nervously at the gangster. "Oh, you don't say."

Finn's brows knitted.

"That is . . . interesting," Cathcart said into the phone, looking not at all interested in hearing this. "Yes, thank you for the call. I'll call you back later."

He hung up the phone and kept looking at it, not wanting to look up at Finn.

"Well?" Finn snapped.

Cathcart nearly jumped. "I just heard some news about the current value of the MacGuffins, in light of the most recent tragic events."

Dorothy glanced at Benchley. "The art world is a smaller place than I'd have thought. News certainly travels fast there."

Cathcart looked up. "News like this does."

Finn grabbed Cathcart by his jacket. "Tell it, damn you. Tell it!"

Cathcart whimpered. The fancy lady stepped back, cringing.

"Another MacGuffin painting just dropped in value by half," Cathcart mumbled. "It went from two thousand down to one."

"Half?" Finn shouted, releasing him with a shove. "Dropped by half?"

Cathcart stumbled back a few steps. "Th-that doesn't mean every MacGuffin painting will lose half its value."

"This one!" Finn pointed to the Brooklyn Bridge painting. "How much is it worth?"

Cathcart adjusted the wireless spectacles on his birdlike nose. "W-well, it's hard to put an exact number—"

Finn stomped his foot. *"How much?"*

Cathcart flinched. "Nineteen hundred. At best."

Finn spoke in a whisper. *"Nineteen hundred. At best."*

He turned to face Dorothy and Benchley. He pointed his shillelagh at them. "You owe me fifty thousand, minus the nineteen hundred!"

"Fifty *thousand?*" she said. "But Mr. Benchley only spent five thousand of your—"

"Fifty thousand!" Finn shouted. "I expected a tenfold return on my investment, and I will surely get a tenfold return on my investment! You have twenty-four hours."

Finn held their gaze a moment longer, snatched up his shillelagh and stormed out of the shop.

"Now, that is beyond the pale," Dorothy muttered to Benchley. "*Absolutely* beyond the pale."

"Absolutely," said the elegant woman, whose own face had gone beyond pale.

Chapter 34

Well, look who it is," Detective O'Rannigan said from behind his messy desk. The desk was piled with papers, manila folders and a tall, half-eaten corned-beef sandwich on a square of waxed paper. "I had a little hunch you'd come sniffing around here today."

"Ah, is that how modern police work is performed these days?" Dorothy asked. "With little hunches?"

"It's certainly not performed with little lunches," Benchley said, looking at O'Rannigan's big, greasy sandwich.

O'Rannigan's half smile of welcome disappeared. "Captain Church knew you were mixed up in this."

"We're not mixed up in any—"

"Save your breath," O'Rannigan snapped. "Captain Church saw Mr. Benchley here at MacGuffin's art auction the other night. Says he knew right away you two were involved somehow—and deeper than just getting Mac-Guffin's suicide note." The detective leaned back in his chair, folding his hands on his big belly. "Did you come here to turn yourselves in?"

"Turn ourselves in?" Dorothy asked.

"Turn ourselves into what?" Benchley asked.

Before O'Rannigan answered, Dorothy asked, "So, *do* you suspect foul play?"

O'Rannigan's face went as blank and hard as a slab of slate. "I didn't say nothing like that."

"You just asked us to turn ourselves in. Clearly you're thinking along those lines?" Dorothy said. "So was MacGuffin's death foul play?"

"I was making a joke. You two fruits make them all the time. You telling me I can't make a joke as a policeman?"

"You already make yourself a joke *of* a policeman. Why beat a dead horse?" she said.

O'Rannigan stood up. "You ain't so smart. You don't think I know your game? You're trying to rattle me. Get me to tell you whatever it is you want to know."

Dorothy lowered her eyes, batting her lashes. "Fine. You figured me out. I take it all back. You are a good detective. You know I'm just trying to get you to tell us how MacGuffin was killed. But you can see right through me."

"Save the sweet talk." O'Rannigan sat down again, smiling and nodding. "I ain't playing that game either. You can't tear me down and you can't butter me up. So just talk straight. What the hell do you want?"

Dorothy spoke plainly. "We know MacGuffin's body was found this morning. But it was found in the street, not in the river."

"The whole city knows that. Don't worry about

289

it. We're looking into it." He chomped off a big bite of his sandwich, speaking with his mouth full. "That it? Anything else bugging you?"

"Yes, there is," she said. "I talked to Ernie MacGuffin the night before last. Now he's dead. That's bugging me."

O'Rannigan stood up, grabbed a paper napkin off his desk, wiped his mouth, crumpled the napkin in his hands and threw it down into a wastebasket. He picked up his small bowler hat and jammed it on his big bald head. "Come on. Let's go talk to the captain."

"Why did you fail to come forward with this information earlier?" Captain Church asked her.

Dorothy had had no intention of coming forward with any information at all. But Church didn't have to know that.

"It was too late and I was too tired to call last night," she fibbed. "I had planned to call from work this morning. But before I could, the news came over the wire that MacGuffin was dead. So as soon as we could get ourselves out of the office, we came here."

Dorothy figured Church didn't have to know about their visit that morning to Cathcart's with Mickey Finn.

Church stood behind his neat, empty desk. He shifted his weight from his good leg to his peg leg. Dorothy could see that he was thinking deeply—

probably skeptically—although his face was blank.

She and Benchley stood before his desk. Detective O'Rannigan stood to one side, against the wall. Dorothy wondered if this would be over quickly or if they would be invited to sit down—or if they'd stand here looking at one another for the next hour or so.

So she sat down in a hard wooden chair facing Church's desk. Benchley sat down, too. He took out his pipe, tobacco and matches and started fixing himself a smoke.

Slowly, Captain Church sat down in his chair. O'Rannigan folded his arms and kept standing. There were no more chairs.

"So," Dorothy began, "if MacGuffin was alive last night, what was he doing dead in the street this morning?"

Church steepled his fingers in thought. Then he reached for his telephone. "This would be an appropriate opportunity to communicate with Chief Medical Examiner Norris."

He dialed a number and asked for the medical examiner. Then he tilted the earpiece away from his ear. They could all hear the man's strident, baritone voice answer, "Norris here."

"Captain Church calling," he said by way of introduction. "I am inquiring about the body of Ernest MacGuffin."

"I'm looking down at the sorry bastard right

now," Norris said. They could hear him puffing on his cigar.

"I have Mrs. Dorothy Parker and Mr. Robert Benchley sitting here in my office. Do you remember meeting them?"

Norris' voice brightened. "I certainly remember that spunky, delectable little Dorothy Parker. I could eat her for dinner."

"She can hear you, Dr. Norris," Church said evenly.

"Then, hello, Mrs. Parker!" He didn't sound ashamed at all. "What I should have said was, could I *meet* you for dinner?"

Church ignored this. "Mrs. Parker stated she saw Ernest MacGuffin alive last night."

"I guess that explains why he wasn't bloated like a sponge and bobbing in the East River," Norris said dryly. "Yeah, I would have told you the same damn thing, Captain, if you'd only waited to receive my report."

Church was unruffled. "Tell us about the body."

Norris exhaled and spoke perfunctorily, as though reciting a case report. "He was found approximately five o'clock this morning by a milkman on his rounds. The body was lying supine in the gutter of the street—"

"Supine?" Dorothy asked.

"Faceup," Norris answered her over the phone. Evidently he could hear her as well as she could hear him. "The body lay perpendicular to the curb of the sidewalk, arms spread wide, the heels of his feet up on the curb, like he was napping in a field of daisies. He was fully dressed, with shoes and jacket, though his hat was found blown against a parked car a dozen yards away."

"What exactly was he wearing?" Dorothy asked.

"Hold on." Norris put down the phone for a moment, and then he picked it back up. They heard the rustle of a paper bag. "Cheap black suit—the label says Penney's," he sneered. "Dingy gray shirt, cuffs stained with streaks of paint. No tie. Nondescript black felt hat. Black shoes, dirty and wet—which isn't so strange considering the rain we just had."

Ernie had told Dorothy he wore dark clothes to move unseen through the alleys. "That's the getup he was wearing the other night," she said.

"Matter of fact," Norris continued, "all his clothes were soaking wet. He must have been lying in the gutter a while before someone reported him."

Church asked, "Are there any injuries? Did you determine the cause of death?"

"Other than the primary insult, no. His hands, forearms and face show no sign of physical violence," Norris said. "No, scratch that—there's a periorbital hematoma of the right eye."

"Perry Orton of Ronkonkoma, Long Island?" Benchley said. "He was my bunkmate at summer camp. Small world."

293

But Dorothy understood exactly what Norris meant by "periorbital hematoma of the right eye." A black eye. The one she gave MacGuffin. She had socked him in the eye in his own basement. And now she knew for sure that the dead body lying in front of the medical examiner really was Ernie MacGuffin. He really was dead. She began to feel the creeping hand of guilt.

"What is the primary insult?" Church asked.

Dr. Norris dropped the medical jargon and spoke in his usual straightforward style. "His head's caved in. Like someone smashed him in the back of the noggin with a slab of concrete."

Dorothy felt a wave of nausea.

O'Rannigan spoke up. "Any slabs of concrete lying nearby?"

Dorothy looked at him. He was serious.

"Nothing of the kind to be found, according to the report I got," Norris said. "But the scene of the crime wasn't far from a construction site, one of the reporting officers said. Rain must have washed most of the blood away, too."

"But he was found in the street," O'Rannigan said. "Car accident maybe?"

"Maybe," Norris said sourly, "if MacGuffin crossed the street bent over—with the back of his head facing into traffic. Good thinking, Detective."

"Every possibility should be explored, Doctor," Church said sharply. "Consider if MacGuffin dropped something into the street. Then he bent over and picked it up. As he was doing so, a car came upon him unexpectedly in the rain and collided directly into his head. You said he was found at five o'clock in the morning. Certainly, if his death occurred at the location in which he was found, it had to have happened shortly before. It would be dark at that time."

"*Hmph,*" Norris grunted. "Possible. But I highly doubt it."

O'Rannigan spoke up. "Up until today, we believed MacGuffin had jumped off the Brooklyn Bridge. Are you sure he didn't drown? Perhaps a passing ship caused the blow to his head. Then for whatever reason, someone dragged him out of the water, pulled him into a car and dumped the body in the street."

Norris grunted again. "Three problems with that theory. Firstly, there was no water in the lungs, so he didn't drown. Secondly, his clothes don't smell like river water. Thirdly, we now have Mrs. Parker's word that she saw him last night . . . *Detective!*"

O'Rannigan's face turned red. "I know that. I was just exploring every possibility."

"Explore on your own time. I have work to do," Norris said.

Dorothy ignored this. "So you don't think it was suicide or an accident? You think maybe it happened deliberately?"

"Can't say. That's for New York's finest to figure out. Could be an accident. Could be cold-blooded murder."

"Murder?" Dorothy said.

MacGuffin had been asking for her help two nights ago. Today he was found murdered? That creeping hand of guilt now tightened around her heart.

"No one said murder," Church grumbled.

"I just did," Norris said.

The word *murder* seemed to hang in the air for a moment before Norris continued. "But if it was murder, the guy would have to be strong as an ox to clobber MacGuffin in the head like that. My guess is it was done with one blow."

Something made Dorothy wonder aloud, "What if it wasn't a guy? What if it was a woman?"

"Doubt it," Norris said. "Not an average woman, anyhow."

"There is no such thing," she said, "as an average woman."

O'Rannigan snorted.

"Every possibility should be explored, gentlemen," Church said again, just as sharply. O'Rannigan's smirk evaporated.

Dorothy asked, "What about an average man—or, for argument's sake, an average woman—with a big shovel or tool of some sort? Couldn't that do the trick?"

"Could be," Norris sighed. "There's just no way

to know for sure. But it'd have to be a very strong-willed man—or woman—to smash in MacGuffin's head with a shovel. It would take a score of blows. But as I said, it looks to me like it was done with just one blow with something really large and heavy."

"But you can't be sure about that?" O'Rannigan said hopefully.

"No, I can't, *Detective,*" Norris said peevishly. "But I wouldn't bet the farm against it either."

"I understand," Church said contemplatively. After a moment's thought, he spoke to Dorothy and Benchley, the phone still in his hand. "We need you to help us. Keep your ears open. You move in these circles, so let us know if you hear anything suspicious."

O'Rannigan snorted again, in disgust.

Dorothy said, "You want us to spy on our friends?"

O'Rannigan said, "If anyone you know had anything to do with the death of MacGuffin, he's no friend of yours."

Church leaned forward. "Say nothing about MacGuffin. We shall inform the press that his death was accidental. If it was murder, this will allow the murderer to lower his defenses and show himself."

"Or *herself,*" Dorothy said. "Dr. Norris said it could have been a strong-willed woman."

"Speaking of strong-willed women"—Norris'

voice turned sweeter—"how about that dinner tonight, Mrs. Parker?"

"How about you go jump off a bridge, Dr. Norris?" she said.

Chapter 35

Y ou should go," Benchley said to Dorothy.

"Go?" she said, pulling off her gloves. "Go where?"

"Out to dinner with that oddball Dr. Norris."

Benchley opened the door for her and they stepped into the familiar lobby of the Algonquin. She was glad Benchley couldn't see her face at the moment, because she couldn't believe he was suggesting this.

She stayed a step in front of him until she could gather her thoughts. She knew he wouldn't show his feelings for her (if indeed he had any). But to push her into the arms of that ghoulish Dr. Norris was not at all what she expected of her best friend.

She said, "Why in heaven's name should I go out to dinner with Norris the Necromaniac?"

"Oh, I'm sure he's not all that bad," Benchley said jovially as he helped her slide off her coat. "At least you'll get a few drinks and a good meal out of it."

She turned and looked at him. Was that what he thought of her? That she was nothing more than one of those women who would go out with a man for a few drinks and a nice meal at a restaurant? That she had no better offers?

"Sure," she said, her words dripping sarcasm.

"Any gal would be happy to go to dinner with a doctor who cuts up the dead all day. I'll ask him to dissect my steak for me. Sounds like an enchanting time."

But then the reality of her statement hit her. Who was she to turn down Dr. Norris? Despite the medical examiner's morbid occupation, he had seemed a quick-witted and pleasant enough gentleman.

Benchley smiled at her encouragingly. "There you are. You'll have a fine time."

A fine time. Well, tonight was Saturday night and she had no other offers, did she? Certainly not an evening at the theater with Benchley—or any other suitors for that matter.

And was it so smart to turn down a good restaurant meal? She had only about seventy-five cents in her purse, which had to cover lunch today and whatever she'd have for dinner tonight.

She sighed, sensing her options (or lack of them) close in around her. She had been feeling very bad about the sudden and mysterious death of MacGuffin, as though there might have been something she could have done to prevent it. And she was still sore about Midge MacGuffin's bestselling, yet blank, book. Now, with her own life looking so dreary, she was beginning to feel even worse. Maybe, by default, she *was* one of those women, after all.

With heavy steps, she entered the hotel's dining room.

"Mrs. Parker!" Alexander Woollcott trilled. "Your magical guest has been waiting anxiously for you."

Sitting next to Woollcott, looking perfectly at home at the Round Table, was Harry Houdini.

Houdini stood up as Dorothy came over to the Round Table. He was the only one who stood.

"Don't stand on ceremony," she said. "Certainly none of the other boys here do."

"*Tosh!*" Woollcott said. "Mrs. Parker *is* one of the boys here."

Nevertheless, she allowed Houdini to pull out her chair and she sat down. Despite his age, Houdini looked as fresh as his starched white monogrammed shirt with the gold *HH*. The late-night scramble through the alleys and the confrontation with MacGuffin hadn't seemed to affect him at all.

"It's a pleasant surprise to see you today," she said.

"I heard the news about the discovery of Ernie MacGuffin's dead body," Houdini said. "I hastened to locate you immediately. I imagined that I might find you here. And indeed I have."

From Houdini's other side, Woollcott leaned across, scolding her. "You've kept him waiting for nearly fifteen minutes, Mrs. Parker. Fortunately for you, Mr. Houdini has remarkable powers of patience, in addition to his amazing powers of prestidigitation."

Woollcott grinned desperately at Houdini, looking like a lapdog hoping for a crumb to fall from the table.

Dorothy smiled. "Yes, he's got tremendous powers for 'some rube,' doesn't he, Aleck?"

Woollcott reddened at his own words from the other night, but he recovered quickly. "I already made my apologies to Mr. Houdini about that. His marvelous disguise could fool his own mother, I'm sure."

Houdini blanched at this heedless mention of his beloved mother. He turned away from Woollcott (who realized he'd made some sort of blunder) toward Dorothy. Houdini quickly redirected the conversation back toward Ernie MacGuffin. "My mind finds it unthinkable that the man found dead in the street this morning is one and the same with the hale and hearty fellow we interrogated Halloween night," Houdini said.

Dorothy would never have described Mac-Guffin—who was as spindly as a scare-crow—as hale and hearty. But she knew what Houdini meant.

"Unthinkable is right," she said. "But we just came from the police. It's MacGuffin, for sure. He's dead for real this time."

Woollcott babbled, "We were all certainly

amazed when Mr. Houdini arrived. And then we were even more amazed when he told us the full, exciting story of how he single-handedly unmasked that unscrupulous phony psychic and that malefactor MacGuffin—"

"Put a sock in it, Aleck," Robert Sherwood said, and faced Dorothy. "What did the police say?"

She exchanged a quick glance with Benchley. Captain Church and Detective O'Rannigan had asked them to keep their ears open and their mouths closed about MacGuffin's death.

But everyone had questions.

Sherwood asked, "Did they tell you how he died?"

"Did they explain why he was found in Water Street, not in the river?" Houdini asked.

"Did anybody see anything?" George Kaufman asked.

"Was he murdered?" Woollcott asked.

Everyone went quiet.

Leave it to Woollcott to jump to the most sensational of explanations, Dorothy thought. Then again, it was the one she suspected as well.

She opened her mouth to speak, but Neysa McMein entered the dining room and rushed to the Round Table. Though she was an artist, Neysa rarely exhibited an 'artistic temperament.' She was usually as calm as the Dead Sea. But not today.

"I just happened to go by Cathcart's shop on my

way here," she said breathlessly. "He told me all about the decline in the value of MacGuffin's paintings—and his encounter with Mickey Finn."

Woollcott was perplexed. "The decline in value? Why would MacGuffin's paintings lose value? He was dead last week. He's still dead today. What's changed?"

Neysa found an empty chair next to Kaufman and plopped down. "MacGuffin's work has little intrinsic value. As art, it's nearly worthless. And as curiosity pieces or investments, their cachet is now gone—"

"Because no one thinks MacGuffin jumped from the bridge after all," Dorothy said.

Neysa nodded. "As a suicide, he was a tortured artist. But as a body in the gutter, he was just a bum."

Dorothy felt another pang of guilt at Neysa's words.

"Tut-tut," Woollcott said, waving his hand as though shooing a fly. "As I promised, my newspaper column this morning glorified the very painting in Benchley's possession. There's no way in all creation that its value can possibly decrease after the lauds I loaded on it."

Neysa looked at him sadly. "Actually, that article is not helping."

"Not helping?" Woollcott reddened.

"Not at all," Neysa said. "If anything, it's making things worse."

"What do you mean?" Woollcott huffed. "Explain yourself."

"Cathcart told me that art experts and critics who discuss these things wonder if your article was intended to inflate the price of the painting."

"Well, indeed it was," Woollcott said. "What's wrong with that?"

"What's wrong with that is that you've fanned the flames of destruction. You've accelerated the speed of its decline."

"How is that possible?" he said. "I wrote nothing but wonderful things about it."

"They think it's puffery," Houdini said. "I know all about that."

Woollcott blanched at Houdini's assessment of his work.

Neysa nodded. "They can see right through it. It put them on the scent, and now they're tearing into it. Overpraised. Overpriced and overvalued."

"Over and done with," Dorothy said morosely.

"Over the love of Pete!" Benchley said drolly, but Dorothy could hear the concern behind his words. "How much are they saying it's worth?"

"It's gone from five thousand when you bought it at auction down to twelve hundred on the street," Neysa said.

" 'On the street'?" Woollcott sneered.

"It's only a figure of speech," Neysa said.

"Just a minute," Dorothy said. "Cathcart told

305

us that he thought it was worth nineteen hundred, not twelve hundred. And Finn expected it to increase tenfold. He expects Mr. Benchley to repay him fifty thousand."

Houdini shook his head. "Fifty thousand for one painting by a nearly unknown contemporary artist? I've bought paintings by European masters for as much. But I wouldn't pay a fraction of that for one of MacGuffin's."

"You and the rest of the world," Benchley said, sinking in his chair.

"But if he was murdered—?" Houdini began.

"The police are saying it was accidental," Dorothy said, phrasing her words carefully.

"But if it *was* murder, the value of his work might indeed skyrocket again after all," Woollcott said, looking to Houdini for approval. "It certainly would be sensational."

Houdini nodded. Woollcott smiled.

"It's possible," Neysa agreed. "But it doesn't sound like much of a murder—if that's even what it was."

Dorothy and Benchley exchanged glances again. If MacGuffin's paintings skyrocketed in value, that would certainly get them out of a jam.

"Okay," she said, "let's say that MacGuffin was murdered, just for argument's sake. If so, who killed him?"

Woollcott threw up his hands. "Who knows? Who cares?"

"No one even knew he was alive," Sherwood said.

"That's not exactly true," Benchley said, his smile slowly returning. "A few people did."

"Who?" Neysa asked.

"Houdini and myself," Dorothy said.

"I think we can rule out you two," Sherwood said.

"MacGuffin's wife knew, of course," Dorothy said.

"Anyone else?" Sherwood asked.

"His mistress, Viola," she said.

"Is that it?"

"His lawyer, Snath," she said.

Kaufman frowned. "A man's wife, his mistress and his lawyer. Sounds like a divorce case, not a murder."

Houdini said, "But if they were the only people who knew he was alive, it must have been one of them."

"Great," Dorothy said sourly. "So now what do we do?"

As she spoke, Luigi the waiter appeared beside the Round Table.

Woollcott sniffed. "We do what we always do at times like these," he said, unfolding his napkin. "We order lunch."

Chapter 36

Late that afternoon, Dorothy was alone in her room. She couldn't stop thinking about Ernie MacGuffin. He was dead, unquestionably dead. It was no prank this time. Dr. Norris, with whom she was about to go on a date this evening, had been examining MacGuffin's body that very morning.

It gave her chills.

She put on her stockings and picked out a dress and a scarf. She powdered her face and sprayed on perfume—lots of perfume. (She feared Dr. Norris might smell of death, and she wanted to cover the smell.)

She tried to think about having a date, even if it was with Dr. Norris. . . .

But she couldn't shake the feeling of guilt. Ernie had begged for her help, and she turned her back on him. *I just want to pretend you're dead, too,* she had said. Now she didn't have to pretend.

But then again, she told herself, it was nobody's fault but his own. She had told him, *You made your bed, you lie in it.* Well, Ernie had dug his own grave, and now he was lying in that.

So she was glad for the distraction when she heard the knock on the door. She looked over at Woodrow Wilson, snoozing on the couch.

"You're some watchdog, Woody," she said.

The dog raised his head at his name, then plopped it down again.

Dorothy opened the door. Lucy Goosey stood in the hallway.

"Miss Goosey. What are you doing here?" Dorothy asked.

"Mickey sent me to give you a reminder. He wants his money."

"Oh, that paltry fifty grand. It nearly slipped my mind," Dorothy said with a casual wave of her hand. "Tell him I'll look through my sofa cushions and coat pockets, and I'll have that money for him in no time."

Lucy nodded but didn't answer. She gazed at Dorothy with a sort of disdainful curiosity, as though looking at a poisonous snake in a zoo's reptile house.

"Was there something else?" Dorothy asked.

Lucy seemed to be debating something in her mind. "I had a very nice evening with Mr. Benchley the other night at the auction. He's a sweetheart," she said.

Dorothy took a step forward. She couldn't hold her tongue. "Keep away from my Benchley."

Lucy didn't back away. "He's not yours."

"He's not yours either. Why are you bothering with him?"

"I'm not bothering with him."

"Like hell you're not."

"I'm not," Lucy said, and glanced at the floor.

"Not anymore anyway. I saw the way you look at him. I wanted to feel like that, that's all. I wanted what you have."

Dorothy was taken aback. "What *I* have? I don't have anything with Benchley."

But Dorothy knew what she had with Benchley. He made her feel like life was a party and she was the center of the party. But she didn't want to admit this to anyone, certainly not to some gangster's moll. Instead she said, "You already have a man."

Lucy folded her arms. "Mickey is his own man, not mine."

"Not yours? He dotes on you like a rich grandfather. Any girl should be so lucky."

"I know, I know. I have him on my arm, but I don't exactly have him here." She tapped a finger over her heart. "Not like you do with Benchley."

This was getting too personal, Dorothy thought. "Mr. Benchley is a married man. I would never do anything to disrupt that. I wouldn't steal another woman's husband."

"Married doesn't matter," Lucy said. "You think of him as yours."

So what if I do? Dorothy thought. But she said, "What's it to you?"

"If I were you, I wouldn't squander it. I wouldn't risk losing it. I'd make it grow."

Dorothy bit her lip. "I'm not sure I can do that. I'm not sure if I *want* to do that."

Lucy looked at her squarely. "Sure you do."

Again, so what if I do? But she said, "What of it?"

Now Lucy took a step forward. "When your chance comes, when you're alone together some sunny day, holding hands under a picture-postcard sky—or even on a smelly empty subway car or the dark backseat of some taxi—show him how you feel. Kiss him, damn it. Kiss him. Show him you're serious."

"Serious is the last word to describe how I feel about Mr. Benchley. Or how he feels about me," Dorothy said. "I could never do that. It would simply ruin our friendship."

"He's devoted to you, you know. Call it friendship or something else, he's devoted to you."

Dorothy sighed. "And I don't want to spoil that."

"It'll spoil your life if you don't do something about it. You can't be that close to a man for so long without something happening. Eventually it'll poison your relationship. One day, you have to show him how you feel."

"Ridiculous," Dorothy said. *But in truth, maybe it wasn't so ridiculous after all.*

"Do you want to live your whole life like someone in an audience, watching life go by without you playing a part in it? Do you want to end up a shriveled, lonely old lady, never having taken your chance?"

A door opened down the hallway. Mrs. Volney, the old nosybody, peeked her silver head out. *Speaking of shriveled, lonely old ladies . . .*

"Good evening to you, Mrs. Parker," the elderly woman said in her threadbare voice. "I heard a disturbance. Is everything quite all right?"

Is everything all right? Dorothy thought, exasperated. *I feel responsible for the death of a third-rate painter. I'm blackballed from my favorite speakeasy as well as every other drinking hole in the city. I have to write a book review for a book with no words in it—when I can't even get a decent contract for my own actual book with actual words in it. Not to mention, Mr. Benchley and I owe a gangster fifty thousand dollars. And on top of that, I'm getting lonely-hearts advice from the gangster's girlfriend.*

But Lucy Goosey was already walking the other way along the corridor, toward the elevator.

"You bet, ma'am," Dorothy said to the old lady. "Everything is just jake."

Chapter 37

Dorothy and Dr. Norris entered through the heavy oak door of the Mansion nightclub. She had never been inside before. Dr. Norris flashed his member's card at the front desk.

A palatial, high-ceilinged rotunda served as the entrance hall. A dignified attendant in a military-style uniform led them up a broad, graceful staircase to a circular barroom with a domed ceiling. A small orchestra of black musicians dressed in immaculate white tuxedos played a quick, up-beat number. (Dorothy spotted the name "Hiram Higginbotham and the Harlem Horns.") But the orchestra was largely ignored by the well-to-do gentlemen and ladies, who brandished glasses of top-shelf whiskey or brandy and puffed carelessly on fifty-cent cigars and Turkish cigarettes.

The attendant led Dorothy and Dr. Norris through the barroom to the quieter but more spacious dining room and showed them to a table for two laid with linen, silver and crystal.

Once they were seated, Dr. Norris immediately ordered a bottle of a newly imported champagne that Dorothy had never heard of before. She felt as though she was dining at Versailles.

When the wine steward left, Norris smiled curiously at Dorothy. "We're much the same, you and I. Wouldn't you agree?"

"We're much the same?" She looked him over—his deep-set eyes, his perfectly groomed goatee, his fashionable clothes, his easygoing affluence. . . . But she wasn't going to be swept away by his extravagant manner or the opulence of the restaurant's surroundings. "How do you figure we're the same? Because we both smell? Me, like perfume. You, like disinfectant?"

"Joke if you like, but I feel we *are* much the same."

"I do like," she said. "But since you're paying the tab, you might as well explain yourself."

An efficient waiter brought the champagne in a bucket stand filled with ice. He showed the bottle to Dr. Norris, who nodded his approval, and then deftly popped the cork and quickly filled a pair of wide-mouthed champagne glasses.

Dorothy accepted the glass greedily. But when she looked over the rim to see Dr. Norris—and not Benchley—gazing back at her . . . well, drinking didn't seem like such fun now.

She took a big sip anyway. She felt she'd need it to get through the evening. "So you were saying, we're the same?"

He smiled. "In many ways, we are. We both work in solitude. You at your typewriter and me at my autopsy table. We both dissect—me with bodies, you with thoughts and words and sentences. We both dig deep for the underlying meaning, the hidden truth. We both aim for the heart of the matter."

"The heart? Don't be so literal. Just because I ponder heartache and you investigate heart attack, don't think we automatically have something in common."

"But we do." He raised his glass to her. "We both wear our hearts on our sleeves. You, figuratively. Me, literally."

She looked at his bleached white shirt cuffs as he sipped from his glass. No atrial blood there, thank goodness. She had anticipated that he'd be creepy. But she didn't expect him to be so amorous, too.

"More champagne?" he asked, and filled her glass without waiting for an answer.

"Don't mind if I do. Keep 'em coming. That's at least one thing we have in common." They clinked glasses and sipped.

"I like you," he said, wagging his finger at her. "You're vivacious and audacious."

"Oh, you old softie, I bet you say that to all the cadavers."

Now the champagne was going down nicely. She held out her glass.

"Another?" he asked.

"Your diagnosis is correct, Doctor."

He watched her drink it, simply enjoying her presence. "I'm not merely a medical examiner, you know. I'm a student of the human condition."

"The human condition? As long as the human is in inert condition." She drained her glass. "Me, I prefer the intoxicated condition."

"You have me all wrong. In contrast to my work, I love life. I love fine restaurants. I live for the opera. I adore all that is transcendent. A day of death brings me to life at night."

"Hmm, which one of us is the poet now?"

"Exactly. My work demands that the poet in me emerge when I'm not at one of my tables."

"I'm not interested in seeing your poet emerge, thank you very much."

"What are you interested in seeing?" He reached for her hand.

"Oh dear." She should have expected as much. She put her glass down. She didn't feel like drinking anymore.

What was she doing here with this man? Was she using him just to get a few drinks and a fancy dinner? Or was she really just looking for a distraction, a way to occupy the evening?

She felt like a heel. She didn't want to be here with this man. She should be spending the evening with Benchley, doing nothing special. Just clowning around.

Damn that Lucy Goosey! She had put these thoughts into Dorothy's head. Now they felt stuck there for good.

Dr. Norris stood up gallantly. "Shall we dance?"

"Not interested." She looked away. "Go find some other warm body."

He was crestfallen. He dropped back into his seat. "Well, you've made yourself abundantly clear."

"Now, don't take it like that," she said. *Great. Now he was going to pout.*

"How else can I take it? Oh, you've no idea what it's like, the way women look at you when you tell them what you do for a living."

"Don't I?" She laughed. "Like being a poet is honorable employment? You wouldn't believe the looks I get. I may as well say I'm the tooth fairy. Men roll their eyes so far back in their heads, they can look at their own tiny brains."

He laughed. "So, do you still think we have nothing in common?"

Before long the evening was going better, now that they had come clean and decided to be friendly. Dorothy was no longer unsociable and Norris was no longer pitching woo. The lights had dimmed. The band had taken five. The dining room had quieted down.

Dr. Norris was telling her tales of the early days of the coroner system in New York. "Before my time, coroners were paid a handsome fee for every body they brought in. So frequently, they'd arrive on the scene simultaneously, and a brawl would ensue over who could lay claim to the corpse."

"Highly professional," she said.

Norris smiled ruefully. "On one particular occasion, a body was found floating in the East River. Coroners from Brooklyn and Manhattan paddled out in rowboats to grab it up. They fought over the body using their oars as clubs, with a crowd of people cheering and jeering from the shore. One of the coroners fell into the water, and the other one grabbed the body and hauled it into his boat."

"They were like pirates," she said. "Only the booty was the body."

"Indeed. Needless to say, that kind of reprehensible behavior no longer occurs with our modern medical examiner system of today. We're paid an annual salary, not a commission for each body."

Dorothy steered the conversation toward the death of Ernie MacGuffin. She wanted to get Norris' insight on whether MacGuffin was actually murdered, and if so, how—and by whom.

"Funny you should ask," Norris said. "Do you know what today is?"

"Saturday?"

"It's also November second, the Mexican Day of the Dead, Día de los Muertos."

"Yes, that *is* funny. You got a hell of a sense of humor, Doc. I'd think every day is the Day of the Dead for you."

"It's the day to pay honor to the deceased."

Norris raised his glass. "So—to Ernie MacGuffin! May he rest in peace."

"To Ernie," Dorothy said, clinking his glass, feeling the guilt return. "We lift our glass to a pain in the ass." She swallowed the champagne in two gulps.

"*De mortuis nil nisi bonum dicendum est*," Norris said with an air of superiority. " 'Of the dead, say nothing but good.' "

"Enough of the pig Latin. Just tell me, what's your professional opinion? Was he murdered?"

Norris set down his glass. "As I said before, I can't be sure how he died. I wasn't at the scene. It was a rainy morning. There's very little evidence to say it *wasn't* some sort of accident."

"But—?"

"But . . ." he said thoughtfully. "It doesn't exactly look like any sort of accident I've seen before."

"When Captain Church had you on the phone this morning, you were the one who said the word *murder*."

Norris didn't answer directly. "I find it odd. If it *was* murder, it's a very odd sort of murder. No weapon. No witnesses that we know of. Nothing, except that his head was smashed in by something like a large block of concrete, which is a very unusual and rather cumbersome way to murder someone."

"But it could have happened?"

He laughed. "Mrs. Parker, *anything* could have happened. That's what I'm trying to tell you. There could be some random explanation that we can't account for."

"Then why did you say *murder* in the first place, if you still think it might be an accident?"

He leaned forward. "Because my gut tells me it wasn't an accident."

She let that sink in a minute. "So now what? Who did it? How?"

"I don't know how." He paused to think. "But as for *who* may have done such a thing . . . If I were the police, I'd look for a tall, strong man."

She instantly thought of Snath. "Why tall?"

"The culprit, assuming it was murder, smashed in the parietal portion of the cranium—the top and back of MacGuffin's skull. It only stands to reason that the person was as tall as or taller than MacGuffin and could hit him on top of the head from behind." His eyes narrowed. "Do you have someone in mind?"

"I do. What should I do?"

"Tell the police."

She frowned at the thought. The police seemed ineffectual to her. "What will they do?"

"Follow the suspect—or suspects."

"Follow the suspects? That's all?"

"Certainly," he said. "What do you think the police do? They have no magic. They knock on doors and ask if anyone saw anything. They shake down sources. They follow people around. They bring them in for questioning. That's about it."

"They don't look for clues?"

"Not like Sherlock Holmes—not much, at any rate. Usually they don't exactly need to. The majority of murders are committed by one spouse getting furious and killing the other spouse. The police come in and find the wife crying at the kitchen table, her husband right there on the floor with the carving knife sticking out of him. Mystery solved."

"And the minority of murders?"

"Nine out of ten of those, it's something like a bar fight. One fellow insults another fellow's baseball team or something. The insults lead to shouting. Shouting leads to punches. Punches lead to a knife or a gun. Next thing you know, one of them is dead on the sidewalk. There's twenty or thirty witnesses, but of course none of them agree. Nevertheless, it's no great mystery."

"You said nine out of ten. What about the one out of ten? Who did that one?"

He gulped his champagne. "The hell if I know. Those are the ones that keep the captains and the detectives up at night." He emptied the rest of the bottle into her glass. "Here, let's have another drink, and let's put an end to this dismal conversation."

Chapter 38

Dorothy walked home alone that night. She turned down Dr. Norris' offer to take her back to the Algonquin. She'd had enough chitchat with Norris—and she'd had more than enough champagne. She needed to clear her head in the cool night air. And, going down Sixth Avenue, the 'Gonk was only a few short blocks away.

The evening with Norris turned out to be fun, after all. Well, perhaps not fun, but at least enjoyable. She didn't plan to go out with him ever again, although she had given him an innocent peck on the cheek when they said good-bye. She didn't care if he might misinterpret it—she wanted to end the night on a positive note. And, in the end, she truly enjoyed his company and appreciated his attention.

She turned the corner from Fifth Avenue—still rather lively even at one in the morning—and strolled down the much quieter Forty-fourth Street. Meanwhile, her thoughts turned to Benchley.

Why did Benchley encourage her to go out with Dr. Norris? Was he tiring of her? Did he not care about her? Or was this *his way* of caring, to encourage her to find some sort of romance?

And what about what Lucy Goosey had said? Show Benchley how she feels, under some picture-postcard sky? Or not even wait until the perfect moment, but grab him and kiss him at the first quiet minute they have alone? Could she— *should she*—do such a thing?

These thoughts, and the champagne, filled her mind—so much so that she didn't notice the car creeping up in the street beside her.

"Lady!" the driver yelled.

She jumped. She couldn't see the man's face in the darkness, but his voice was deep, rough and unfamiliar. Instinct (bred by a lifetime of city living) told her to keep walking—fast.

"Stop, damn it!" the man said as the car prowled along beside her. "I got something for you."

She turned around and hurried back the way she had come, to Fifth Avenue. The car—by now she realized it was a taxi—came to a quick stop, then started in reverse.

"Get back here, you stupid broad!" the driver's deep voice yelled.

She reached Fifth and she heard the taxi's brakes scream. She risked a glance over her shoulder and saw that the car had stopped abruptly. The driver got out. She could see his figure outlined by the passing headlights. He was a big, heavyset man.

She remembered how Dr. Norris described MacGuffin's potential murderer: *a tall, strong man.*

Dorothy kept moving, faster now. But she could

hear the man's heavy footsteps a few paces behind her.

"Where do you think you're going, lady?" he snarled. He was getting closer. "I said wait!"

She tried to run, but her shoes slowed her down. *Why did she wear these high-heeled pumps?* She was short already; did her feet—and maybe her life—have to suffer for it, too?

She had to find a crowd. She'd be safe among people.

Behind her, the man's breath was coming in gasps. He may have been big and strong, but he was no athlete. Still, he was coming nearer. Soon she'd be within his grasp.

Up ahead, bright light from a shop window spilled onto the sidewalk. Dorothy could smell baking pastry and powdered sugar. A doughnut shop. Neon flashed: OPEN 24 HRS.

The man's ragged breathing and heavy footsteps were right behind her now. She grabbed the door handle and flung open the door. She flew inside. Two workers, in folded white paper hats and faces dusted in flour, turned to look at her.

"Help," she gasped. "A man is trying to attack me!"

But then the big man burst through the door, his barrel chest rising and falling, his face coated in sweat. He was older than she had expected—quite a bit older. And fatter, too. Dorothy had seen him somewhere before, but she couldn't place where.

"Got you!" he wheezed. He lowered his head and lumbered at her. He thrust out his hand toward her. Dorothy flinched and covered her face.

But nothing happened. Slowly, she lowered her hands.

The man stood there, catching his breath. In his hand was a long piece of rich wool cloth. "Your scarf! Just dropped off a guy . . . Doctor . . . Paid me five bucks to track back and find you . . . Return it . . . Left it at the restaurant."

"Oh," she said, taking the scarf. She realized her heart was pounding. She had been afraid—afraid for her life.

The bakers behind the counter stared wide-eyed at her and the cabdriver.

She didn't know what to say to the big old man. "Can I offer you a doughnut?"

The driver looked up. Recognition dawned on his flushed face. "It's you! That crazy lady! You were in my cab a week ago."

Ohhhh! Now she recognized him, too.

He wheezed, "I drove you and some other lunatic to the Brooklyn Bridge. We was chased by another crazy lady and her devil kid!" The cabbie recoiled, holding up his hands. "Get away from me. Just leave me alone!"

He retreated, nearly crashing through the door as he made his escape.

She turned and looked innocently at the bakers.

325

"I guess he doesn't like doughnuts," she said. "And he thinks *I'm* crazy?"

Back out on the dark sidewalk, she held the scarf to her beating chest. She tried to calm herself down.

Why had she panicked? Was it the stress of the past few days? Was it all the talk of death? Or was it just too much champagne? She could already feel a headache coming on.

She knew this much: She couldn't keep on like this. She had to do something.

Chapter 39

Y ou want us to follow the *suspects?*" Benchley said in a prickly mood. "Mrs. Parker, it's nine o'clock on a Sunday morning. No self-respecting suspect is even awake at this hour!"

Why should he be so cranky? Dorothy wondered. Just because he had to ride in on the early train from the suburbs on a Sunday, that didn't give him the right to be so irritable. After all, she was the one with the hangover and raging headache.

She wouldn't touch another drop of champagne until New Year's Eve; that was for sure. It figured that she would go for more than a week of imposed teetotaling, and then, after a one-night binge, want to swear off the hooch for the foreseeable future.

Robert Sherwood yawned and stretched. "Mrs. Parker, what makes you so sure that MacGuffin was actually murdered?"

It was just the three of them again in the editorial office of *Vanity Fair*. She had called them to meet with her there and form some kind of plan.

"Because MacGuffin is simply not the type to commit suicide. I know that for sure now. Also, I feel in my gut that it was no accident. And Dr. Norris agrees with me on that point."

"And how is the good doctor?" Benchley asked,

an unusual tension in his voice. "How was the fancy date last night?"

Sherwood sat up at this. "A date?"

Dorothy lit a cigarette and shook the flame out of the match. "It was no date. We talked mostly of MacGuffin. Norris agreed that he was likely murdered."

"Not a date?" Benchley said. "Was it just the two of you? Did he buy you dinner? Were there drinks? And candlelight?"

"Yes. Yes. Yes. And yes," she said. "If you must know, it started off as a date, but we ended the night as friends."

Benchley and Sherwood exchanged a knowing glance and nodded.

"Can we *please* just get back to talking about who killed Ernie MacGuffin?" she said.

"Of course." Benchley pulled out his pipe and tobacco. "But what's the mystery? Without a doubt it was Snath, his lawyer. Snath was the only one who could have done it."

"What makes you so sure about Snath?" Sherwood stood and put a kettle on an electric hot plate. "By the way, anyone for a cup of tea?"

"Tea for me," Dorothy said. "As for Snath—"

"No tea for him," Benchley said. "He drinks only engine oil."

She ignored him. "Snath is the only one tall enough and strong enough to have smashed in the top of Ernie's head."

"The only one?" Sherwood repeated. "The other suspects are his wife and his mistress?"

"They're the only ones who knew Ernie was alive," she said.

Benchley leaned back in his chair, a cloud of smoke enveloping him as he pulled on his pipe. "If one may take this seriously for a moment—"

"But only for a moment, Mr. Benchley," Sherwood said.

"It occurs to me," Benchley continued, "that his wife, Midge, is tall enough to strike the back of Ernie's head. If memory serves, she even was an inch or two taller than he was. Perhaps—"

"Perhaps nothing," Dorothy said. "Midge is as hard and indifferent as a statue. Certainly she could have done it . . . somehow."

"Somehow?" Sherwood said.

"Dr. Norris thinks that Ernie died by a single hard blow to the back of his head. He suggested he was hit with something like a large block of concrete."

"But there was no such thing where Ernie was found," Benchley explained to Sherwood.

"Still," she said, "Norris also said there was some kind of construction site nearby. Perhaps Midge somehow used a heavy tool or a cinder block to clock Ernie on the head, and then tossed it back over the fence—or something."

"From what little I know of Midge," Sherwood said, "she doesn't seem the type to do such a thing."

"I didn't think she was the type to help Ernie stage his own fake suicide," Dorothy said. "But now I know that she did just that. Who knows what, if anything, is going on behind that porcelain facade?"

Sherwood handed Dorothy a cup of tea. "And the mistress?"

"She seems even less likely to do such an atrocious act," Benchley said.

"Why?" Dorothy asked. "Just because she's a sweet young thing who takes her clothes off for money?"

Benchley smiled. "That may be part of it. But I was actually thinking she couldn't have done it because she's neither tall nor strong."

"But Viola *is* willing to bend or break the law," she said. "She had no compunction against fleecing gullible dupes and coercing Ernie into dropping by for a fake phantasmic visit. She doesn't exactly have the moral fiber of a Sunday school teacher."

"That doesn't mean she killed him," Benchley said. "After all, he was putting money in her pocket."

"And wasn't he doing the same for Midge?" Sherwood said to Dorothy. "The money Ernie was making *after* his death allowed her to live in the lap of luxury—or at least on the kneecaps of comfort."

That was absolutely true, Dorothy realized. She

slumped in her chair. "Come to think of it, that goes double for Snath," she said glumly. "To hear Ernie tell it, Snath was working him to the bone to create more and more 'posthumous' paintings."

Indeed, on Halloween night, Ernie had begged her to help him out of the corner he had quite literally painted himself into—to help him out of the snare in which Snath had him trapped.

Sherwood sipped his tea. "So we have three suspects but absolutely no motive. If anything, each of them wanted him *alive,* not dead. Alive, he could continue to churn out paintings that brought in money. Dead, he was of no use to them whatsoever."

"True enough," Benchley said. "Why would any of them want to kill the goose that lays the golden eggs?"

Dorothy gulped her tea. "So, of the three, which of them *did* want Ernie's goose cooked?"

Dorothy came back to the decision that had brought them here in the first place. "We need to follow them."

"But why, Mrs. Parker?" Benchley said.

She didn't want to admit that Norris had put the idea into her head. "Because that's what the cops do."

"So let them do it," Benchley said.

"We can't afford to, remember? Who knows how long they'll take."

Benchley nodded, clearly remembering the deadline that Mickey Finn had set.

"If we do follow them, how do we go about it?" Sherwood asked.

"We'll split up," she said. "There's three of them and three of us. One per customer."

"Won't they recognize us?" Benchley said.

Dorothy would not wear a costume again, as Houdini had required her to do.

"We'll each follow the suspect who may recognize us the least," she said. "Both Midge and Viola probably know me too well—after I scolded Midge and set Viola's wig on fire. So I had better follow Snath."

Benchley yanked the pipe out of his mouth. "You can't follow him alone. He's a hothead. What if he's dangerous? Perhaps—"

Perhaps we should follow him together, was what he was thinking, Dorothy knew. But Benchley didn't come out and say it.

"Not to worry, Fred," she said. "I'll get Houdini to go with me."

"Houdini?" he said. "The man is in his fifties."

"And he's as strong as a gorilla and as quick as a cobra."

"And he smells like a zoo. But will he protect you?"

Dorothy was touched by his concern. "Oh, Fred, I don't need that much protecting. Don't be worried."

Benchley frowned. "I'm not worried, Mrs. Parker. And stop calling me Fred."

"Then worry about yourself, Mr. Benchley, because you'll have to follow Midge." She didn't want him following that hotsy-totsy phony spiritualist. "Mr. Sherwood, *you* find and follow Viola."

Sherwood perked up. "The nude artist's model? I'm on top of her. You can count on me." He stood up immediately.

The door opened and their boss, Frank Crowninshield, entered. As usual, he was dressed with Old World dignity in his Sunday best. "What are you young whelps doing in the office on the weekend? Certainly you're not working."

"Certainly not," Benchley said. "Just enjoying a nice cup of tea."

Crowninshield folded his arms. "As I've said before, this is not your private clubhouse. This office is a place of work and business, in a building that's a cathedral of editorial craftsmanship. I'm consternated at your laissez-faire attitude."

As he spoke, Dorothy, Benchley and Sherwood grabbed their coats. "You're what?" she asked.

Crowninshield's impeccable white mustache twitched with frustration. "I'm consternated, that's what!"

"Go see your doctor." She pushed him into his private office. "And eat more roughage."

She closed his office door. They hurried out into the hallway and waited for the elevator. When it arrived, Sherwood stepped in but Dorothy hesitated, laying a hand on Benchley's arm.

"Going my way?" Sherwood said.

"We'll take the next one," she said. "Let's meet at the 'Gonk around dinnertime. Good luck, and be careful."

Sherwood tipped his hat as the elevator doors closed.

Alone in the corridor, Dorothy turned to Benchley.

"Something the matter?" he asked.

"It's very rare to see you upset," she said. "You're not really angry with me, are you?"

He smiled and spoke tenderly, looking at her with those sweet, merry eyes. "Dottie dear, I've never been angry with you in my entire life." Then he gave her a quick kiss on the forehead. "Now, enough of this. Let's get going."

A kiss on the forehead? What the hell did that mean?

They waited for the next elevator to arrive. She was silent and thoughtful as they descended to the lobby.

Chapter 40

Robert Sherwood had never met an artist who actually wore a beret.

Sherwood stood at the door of the Hudson River School of Art facing the beret-wearing man. To match the black beret, the man also had on a stained, black turtleneck sweater. A thin, vile-smelling cigarette dangled from his dry lips. He held a broom in one hand.

"Viola the model, huh?" the man said in response to Sherwood's question. "Sorry, pal—she's no longer here."

"No longer? What do you mean? Did something happen to her?"

"Are you pulling my leg? Don't you read the news?"

"No, I don't bother. Friends of mine write it. They usually just tell me."

The man looked askance at Sherwood, not sure whether to take him seriously. "Well, Viola was running a bogus spiritualism thing. It turned out to be a big sham."

"Yes, a séance. I've heard as much."

"She was working it with her mother and with Ernie MacGuffin. Have you heard of *him?*"

"Yes. I knew him."

"Yeah, we all knew him around here," the man said. "When we found out Viola was running a fraud voodoo operation, we fired her. And now Ernie is found dead. Not suicide, but dead just the same. If we'd known this before, we would have done more than fire Viola."

"Done more?" Sherwood asked. "Do you think Viola had something to do with Ernie's death?"

"She knew he was alive, didn't she? Then her phony operation gets exposed, and before that news is hardly even out, Ernie turns up dead." The man narrowed his eyes. "His whole suicide was a sham, see? So to answer your question—yeah, I think Viola had something to do with it."

"Do you know where I can find her?"

He nodded, a knowing look on his face. "Try the Peek-a-Boo Revue, at the Spotlight Theater."

"The Peek-a-Boo Revue? You mean—"

"Yeah, she's strutting her stuff again. It was what she was doing before she became an artist's model here." He plucked the cigarette from his bottom lip and spat on the sidewalk. "What else is she good for?"

Sherwood checked his pocket watch. "It's early yet. Do you know where I can find her right now?"

"Try her mother's. She lives here in the Village, off Wooster Street." The man gave Sherwood the exact address.

"Thanks." Sherwood extended his hand. "You know, I don't think I've ever met an artist who actually wore a beret."

"Artist?" The man dropped Sherwood's hand. "I'm no artist. I'm the janitor!"

He slammed the door in Sherwood's face.

"Mrs. Parker!" Houdini shouted from somewhere within the jungle of books and papers. For every bookcase in the room, there were also a half dozen chest-high stacks of books piled on the floor. On top of all these were papers, pamphlets and news clippings overflowing like palm leaves. "What brings you here?"

Dorothy called out, "Your wife, Sacagawea, brought me here. And now she'll have to lead me through this untamed wilderness to find you in person."

Dorothy and Houdini's wife—who had introduced herself as Bess—had just climbed the stairs to the attic of Houdini's large town house. Moments earlier, when Dorothy had arrived and introduced herself, Bess had warned her about venturing into Houdini's overstuffed attic library. Now Dorothy understood what Bess had meant.

They weaved through the forest of books and papers and eventually found Houdini in a corner of the library. He sat on the edge of a leather-backed swivel chair, hunched over a very messy desk. He took off his half-moon reading glasses and stood to welcome them, knocking over a pile of books in the process.

"Good morning, Mrs. Parker. Even in my wildest imagination, I didn't expect you to come calling. What can I do for you?"

"Are you looking for something to do today?"

Houdini glanced, with a concerned expression, at the pile of papers and scrapbooks on his desk. "I really do have so much to do. . . ."

Bess chided him. "My love, no one but yourself is compelling you to put your library in order. It's Sunday, a day of rest for most people. Give yourself the day off." She turned to Dorothy. "He has the largest collection of books and papers on magic and illusion in the world, as well as the largest collection on the dramatic arts this side of Harvard."

Houdini said, "And it will never get organized, my love, if I don't do it." He turned to Dorothy dismissively. "Just what type of outing do you have in mind, Mrs. Parker? A carriage ride? A visit to the museums? A stroll in the park?"

Dorothy shook her head. "Adventure. Danger. Excitement. Maybe we'll stop for a nice lunch."

Houdini's mesmerizing eyes lit up. "I'll get my coat!"

He raced out of the jam-packed room, a flutter of papers flying in his wake.

"Bess! Tell Henry to bring the Rolls around!" Houdini yelled as he clambered down the stairs. "Well, come on, Mrs. Parker. Let's be on with it!"

338

• • •

Across the street from Midge MacGuffin's house, Benchley stood leaning against a tree. He watched her front window. For the second time in ten minutes, Midge appeared in the window and looked nervously up and down the street. Both times, Benchley thought Midge would notice him looking at her. But she didn't. She had her eyes out for someone else.

What is she up to? Benchley wondered. Something did not seem right.

It was a quiet street of modest little town houses, and Benchley felt rather conspicuous just standing against a tree with no business being there. What would he say if anyone bothered to ask him why he was loitering around? He tried to occupy his thoughts with an answer. So far, he had nothing.

A few minutes later, the front door opened. Midge stepped halfway out. She had her coat on. Again she looked both up and down the street. This time, she did glance at Benchley. He pulled down the brim of his hat, but she was already back inside, the door closed.

He didn't think she had paid any attention to him. She had glanced at him, realized he wasn't whom she was looking for, and gone back inside.

At least that was what he hoped had happened. It was possible that she had seen him, recognized him, and quickly retreated into her house. He didn't think so . . . but he couldn't be sure.

Now he really felt conspicuous. He pulled out his pipe, filled the bowl (and spilled half of his tobacco in his haste) and tried desperately to light it. A man standing around smoking a pipe might not seem quite so suspicious. Why *wouldn't* a man stop on a nice quiet street and have a pleasant little smoke? Happens all the time, right?

"Hello," a high-pitched voice said. "What are you doing here?"

Benchley, startled, spilled the rest of his tobacco. He turned quickly. He looked down to see a very young girl with a miniature poodle.

"Who are you?" she asked. "What are you doing here?"

Benchley smiled. Without thinking, he answered, "I'm the tooth fairy. Just taking a break."

She was befuddled. "Taking a break? The tooth fairy takes breaks?"

What a sweet little cherub, Benchley thought. "Yes, indeed, I'm very busy. Why, I'm taking a tooth from every child on this block."

The little girl's eyes went wide in alarm. Her hands flew to her mouth. "Don't take my teeth. Don't take any of my teeth!"

The poodle growled at Benchley, baring its sharp, tiny fangs. The little girl spun around and yelled at the top of her voice. "*Mommy!* He's going to take my teeth! He just said so!"

Benchley looked up to see a stern-faced woman

pushing a baby carriage. The woman's expression went from stern to threatening. "He said *what?*"

The little girl began to sob. The dog was now yapping, darting back and forth at Benchley's feet. The carriage jiggled on its own; the baby inside was stirring. Then it let loose a piercing wail.

Well, Benchley thought as he backed away, *so much for being inconspicuous.*

Robert Sherwood found the dingy street and soon knocked at the door of Viola's mother's house.

The door flew open. An enormous, broad-shouldered woman filled the threshold. The woman wore an old cotton robe sprinkled with coffee stains. Sherwood was taken aback. The woman's hair was askew—until he realized it was a wig.

"Who are you?" she spat. Before Sherwood could answer, she ranted, "Another dissatisfied customer? Well, get out! No refunds! It's all over with. Or don't you read the news?"

Sherwood pulled himself up to every inch of his six-foot-seven height. He wouldn't be intimidated by this woman—no matter how intimidating she was.

"No, I don't bother to read the news," he said, using the same retort he gave to the janitor at the art school. "Friends of mine write it. They usually just tell me."

The woman took a deep breath. She seemed to

expand to twice her size. "So you're one of those bloodsucking reporters? I've half a mind to beat you into a bloody pulp for the way you've raked my little princess over the coals."

Sherwood instinctively stepped back. He almost expected her to roll up her sleeves and display a pair of muscled, tattooed forearms.

He raised his hands as if to calm her down. "Your little princess—that's who I'm looking for. I just want to see Viola."

"Oh, another one of those guys!" The big woman rolled her eyes. Then she pointed a thick, accusing finger at Sherwood. "If you want to see my daughter disgrace herself, and forget every lesson I've ever taught her about how to act like a proper lady, you go right ahead down to that flea-bitten theater and you pay for a ticket like all the other perverts!"

She slammed the door so hard that the force of it shoved Sherwood backward. For a second, he thought the door might crack and splinter to bits. He stood dumbfounded for just a moment, then turned quickly to leave.

Mrs. Parker was right, after all, he thought. *Maybe the murderer was a woman. Certainly a woman as big and as angry as Viola's mother could have smashed in Ernie's head.* Right after Sherwood looked in on Viola at the Peek-a-Boo Theater, he'd have to give Dorothy an earful about this.

• • •

Up the street from Abraham Snath's law office, Dorothy Parker and Harry Houdini sat waiting in the back of his Rolls-Royce. They had driven by the dismal building, and Dorothy saw the sign posted on the door announcing another auction of MacGuffin's art at "rock bottom" prices. The auction was scheduled to begin at eleven o'clock, but it wasn't quite time yet. So Dorothy and Houdini decided to wait in the comfort of the Rolls.

Houdini was relating a story of his earlier days, how he would drum up interest in each town he visited on his tours. He explained how he would be tied into a straitjacket and suspended upside down ten stories above the street. The stunt would draw so many people that traffic would come to a complete standstill.

"The easiest way to attract a crowd," he said, "is to let it be known that at a given time and a given place, someone is going to attempt something that, in the event of failure, will mean sudden death."

Dorothy listened halfheartedly, gazing out the window. She watched a mounted policeman go by. His chestnut brown horse ambled along the street, in no rush whatsoever.

After a thoughtful moment, she turned to Houdini, interrupting him. "I know how you made that horse disappear!"

"Horse?" he asked, annoyed at the interruption. "What horse?"

"At the professional football game. You made a mounted policeman's Clydesdale disappear. I know how you did it!"

He laughed scornfully and playfully slapped her knee. "Like fun you do, you silly girl."

She didn't like being treated like a *silly girl*. "How much do you want to bet?"

"Bet?" He laughed.

"Are you a gambling man?"

He stopped laughing. "I've been known to make a wager on occasion."

"Then how much do you want to bet I know how you did that disappearing trick?"

Now he started to get annoyed. "Impossible. Don't toy with me."

"Never," she said innocently. "I'm as serious as a heart attack. How much?"

"No one knows how I do my tricks. Not even my wife, and she used to be my assistant!"

"Then what do you have to lose? Five bucks? Ten bucks?"

He turned and stared ahead. "Impossible."

"A hundred? Five hundred?" she asked. "Five hundred bucks says I know how you did that trick."

He looked at her a moment, his expression as hard as stone. "Fine. Go ahead, tell me."

She stuck out her hand and he eventually shook it.

"You faked it," she said.

He frowned. "Of course I faked it. It's a trick."

"I mean, the whole thing was a fake. The horse, the policeman, the stage."

He smiled slyly. "I assure you, the horse was quite real."

"But it wasn't a police horse; it was a plant. What was it, a circus horse? A trained horse used in a vaudeville show?"

His mouth tightened. She'd gotten it right, she knew.

"And the policeman—he was a plant, too," she continued. "Let me guess: He and the horse worked together in vaudeville. The horse did tricks—counting numbers and stomping his hoof, right?"

"You haven't figured it out," Houdini grumbled. "You haven't explained my trick at all."

"Onstage, you raised a box around the horse. Inside the box, the floor of the stage lowers—it's a ramp. The horse is trained to go down the ramp and hide under the stage."

Houdini's voice was tight. "There was no room under the stage. And you saw for yourself that the policeman looked and didn't find the horse there."

"Oh, right," she said. "The policeman jumped off the stage, looked underneath it and threw up his hands like the horse wasn't there."

"Precisely."

"Only the horse *was* there! As I said, the

345

policeman was an actor, and so was the horse. The horse was trained to crouch down in such a small space. And the phony cop only pretended he didn't see the horse."

"Absurd!" Houdini's breath came in quick bursts. "That's buffoonery, not magic. I assure you that was a real police horse and a real policeman. What devil would possess you to say anything to the contrary?"

She smiled and spoke softly. "Did you see that mounted policeman who just went by? He was riding a small chestnut horse."

"So?"

"So, the New York City Mounted Police doesn't use Clydesdales. I just realized I've never seen even one."

"That doesn't prove—"

Dorothy rolled down the window. "Officer! Officer! Please help!"

Half a block away, the policeman stopped, turned his horse around and cantered back to the Rolls-Royce.

"This is absolutely unnecessary." Houdini glowered.

"What's that smell?" she asked the magician.

"Horseshit."

"Smells like five hundred bucks to me," she said.

The mounted policeman rode up to the car. "Is there a problem here, lady?"

"Yes," Dorothy said, and reached out to scratch the horse above its muzzle. "Do any officers ride a Clydesdale? Even one?"

"That your emergency?"

"Yes," she said sweetly, patting the horse.

Houdini turned away, trying to remain unrecognized.

The policeman shrugged, evidently happy to talk. "Nah, no Clydesdales. Morgan horses and quarter horses, usually geldings. Need a calm, relaxed horse for walking through crowds and loud traffic. Clydesdale is too big, too unruly."

"Thank you, Officer. I wish I had an apple for your horse."

"No feeding the horse, miss." The policeman yanked the reins and ambled away.

She turned to Houdini and held out her hand, palm up. "Five hundred dollars, please."

"I never agreed to such a wager," he muttered.

"You shook on it!"

"I never verbally agreed," he said, turning away. "Look. People are going into the lawyer's office. The auction is beginning."

He hastily opened the door and stepped out to the curb. He held the door open for Dorothy.

Was Houdini—perhaps the wealthiest performer in the United States, maybe the world—trying to weasel out of their bet?

"I guess you were right," she said as she got out. "I do smell horseshit."

Chapter 41

Oh, you're going to pay for this, Mr. Brown Oxford," wheezed Rudy the shoe-shine man. He and Benchley were carrying his large, heavy shoe-shine stand down the sidewalk.

"Please," Benchley gasped. "Don't call me Mr. Brown Oxford. It's sweet old Bob. We've known each other for years."

"Sweet old Bob, huh?" Rudy huffed. "Does that mean SOB?"

The stand was a large wooden platform, with two chairs mounted on the top and a footrest in front of each chair. Benchley and Rudy had carried, struggled and weaved it through pedestrians for nearly three blocks. Benchley's forearms were burning, and he knew he was going to feel it in his back the next day.

They shuffled to the corner of Midge Mac-Guffin's quiet street.

"Okay," Benchley puffed. "Just down this block here."

"This block here?" Rudy cried. "No, no. I can't put my stand on a residential street. I don't even have a permit to put it anywhere but where it was. What did you get me into?"

"Rudy—"

"No, *sweet old Bob!* I'm putting it down here. I can't go another step."

He set down his end of the stand. Benchley, realizing he wasn't going anywhere without Rudy's help, dropped his end of the stand onto the sidewalk with a thud.

"Be careful, Brown Oxford! That's my livelihood you're throwing around there."

"Sorry," Benchley said.

He climbed into one of the chairs and peered along the sidewalk to get a look at Midge's house. From up on the shoe-shine stand, he had a clear view to the MacGuffins' front stoop.

Yes, he thought, *this is a good vantage point after all, and not at all conspicuous.*

"Oh, you want a shine now?" Rudy said, exasperated, still catching his breath.

"Would you?" Benchley asked, though he didn't like pushing his luck with Rudy. "It would look strange if I just sat here reading the newspaper."

Rudy shook his head and mumbled to himself. But he fished out his shoe-shine polish, brushes and rags from a drawer in the bottom of the stand.

As Rudy started cleaning his shoes, Benchley uncapped a fountain pen and used it to poke two holes into a newspaper. He held it up and found he could look through the holes and see directly to Midge's house. Perfect!

"If you're trying not to look strange," Rudy said, "then you might want to turn your newspaper right side up."

Benchley saw that Rudy was right—he was holding the paper upside down. As he turned it around, Bert Clay walked right past the shoe-shine stand. Benchley jumped in his seat.

"What the—?" Rudy cried as the toe of Benchley's brown oxford came within an inch of his chin.

Benchley hurried to bring the newspaper up in front of his face—but it didn't matter. Clay hadn't noticed them. He was hurrying toward Midge's house. And he was carrying a large new suitcase.

Midge opened the door before Clay even reached the stoop. He disappeared inside.

"There," Rudy said, relieved. "All done. That'll be two bits, *sweet old Bob*."

"Give me another," Benchley said. He couldn't leave yet. Not now.

"Another shine?" Rudy asked. "I just shined them. You got some fine shoes, but they are not going to get any shinier!"

Benchley felt bad for Rudy, but someone had to keep an eye on Midge and Clay. He stood up. "I'll shine *your* shoes, then. Just keep a lookout on that house—"

Rudy held up a weather-beaten hand. "No, sir, thank you very much! I don't want you touching my shoes or my polishing equipment. Sit down," he sighed. "I'll give you another."

Benchley sat down.

• • •

Robert Sherwood stood outside the box office of the Spotlight Theater. He had attended countless plays on Broadway, and as the film reviewer for *Vanity Fair*, he had seen dozens upon dozens of silent pictures. But he had never been to a girlie show before, and he felt a certain thrill about it. He had heard about the titillating Dance of the Seven Veils, which could bring an audience to its knees. And there was a sinuous dancer who covered herself in nothing but a boa constrictor. Another used origami butterflies to astounding effect. . . .

The box office opened and a few men quickly got in line. Sherwood took his place behind them. An unusual crowd for a Sunday near lunchtime. The men cast furtive looks away or simply stared ahead. Sherwood paid his fifty cents to a bored attendant in the box office, and then strolled into the theater.

Inside, the lobby was poorly lit and smelled of mold. The auditorium itself was quiet and almost as dark as a cave. There were no ushers to show him to his seat, so he picked one at random halfway to the stage. He had to wait a few minutes before the show started, as the five-piece "orchestra" tuned up. He counted the number of people (all men, of course) in the audience: seven.

Finally, the orchestra struck up a brassy, saucy tune, the lights went up, and a short chorus line of five girls danced out. They wore high-hemmed, low-cut, sequined flapper dresses, which shook with much more excitement than the dancers themselves did. Most of the bedraggled girls, Sherwood thought, looked like they'd just woken up.

Five girls onstage, five players in the orchestra, and seven people in the seats—the performers outnumbered the audience! Sherwood thought.

He identified Viola easily, thanks to Dorothy and Benchley's description. She must have run out and bought a new platinum blond wig. She looked terrific, but what a frightful dancer! He'd seen dancing bears with better timing.

He sank in his seat. This girlie show was not all it was cracked up to be.

He had a peculiar wish that he'd stayed and kept an eye on Viola's mother. At least that big woman was interesting.

Dorothy and Houdini sat silently on folding chairs in a cavernous unheated room on the ground floor of Snath's dilapidated office building. This was a far cry from the fancy auction that Benchley had described.

Dorothy looked around. The large, hollow room was grim, both in appearance and in atmosphere. The walls were a dull, pallid gray. They had once been painted some neutral color, she figured, but that had faded years and years ago. When the cold draft whispered through, lacy spiderwebs fluttered at the corners of the cracked ceiling. Only a dozen stragglers occupied the hundred or so empty metal folding chairs, occasionally making an echoing screech on the marble floor.

Abraham Snath, Esquire, appeared and stalked toward the front of the room. He wore the same type of impeccable black suit she had seen him in previously. His face, however, was even more drawn and sharp than before.

Snath, his large hands tightly gripping the sides of the podium, stood surveying the small audience. His face clearly showed disgust and even anger. Dorothy followed his disdainful gaze around the room at the other bidders—most of these folks looked like they belonged at a racetrack, not at an art auction. These weren't rich, high-society art connoisseurs. These were shrewd sharpers and hagglers looking for a bottom-dollar bargain.

She took a quick glance at Houdini. He had put on a "disguise"—a large handlebar mustache—to avoid being recognized. He continued to avoid looking at her or speaking with her. She wondered why he still came along, if he was so angry about her figuring out his disappearing-horse trick.

At the podium, Snath gathered himself and spoke in his smoothest, deepest voice. "Good afternoon, and welcome to another fine auction brought to you by the Snath Art Emporium. Today, we will delight you with prized, one-of-a-kind offerings by the artistic genius, and untimely deceased, Ernest MacGuffin."

Dorothy wondered whom Snath meant by "we." He was the only one at the podium.

Snath lifted up a painting and put it on an easel. Dorothy had seen it before, upstairs in the lawyer's own office. It was the "genre work," as he described it, of two gunslingers. MacGuffin had done it as a "rush job" for *Old West Magazine*, as Dorothy recalled, and had earned only a hundred bucks for it.

"This is one of MacGuffin's finest, and most . . . accessible works," Snath said, choosing his words with care. "Shall we start the bidding at eight hundred?"

The lawyer hadn't even supplied the bidders with paddles. They were simply left to raise a hand—but no one did. No one moved a muscle.

"Eight hundred dollars for this spectacular, unique work of art?"

Snath stood there through a long, uncomfortable silence.

Finally, a man yelled out, "Seven hundred."

A few people snickered. Snath ignored the bid as well as the chuckles. "Eight hundred for this provocative, historic painting? Who will make the first bid?"

The man who bid before spoke again. "I'll give you seven hundred, final offer."

More laughs from the audience. Snath was

compelled to answer the man. "I'm afraid you misunderstand. The bidding is supposed to go up, not down."

"I understand perfect," the man said. "Seven hundred. Take it or leave it."

Snath chose to ignore him. "Eight hundred—"

"Six hundred!" said a hard-voiced woman at the back of the room.

"No, that is not how it's done—" Snath said, clearly losing what little patience he had.

Houdini raised his hand. "Five hundred. I'll give you five hundred in cash, right now!"

Dorothy elbowed him hard. "If you're handing out five hundred, I'm first in line."

Snath's face colored from gray to purple. He finally burst out in rage. "You brainless, toothless morons! You pathetic cretins! For the last time, the auction price goes up, not down!"

The man who had made the first bid stood up. "Who are you calling a moron? The price is what the market will bear! And the price for that piece of crap is currently five hundred and falling."

"Get out!" Snath screamed, as his carefully slicked-back hair came undone. "All of you, get out! Be gone from my sight! You dull-witted, un-sophisticated dunderheads! This auction is over!"

The bidders got to their feet to leave. Dorothy and Houdini stood, too, but they took their time. They watched Snath out of the corners of their eyes. He pulled out a pile of a dozen or so other canvases, which he'd kept out of view behind the podium. Then he grabbed the cowboy painting off the easel and added it to the stack. Cursing to himself, he carried the stack of canvases in his arms and ducked through an archway at the front of the room.

Once he was out of sight, Dorothy and Houdini quickly followed him through the archway. They found themselves in a wide hallway. A door at the end of the hallway stood open, and milky daylight beamed in. They heard a clatter and another bitter curse and went quickly to investigate. Houdini was about to rush through the open door, but Dorothy held him back. She crouched by the door and peeked out.

Snath stood in a wide, dirty alleyway. On the stained concrete at his feet was the pile of MacGuffin's paintings. Snath searched his pockets and pulled out a gold flask. He poured the contents of the flask on the paintings. Dorothy detected the smell of cheap, sweet brandy. Then Snath put the flask back in his jacket and pulled out a box of matches. He struck one against the brick wall. It blossomed into flame.

"Here's to you, Ernie," he spat bitterly. "Wherever you are, I hope you're burning, too."

He flung the match onto the pile of paintings. It ignited the vapors of the alcohol and—*voom!*— burst into a cloud of flame. Snath staggered backward from the flare.

356

Chapter 42

Rudy was in the middle of giving Benchley's shoes yet another shine when Bert Clay emerged from Midge MacGuffin's house.

"It's him!" Benchley said to Rudy.

Rudy turned to look.

"Don't look," Benchley said, whipping up the newspaper and gazing through the peepholes.

Clay walked quickly and purposefully, a man on a mission. As he approached, Benchley could see the determined and almost angry look on his face. And Clay no longer carried the suitcase. He must have left it inside Midge's house.

What was he up to? What were *they* up to?

Clay slowed down as he neared the shoe-shine stand. He looked curiously at Rudy and the stand. Benchley could almost read Clay's thoughts: *There was never a shoe-shine stand here before.* Clay looked up at Benchley and frowned. Benchley's hands began to shake; the newspaper started to rustle. Clay shook his head and moved on.

After Clay was a few paces away, Rudy whispered, "You got the dang newspaper upside down again."

Nevertheless, Benchley exhaled in relief now that Clay was on his way. The man seemed like a bully, and Benchley didn't want to cross him.

Clay not only was physically imposing, but also seemed temperamental and aggressive—a rotten combination. And now Benchley started to wonder. . . .

They had three suspects—Snath, Midge and Viola. But what about Clay? They hadn't even considered him. . . .

Benchley dropped the newspaper and looked back and forth between Midge's house and the receding figure of Clay. What should he do? Should he stay and keep an eye on Midge? Or should he follow Clay and see what the big man was up to?

He reasoned that Clay would come back sooner or later—he had left his suitcase behind, after all. And if he was coming back, that probably meant that Midge would stay put until he did. But where was Clay headed?

Benchley decided to follow him. He jumped down from the shoe-shine stand.

"Hey!" Rudy cried. "That's the second time you almost kicked me in the chin. And where do you think you're going?"

"I need to follow that big fellow," Benchley said hastily, pointing in Clay's direction.

"Oh no, you don't!" Rudy said, hands on his hips. "You need to help me carry this big old shoe-shine stand back to where it belongs. And you owe me for at least three shines!"

Benchley pulled out his wallet. Perhaps he could

make it worth Rudy's while. But other than his train ticket, his wallet was empty.

Rudy stepped closer, seeing the empty wallet. "Oh, I should have known!"

"Rudy, I'll make it up to you, I promise," Benchley pleaded, shoving the wallet back in his pocket. "But right now I have to go."

"Oh, you'll make it up to me, all right." He eyed Benchley's exquisitely polished brown oxfords. "You can make it up to me right here and now, *sweet old Bob*."

Benchley sighed. How fast could he follow Clay in his stocking feet?

He kicked off his shoes. He was about to find out.

Robert Sherwood nearly dozed off in his seat. The orchestra still played. Onstage, the performers were now doing a fan dance. But their peacock-feather fans were so large, and their moves so quick, that it was hardly worth getting excited over. Or even paying attention to.

Sherwood was determined to stay awake for the finale. . . . But when he opened his eyes again, the music had stopped and the houselights were up.

Was the show over? He looked at his watch. No, it was only the intermission. It felt as though he had been sitting here for hours, yet only one hour had passed.

He was terrifically bored. Perhaps a snack would keep him awake. He stood, stretched and strolled up the aisle to the lobby. At the concession stand, he bought a bag of peanuts. The lobby lights flickered—the show was about to resume—so he reluctantly went back to his seat.

He cracked a few peanuts and carelessly threw the shells on the dirty floor. Peanut shells were certainly not the worst thing this floor had seen. The orchestra, like an old cat dragging itself to its feet, slowly lurched into a discordant ditty.

But as the houselights dimmed, before the curtain went up, something strange happened. A hard red ball came hurtling down the aisle, rumbling toward the orchestra pit. It bounced twice, hit the balustrade that separated the audience from the orchestra, and flew up in a narrow arc. It came down hard in the orchestra pit, crashing loudly onto a cymbal and knocking over the percussionist, who fell backward into the saxophone player. The sax player's feet upturned two music stands, which brought the entire orchestra to a loud, disruptive halt. Pages of sheet music fluttered down like pigeons shot from the sky. The musicians—those who weren't lying on the floor—stood shocked and stunned.

But Sherwood wasn't quite so surprised. He turned toward the top of the aisle. Two dark figures were silhouetted in the doorway to the lobby.

"Woollcott! Harpo!" Sherwood called. "What the devil do you think you're up to?"

Alexander Woollcott, wearing his croquet whites and carrying his mallet, came sauntering down the aisle. Harpo Marx, also wearing his whites as well as a mischievous grin, followed close behind.

"What are we up to?" Woollcott asked. "Nineteen to twelve, my lead!"

"Ha!" cried Harpo. "Your ball's in the rough. It'll take you a dozen strokes to get it out of there."

"What kind of insane form of croquet is this?" Sherwood asked.

"Not insane at all, my lanky lad," Woollcott said coolly. "Standard croquet rules, just altered slightly for the urban landscape." He turned to Harpo. "As for getting my ball out of the rough, I won't need a dozen strokes. Not even one, because you owe me a mulligan."

Harpo raised his mallet. "A mulligan, my eye!"

"But I let you have a wicket on that old gent with the cane," Woollcott argued.

"That old guy was on crutches, and my ball sailed right between 'em. That was a wicket, fair and square. You didn't *let* me have anything!"

Sherwood noticed that the musicians had gathered themselves together. They were climbing over the balustrade, instruments in hand. And they looked angry.

"Listen, boys," he said urgently to Harpo and Woollcott. "Let's take this out of here."

Woollcott said, "But I haven't retrieved my ball."

"Here it comes now!" Sherwood said, as the percussionist hurled it with deadly aim. But Harpo was quicker. He snatched the soft white fedora from Woollcott's head, held it like a catcher's mitt and caught the ball easily.

"Your ball, your highness," Harpo said, offering it to Woollcott.

"You've dented my chapeau!" Woollcott cried, taking both the ball and the hat.

"They'll dent our craniums in a minute," said Sherwood of the menacing musicians. "Let's go."

He grabbed them each by the shoulder and led them quickly up the aisle. But when they got to the entrance to the lobby, Sherwood stopped.

Someone was blocking the way. A very large someone.

"You!" Viola's mother shouted at Sherwood. "So you did come to get an eyeful of my daughter, you dirty pervert."

Sherwood glanced over his shoulder. The musicians were getting closer, their instruments raised like weapons. He turned back to Viola's mother, who stood like a brick wall in front of him.

He had never struck a woman before, and he decided this was absolutely, positively, most definitely *not* the time to give it a try.

Chapter 43

Dorothy and Houdini watched the flames dance and destroy the stack of MacGuffin's paintings. Snath stood over the pyre, as though to make sure no canvas might somehow escape.

Dorothy tugged Houdini's sleeve. "Let's go around to the front of the alley," she whispered. "He's bound to come back this way eventually."

They tiptoed back along the hallway and through the large room used for the auction. They went out the front door and around the corner and soon stood near the entrance to the alley, peeking in. From this vantage point, Snath was much farther away—perhaps twenty yards. But they could see that the canvases were already blackening, the oil paint sizzling in the heat of the fire.

Dorothy whispered to Houdini. "There goes the career of Ernie MacGuffin. Up in smoke."

"A flash in the pan," added Robert Benchley, who suddenly appeared behind them.

Dorothy and Houdini spun around in surprise.

"What are you doing here?" she asked. "You're supposed to be watching Midge!"

"I was, but—" Benchley looked curiously at Houdini. "Why are you wearing that strange mustache?"

Houdini, taking off the mustache, looked with

equal curiosity at Benchley. "Why are you not wearing shoes?"

They looked down at the soiled socks on Benchley's feet.

"Now, that's a funny story," he began.

"Tell us later," Dorothy said sharply. "Why aren't you watching Midge?"

"I'm following Bert Clay."

"Clay?" she asked.

"He stopped by Midge's house with a suitcase. It occurred to me he could be our suspect. He's big enough, and rough around the edges."

"So's the Rock of Gibraltar, that doesn't make it a suspect," she said. "So where is he?"

"He just went into this building by the front entrance. He must be looking for Snath. I saw him go inside, but I also saw you two lurking here." Benchley took another peek around the corner into the alley. "What is Snath up to? Why the bonfire?"

Dorothy and Houdini quickly explained the auction debacle.

"There he is!" Benchley said, looking up the alleyway. Bert Clay stood in the doorway where, moments ago, Dorothy and Houdini had crouched.

"There you are!" Clay said to Snath with a mean smile.

"Who the hell are you?" Snath said.

"Harriet sent me. You owe her a share of the profits for the paintings."

"*Harriet?* I know no—"

"Midge MacGuffin!" Clay spat out the words, as though it pained him to say it. "I'm here for her share of the profits."

"Profits?" Snath laughed. "What profits? These paintings are worthless. They're less than worthless! That's why I'm burning them, you dolt."

Clay stepped forward, fists out. Snath, who was about Clay's size, didn't move a muscle.

"The paintings you sold the other night. Where's the money for those?" Clay shouted. "You raked in tens of thousands of dollars at that highfalutin auction. It was all over the newspapers. You owe her a fortune. And I've come to collect."

"In due time." Snath folded his arms. "There are forms to fill out. Procedures to follow."

"Procedures, like hell!" Clay growled, stepping closer, inches from Snath's face. "Hand it over. Now!"

Snath looked down his pointy nose at Clay. "You lowly underling. I don't carry such sums—"

With one hand, Clay grabbed Snath by the collar. With his other hand, he punched Snath hard in the mouth. Snath cried out. Clay punched again, but it glanced off Snath's sharp chin.

Snath brought up his knee toward Clay's groin, but Clay managed to turn aside. Snath lost his balance and fell backward, nearly pulling Clay down with him. But Clay let go of Snath's collar, and Snath hit the concrete with a thud.

On his back now, Snath tried to scramble away like a crab. But Clay leaned out and grabbed his legs.

"Give me the money, you shyster!" Clay yelled. "I want it. Now!"

Back at the alley's entrance, Dorothy turned to Benchley and Houdini. "Should we lend a hand?"

"To whom?" Benchley asked. "To help Snath escape, or to help Clay beat the snot out of him?"

Houdini laid a reassuring hand on her shoulder. "Don't trouble yourself. They're grown men. Let them deal with the matter as they choose."

Clay clutched Snath by the ankles. Snath couldn't pull free, no matter how he flailed. Now Clay dragged Snath toward the bonfire of Mac-Guffin's paintings.

"I don't like the look of this," Dorothy muttered.

Snath started grunting, jerking even more violently. His arms flailed as though he were doing the backstroke, but Clay only pulled him inexorably forward toward the large, crackling fire.

"The money," Clay demanded through gritted teeth. "Where is Harriet's money?"

Snath weakened as Clay brought him close to the bonfire. "I will get it for you, sir, I assure you. It's in my safe. Upstairs."

"Bullshit!" Clay snarled. He dragged Snath the last few inches and literally held his feet to the fire. Snath wailed. But Clay kept talking. "I know the kind of man you are. I know you're not afraid to carry around that kind of cash. You like to keep it on you, don't you? You think it's safer with you than hidden away in a safe."

Snath was breathless now. He couldn't even scream for help. The flames licked at his heels. His leather shoe uppers began to smoke.

Dorothy turned to Houdini and Benchley. "Do something!"

Houdini tightened his jaw, prepared to step forward. "You're right. I'm the man to—"

"Not yet," Benchley said, grabbing Houdini's sleeve. "Look."

Snath had reached inside his jacket pocket. He pulled out a small leather case, just large enough to hold a thick wad of bills. He flung it at Clay.

Clay dropped Snath's feet and snatched the case out of the air.

Snath's legs landed in the midst of the fire. Snath howled and pulled his legs out immediately. The leather of his shoes still emitted wisps of smoke, and his heels and pants were blackened with soot. But he was otherwise unharmed.

Clay unzipped the case and thumbed through the money. Satisfied, he closed it up again and stuffed it in his jacket. Without a second look, he turned away from Snath and strolled back into the building.

Snath lay on the ground, moaning.

Dorothy, Benchley and Houdini hurried to him.

They reached down to lift him up. But Snath's eyes went wide when he saw them. He flung up his arms protectively and even kicked out his smoking feet. "Get away, you vultures!"

His left leg caught Houdini by surprise, jabbing him in the side like a kidney punch. Houdini doubled over and stumbled backward, about to back into the fire. Realizing this, Houdini contorted himself, pulling his knees up and falling onto his side. He landed hard, just a foot from the flames, making a pathetic yelp.

Dorothy turned away from Snath and was at Houdini's side in a flash. "Are you hurt?"

Houdini nodded; his eyes were like slits. His face had gone ashen. "My arm. It may be broken."

Dorothy helped him to his feet.

Meanwhile, Benchley attempted to calm down Snath. "We're not robbers or thieves, Mr. Snath! We're here to help you." He spoke over his shoulder to Dorothy. "I think we should call for an ambulance, Mrs. Parker."

"I fully agree, Mr. Benchley."

She helped Houdini hobble to the doorway and stood him against the jamb.

"I'll be fine in a moment," he insisted, though his voice was weak. "I've nearly died several times. I dislocated my shoulder on countless occasions. That straitjacket escape was ruinous to my body, but I happily performed it twice a night."

The show must go on, Dorothy thought. She left him leaning somewhat unsteadily in the doorway and ran inside to find a telephone. She hoped she wouldn't also find Bert Clay still hanging around.

The first phone she found was upstairs in the reception room in front of Snath's office. It was an old wall-mounted crank-winding phone. No wonder Snath couldn't keep a secretary, the cheap bastard. She turned the crank, tapped the switch hook and soon had the operator on the line.

Moments later she was back in the alley. Houdini was looking better. His color had improved from gray to sallow pink. Benchley was huddled over Snath, who still lay on the ground. Benchley had removed Snath's shoes.

"How're his feet?" she asked.

"Odorous," Benchley said. "But they won't require amputation, I don't think."

"Amputation?" Snath cried. He was sweating, but it appeared to Dorothy to be a sickly, cold sweat.

Soon, the ambulance arrived at the end of the alley. Two orderlies with a wooden stretcher came hurrying forward.

Behind the ambulance, a long white limousine cruised to a stop.

"Fred, look!" Dorothy said. "Is that Mickey Finn come to find us?"

"Come to *fine* us, I think," Benchley said.

"Finn the bootlegger?" Houdini said. "He struck me as a hot-tempered sort of fellow."

"He's not the forgiving sort," Dorothy said. "Especially when it comes to debts."

Benchley turned back to Snath. "We have to run." He held up Snath's blackened shoes so the lawyer could see them. "Mind if I borrow these?"

Chapter 44

Viola's mother folded her big, flabby arms over her broad chest. In one hand, she held a brown paper sack. "I'm here to see my daughter, too. But not the same way you're here to see her." She narrowed her eyes at Sherwood, Woollcott and Harpo. "And I see you've brought some low-life pervert friends."

"Madame, withdraw that imputation," Woollcott said haughtily, holding up his croquet mallet like a walking stick. "Perverts? Perhaps. Lowlifes? Never!"

Sherwood glanced again over his shoulder. The musicians were only a few paces behind them now.

Harpo didn't say a word. He simply snatched the paper bag from the woman's chubby hand.

"Give that back!" she cried, reaching toward Harpo. "That's my daughter's lunch."

Harpo easily ducked under her swinging arm and darted past her into the theater lobby. She turned and lumbered after him. Sherwood and Woollcott quickly followed. As soon as she was out of the doorway, they circled around her and caught up to Harpo.

She couldn't move as fast as they, but she pursued them like a charging rhino. Harpo held out the bag, taunting her.

"Enough of that," Sherwood said. "Time to go." He pulled Harpo by the back of his sweater and grabbed Woollcott by the elbow, steering them out of the theater's front doors.

They hurried along the sidewalk. Their only destination in mind was to get away. As they rounded the corner, Sherwood took a glance behind. Viola's mother doggedly followed them, her fists pumping, her dress swaying as she ran. They may have been faster, but she had the single-minded determination of a bloodhound. At least the musicians had stayed behind at the theater.

Harpo slowed as they neared the iron stairway leading up to the elevated train station.

"Come on," he said, a wide grin on his puckish face. "Let's take the El. We'll lose her."

They clambered up the stairs. But the station platform was empty. No trains were departing or arriving. They paced back and forth a moment, not yet sure what to do. Sherwood stepped on something that crunched. He looked down. It was a peanut. Just then, they heard the woman's footsteps clanging heavily up the stairs.

"Ah, nuts!" Sherwood said.

"Yes, she's coming," Woollcott said.

"No, *nuts,*" Sherwood repeated. "I have a bag of peanuts in my jacket pocket. They've been falling out. I've been leaving behind a trail of peanuts like Hansel and Gretel leaving a trail of bread crumbs."

"And here comes the wicked witch of the forest!" Harpo said.

Sherwood silently cursed himself. He was supposed to be unobtrusively following Viola. Instead, Viola's mother—a potential murderer—was the one following him. He did not think this was what Mrs. Parker had in mind when she assigned him to this task.

The woman appeared at the top of the stairs.

"Fun and games are over, Harpo," Woollcott huffed, his face flushed from running. "Just give her back the lunch bag."

"No, don't." Sherwood had an idea. "Keep the lunch. Now I *want* her to follow us. Come on!"

He reached in his pocket for change. Somehow they had to get around the woman and back down the stairs. He handed a nickel each to Harpo and Woollcott and had one for himself.

He rushed toward the turnstile and dropped in his nickel. Harpo and Woollcott quickly followed. Now that they were on the other side of the gate, they passed by Viola's mother, who stared at them in anger. They exited through a different set of turnstiles and found themselves near the top of the stairs. They hurried down to the sidewalk. The woman's heavy footsteps again clanged behind them as she, too, descended the stairway.

When they reached the sidewalk, Sherwood directed them south. He began dropping peanuts as they went.

"Why in heaven's name," wheezed Woollcott, "do you want her to follow us?"

"I think this woman killed Ernie MacGuffin," Sherwood said. "We need to lead her to Dottie."

Just then, an ambulance sped past them in the street, its siren wailing. And who, of all people, did Sherwood see in the back window?

"Bless my stars!" he said. "There goes Dottie now."

Chapter 45

Inside the crowded ambulance, Dorothy thanked the orderlies for giving them a ride. They didn't look at her as they responded. "Anything for Mr. Houdini," one said.

The magician smiled. "It's just Houdini, boys. Everyone calls me Houdini."

A little adulation and he's right as rain, Dorothy thought.

In the center, Snath lay on the stretcher. He, too, seemed to be returning to his typical ill-tempered self. Crowded around him were Dorothy, Benchley, Houdini and the two orderlies.

"I reiterate," Snath said, "I have changed my mind. I do not need to go to the hospital."

The orderlies ignored him. One of them just finished putting Houdini's arm in a sling.

"Tell us, Mr.—I mean, Houdini," the orderly said. "Can you still perform a trick with a sprained wrist?"

"Well, boys"—Houdini's smile faded—"I'm afraid that would be impossible for any magician."

"Awww," the orderlies said in unison.

Then Houdini smiled even wider than before, his eyes alight. "But I'm not just any magician. And the impossible is my stock-in-trade!"

The orderlies actually cheered. Dorothy shook her head.

With his good arm, Houdini reached in his pocket for a deck of cards. But the ambulance slowed and came to a stop before he barely had a chance to show the orderlies that he could shuffle with one hand.

"Show's over," Dorothy said. "We're here."

"I tell you again," Snath cried. "I don't need to go to the hospital."

"This is our stop," Dorothy said. "Not yours."

She pushed open the ambulance's back door and hopped out. A shoe-shine stand, which she'd never noticed before, blocked her view of Midge MacGuffin's house. Benchley got out and stood beside her.

"Where did this shoe-shine stand come from?" she asked.

"Now, that's another funny story—" he said.

"*Shh,*" Dorothy hissed, pointing ahead. "There he goes."

They inched forward and peered around the shoe-shine stand. Just on the other side, Bert Clay strolled down the sidewalk. Now they could see that he was headed toward Midge MacGuffin's house.

Clay moved quickly, but there was a spring in his step, a cheerful jauntiness in his stride. His hat was tipped back ever so slightly, as if to catch a few extra rays of hazy autumn sunshine.

The moment he reached the steps, the door opened and Midge appeared. Clay stopped at the bottom step, reached in his jacket and pulled out the leather money case he had taken from Snath. He held it up triumphantly. Midge raced down the steps and into Clay's arms.

"Now what do you think they're up to?" Dorothy muttered, looking at Benchley. He shook his head.

After their embrace, Midge and Clay skipped up the steps and into the house. The door remained open.

"What's going on back here?" said a familiar scratchy voice. Then Rudy appeared from around the front of the shoe-shine stand. His face fell when he saw Benchley. "Oh no, it's you again."

Looking past Rudy, they saw Midge and Clay reappear at the door. Midge wore a bright green coat and Clay now had two suitcases—a green one to match Midge's coat and his own shiny new one. Bert Clay looked up, the ambulance apparently now catching his eye.

Benchley pulled Dorothy away, flattening them both against the back of the shoe-shine stand. He had his hand on her arm. How comforting that felt! She was tempted to entwine her fingers in his.

But then Rudy spoke. "What are you two up to?"

"We're wondering the same thing—but about them," Benchley whispered, with a nod of his head toward the house.

Rudy turned and looked.

Benchley said, "What are they doing?"

"The woman is closing the door, locking it," Rudy reported. "Man is picking up the bags, and down the stairs they go. Coming this direction now."

Houdini poked his head out of the ambulance. "Whatever is going on out here?"

"Get back inside or they'll see you," Dorothy said quietly. "Shut the door."

Houdini nodded and disappeared, soundlessly closing the ambulance's back door.

"Rudy," Benchley murmured. "Where are they now?"

Rudy faced the sidewalk, one arm leaning against the corner of the shoe-shine stand. "Good afternoon, folks," he said enthusiastically.

Midge's voice came from the other side of the stand. She spoke blissfully. "A *lovely* afternoon."

Rudy nodded and tipped his cap as Midge and Clay passed by. A few moments later, he turned back to Dorothy and Benchley. His enthusiastic voice and smile had vanished. "They're gone, okay? Now, how about you get going, too."

Benchley nodded. "My thoughts exactly."

He grabbed Dorothy's hand—or had she grabbed his?—and they climbed back into the ambulance.

"Houdini," Dorothy said pleasantly. "Can you

please request the driver to follow that couple strolling up the street—a tall woman in a green coat and a large man carrying suitcases?"

Before Houdini could answer, Snath sat up. "A tall woman? And a large man! Don't tell me—"

Snath jumped up and poked his head into the driver's compartment. "It's him! That violent, monstrous thief! It's a good thing for him we're in an ambulance, because he's going to need it."

Houdini laid a hand on Snath's arm. "There, there, my good man. All in good time. As Mrs. Parker says, let's see what they're up to."

"He'll be up to twenty years in prison before I'm through with him!" Snath said. "And he's with Midge, no less. She's a good woman. She should know better."

Dorothy spoke thoughtfully. "Perhaps she does."

Houdini leaned into the driver's compartment and told him to follow Midge and Clay.

"As inconspicuously as an ambulance can," Dorothy added.

The ambulance started up and moved forward slowly, the driver following twenty yards behind the couple.

Dorothy turned to Snath, who had sat back down on the stretcher. He craned his neck forward to look out the front window.

"Where are they going?" she asked.

Snath looked at her, perplexed. "How the deuce should I know?"

"Midge is your client. Did she say anything about packing up and leaving?"

Snath's expression hardened. "She certainly did not."

"Are you in love with her?"

His eyes went wide. The thought seemed to disgust him. "How dare you! She was not only my client, but also the wife of my now deceased client, Ernest MacGuffin!"

"Just asking," she said.

"Look," Houdini said. "She's carrying tickets."

Dorothy could see only that Midge held a couple of slips of paper. "What kind of tickets, do you suppose?"

"Not theater tickets," Benchley said.

"Not train tickets," Houdini said. "Penn Station and Grand Central are uptown."

"Then what?" Dorothy asked. "What's south?"

"Liberty Island Ferry?" Benchley joked.

"Not with suitcases," Houdini said seriously. "But what about an ocean liner? There are several ports."

"Of course," Dorothy said.

Snath muttered, "I never expected her to surprise us all and try to skip town with the money."

Now Dorothy understood. "No. That's what *you* hoped to do."

Like a prudent lawyer, Snath didn't answer that statement.

Clay and Midge walked several blocks farther. Clay didn't seem to tire from carrying the suitcases.

But Dorothy and everyone else inside the ambulance began to grow weary. "What are they doing now?" one of the orderlies asked.

"Still walking and talking and tripping the light fantastic," Dorothy said.

"This will take all day," Benchley sighed. "Let's just pull over already and give them a ride."

"Not on your life!" Snath snapped. "That Clay is going to get what's coming to him."

Dorothy turned to the lawyer. "Did you give Ernie what was coming to him?"

"What do you mean?" Snath said, his voice rising. "His share of the profits? Sadly, I did not have the opportunity to remunerate him before his untimely death, and I don't like your insinuation—"

"No," she said. "I'm asking did you *cause* his untimely death?"

"Slander!" Snath shouted. "You all heard it. This viper just slandered me. You witnessed it!"

Dorothy turned to one of the orderlies. "Can you bandage his mouth?"

"How about stitches instead?" Benchley asked.

"Look," Houdini said. "They've stopped. Clay is saying something."

At a corner not far ahead, Clay seemed to indicate he wanted to go in a different direction.

Midge looked south, the direction they had been headed. She pointed that way with the tickets in hand.

Clay shook his head, a playful smile on his face. He tilted his head toward the east.

Midge reacted with an equally playful stomp of her foot, then laughed. She linked her arm through his, and they turned east.

"What's he have in mind?" Dorothy asked. "A surprise for her?"

The ambulance driver continued to follow them for two or three more blocks. "Water Street," he said.

"Water Street?" Benchley turned to Dorothy. "Why does that ring a bell?"

She spoke quietly. "It was where Ernie's body was found."

Chapter 46

Midge and Clay continued along Water Street for a short distance. Then Clay stopped, put down the suitcases with a sort of ceremonious finality and gestured with his arms wide.

Midge shook her head. She didn't seem to understand.

They stood in the shadow of a nearly completed skeleton of a building under construction. Clay threw his hands up as if to encompass the entire edifice, as if to show her all that he had done.

"It must be his skyscraper!" Benchley said.

"*His* skyscraper?" Dorothy and Houdini asked in unison.

"He's the main engineer. He told me so himself." Benchley looked up seventy stories toward the uncompleted top of the building. "A skyscraper is the embodiment of a man's dreams, he said. Quite the poet."

Dorothy and Houdini looked up as well. The latticework of steel and stone reached high in the blue sky, as though to obscure the sun itself.

Dorothy looked down to the sidewalk. "Damn! Where did they go?"

Across the street, Clay and Midge had disappeared.

She looked up and down the street, which was nearly empty of cars and foot traffic. They weren't anywhere to be seen.

"Inside," she said. "They must have gone inside the skyscraper."

Benchley opened the ambulance's back door and jumped out. Dorothy and Houdini quickly followed. They looked again across the street to the sidewalk where Midge and Clay had recently stood. And again up and down the street. No sign of them.

"Wait for me!" Snath said from the ambulance. "I must see this thing through."

"The only thing you're seeing is a hospital room," Dorothy said, and turned to the orderlies. "Take him away, boys."

But Snath moved with surprising speed. He got up from the stretcher and hopped out of the ambulance. He stood in his bandaged feet, arms folded, unwilling to be moved.

"You can't force me to go to the hospital if I choose not to go," he said.

The orderlies shrugged their shoulders. "He's right," one said.

"His feet weren't hurt that bad," the other added. "Not even first-degree burns."

Snath nodded, as though this decided the matter. He turned to Benchley. "I'll have my shoes back now, thank you."

As Benchley reluctantly removed the blackened

384

shoes, the orderlies closed the door and the ambulance drove away.

"We're wasting valuable time," Houdini said, pointing to the skyscraper. "Who knows what that madman is about to do to that defenseless woman?"

"I know exactly what he's going to do to her," Dorothy said, speaking with a calmness she didn't feel. She had finally figured it out. "Clay's going to shove her off the building. Like he did to Ernie."

"Shove her off the building?" Houdini said. "I thought you said Ernie was hit with some large and heavy object."

"That's what Dr. Norris said." Dorothy looked at the sidewalk in front of the building. Ernie's body must have been found there. "Dr. Norris actually guessed that Ernie was hit by a big block of concrete. I suppose he didn't figure that Ernie was the one to hit the concrete instead."

The thought of it made her feel sick. She glanced at Snath, who had finished tying on his burned shoes. Benchley was back in his thread-bare, dirty socks.

"Come on," she said. "Let's go."

But all of a sudden, she was caught by surprise. A long white limousine blocked their way.

Mickey Finn got out. He looked annoyed—and dangerous. Lucy Goosey stepped out, too. She looked somewhat guilty.

"You're going nowhere," the gangster said. "Not until you pay me my fifty grand."

Benchley seemed to find this preposterous. "Just a minute. How did you even find us?"

"That doesn't matter a whit," Finn said. "Point is, I found you."

Lucy pointed at Snath. "We knew you'd be looking for him because of the paintings. So we went by his office, and we saw you get into the ambulance. Then we followed the ambulance here. No big mystery."

Finn turned to her sharply. "How about I do the talking, since this is my business?"

Lucy bit her lip.

Dorothy and Benchley glanced at each other. They had never heard Finn speak roughly to Lucy before. Usually, it was the other way around.

"Now," Finn said, stepping closer, holding up his silver-tipped shillelagh. "You know you owe me the money today. Where is it?"

Houdini spoke up, stepping closer to Finn. He wasn't intimidated by the gangster at all. "The day is far from over, Mr. Finn. Please allow us to proceed with our very urgent business right now, and perhaps Mrs. Parker and Mr. Benchley will reimburse you later in the day."

Now Finn took a step closer. They were almost nose to nose. He seemed to have lost his awe of the magician. "*Perhaps* they will reimburse me?"

he growled, his rotten yellow teeth practically chewing on the words. "No perhaps about it. The bill is due now, and I've come to collect."

Dorothy looked to Houdini. "How about a little magic?"

He turned to her, surprised. "What?"

"I've seen you make a horse disappear and even a five-ton elephant disappear. Why can't you make this two-bit hoodlum disappear?"

"Aye," Finn jeered. "Not so amazing now, are you? Tricks are easy on the stage. But out here on the street, it's a different story, isn't it?"

"This is hardly fair." Houdini seemed to shrink in stature. "My arm is incapacitated."

"But the impossible is your stock-in-trade," Dorothy said. "Go on, make him disappear. Use your magic."

Houdini began to sweat. But he didn't back down from Finn.

The gangster laughed in Houdini's face. "Aye, come, now. No tricks up your sleeve?"

Then Houdini smiled. "Just this. Your shoes are untied."

Finn held back a laugh for a moment, but only a moment. "Haven't heard that one since I was a child," he burst out. "You expect me to fall for that one?"

"Yes," Houdini said. "That's exactly what I expect you to do."

The magician backed away. Finn stepped

forward—then he fell flat on his face, nearly bringing Lucy Goosey down with him.

"Did I say your shoes were untied?" Houdini called over his shoulder. "I mean, they are tied."

Dorothy saw that Houdini was right. The laces of Finn's expensive wingtips were tied together. Finn pulled his feet toward him and grabbed at his shoes and laces.

Dorothy didn't waste another moment. She grabbed Benchley's hand and they hurried after Houdini, who was already entering the skyscraper's large main entrance. She heard Snath follow them.

"Come on," she said to Benchley. "Clay killed Ernie. Now he's going to kill Midge, too. We should have included him among our suspects right from the beginning."

"But we didn't know that Clay knew that Ernie was alive—"

"Clay didn't know," Dorothy said, "until he overheard us tell Midge the other morning. Remember how he jumped out of the closet like a jack-in-the-box?"

"And Ernie was found dead by the following morning."

"Below this skyscraper!"

They pushed open the unlocked door and ran inside. Because it was Sunday, no work was being done and no workmen were about. The skyscraper's lobby was quiet and spacious. No lights were on, but the afternoon sunshine poured through yellow-tinted glass windows, casting gleaming golden rectangles across the floor.

They crossed the lobby quickly and headed to the bank of elevators, which were highlighted with art deco touches of black, silver and gold. Dorothy punched the UP elevator button. All the elevators except one whooshed open.

"The top floor," Dorothy shouted, and pointed at the one closed elevator. "They must have taken that one to the top. Let's go."

She raced into the nearest elevator and pressed the highest-numbered button: seventy. Benchley, Houdini and Snath followed her in.

"No elevator operator," she said. "How modernized!"

There was a tense moment when they wondered if Finn might appear, but the doors closed silently and the elevator ascended quickly.

Dorothy had never been on such a fast elevator. She felt her stomach flip and her ears pop. To distract herself, she turned to Houdini.

"How did you manage to tie Finn's shoelaces?"

"Yes," Benchley said. "What magic did you use to do that?"

"No magic," Houdini said with a proud smile. "Just amazing physical dexterity combined with hours of practice using my toes like fingers. I've called upon such skills to escape from innumerable traps and confinements. If you wish to call that magic, I shall not stop you."

"You did the same thing at the séance," Dorothy said. "You slipped off your shoes and used your toes to find that radio wire."

Houdini made a slight bow.

Suddenly, the elevator stopped and the doors opened. Dorothy was taken by surprise when fresh air and afternoon daylight poured in.

She stepped out of the elevator. Not only were they on the very top floor; they were on the very top of the building. There was no ceiling, no walls, no windows. Just a flat expanse of unfinished floor under her feet and a spectacular, wide-open view of the city in all directions.

The city looked so perfect from such a height. To the north, Manhattan's landscape of buildings stretched as far as the eye could see, broken only by the rectangle of Central Park, with its autumn trees awash in gold, red and orange. To the east, the Brooklyn Bridge spanned the glittering, brilliant East River. To the south, the Statue of Liberty appeared like a bronze toy in the vast green harbor. To the west . . . two figures were dangerously close to the roof's edge, silhouetted against the afternoon sun.

"Mrs. Parker—" Benchley said, looking in the same direction.

"I see them," she said. "Houdini, come on! It's Clay. He's going to push Midge off."

Chapter 47

Dorothy and Benchley ran. Houdini, distracted by the view, turned abruptly and followed them.

Dorothy couldn't make out what Clay was doing to Midge. The bright afternoon sun was in her eyes. The two were close together and perilously near the building's edge—she could see that much.

"Ouch!" Benchley yelled. He stopped and grabbed his foot. Dorothy looked down. He had stubbed his stocking feet into a scattered pile of five-inch steel rivets.

"Go on," he yelled, waving at Dorothy to keep going.

Houdini caught up to her and they ran side by side, only a dozen paces now from Clay and Midge.

One of the figures was standing; one was crouching low. This didn't look good at all, Dorothy thought.

Houdini gasped, and then suddenly went down. Dorothy paused to look. Houdini had stumbled and fallen inside a large, low wooden box— some kind of big tool chest. The impact of his fall brought the lid down with a bang. Houdini was shut inside as if it was a coffin.

The bang of the tool chest brought a soft cry of

surprise. The cry sounded like Midge's voice. Dorothy held up her hand to block the blinding sunlight. Just a few yards ahead, she saw Midge and Clay. But Midge was the one standing. Clay was on his knees.

"Don't move another inch!" Dorothy said to them.

"Mrs. Parker," Midge said, surprised and bewildered. "What are you doing here?"

Benchley hobbled up to stand beside Dorothy, blocking the sun with his hat. "We could ask you the same thing. As a matter of fact, we will. What are *you* doing here?"

Clay got up from his knees—and now they saw the glitter of the gold ring in his hand. "I brought Harriet up here to propose," he said breathlessly. "Look around you. The sun, the sky, the magnificent city spread in all directions. The marvel of construction under your feet, holding you up to the heavens. Can you picture anything more beautiful?"

Dorothy and Benchley turned to each other, silently mouthing, *Propose?*

Clay took a step closer to Midge. "I can think of only one thing more beautiful." He took her hands and looked deeply into her eyes. "You."

Midge smiled in return, clasping Clay's hands enthusiastically.

A muffled grunt came from Houdini in the tool chest. But with the rustling wind, Midge and

Clay didn't hear it. Dorothy and Benchley ignored it, for now.

Benchley chuckled. "Well, I guess we have egg on our faces." He gently grasped Dorothy's hand and began to back away. "We didn't know you came up here to propose. We'll leave you to it, then."

Midge and Clay gave them a puzzled look.

"So," Midge asked, "why did you think we came up here?"

Benchley stopped and stood uncomfortably. He fanned himself with his hat, though it wasn't particularly warm. "Oh, nothing much."

Now Dorothy chuckled. "It's kind of a funny story—when you think about it."

"What story?" Midge asked.

"Wait a minute," Clay argued to Midge, playfully yet petulantly. He wrapped his hands around hers, enveloping them in his. "You've had my proposal, my dear Harriet. Now, what's your answer?"

"My—my answer?" she stammered.

"Your answer," he insisted with a smile.

Dorothy coughed quietly. She and Benchley took another step backward. "We'll just leave you two lovebirds to yourselves—"

"Wait," Midge said, distracted, turning toward Dorothy. "Why *did* you follow us up here?"

"Well, the fact is . . ." Dorothy was reluctant to explain. "The fact is, we thought your Mr.

Bertram Clay here might not be quite so fond of you after all."

"Not fond of Harriet?" Clay sputtered. "My heart belongs to her!"

"Yes, dear," Midge said to him sweetly and just the slightest bit impatiently. "That's lovely how you keep repeating that so often." She turned back to Dorothy and Benchley. "What do you mean, not so fond?"

Benchley cleared his throat. "We—that is, Mrs. Parker and I, as well as Mr. Houdini"—he gestured to the tool chest—"who I'm sure will make a magnificent escape from that box at any moment . . . We had the strange idea—and a rather funny one when you think about it, as I'm sure you will—that your Mr. Clay here had come up here to . . . Well, he had designs to . . ."

"To kill you," Dorothy said with as much cheer and humor as she could muster. "To throw you off the roof. Isn't that a laugh?"

Even with the sun in their eyes, they could see Clay stiffen. Midge lowered her hands from his but didn't quite let go—he wouldn't let her let go.

"No," Midge said seriously. "I don't think that's funny at all. Perhaps you'd better leave."

Dorothy tried to explain. "We let our imagination get the best of us, I'm afraid. You see, when we came to your house that morning, the day before Ernie was murdered—"

"Murdered?" Midge said sharply.

Oh damn! Dorothy bit her lip. *O'Rannigan did warn me not to say that to anyone. Of course Midge wouldn't know! It's not exactly public knowledge.*

Now Midge let go of Clay's hands. She staggered toward Dorothy and Benchley, her voice still shrill. "What do you mean, *murdered?*"

Another muffled cry and then a thump came from the tool chest.

"Harriet dear," Clay pleaded, reaching toward her. "Let's stop this tomfoolery—"

A loud voice called across the rooftop. "Mrs. Parker!"

Dorothy and Benchley knew that voice. They turned to face Robert Sherwood running full tilt at them. As he ran, he held up a small brown paper bag. A hefty older woman in a voluminous flowered dress came pounding after him, her ash blond wig askew on her big, sweaty head.

"Mrs. Parker!" Sherwood yelled again, jerking a thumb over his shoulder. "I have her. She did it. She killed Ernie. She has the motive—and the muscle!"

Then Sherwood made the same error as Houdini. He stumbled against the low tool chest, landing on top of the lid with a thud. Inside, Houdini emitted a muffled groan.

Viola's mother thundered to a stop at the foot of the tool chest, breathing heavily. Sherwood spun around to face her, as helpless as a turtle on its back.

"I heard that." She gasped for air, holding one chubby hand over her bosom. "But I had no wish to kill Ernie. He was like a son to me."

Something here certainly doesn't add up, Dorothy thought. "Then who—?"

"Who do you think?" Viola's mother pointed a thick finger to her right, to Abraham Snath. "It was him! Look at him. A sleazy lawyer. A villain through and through. He's been horrible to my poor Viola."

Snath? Dorothy had nearly forgotten all about him. He must have sidled up as she and Benchley talked with Midge and Clay.

"Me?" Snath cried, his hands out, pleading. "Why would I, of all people, kill Ernest Mac-Guffin? I lost a fortune when they found him dead!"

Midge made a small cry.

Snath stomped his foot—then winced because it was still tender. "How I wish Ernie were still alive. I wish a dozen of him were alive!"

"A dozen?" Clay said disgustedly. "One Mac-Guffin was plenty. Matter of fact, one MacGuffin was more than enough."

Everyone turned toward Clay.

"What do you mean, one MacGuffin was more than enough?" Dorothy asked.

Clay didn't answer right away. He looked at

Midge with devotion, anxiety and—was it guilt?—written on his face.

Oh no, Dorothy realized, *I was right about Clay all along. He* did *kill Ernie.*

"Bertram, what do you mean?" Midge asked. When he didn't answer, she turned to Dorothy, her voice rising. "What did he mean?"

"Tell her," Dorothy said to Clay. The look in Clay's eyes almost made Dorothy's heart want to break. Did she look at Benchley that way—so desperately, so piteously?

And now Dorothy fully understood. Clay didn't kill Ernie for money, or anger, or revenge, or jealousy. Clay murdered Ernie for love—his crazy, foolish, undying love for Midge.

Midge choked on her words. "Did you—?"

Clay looked at her morosely. "I did what I had to do, for us to be together."

Midge didn't move. Didn't speak.

Clay moved toward her. He held her hands. "I love you, my darling. I've loved you for years. I'd do anything for you. Anything for *us* to be together. Forever."

Dorothy didn't like Clay standing so close to Midge—and both of them so close to the building's edge.

"B-but—" Midge stammered.

"But nothing, my love," Clay said, silencing her with a finger to her lips. Then his voice turned angry. "He wasn't worthy of you. He called

397

himself an artist. But he was just another money-grubbing hack. An artist lives for love and beauty. That's me! People see me and they think I'm merely an engineer. No! *I'm* the artist. *I'm* the romantic!"

"Y-you?" Midge repeated, dazed, unable to take all this in.

"Yes, a romantic! A hundred times, yes!" Clay said, clutching her hands even tighter, his eyes pleading. "My heart soars now. It floats on your love. I spent years thinking about you, devoted to you, imprisoned by the thought of you. I built this building as a monument of my love for you. And then—" Tears filled his eyes.

Midge couldn't respond.

"Then what?" Dorothy asked, impatient for Midge to understand. "Tell her."

Clay's gaze never wavered from Midge. "Then when I read in the newspaper that Ernie had jumped off the bridge, I thought my heart would burst. A second chance with you! I found you as soon as I could." He was nearly weeping. "And then—and then my dream came true. You thought so, too! You were so happy for us to be reunited after so many years apart. And so was I. So very happy."

"I thought—" Midge mumbled.

Clay's eyes darkened. He shot a fierce glance at Dorothy and Benchley. "But when these two jackasses showed up at your house and said that

Ernie was still alive—well, it was more than I could bear! I wouldn't let him take you away from me again. Not again! So I dragged him here just as soon as I could. And what a spineless jellyfish he was. He squirmed and he squealed. I tried to bring him up to the roof, but I couldn't get him farther than the sixth floor—the coward! So I threw him out the window like a piece of trash. Oh, my darling, had you seen him, you'd have been so ashamed that you ever took his name. He didn't care about you. I had seen him around with some dirty little blonde—"

Viola's mother made an angry guttural sound. She took half a step toward Clay.

"That's it, lady," Dorothy muttered. "Sic him!"

Then Viola's mother collapsed in a dead faint, landing squarely on top of Sherwood.

Sherwood groaned with the crush of the woman's unconscious body, the air flattened right out of him. Inside the tool chest, Houdini emitted a stifled, bewildered yelp.

Clay didn't look up. He gazed only at Midge. His voice softened again, his eyes welling up. "Our path is clear now. Marry me, my darling Harriet. Marry me and make me the happiest man alive!"

Midge tore her hands away from his. She backed away in fear. Backed away too close to the building's edge, Dorothy thought.

"No, Bertram," Midge said like a vow. "Never. Never will I marry you."

"No? *Never?*" he gasped. His face became a storm of emotions—love, devotion, anger, fear, confusion. . . . He stepped toward her.

"I could never marry you." She backed away from him again. "You killed my husband."

"Your—your *husband?* But you were through with him. You told me so."

"But I didn't want him dead. Ernie still provided for me, and I still cared for him."

Betrayal was etched painfully on Clay's face. "You still *cared* for him? Even after we were together?"

"Yes," she said. "I was no longer in love with him, I suppose. But I still loved him."

Clay was shattered, his voice as edgy as broken glass. "How can you say you loved him? You're with me now! You agreed to take an ocean liner away with *me!*" He moved one step closer to her.

Hmm, ocean liner, Dorothy thought. *Houdini had guessed it right.* She'd have to tell him later.

"I can't go with you now," Midge sobbed. "I can't ever be with you."

Clay's face turned as pale as a ghost. He clutched at her arm. She was inches from the building's edge. Seventy stories below, the traffic was barely audible. She tried to pull away.

"If you won't be with me in this life," he pleaded to her, "be with me in the next one. Together—forever!"

Clay wrapped his arms around her middle,

pinning her arms to her sides. He stepped toward the precipice, ready to pull her over with him. Midge screamed. She pulled one arm free, reaching out.

Dorothy was closest to her. She grabbed Midge's hand. Midge held hers tightly, desperately.

Clay spun around with a malevolent look at Dorothy. He released one arm from Midge and grabbed Dorothy by the shoulder, trying to shove her backward.

Benchley stepped forward and gripped Clay's forearm with both his hands.

The four were locked together, teetering just one step away from the building's edge.

Too close, Dorothy thought. She felt the wind whip upward. Saw the tiny black ribbon of street far, far below. Fear scized her. This was Ernie's view, just before he died.

She looked desperately at Benchley. He turned his gaze away from Clay and met her eyes. Then . . . he smiled.

What the hell, she thought. *Dear, sweet Benchley!*

Suddenly, something red flew right by her vision. It struck Clay on the forehead with a loud, dull knock. His head whipped back with the force of it.

Clay's hand released its pressure on Dorothy. Benchley let go of Clay's arm. Midge, also freed, collapsed to Dorothy's side.

Dorothy turned to see where the object had come from.

"Tremendous shot!" Harpo jumped up and down. "You croqueted that ball with his brain."

Woollcott proudly rested his croquet mallet on one shoulder. "Yes, quite a sticky wicket, if I say so myself. Yet I lost the ball."

Dorothy turned back around. Clay faced her, his heels on the brink of the precipice, horror on his face. He slowly teetered backward over the abyss, his arms pinwheeling.

Midge jumped up to pull him back. She reached out to grab him. But it was a moment too late. She reached too far. He clutched at her hands. She screamed.

In a terrifying instant, she and Clay disappeared together over the edge. They were gone.

Dorothy held her breath. She couldn't look down. But she couldn't *not* look down. She glanced at Benchley.

Benchley nodded. He understood. He moved cautiously to the edge and peered down. Then he chuckled. "I guess that's the last time she'll fall for him."

Dorothy was aghast.

Benchley turned to her, a smile of relief on his face. "Don't worry. They're safe. Take a look."

She stepped forward tentatively, grabbing Benchley's arm for safety. She looked down.

One floor below, Midge and Clay lay on the

narrow platform of a wooden scaffold. Midge turned and looked up at them—shock and wonderment on her face. She had landed on top of Clay. His eyes were closed, his mouth agape. One leg seemed to be twisted at an unnatural angle.

Benchley called down. "Are you all right?"

"Fine," Midge said. "Alive. But Bertram is unconscious."

"And soon to be under arrest," Dorothy muttered to Benchley. Then to Midge, she called, "Stay there. We'll send someone down to get you."

By this time, Snath, Harpo and Woollcott had joined Dorothy and Benchley at the building's edge.

"We'll go down and rescue the fair damsel," Woollcott said. "And call the authorities to scrape up the Clay."

He and Harpo turned toward the elevators, chatting about their game.

Next to Dorothy, Snath yelled down, "Can you hear me, Clay? You'd better have a terrific lawyer. You're going to need one before I get through with you." He turned to her and Benchley. "You heard his confession. We all heard it. That won't be the last scaffold he'll ever see. The next one will have a noose hanging above it."

He spun on his heel and followed Harpo and Woollcott, marching past Viola's mother, still collapsed on top of Sherwood.

Sherwood writhed out from under her, managing to leave her inert body on top of the tool chest. He stood and came over to them, smoothing out his clothes as he risked a quick look down.

"I really thought it was her." He nodded over his shoulder to Viola's mother. He sighed, looking at the big woman's motionless body. "I guess I should go get a few strong fellows—and a hoist—to lift her. Or at least fetch some smelling salts. Be back in a few minutes." Sherwood left for the elevators.

When Sherwood was gone, Dorothy turned to Benchley. She still clung to his arm. She couldn't let go. Not now.

Clay was right about one thing. It was beautiful up here, Dorothy thought. From this height, the city was peaceful. The sky was brilliant blue. The sun was golden yellow and warm on their faces.

She looked at Benchley. Without his shoes on, he wasn't much taller than she was. They were closer to eye level now. His eyes were so happy, she wanted to drink it in. He smiled at her—that merry, carefree and tender smile. She realized to her relief that she didn't feel pathetic or needy with Benchley. She just felt . . . happy.

Lucy Goosey's words came back to her. *When you're alone together some sunny day, holding hands under a picture-postcard sky . . . show him how you feel. Kiss him, damn it. Kiss him.*

She lifted her face to his. His smile widened, softened. He tilted his face to hers. . . .

"Enough!" Houdini yelled from the tool chest. "I give up. I can't escape this damned thing." From inside, he thumped on the wooden box angrily. "Get me out of here!"

Benchley laughed. Then so did she. And the magic vanished. They were two friends just sharing a laugh.

They parted. Dorothy let go of Benchley's arm with a little affectionate pat. They moved to the tool chest.

"You call yourself an escape artist?" she said, loud enough for Houdini to hear. "Go back to art school."

Chapter 48

The next morning, a gray and chilly Monday, Dorothy was summoned down to the lobby desk at the Algonquin for a phone call. She didn't yet have a telephone installed in her room. She didn't yet have the money to pay for it.

"Hello?" she said.

A woman's voice was on the other end. "Mrs. Parker? This is Bess Houdini. Would you please come up to the house? We're sending the car for you."

Dorothy was puzzled. Was Houdini all right?

"He's fine," Bess replied. "Between you and me, his pride is a little wounded, that's all. And bring that painting, please."

Fortunately, Benchley had left MacGuffin's Brooklyn Bridge painting in her room.

Within an hour, Dorothy stood in Houdini's disheveled attic office and library. She set the painting against a chest-high stack of books.

"How much?" Houdini grumbled from his desk. He'd had the sling on his arm replaced with a better one.

"How much?" Dorothy repeated. "How much what?"

He looked up at her, his brows furrowed. "How much do you want for it?"

406

"The painting, you mean?" She was amazed. "You want to buy it?"

"An investment," he said, tight-lipped. "What's its value?"

Cripes, she thought. Last she could remember, Cathcart put it at a lousy twelve hundred.

Houdini seemed to take her lack of response as a bargaining tactic.

"Fine. You may have thirty for it."

Thirty dollars? She figured Houdini was tight-fisted with his vast amount of money, but this was ridiculous. "That's insultingly low."

He gritted his teeth. "Is that how it is? Very well. Forty. Take it or leave it." He slapped a checkbook as big as a ledger tablet onto his desk blotter. "Forty thousand is more than a fair price."

Forty *thousand?* Had he hit his head too hard inside that toolbox? "Are you sure about that?"

He sat back, insulted. "Enough. I knew you were a hard woman at bottom, but you've pressed me to my limit. I'll haggle no further. Fifty thousand, my final offer. Take it or leave it."

Fifty thousand! She couldn't believe it. She could pay back their debt to Mickey Finn, and perhaps Finn might not even send some thug to break their kneecaps, just for good measure.

"I'll take it," she said quickly, before Houdini changed his mind.

Angrily, he flipped open his checkbook. He snatched up a pen and dipped it in a bottle of ink.

What had made Houdini do this? Not for some fondness for her, Dorothy reasoned. He seemed to hardly stand the sight of her now. Fifty grand would be, well, grand . . . but, she needed even more money to pay their tab at Tony Soma's.

"Just a minute," she said.

His pen froze over the checkbook. "Yes?"

"Make it fifty thousand and five hundred," she said. "Fifty thousand for the painting and five hundred for the bet you lost to me."

Houdini fumed, his pen poised over the check. Had she pushed him too far? After a long moment, he started writing again. The pen scratched irritably against the paper. He scribbled his taut signature, blew on the ink, tore out the big check and handed it to her without another word. She cautiously accepted it and left behind the painting.

Benchley's fork froze between his plate and his mouth. "Fifty *thousand?*"

Dorothy corrected, "Fifty thousand and *five hundred*. But that's not the whole story."

It was lunchtime at the Algonquin. As usual, they were gathered at the Round Table.

Dorothy explained that on her way out of Houdini's town house, Bess Houdini stopped her on the stairs. Dorothy held the check in her hand.

"Bess told me, 'Just to be clear, that's for the painting, as well as your discretion.' Then she put a finger to her lips as a sign for silence."

The Round Tablers nodded. Benchley clucked his tongue. "That's why Houdini was willing to pay so much. He bought the painting, but he was paying for our silence."

"Yes," Dorothy said, sipping her tea. "The great Houdini can't have the world knowing he couldn't escape from a plain wood toolbox with just a fat woman on it."

"What about Bert Clay?" asked Frank Adams. "Incarcerated, I hope."

"Soon," Dorothy said. "Currently he's in Bellevue Hospital with a broken leg and a concussion. But he's under police guard. Even if he could get up, he couldn't get away. And then he goes to trial. So Abraham Snath could be right—the next scaffold Clay sees may belong to the hangman."

"And Midge?" Sherwood asked. "What will she do now?"

Dorothy frowned. "No need to worry about her. She'll be just fine. Her blank book is a big best-seller. And I heard from that slimy limey Jasper Welsh that she's got a sequel to be released soon. Another blank book."

"Oh dear," Sherwood said. "What's it called?"

"*Untold Loss: Silence Speaks Volumes, Volume Two*," Harold Ross answered. "By the way, Dottie, did you ever write the book review for her first book?"

Benchley answered for her. He spoke proudly.

"Yes, she did. It's only thirteen words long and it's pure Mrs. Parker: 'My review is just like Midge MacGuffin's book: the less said, the better.'"

"Well, forget it," Ross said glumly. "I don't need it. Matter of fact, I won't need the article about Ernie MacGuffin either."

"You won't? But it will be tremendous," Benchley said.

Dorothy glanced at Benchley, and he smiled back playfully. The truth was, they hadn't even started writing it. They were too busy taking part in it.

"Nah, *The New Yorker* is dead in the water, for now anyway." Ross wiped his mouth and flung down his napkin. "Fleischmann is getting cold feet. He's delaying the loan."

"How about that?" Woollcott chuckled. "The yeast tycoon can't raise the dough."

Benchley slid back his chair. "Speaking of dough, I'd guess we'd better take that fifty thousand right over to Mickey Finn—before he comes after us again."

Dorothy put her hand on Benchley's arm. "Don't worry. I already did it. I went over to Finn's hideaway immediately after I left Houdini's house. After calming him down and explaining why I was there, I signed the check over to him. And he was kind enough to give me the extra five hundred in cash."

"And he bore no grudge that you didn't pay him

on time?" Woollcott asked. "Or that Houdini tripped him up in broad daylight?"

"Finn is probably still too awestruck by Houdini to hold a grudge against him," Dorothy said. "As for not paying on time, he seemed to forget all about it once he got the check. He had another problem that was bothering him."

"And what is that?" Woollcott said disinterestedly, scooping up a large spoonful of custard.

"Seems a red croquet ball fell out of the sky like a meteor," she said. "It punched a hole right through the roof of his fancy white limousine."

Woollcott froze, his mouth full of custard. "And what did you say?"

"I wished him well in figuring out who to blame and how to get it fixed," she said. "So, how's your croquet game going?"

"Oh, we've just given it up." Woollcott gulped down the custard hastily. "Winter will soon be upon us, and it's too—too inhospitable to play outdoors these days. Hazardous to one's health. No, I think Harpo and I will take up indoor pursuits—cribbage, charades, twenty questions and the like."

Sherwood asked, "What's that game you keep bothering us about? The one in which everyone plays detective?"

Woollcott lowered his chin theatrically and spoke deeply. *"Murder!"*

411

Dorothy set down her cup. "I think we've had quite enough of that for a while."

Adams said, "But speaking of that, I saw you talking to Detective O'Rannigan in the lobby before lunch."

"Ah, yes, Detective Orangutan," Benchley said. "What did he want?"

Dorothy did her best imitation of the detective, which was far from accurate. She spoke roughly, "'I thought I told youse to keep your stupid mouths shut.'"

"And what did you say?" Benchley asked.

"I told him, 'It would take an act of Congress to keep my mouth shut, Detective.'"

Dorothy went on to explain that O'Rannigan had told her that Dr. Norris was beside himself. "Norris said he should have realized that Mac-Guffin fell and hit the concrete, not that he was hit *with* concrete," she said.

"Yes, why didn't he realize that?" Sherwood asked.

"O'Rannigan said that in Dr. Norris' defense, it had been a rainy morning, which could have washed away the telltale spatter of blood on the ground," she said. "And Norris wasn't there to see it anyway. There were some 'greenhorn police officers' on the scene, as O'Rannigan put it. Now Norris is going to have a telephone switchboard installed at the morgue at Bellevue, so that if the cops ever have questions or need a medical

412

examiner, they can call anytime, day or night. Apparently, in his little sphere, Dr. Norris is quite the reformer."

"He didn't reform you, though, did he?" Benchley asked her playfully—and did she detect a little jealousy?

She shook her head. "The next time I'm at a table with Dr. Norris will be in his autopsy room, and I'll be the one lying on it."

As she said this, Neysa McMein came in like a whirlwind. She didn't bother with saying her hellos. "Well, Abraham Snath should be happy. The talk around town is that the value of Ernie MacGuffin's paintings are higher than ever, now that everyone knows his death was actually a murder."

Dorothy felt a little sorry for Snath, but she had to laugh as well. "That news won't make Snath happy one bit. He burned all of Ernie's paintings."

Neysa couldn't help but chuckle, too. "Oh, then you're right. He won't be happy at all. Ernie's paintings are skyrocketing again."

"Just because he was murdered?" Adams scowled. "That's abominable."

"That's human nature," Woollcott said. "People love it when a terrible juicy story is involved."

Benchley said, "Just imagine people in their living rooms, pointing to the painting above the mantel. That's a murdered MacGuffin right there!"

"You can't put a price on cachet," Woollcott agreed.

"No, Aleck. You most certainly *can* put a price on cachet," Neysa said. "I just heard all this at Cathcart's. Houdini had been there this morning. He sold the Brooklyn Bridge painting to Cathcart for eighty grand."

Dorothy almost spit out her tea. "Eighty?" she cried. "But I just sold it to him for fifty! Houdini made thirty grand in one day?"

Benchley shook his head. "He knows how to make elephants disappear and money reappear."

Dorothy turned to him, a wry smile on her face. "That money could have been ours, if we had only known!"

"Don't feel so bad," Benchley said softly. "After all, Ernie got the worst part of the bargain, not us."

"I suppose you're right," she sighed. "But, oh, what we could have done with a spare thirty grand in our pockets!"

He looked at her knowingly and smiled. "We would have done the same thing we'll do with the spare five hundred you have, Mrs. Parker. We'll take it to Tony Soma's."

Dorothy raised her cup of plain old tea. "I'll drink to that, Mr. Benchley."

HISTORICAL NOTE

This fictional story is full of improbable and sometimes impossible incidents. History, too, is full of improbable and often unbelievable people and events. The following explanation attempts to distinguish the two.

First of all, the members of the Algonquin Round Table were real people, although this story takes some liberties with timelines and events. Dorothy Parker, Robert Benchley and Robert Sherwood (along with their editor, Frank Crowninshield) worked together at *Vanity Fair* magazine. Ernie MacGuffin, however, is fictional.

This story makes reference to Dorothy Parker's attempts at suicide. Like her attempts at writing a novel, she failed each time she tried. Her friends doubted her seriousness about suicide. They joked with her about it when they came to visit her in the hospital after one attempt. She joked right along with them. It was easier to do that than to try to explain the pain she felt.

Also, it bears repeating that in reality Dorothy and Benchley were not romantically involved, although they were the best of friends.

Alexander Woollcott, as improbable as he seemed, was real, and he had a real passion for croquet, as well as many other games. He hated to lose. "Their croquet was a kind of ferocious golf, with the wrong tools, and no limits. Once, when Woollcott drove Harpo Marx's ball into the woods for the third time, Bea Kaufman found Harpo sobbing his heart out against a tree," wrote Margaret Case Harriman (daughter of Algonquin Hotel owner Frank Case) in her book *The Vicious Circle: The Story of the Algonquin Round Table*. Despite this one-upmanship, Woollcott and Harpo Marx were close friends. They once rented a house together for the summer in the south of France. (But that's an entirely different story.)

There was indeed a speakeasy called Tony Soma's and a man by the same name. (In real life, the speakeasy was in the basement, not on the first floor as in this story.) Carlos, described as a "dull-witted Basque . . . uninspired in his work with the shaker and bottle," was the bartender. Tony reportedly would stand on his head and sing opera to entertain the speakeasy's drinkers. Interestingly, Tony's daughter, Enrica Soma, was a ballerina and fashion model who married John Huston, the director of *The Maltese Falcon*, *The Treasure of the Sierra Madre*, *The African Queen*, and *Prizzi's Honor*. Their daughter is actress Angelica Huston.

Here are some other real people (who were also real characters):

Harold Ross
Harold Ross and his wife, Jane Grant, founded *The New Yorker* magazine after a few financial fits and

starts. Half of the start-up money came from Raoul Fleischmann, who joined in the Round Tablers' Saturday night poker games. Fleischmann was an heir to the General Baking Company and a relation to the owners of the Fleischmann Yeast Company. The original *New Yorker* office was not in the fictional "Fleischmann Building" but in a nondescript office building on Forty-fifth Street.

In the beginning, Ross used the names of several Round Tablers as advisory editors. But Dorothy Parker and Robert Benchley contributed very little, and some of the others didn't contribute at all. Ross paid only peanuts in those early lean years, and sometimes handed out stock instead, which was worth almost nothing at the time. (Ross once bumped into Dorothy Parker unexpectedly. "I thought you were coming into the office to write a piece last week. What happened?" he asked. "Somebody was using the pencil," she answered.) But soon the magazine took off. Ten or more years later, even during the Depression, stock in *The New Yorker* was worth quite a pretty penny.

The name for *The New Yorker* is credited to John Peter Toohey, a Broadway writer and publicist and a founding member of the Round Table.

Harry Houdini
Bestselling author Edna Ferber, an occasional Algonquin Round Table member, grew up in

Houdini's hometown, Appleton, Wisconsin. At age nineteen, when she was a cub reporter (and the first female reporter) for the Appleton newspaper, Ferber interviewed Houdini. She described him as "a medium sized, unassuming, pleasant faced, young fellow, with blue eyes that are very much inclined to twinkle." Other than this incident, Houdini had little connection to the members of the Algonquin Round Table. He never befriended Dorothy Parker as portrayed in this story.

But that's not to say that they never met. In the mid-1920s, Houdini did have a six-week run at the New York Hippodrome, which was located across the street from the Algonquin Hotel. So it's very possible they crossed paths at some point.

Houdini achieved fame and success not only as a magician and escape artist, but also as a skeptic and debunker of fraudulent spiritualists. (In 1924, Houdini was a member of a committee organized by *Scientific American* magazine. The magazine offered a cash prize for a medium who could produce, under test conditions, an "objective psychic manifestation of physical character.") Houdini incorporated this into his stage act by demonstrating how phony mediums pulled their tricks during séances. His longtime friendship with Arthur Conan Doyle, the creator of Sherlock Holmes and a fervent spiritualist, went to pieces because of their opposing views on the matter.

Although Houdini did not appear as the half-time entertainment, the first professional football game in New York was indeed held at the New York Polo Grounds between the New York Football Giants and the Frankford (Philadelphia) Yellow Jackets. (The actual game was played on a Sunday, not a Tuesday afternoon as depicted in this story. And, unfortunately, the home team lost.)

Houdini died on Halloween 1926. As he had instructed, he was buried in his coffin with a packet of his mother's letters for a pillow.

Charles Norris, MD

Dr. Norris brought forensic medicine in New York City out of the dark ages. Before his appointment in 1918 as New York's first chief medical examiner, the city got by with a motley assortment of ill-equipped and often wrong-headed coroners, none of whom had the medical training required for forensic science. Because the coroners were paid on commission for every body they examined, some corpses wound up being autopsied several times over while the coroners lined their pockets. It was a "system which fosters ignorance, prejudice and graft," Dr. Norris wrote.

Even among the many outrageous and outsized personalities of the Roaring Twenties, Charles Norris stood out. He came from a wealthy family, was educated in Europe, and had the genteel manners and aristocratic nature of his station. He wore fashionable suits and cut a dashing figure going into and out of expensive restaurants. But for all his sophisticated elegance, he had the grit and tenacity of a bare-knuckle prizefighter when it came to his job. He pestered city officials for better equipment and personnel—but he paid for most of the lab instruments from his own deep pockets.

In this story, his infatuation with Dorothy Parker is pure fiction. But as with Houdini, there's a sporting chance they might have met at some ritzy speakeasy or celebrity's party. Incidentally, the Mansion nightclub was real, and its membership was very exclusive—just the kind of place Dr. Norris might frequent. Members showed a unique wooden calling card to gain entrance.

ACKNOWLEDGMENTS

I owe considerable thanks and recognition to:

Dorothy Parker—although she had some sad times in her life, she continued to utter every cynical remark with a bright, sparkling joke. Every bookshelf should contain *The Portable Dorothy Parker*.

Robert Benchley and the rest of the Algonquin Round Table, whose happy and easygoing attitude toward work and desperate pursuit of fun should not be entirely rejected these days.

Harry Houdini for his charmingly skeptical account of the paranormal, *Magician Among the Spirits*.

Kenneth Silverman for his colorful and detailed biography, *Houdini!!! The Career of Ehrich Weiss*.

Colin Evans for his authoritative book, *Blood on the Table: The Greatest Cases of New York City's Office of the Chief Medical Examiner.*

Deborah Blum for her funny and frightening *Poisoner's Handbook: Murder and the Birth of Forensic Medicine in Jazz Age New York*.

Al Hirschfeld for his wonderfully illustrated and humorously written field guide of Prohibition-era watering holes, *The Speakeasies of 1932*.

James Thurber for his fantastical chronicle of the early years of *The New Yorker* magazine and its founder Harold Ross, *My Years with Ross*.

Brian Kreydatus, chair of the Art and Art History Department at the College of William and Mary, for his insight inside the art world.

Kaitlyn Kennedy for helping to spread the word and listening to some cockamamie ideas.

Editor Sandra Harding for her lightheartedness and her light use of the red pen.

Michael Gibbons and the members of the Between Books Critique Group (a division of the Delaware Valley Sisters in Crime) for their editorial assistance with the first draft.

Karin, as always, for her positive attitude and continued support.

About the Author

J. J. Murphy grew up as the child of circus performers. But life under the big top was monotonous and dreary for an inquisitive youth. So one night, J.J. ran away from the dull and dismal circus to join the thrilling, razzmatazz world of business-to-business trade publishing. After a highly lucrative and award-winning career in corporate journalism, J.J. sought a totally new challenge: writing the sayings in fortune cookies. Soon, by piecing together thousands of these random sayings, J.J. realized that this collection was actually a (somewhat) coherent novel—the first Algonquin Round Table Mystery—and had serendipitously embarked on a new career!

CONNECT ONLINE

www.RoundTableMysteries.com
www.facebook.com/RoundTableMysteries

Center Point Large Print
600 Brooks Road / PO Box 1
Thorndike ME 04986-0001 USA

(207) 568-3717

US & Canada:
1 800 929-9108
www.centerpointlargeprint.com